THE ASTOUNDING ADVENTURES OF DR. BIRD

By Captain S. P. Meek
Edited by Greg Fowlkes

Includes the Special Bonus Story
AND NOW A MESSAGE . . .
By Greg Fowlkes

THE ASTOUNDING ADVENTURES OF DR. BIRD

© 2010 Resurrected Press
www.ResurrectedPress.com

Published by Intrepid Ink, LLC

Intrepid Ink, LLC provides full publishing services to authors of fiction and non-fiction books, eBooks and websites. From editing to formatting, to publishing, to marketing, Intrepid Ink gets your creative works into the hands of the people who want to read them.
Find out more at www.IntrepidInk.com.

ISBN 13: 978-1-935774-38-9

Printed in the United States of America

OTHER RESURRECTED PRESS
SCIENCE FICTION

FOREWORD

During the 1930's *Astounding Stories* was the premier venue for tales of adventure and science fiction. It is a mark of the popularity of the Dr. Bird stories that from 1930 to 1932 eleven stories featuring the character appeared in the magazine as well as several other stories by the author, Sterner St. Paul Meek, writing as Capt. S. P. Meek.

Each of the stories features a remarkable threat based on some scientific principle or fact and it was the task of the doctor to thwart the threat using his superior scientific knowledge. To assist him, he could always count on the help of Secret Service Operative Carnes, and it was often Carnes who brought the problem to the doctor's attention.

While the threats (and sometimes the solutions) may seem farfetched and unrealistic today, the background science presented was often very good and holds up well for the modern reader. As an example, there is no element, Lunium, as described in The Ray of Madness, whose radiation causes insanity, but the descriptions of quartz windows and ultra-violet spectroscopy are quite accurate.

But leaving the science aside, these are tales of adventure, with Dr. Bird and Carnes working against the likes of Saranoff and other villains who are seeking to damage the United States. They are as likely to bust down doors and shoot to kill as they are to wield a spectrascope or other scientific device.

The doctor, rather than being portrayed as the typical scientist of the era, is described as six feet tall and over two hundred pounds. More than once he pushes the smaller Carnes aside to lend a shoulder to breaking down a door.

These stories are as enjoyable today as they were in the 30's. Resurrected Press is happy to publish *The Astounding Adventures of Dr. Bird* for your reading pleasure.

About the Author

Capt. S. P. Meek was the pen name of Sterner St. Paul Meek (April 8, 1894-June 10, 1972). Meek was an early science fiction author before turning his talents to children's books. As a children's author he wrote over 20 books mostly about dogs or horses including the popular *Pat: the Story of a Seeing Eye Dog*.

Greg Fowlkes
Editor-In-Chief
Resurrected Press
www.ResurrectedPress.com

Table Of Contents

THE THIEF OF TIME

ORIGINALLY PUBLISHED IN *ASTOUNDING STORIES OF SUPER-SCIENCE*
FEBRUARY 1930

THE THIEF OF TIME

Harvey Winston, paying teller of the First National Bank of Chicago, stripped the band from a bundle of twenty dollar bills, counted out seventeen of them and added them to the pile on the counter before him.

"Twelve hundred and thirty-one tens," he read from the payroll change slip before him. The paymaster of the Cramer Packing Company nodded an assent and Winston turned to the stacked bills in his rear currency rack. He picked up a handful of bundles and turned back to the grill. His gaze swept the counter where, a moment before, he had stacked the twenties, and his jaw dropped.

"You got those twenties, Mr. Trier?" he asked.

"Got them? Of course not, how could I?" replied the paymaster. "There they are...."

His voice trailed off into nothingness as he looked at the empty counter.

"I must have dropped them," said Winston as he turned. He glanced back at the rear rack where his main stock of currency was piled. He stood paralyzed for a moment and then reached under the counter and pushed a button.

The bank resounded instantly to the clangor of gongs and huge steel grills shot into place with a clang, sealing all doors and preventing anyone from entering or leaving the bank. The guards sprang to their stations with drawn weapons and from the inner offices the bank officials came swarming out. The cashier, followed by two men, hurried to the paying teller's cage.

"What is it, Mr. Winston?" he cried.

"I've been robbed!" gasped the teller.

"Who by? How?" demanded the cashier.

"I–I don't know, sir," stammered the teller. "I was counting out Mr. Trier's payroll, and after I had stacked the twenties I turned to get the tens. When I turned back the twenties were gone."

"Where had they gone?" asked the cashier.

"I don't know, sir. Mr. Trier was as surprised as I was, and then I turned back, thinking that I had knocked them off the counter, and I saw at a glance that there was a big hole in my back racks. You can see yourself, sir."

The cashier turned to the paymaster.

"Is this a practical joke, Mr. Trier?" he demanded sharply.

"Of course not," replied the paymaster. "Winston's grill was closed. It still is. Granted that I might have reached the twenties he had piled up, how could I have gone through a grill and taken the rest of the missing money without his seeing me? The money disappeared almost instantly. It was there a moment before, for I noticed when Winston took the twenties from his rack that it was full."

"But someone must have taken it," said the bewildered cashier. "Money doesn't walk off of its own accord or vanish into thin air–"

A bell interrupted his speech.

"There are the police," he said with an air of relief.
"I'll let them in."

*   *   *   *   *

The smaller of the two men who had followed the cashier from his office when the alarm had sounded stepped forward and spoke quietly. His voice was low and well pitched yet it carried a note of authority and power that held his auditors' attention while he spoke. The voice harmonized with the man. The most noticeable point about him was the inconspicuousness of his voice and manner, yet there was a glint of steel in his gray eyes that told of enormous force in him.

"I don't believe that I would let them in for a few moments, Mr. Rogers," he said. "I think that we are up against something a little different from the usual bank robbery."

"But, Mr. Carnes," protested the cashier, "we must call in the police in a case like this, and the sooner they take charge the better chance there will be of apprehending the thief."

"Suit yourself," replied the little man with a shrug of his shoulders. "I merely offered my advice."

"Will you take charge, Mr. Carnes?" asked the cashier.

"I can't supersede the local authorities in a case like this," replied Carnes. "The secret service is primarily interested in the suppression of counterfeiting and the enforcement of certain federal statutes, but I will be glad to assist the local authorities to the best of my ability, provided they desire my help. My advice to you would be to keep out the patrolmen who are demanding admittance and get in touch with the chief of police. I would ask that his best detective together with an expert finger-print photographer be sent here before anyone else is admitted. If the patrolmen are allowed to wipe their hands over Mr. Winston's counter they may destroy valuable evidence."

"You are right, Mr. Carnes," exclaimed the cashier. "Mr. Jervis, will you tell the police that there is no violence threatening and ask them to wait for a few minutes? I'll telephone the chief of police at once."

*   *   *   *   *

As the cashier hurried away to his telephone Carnes turned to his companion who had stood an interested, although silent spectator of the scene. His companion was a marked contrast to the secret service operator. He stood well over six feet in height, and his protruding jaw and shock of unruly black hair combined with his massive shoulders and chest to give him the appearance of a man who labored with his hands—until one looked at them. His hands were in strange contrast to the rest of him. Long, slim, mobile hands they were, with tapering nervous fingers—the hands of a thinker or of a musician. Telltale splotches of acid told of hours spent in a laboratory, a tale that was confirmed by the almost imperceptible stoop of his shoulders.

"Do you agree with my advice, Dr. Bird?" asked Carnes deferentially.

The noted scientist, who from his laboratory in the Bureau of Standards had sent forth many new things in the realms of chemistry and physics, and who, incidentally, had been instrumental in solving some of the most baffling mysteries which the secret service had been called upon to face, grunted.

"It didn't do any harm," he said, "but it is rather a waste of time. The thief wore gloves."

"How in thunder do you know that?" demanded Carnes.

"It's merely common sense. A man who can do what he did had at least some rudiments of intelligence, and even the feeblest-minded crooks know enough to wear gloves nowadays."

Carnes stepped a little closer to the doctor.

"Another reason why I didn't want patrolmen tramping around," he said in an undertone, "is this. If Winston gave the alarm quickly enough, the thief is probably still in the building."

"He's a good many miles away by now," replied Dr. Bird with a shrug of his shoulders.

*   *   *   *   *

Carnes' eyes opened widely. "Why?—how?—who?" he stammered. "Have you any idea of who did it, or how it was done?"

"Possibly I have an idea," replied Dr. Bird with a cryptic smile. "My advice to you, Carnes, is to keep away from the local authorities as much as possible. I want to be present when Winston and Trier are questioned and I may possibly wish to ask a few questions myself. Use your authority that far, but no farther. Don't volunteer any information and especially don't let my name get out. We'll drop the counterfeiting case we were summoned here on for the present and look into this a little on our own hook. I will want your aid, so don't get tied up with the police."

"At that, we don't want the police crossing our trail at every turn," protested Carnes.

"They won't," promised the doctor. "They will never get any evidence on this case, if I am right, and neither will we—for the present. Our stunt is to lie low and wait for the next attempt of this nature and thus accumulate some evidence and some idea of where to look."

"Will there be another attempt?" asked Carnes.

"Surely. You don't expect a man who got away with a crime like this to quit operations just because a few flatfeet run around and make a hullabaloo about it, do you? I may be wrong in my assumption, but if I am right, the most important thing is to keep all reference to my name or position out of the press reports."

The cashier hastened up to them.

"Detective-Captain Sturtevant will be here in a few minutes with a photographer and some other men," he said. "Is there anything that we can do in the meantime, Mr. Carnes?"

"I would suggest that Mr. Trier and his guard and Mr. Winston go into your office," replied Carnes. "My assistant and I would like to be present during the questioning, if there are no objections."

"I didn't know that you had an assistant with you," answered the cashier.

Carnes indicated Dr. Bird.

"This gentleman is Mr. Berger, my assistant," he said. "Do you understand?"

"Certainly. I am sure there will be no objection to your presence, Mr. Carnes," replied the cashier as he led the way to his office.

*   *   *   *   *

A few minutes later Detective-Captain Sturtevant of the Chicago police was announced. He acknowledged the introductions gruffly and got down to business at once.

"What were the circumstances of the robbery?" he asked.

Winston told his story, Trier and the guard confirming it.

"Pretty thin!" snorted the detective when they had finished. He whirled suddenly on Winston.

"Where did you hide the loot?" he thundered.

"Why—uh—er—what do you mean?" gulped the teller.

"Just what I said," replied the detective. "Where did you hide the loot?"

"I didn't hide it anywhere," said the teller. "It was stolen."

"You had better think up a better one," sneered Sturtevant. "If you think that you can make me believe that that money was stolen from you in broad daylight with two men in plain sight of you who didn't see it, you might just as well get over it. I know that you have some hiding place where you have slipped the stuff and the quicker you come clean and spill it, the better it will be for you. Where did you hide it?"

"I didn't hide it!" cried the teller, his voice trembling. "Mr. Trier can tell you that I didn't touch it from the time I laid it down until I turned back."

"That's right," replied the paymaster. "He turned his back on me for a moment, and when he turned back, it was gone."

"So you're in on it too, are you?" said Sturtevant.

"What do you mean?" demanded the paymaster hotly.

"Oh nothing, nothing at all," replied the detective. "Of course Winston didn't touch it and it disappeared and you never saw it go, although you were within three feet of it all the time. Did *you* see anything?" he demanded of the guard.

"Nothing that I am sure of," answered the guard. "I thought that a shadow passed in front of me for an instant, but when I looked again, it was gone."

*   *   *   *   *

Dr. Bird sat forward suddenly. "What did this shadow look like?" he asked.

"It wasn't exactly a shadow," said the guard. "It was as if a person had passed suddenly before me so quickly that I couldn't see him. I seemed to feel that there was someone there, but I didn't rightly *see* anything."

"Did you notice anything of the sort?" demanded the doctor of Trier.

"I don't know," replied Trier thoughtfully. "Now that Williams has mentioned it, I did seem to feel a breath of air or a motion as though something had passed in front of me. I didn't think of it at the time."

"Was this shadow opaque enough to even momentarily obscure your vision?" went on the doctor.

"Not that I am conscious of. It was just a breath of air such as a person might cause by passing very rapidly."

"What made you ask Trier if he had the money when you turned around?" asked the doctor of Winston.

"Say-y-y," broke in the detective. "Who the devil are you, and what do you mean by breaking into my examination and stopping it?"

Carnes tossed a leather wallet on the table.

"There are my credentials," he said in his quiet voice. "I am chief of one section of the United States Secret Service as you will see, and this is Mr. Berger, my assistant. We were in the bank, engaged on a counterfeiting case, when the robbery took place. We have had a good deal of experience along these lines and we are merely anxious to aid you."

Sturtevant examined Carnes' credentials carefully and returned them.

"This is a Chicago robbery," he said, "and we have had a little experience in robberies and in apprehending robbers ourselves. I think that we can get along without your help."

"You have had more experience with robberies than with apprehending robbers if the papers tell the truth," said Dr. Bird with a chuckle.

*　　*　　*　　*　　*

The detective's face flushed.

"That will be enough from you, Mr. Sherlock Holmes," he said. "If you open your mouth again, I'll arrest you as a material witness and as a possible accomplice."

"That sounds like Chicago methods," said Carnes quietly. "Now listen to me, Captain. My assistant and I are merely trying to assist you in this case. If you don't desire our assistance we'll proceed along our own lines without interfering, but in the meantime remember that this is a National Bank, and that our questions will be answered. The United States is higher than even the Chicago police force, and I am here under orders to investigate a counterfeiting case. If I desire, I can seal the doors of this bank and allow no one in or out until I have the evidence I desire. Do you understand?"

Sturtevant sprang to his feet with an oath, but the sight of the gold badge which Carnes displayed stopped him.

"Oh well," he said ungraciously. "I suppose that no harm will come of letting Winston answer your fool questions, but I'll warn you that I'll report to Washington that you are interfering with the course of justice and using your authority to aid the getaway of a criminal."

"That is your privilege," replied Carnes quietly. "Mr. Winston, will you answer Mr. Berger's question?"

"Why, I asked him because he was right close to the money and I thought that he might have reached through the wicket and picked it up. Then, too–"

He hesitated for a moment and Dr. Bird smiled encouragingly.

"What else?" he asked.

"Why, I can't exactly tell. It just seemed to me that I had heard the rustle that bills make when they are pulled across a counter. When I saw them gone, I thought that he might have taken them. Then when I turned toward him, I seemed to hear the rustle of bills behind me, although I knew that I was alone in the cage. When I looked back the money was gone."

"Did you see or hear anything like a shadow or a person moving?"

"No–yes–I don't know. Just as I turned around it seemed to me that the rear door to my cage had moved and there may have been a shadow for an instant. I don't know. I hadn't thought of it before."

"How long after that did you ring the alarm gongs?"

"Not over a second or two."

"That's all," said Dr. Bird.

"If your high and mightiness has no further questions to ask, perhaps you will let me ask a few," said Sturtevant.

*   *   *   *   *

"Go ahead, ask all you wish," replied Dr. Bird with a laugh. "I have all the information I desire here for the present. I may want to ask other questions later, but just now I think we'll be going."

"If you find any strange finger-prints on Winston's counter, I'll be glad to have them compared with our files," said Carnes.

"I am not bothering with finger-prints," snorted the detective. "This is an open and shut case. There would be lots of Winston's finger-prints there and no others. There isn't the slightest doubt that this is an inside case and I have the men I want right here. Mr. Rogers, your bank is closed for to-day. Everyone in it will be searched and then all those not needed to close up will be sent away. I will get a squad of men here to go over your building and locate the hiding place. Your money is still on the premises unless these men slipped it to a confederate who got out before the alarm was given. I'll question the guards about that. If that happened, a little sweating will get it out of them."

"Are you going to arrest me?" demanded Trier in surprise.

"Yes, dearie," answered the detective. "I am going to arrest you and your two little playmates if these Washington experts will allow me to. You will save a lot of time and quite a few painful experiences if you will come clean now instead of later."

"I demand to see my lawyer and to communicate with my firm," said the paymaster.

"Time enough for that when I am through with you," replied the detective.

He turned to Carnes.

"Have I your gracious permission to arrest these three criminals?" he asked.

"Yes indeed, Captain," replied Carnes sweetly. "You have my gracious permission to make just as big an ass of yourself as you wish. We're going now."

*　　*　　*　　*　　*

"By the way, Captain," said Dr. Bird as he followed Carnes out. "When you get through playing with your prisoners and start to look for the thief, here is a tip. Look for a left-handed man who has a thorough knowledge of chemistry and especially toxicology."

"It's easy enough to see that he was left-handed if he pulled that money out through the grill from the positions occupied by Trier and his guard, but what the dickens led you to suspect that he is a chemist and a toxicologist?" asked Carnes as he and the doctor left the bank.

"Merely a shrewd guess, my dear Watson," replied the doctor with a chuckle. "I am likely to be wrong, but there is a good chance that I am right. I am judging solely from the method used."

"Have you solved the method?" demanded Carnes in amazement. "What on earth was it? The more I have thought about it, the more inclined I am to believe that Sturtevant is right and that it is an inside job. It seems to me impossible that a man could have entered in broad daylight and lifted that money in front of three men and within sight of a hundred more without some one getting a glimpse of him. He must have taken the money out in a grip or a sack or something like that, yet the bank record shows that no one but Trier entered with a grip and no one left with a package for ten minutes before Trier entered."

"There may be something in what you say, Carnes, but I am inclined to have a different idea. I don't think it is the usual run of bank robbery, and I would rather not hazard a guess just now. I am going back to Washington to-night. Before I go any further into the matter, I need some rather specialized knowledge that I don't possess and I want to consult with Dr. Knolles. I'll be back in a week or so and then we can look into that counterfeiting case after we get this disposed of."

"What am I to do?" asked Carnes.

"Sit around the lobby of your hotel, eat three meals a day, and read the papers. If you get bored, I would recommend that you pay a visit to the Art Institute and admire the graceful lions which adorn the steps. Artistic contemplations may well improve your culture."

"All right," replied Carnes. "I'll assume a pensive air and moon at the lions, but I might do better if you told me what I was looking for."

"You are looking for knowledge, my dear Carnes," said the doctor with a laugh. "Remember the saying of the sages: To the wise man, no knowledge is useless."

*   *   *   *   *

A huge Martin bomber roared down to a landing at the Maywood airdrome, and a burly figure descended from the rear cockpit and waved his hand jovially to the waiting Carnes. The secret service man hastened over to greet his colleague.

"Have you got that truck I wired you to have ready?" demanded the doctor.

"Waiting at the entrance; but say, I've got some news for you."

"It can wait. Get a detail of men and help us to unload this ship. Some of the cases are pretty heavy."

Carnes hurried off and returned with a gang of laborers, who took from the bomber a dozen heavy packing cases of various sizes, several of them labelled either "Fragile" or "Inflammable" in large type.

"Where do they go, Doctor?" he asked when the last of them had been loaded onto the waiting truck.

"To the First National Bank," replied Dr. Bird, "and Casey here goes with them. You know Casey, don't you, Carnes? He is the best photographer in the Bureau."

"Shall I go along too?" asked Carnes as he acknowledged the introduction.

"No need for it. I wired Rogers and he knows the stuff is coming and what to do with it. Unpack as soon as you get there, Casey, and start setting up as soon as the bank closes."

"All right, Doctor," replied Casey as he mounted the truck beside the driver.

"Where do we go, Doctor?" asked Carnes as the truck rolled off.

"To the Blackstone Hotel for a bath and some clean clothes," replied the doctor. "And now, what is the news you have for me?"

"The news is this, Doctor. I carried out your instructions diligently and, during the daylight hours, the lions have not moved."

*   *   *   *   *

Dr. Bird looked contrite.

"I beg your pardon, Carnes," he said. "I really didn't think when I left you so mystified how you must have felt. Believe me, I had my own reasons, excellent ones, for secrecy."

"I have usually been able to maintain silence when asked to," replied Carnes stiffly.

"My dear fellow, I didn't mean to question your discretion. I know that whatever I tell you is safe, but there are angles to this affair that are so weird and improbable that I don't dare to trust my own conclusions, let alone share them. I'll tell you all about it soon. Did you get those tickets I wired for?"

"Of course I got them, but what have two tickets to the A. A. U. track meet this afternoon got to do with a bank robbery?"

"One trouble with you, Carnes," replied the doctor with a judicial air, "is that you have no idea of the importance of proper relaxation. Is it possible that you have no desire to see Ladd, this new marvel who is smashing records right and left, run? He performs for the Illinois Athletic Club this afternoon, and it would not surprise me to see him lower the world's record again. He has already lowered the record for the hundred yard dash from nine and three-fifths to eight and four-fifths. There is no telling what he will do."

"Are we going to waste the whole afternoon just to watch a man run?" demanded Carnes in disgust.

"We will see many men run, my dear fellow, but there is only one in whom I have a deep abiding interest, and that is Mr. Ladd. Have you your binoculars with you?"

"No."

"Then by all means beg, borrow or steal two pairs before this afternoon. We might easily miss half the fun without them. Are our seats near the starting line for the sprints?"

"Yes. The big demand was for seats near the finish line."

"The start will be much more interesting, Carnes. I was somewhat of a minor star in track myself in my college days and it will be of the greatest interest to me to observe the starting form of this new speed artist. Now Carnes, don't ask any more questions. I may be barking up the wrong tree and I don't want to give you a chance to laugh at me. I'll tell you what to watch for at the track."

*   *   *   *   *

The sprinters lined up on the hundred yard mark and Dr. Bird and Carnes sat with their glasses glued to their eyes watching the slim figure in the colors of the Illinois Athletic Club, whose large "62" on his back identified him as the new star.

"On your mark!" cried the starter. "Get set!"

"Ah!" cried Dr. Bird. "Did you see that Carnes?"

The starting gun cracked and the runners were off on their short grind. Ladd leaped into the lead and rapidly distanced the field, his legs twinkling under him almost faster than the eye could follow. He was fully twenty yards in the lead when his speed suddenly lessened and the balance of the runners closed up the gap he had opened. His lead was too great for them, and he was still a good ten yards in the lead when he crossed the tape.

The official time was posted as eight and nine-tenths seconds.

"Another thirty yards and he would have been beaten," said Carnes as he lowered his glasses.

"That is the way he has won all of his races," replied the doctor. "He piles up a huge lead at first and then loses a good deal at the finish. His speed doesn't hold up. Never mind that, though, it is only an additional point in my favor. Did you notice his jaws just before the gun went?"

"They seemed to clench and then he swallowed, but most of them did some thing like that."

"Watch him carefully for the next heat and see if he puts anything into his mouth. That is the important thing."

Dr. Bird sank into a brown study and paid no attention to the next few events, but he came to attention promptly when the final heat of the hundred yard dash was called. With his glasses he watched Ladd closely as the runner trotted up to the starting line.

"There, Carnes!" he cried suddenly. "Did you see?"

"I saw him wipe his mouth," said Carnes doubtfully.

"All right, now watch his jaws just before the gun goes."

*   *   *   *   *

The final heat was a duplicate of the first preliminary. Ladd took an early lead which he held for three-fourths of the distance to the tape, then his pace slackened and he finished only a bare ten yards ahead of the next runner. The time tied his previous world's record of eight and four-fifths seconds.

"He crunched and swallowed all right, Doctor," said Carnes.

"That is all I wanted to be sure of. Now Carnes, here is something for you to do. Get hold of the United States Commissioner and get a John Doe warrant and go back to the hotel with it and wait for me. I may phone you at any minute and I may not. If I don't, wait in your room until you hear from me. Don't leave it for a minute."

"Where are you going, Doctor?"

"I'm going down and congratulate Mr. Ladd. An old track man like me can't let such an opportunity pass."

"I don't know what this is all about, Doctor," replied Carnes, "but I know you well enough to obey orders and to keep my mouth shut until it is my turn to speak."

Few men could resist Dr. Bird when he set out to make a favorable impression, and even a world's champion is apt to be flattered by the attention of one of the greatest scientists of his day, especially when that scientist has made an enviable reputation as an athlete in his college days and can talk the jargon of the champion's particular sport. Henry Ladd promptly capitulated to the charm of the doctor and allowed himself to be led away to supper at Bird's club. The supper passed off pleasantly, and when the doctor requested an interview with the young athlete in a private room, he gladly consented. They entered the room together, remained for an hour and a half, and then came out. The smile had left Ladd's face and he appeared nervous and distracted. The doctor talked cheerfully with him but kept a firm grip on his arm as they descended the stairs together. They entered a telephone booth where the doctor made several calls, and then descended to the street, where they entered a taxi.

"Maywood airdrome," the doctor told the driver.

*   *   *   *   *

Two hours later the big Martin bomber which had carried the doctor to Chicago roared away into the night, and Bird turned back, reentered the taxi, and headed for the city alone.

When Carnes received the telephone call, which was one of those the doctor made from the booth in his club, he hurried over to the First National Bank. His badge secured him an entrance and he found Casey busily engaged in rigging up an elaborate piece of apparatus on one of the balconies where guards were normally stationed during banking hours.

"Dr. Bird said to tell you to keep on the job all night if necessary," he told Casey. "He thinks he will need your machine to-morrow."

"I'll have it ready to turn on the power at four A.M.," replied Casey.

Carnes watched him curiously for a while as he soldered together the electrical connections and assembled an apparatus which looked like a motion picture projector.

"What are you setting up?" he asked at length.

"It is a high speed motion picture camera," replied Casey, "with a telescopic lens. It is a piece of apparatus which Dr. Bird designed while he was in Washington last week and which I made from his sketches, using some apparatus we had on hand. It's a dandy, all right."

"What is special about it?"

"The speed. You know how fast an ordinary movie is taken, don't you? No? Well, it's sixteen exposures per second. The slow pictures are taken sometimes at a hundred and twenty-eight or two hundred and fifty-six exposures per second, and then shown at sixteen. This affair will take half a million pictures per second."

"I didn't know that a film would register with that short an exposure."

*   *   *   *   *

"That's slow," replied Casey with a laugh. "It all depends on the light. The best flash-light powder gives a flash about one ten-thousandth of a second in duration, but that is by no means the speed limit of the film. The only trouble is enough light and sufficient shutter speed. Pictures have been taken by means of spark photography with an exposure of less than one three-millionth of a second. The whole secret of this machine lies in the shutter. This big disc with the slots in the edge is set up before the lens and run at such a speed that half a million slots per second pass before the lens. The film, which is sixteen millimeter X-ray film, travels behind the lens at a speed of nearly five miles per second. It has to be gradually worked up to this speed, and after the whole thing is set up, it takes it nearly four hours to get to full speed."

"At that speed, it must take a million miles of film before you get up steam."

"It would, if the film were being exposed. There is only about a hundred yards of film all told, which will run over these huge drums in an endless belt. There is a regular camera shutter working on an electric principle which remains closed. When the switch is tripped, the shutter opens in about two thirty-thousandths of a second, stays open just one one-hundredth of a second, and then closes. This time is enough to expose nearly all of our film. When we have our picture, I shut the current down, start applying a magnetic brake, and let it slow down. It takes over an hour to stop it without breaking the film. It sounds complicated, but it works all right."

"Where is your switch?"

*   *   *   *   *

"That is the trick part of it. It is a remote control affair. The shutter opens and starts the machine taking pictures when the back door of the paying teller's cage is opened half an inch. There is also a hand switch in the line that can be opened so that you can open the door without setting off the camera, if you wish. When the hand switch is closed and the door opened, this is what happens. The shutter on the camera opens, the machine takes five thousand pictures during the next hundredth of a second, and then the shutter closes. Those five thousand exposures will take about five minutes to show at the usual rate of sixteen per second."

"You said that you had to get plenty of light. How are you managing that?"

"The camera is equipped with a special lens ground out of rock crystal. This lens lets in ultra-violet light which the ordinary lens shuts out, and X-ray film is especially sensitive to ultra-violet light. In order to be sure that we get enough illumination, I will set up these two ultra-violet floodlights to illumine the cage. The teller will have to wear glasses to protect his eyes and he'll get well sunburned, but something has to be sacrificed to science, as Dr. Bird is always telling me."

"It's too deep for me," said Carnes with a sigh. "Can I do anything to help? The doctor told me to stand by and do anything I could."

"I might be able to use you a little if you can use tools," said Casey with a grin. "You can start bolting together that light proof shield if you want to."

*　　*　　*　　*　　*

"Well, Carnes, did you have an instructive night?" asked Dr. Bird cheerfully as he entered the First National Bank at eight-thirty the next morning.

"I don't see that I did much good, Doctor. Casey would have had the machine ready on time anyway, and I'm no machinist."

"Well, frankly, Carnes, I didn't expect you to be of much help to him, but I did want you to see what Casey was doing, and a little of it was pretty heavy for him to handle alone. I suppose that everything is ready?"

"The motor reached full speed about fifteen minutes ago and Casey went out to get a cup of coffee. Would you mind telling me the object of the whole thing?"

"Not at all. I plan to make a permanent record of the work of the most ingenious bank robber in the world. I hope he keeps his word."

"What do you mean?"

"Three days ago when Sturtevant sweated a 'confession' out of poor Winston, the bank got a message that the robbery would be repeated this morning and dared them to prevent it. Rogers thought it was a hoax, but he telephoned me and I worked the Bureau men night and day to get my camera ready in time for him. I am afraid that I can't do much to prevent the robbery, but I may be able to take a picture of it and thus prevent other cases of a like nature."

"Was the warning written?"

"No. It was telephoned from a pay station in the loop district, and by the time it was traced and men got there, the telephoner was probably a mile away. He said that he would rob the same cage in the same manner as he did before."

"Aren't you taking any special precautions?"

"Oh, yes, the bank is putting on extra guards and making a lot of fuss of that sort, probably to the great amusement of the robber."

"Why not close the cage for the day?"

"Then he would rob a different one and we would have no way of photographing his actions. To be sure, we will put dummy money there, bundles with bills on the outside and paper on the inside, so if I don't get a picture of him, he won't get much. Every bill in the cage will be marked as well."

"Did he say at what time he would operate?"

"No, he didn't, so we'll have to stand by all day. Oh, hello, Casey, is everything all right?"

"As sweet as chocolate candy, Doctor. I have tested it out thoroughly, and unless we have to run it so long that the film wears out and breaks, we are sitting pretty. If we don't get the pictures you are looking for, I'm a dodo, and I haven't been called that yet."

"Good work, Casey. Keep the bearings oiled and pray that the film doesn't break."

*   *   *   *   *

The bank had been opened only ten minutes when the clangor of gongs announced a robbery. It was practically a duplicate of the first. The paying teller had turned from his window to take some bills from his rack and had found several dozens of bundles missing. As the gongs sounded, Dr. Bird and Casey leaped to the camera.

"She snapped, Doctor!" cried Casey as he threw two switches. "It'll take an hour to stop and half a day to develop the film, but I ought to be able to show you what we got by to-night."

"Good enough!" cried Dr. Bird. "Go ahead while I try to calm down the bank officials. Will you have everything ready by eight o'clock?"

"Easy, Doctor," replied Casey as he turned to the magnetic brake.

By eight o'clock quite a crowd had assembled in a private room at the Blackstone Hotel. Besides Dr. Bird and Carnes, Rogers and several other officials of the First National Bank were present, together with Detective-Captain Sturtevant and a group of the most prominent scientists and physicians gathered from the schools of the city.

"Gentlemen," said Dr. Bird when all had taken seats facing a miniature moving picture screen on one wall, "to-night I expect to show you some pictures which will, I am sure, astonish you. It marks the advent of a new departure in transcendental medicine. I will be glad to answer any questions you may wish to ask and to explain the pictures after they are shown, but before we start a discussion, I will ask that you examine what I have to show you. Lights out, please!"

He stepped to the rear of the room as the lights went out. As his eyes grew used to the dimness of the room he moved forward and took a vacant seat. His hand fumbled in his pocket for a second.

"Now!" he cried suddenly.

In the momentary silence which followed his cry, two dull metallic clicks could be heard, and a quick cry that was suddenly strangled as Dr. Bird clamped his hand over the mouth of the man who sat between him and Carnes.

"All right, Casey," called the doctor.

*   *   *   *   *

The whir of a projection machine could be heard and on the screen before them leaped a picture of the paying teller's cage of the First National Bank. Winston's successor was standing motionless at the wicket, his lips parted in a smile, but the attention of all was riveted on a figure who moved at the back of the cage. As the picture started, the figure was bent over an opened suitcase, stuffing into it bundles of bills. He straightened up and reached to the rack for more bills, and as he did so he faced the camera full for a moment. He picked up other bundles of bills, filled the suitcase, fastened it in a leisurely manner, opened the rear door of the cage and walked out.

"Again, please!" called Dr. Bird. "And stop when he faces us full."

The picture was repeated and stopped at the point indicated.

"Lights, please!" cried the doctor.

The lights flashed on and Dr. Bird rose to his feet, pulling up after him the wilted figure of a middle-aged man.

"Gentlemen," said the doctor in ringing tones, "allow me to present to you Professor James Kirkwood of the faculty of the Richton University, formerly known as James Collier of the Bureau of Standards, and robber of the First National Bank."

Detective-Captain Sturtevant jumped to his feet and cast a searching glance at the captive.

"He's the man all right," he cried. "Hang on to him until I get a wagon here!"

"Oh, shut up!" said Carnes. "He's under federal arrest just now, charged with the possession of narcotics. When we are through with him, you can have him if you want him."

"How did you get that picture, Doctor?" cried the cashier. "I watched that cage every minute during the morning and I'll swear that man never entered and stole that money as the picture shows, unless he managed to make himself invisible."

*   *   *   *   *

"You're closer to the truth than you suspect, Mr. Rogers," said Dr. Bird. "It is not quite a matter of invisibility, but something pretty close to it. It is a matter of catalysts."

"What kind of cats?" asked the cashier.

"Not cats, Mr. Rogers, catalysts. Catalysts is the name of a chemical reaction consisting essentially of a decomposition and a new combination effected by means of a catalyst which acts on the compound bodies in question, but which goes through the reaction itself unchanged. There are a great many of them which are used in the arts and in manufacturing, and while their action is not always clearly understood, the results are well known and can be banked on.

"One of the commonest instances of the use of a catalyst is the use of sponge platinum in the manufacture of sulphuric acid. I will not burden you with the details of the 'contact' process, as it is known, but the combination is effected by means of finely divided platinum which is neither changed, consumed or wasted during the process. While there are a number of other catalysts known, for instance iron in reactions in which metallic magnesium is concerned, the commonest are the metals of the platinum group.

"Less is known of the action of catalysts in the organic reactions, but it has been the subject of intensive study by Dr. Knolles of the Bureau of Standards for several years. His studies of the effects of different colored lights, that is, rays of different wave-lengths, on the reactions which constitute growth in plants have had a great effect on hothouse forcing of plants and promise to revolutionize the truck gardening industry. He has speeded up the rate of growth to as high as ten times the normal rate in some cases.

"A few years ago, he and his assistant, James Collier, turned their attention toward discovering a catalyst which would do for the metabolic reactions in animal life what his light rays did for plants. What his method was, I will not disclose for obvious reasons, but suffice it to say that he met with great success. He took a puppy and by treating it with his catalytic drugs, made it grow to maturity, pass through its entire normal life span, and die of old age in six months."

*　　*　　*　　*　　*

"That is very interesting, Doctor, but I fail to see what bearing it has on the robbery."

"Mr. Rogers, how, on a dark day and in the absence of a timepiece, would you judge the passage of time?"

"Why, by my stomach, I guess."

"Exactly. By your metabolic rate. You eat a meal, it digests, you expend the energy which you have taken into your system, your stomach becomes empty and your system demands more energy. You are hungry and you judge that some five or six hours must have passed since you last ate. Do you follow?"

"Certainly."

"Let us suppose that by means of some tonic, some catalytic drug, your rate of metabolism and also your rate of expenditure of energy has been increased six fold. You would eat a meal and in one hour you would be hungry again. Having no timepiece, and assuming that you were in a light-proof room, you would judge that some five hours had passed, would you not?"

"I expect so."

"Very well. Now suppose that this accelerated rate of digestion and expenditure of energy continued. You would be sleepy in perhaps three hours, would sleep about an hour and a quarter, and would then wake, ready for your breakfast. In other words, you would have lived through a day in four hours."

"What advantage would there be in that?"

"None, from your standpoint. It would, however, increase the rate of reproduction of cattle greatly and might be a great boom to agriculture, but we will not discuss this phase now. Suppose it were possible to increase your rate of metabolism and expenditure of energy, in other words, your rate of living, not six times, but thirty thousand times. In such a case you would live five minutes in one one-hundredth of a second."

"Naturally, and you would live a year in about seventeen and one-half minutes, and a normal lifespan of seventy years in about twenty hours. You would be as badly off as any common may-fly."

*   *   *   *   *

"Agreed, but suppose that you could so regulate the dose of your catalyst that its effect would last for only one one-hundredth of a second. During that short period of time, you would be able to do the work that would ordinarily take you five minutes. In other words, you could enter a bank, pack a satchel with currency and walk out. You would be working in a leisurely manner, yet your actions would have been so quick that no human eye could have detected them. This is my theory of what actually took place. For verification, I will turn to Dr. Kirkwood, as he prefers to be known now."

"I don't know how you got that picture, but what you have said is about right," replied the prisoner.

"I got that picture by using a speed of thirty thousand times the normal sixteen exposures per second," replied Dr. Bird. "That figure I got from Dr. Knolles, the man who perfected the secret you stole when you left the Bureau three years ago. You secured only part of it and I suppose it took all your time since to perfect and complete it. You gave yourself away when you experimented on young Ladd. I was a track man myself in my college days and when I saw an account of his running, I smelt a rat, so I came back and watched him. As soon as I saw him crush and swallow a capsule just as the gun was fired, I was sure, and got hold of him. He was pretty stubborn, but he finally told me what name you were running under now, and the rest was easy. I would have got you in time anyway, but your bravado in telling us when you would next operate gave me the idea of letting you do it and photographing you at work. That is all I have to say. Captain Sturtevant, you can take your prisoner whenever you want him."

*   *   *   *   *

"I reckoned without you, Dr. Bird, but the end hasn't come yet. You may send me up for a few years, but you'll never find that money. I'm sure of that."

"Tut, tut, Professor," laughed Carnes. "Your safety deposit box in the Commercial National is already sealed until a court orders it opened. The bills you took this morning were all marked, so that is merely additional proof, if we needed it. You surely didn't think that such a transparent device as changing your name from 'James Collier' to 'John Collyer' and signing with your left hand instead of your right would fool the secret service, did you? Remember, your old Bureau records showed you to be ambidextrous."

"What about Winston's confession?" asked Rogers suddenly.

"Detective-Captain Sturtevant can explain that to a court when Mr. Winston brings suit against him for false arrest and brutal treatment," replied Carnes.

"A very interesting case, Carnes," remarked the doctor a few hours later. "It was an enjoyable interlude in the routine of most of the cases on which you consult me, but our play time is over. We'll have to get after that counterfeiting case to-morrow."

Cold Light

Originally Published in *Astounding Stories of Super-Science*
March 1930

How could a human body be found actually splintered--broken into sharp fragments like a shattered glass! Once again Dr. Bird probes deep into an amazing mystery.

COLD LIGHT

"Confound it, Carnes, I am on my vacation!"

"I know it, Doctor, and I hate to disturb you, but I felt that I simply had to. I have one of the weirdest cases on my hands that I have ever been mixed up in and I think that you'll forgive me for calling you when I tell you about it."

Dr. Bird groaned into the telephone transmitter.

"I took a vacation last summer, or tried to, and you hauled me away from the best fishing I have found in years to help you on a case. This year I traveled all the way from Washington to San Francisco to get away from you and the very day that I get here you are after me. I won't have anything to do with it. Where are you, anyway?"

"I am at Fallon, Nevada, Doctor. I'm sorry that you won't help me out because the case promises to be unusually interesting. Let me at least tell you about it."

Dr. Bird groaned louder than ever into the telephone transmitter.

"All right, go ahead and tell me about it if it will relieve your mind, but I have given you my final answer. I am not a bit interested in it."

"That is quite all right, Doctor, I don't expect you to touch it. I hope, however, that you will be able to give me an idea of where to start. Did you ever see a man's body broken in pieces?"

"Do you mean badly smashed up?"

"No indeed, I mean just what I said, broken in pieces. Legs snapped off as though the entire flesh had become brittle."

"No, I didn't, and neither did anyone else."

"I have seen it, Doctor."

"Hooey! What had you been drinking?"

Operative Carnes of the United States Secret Service chuckled softly to himself. The voice of the famous scientist of the Bureau of Standards plainly showed an interest which was quite at variance with his words.

"I was quite sober, Doctor, and so was Hughes, and we both saw it."

"Who is Hughes?"

"He is an air mail pilot, one of the crack fliers of the Transcontinental Airmail Corporation. Let me tell you the whole thing in order."

"All right. I have a few minutes to spare, but I'll warn you again that I don't intend to touch the case."

*   *   *   *   *

"Suit yourself, Doctor. I have no authority to requisition your services. As you know, the T. A. C. has been handling a great deal of the transcontinental air mail with a pretty clean record on accidents. The day before yesterday, a special plane left Washington to carry two packages from there to San Francisco. One of them was a shipment of jewels valued at a quarter of a million, consigned to a San Francisco firm and the other was a sealed packet from the War Department. No one was supposed to know the contents of that packet except the Chief of Staff who delivered it to the plane personally, but rumors got out, as usual, and it was popularly supposed to contain certain essential features of the Army's war plans. This much is certain: The plane carried not only the regular T. A. C. pilot and courier, but also an army courier, and it was guarded during the trip by an army plane armed with small bombs and a machine-gun. I rode in it. My orders were simply to guard the ship until it landed at Mills Field and then to guard the courier from there to the Presidio of San Francisco until his packet was delivered personally into the hands of the Commanding General of the Ninth Corps Area.

"The trip was quiet and monotonous until after we left Salt Lake City at dawn this morning. Nothing happened until we were about a hundred miles east of Reno. We had taken elevation to cross the Stillwater Mountains and were skimming low over them, my plane trailing the T. A. C. plane by about half a mile. I was not paying any particular attention to the other ship when I suddenly felt our plane leap ahead. It was a fast Douglas and the pilot gave it the gun and made it move, I can tell you. I yelled into the speaking tube and asked what was the reason. My pilot yelled back that the plane ahead was in trouble.

"As soon as it was called to my attention I could see myself that it wasn't acting normally. It was losing elevation and was pursuing a very erratic course. Before we could reach it it lost flying speed and fell into a spinning nose dive and headed for the ground. I watched, expecting every minute to see the crew make parachute jumps, but they didn't and the plane hit the ground with a terrific crash."

"It caught fire, of course?"

*   *   *   *   *

"No, Doctor, that is one of the funny things about the accident. It didn't. It hit the ground in an open place free from brush and literally burst into pieces, but it didn't flame up. We headed directly for the scene of the crash and we encountered another funny thing. We almost froze to death."

"What do you mean?"

"Exactly what I say. Of course, it's pretty cold at that altitude all the time, but this cold was like nothing I had ever encountered. It seemed to freeze the blood in our veins and it congealed frost on the windshields and made the motor miss for a moment. It was only momentary and it only existed directly over the wrecked plane. We went past it and swung around in a circle and came back over the wreck, but we didn't feel the cold again.

"The next thing we tried to do was to find a landing place. That country is pretty rugged and rough and there wasn't a flat place for miles that was large enough to land a ship on. Hughes and I talked it over and there didn't seem to be much of anything that we could do except to go on until we found a landing place. I had had no experience in parachute jumping and I couldn't pilot the plane if Hughes jumped. We swooped down over the wreck as close as we dared and that was when we saw the condition of the bodies. The whole plane was cracked up pretty badly, but the weird part of it was the fact that the bodies of the crew had broken into pieces, as though they had been made of glass. Arms and legs were detached from the torsos and lying at a distance. There was no sign of blood on the ground. We saw all this with our naked eyes from close at hand and verified it by observations through binoculars from a greater height.

"When we had made our observations and marked the location of the wreck as closely as we could, we headed east until we found a landing place near Fallon. Hughes dropped me here and went on to Reno, or to San Francisco if necessary, to report the accident and get more planes to aid in the search. I was wholly at sea, but it seemed to be in your line and as I knew that you were at the St. Francis, I called you up."

*   *   *   *   *

"What are your plans?"

"I made none until I talked with you. The country where the wreck occurred is unbelievably wild and we can't get near it with any transportation other than burros. The only thing that I can see to do is to gather together what transportation I can and head for the wreck on foot to rescue the packets and to bring out the bodies. Can you suggest anything better?"

"When do you expect to start?"

"As soon as I can get my pack train together. Possibly in three or four hours."

"Carnes, are you sure that those bodies were broken into bits? An arm or a leg might easily be torn off in a complete crash."

"They were smashed into bits as nearly as I could tell, Doctor. Hughes is an old flier and he has seen plenty of crashes but he never saw anything like this. It beats anything that I ever saw."

"If your observations were accurate, there could be only one cause and that one is a patent impossibility. I haven't a bit of equipment here, but I expect that I can get most of the stuff I want from the University of California across the bay at Berkeley. I can get a plane at Crissy Field. I'll tell you what to do, Carnes. Get your burro train together and start as soon as you can, but leave me half a dozen burros and a guide at Fallon. I'll get up there as soon as I can and I'll try to overtake you before you get to the wreck. If I don't, don't disturb anything any more than you can help until my arrival. Do you understand?"

"I thought that you were on your vacation, Doctor."

"Oh shut up! Like most of my vacations, this one will have to be postponed. I'll move as swiftly as I can and I ought to be at Fallon to-night if I'm lucky and don't run into any obstacles. Burros are fairly slow, but I'll make the best time possible."

"I rather expected you would, Doctor. I can't get my pack train together until evening, so I'll wait for you right here. I'm mighty glad that you are going to get in on it."

*　　*　　*　　*　　*

Silently Carnes and Dr. Bird surveyed the wreck of the T. A. C. plane. The observations of the secret service operative had been correct. The bodies of the unfortunate crew had been broken into fragments. Their limbs had not been twisted off as a freak of the fall but had been cleanly broken off, as though the bodies had suddenly become brittle and had shattered on their impact with the ground. Not only the bodies, but the ship itself had been broken up. Even the clothing of the men was in pieces or had long splits in the fabric whose edges were as clean as though they had been cut with a knife.

Dr. Bird picked up an arm which had belonged to the pilot and examined it. The brittleness, if it had ever existed, was gone and the arm was limp.

"No *rigor mortis*," commented the Doctor. "How long ago was the wreck?"

"About seventy-two hours ago."

"Hm-m! What about those packets that were on the plane?"

Carnes stepped forward and gingerly inspected first the body of the army courier and then that of the courier of the T. A. C.

"Both gone, Doctor," he reported, straightening up.

Dr. Bird's face fell into grim lines.

"There is more to this case than appears on the surface, Carnes," he said. "This was no ordinary wreck. Bring up that third burro; I want to examine these fragments a little. Bill," he went on to one of the two guides who had accompanied them from Fallon, "you and Walter scout around the ground and see what you can find out. I especially wish to know whether anyone has visited the scene of the wreck."

*　　*　　*　　*　　*

The guides consulted a moment and started out. Carnes drove up the burro the Doctor had indicated and Dr. Bird unpacked it. He opened a mahogony case and took from it a high powered microscope. Setting the instrument up on a convenient rock, he subjected portions of the wreck, including several fragments of flesh, to a careful scrutiny. When he had completed his observations he fell into a brown study, from which he was aroused by Carnes.

"What did you find out about the cause of the wreck, Doctor?"

"I don't know what to think. The immediate cause was that everything was frozen. The plane ran into a belt of cold which froze up the motor and which probably killed the crew instantly. It was undoubtedly the aftermath of that cold which you felt when you swooped down over the wreck."

"It seems impossible that it could have suddenly got cold enough to freeze everything up like that."

"It does, and yet I am confident that that is what happened. It was no ordinary cold, Carnes; it was cold of the type that infests interstellar space; cold beyond any conception you have of cold, cold near the range of the absolute zero of temperature, nearly four hundred and fifty degrees below zero on the Fahrenheit scale. At such temperatures, things which are ordinarily quite flexible and elastic, such as rubber, or flesh, become as brittle as glass and would break in the manner which these bodies have broken. An examination of the tissues of the flesh shows that it has been submitted to some temperature that is very low in the scale, probably below that of liquid air. Such a temperature would produce instant death and the other phenomena which we can observe."

"What could cause such a low temperature, Doctor?"

"I don't know yet, although I hope to find out before we are finished. Cold is a funny thing, Carnes. Ordinarily it is considered as simply the absence of heat; and yet I have always held it to be a definite negative quantity. All through nature we observe that every force has its opposite or negative force to oppose it. We have positive and negative electrical charges, positive and negative, or north and south, magnetic poles. We have gravity and its opposite apergy, and I believe cold is really negative heat."

"I never heard of anything like that, Doctor. I always thought that things were cold because heat was taken from them—not because cold was added. It sounds preposterous."

* * * * *

"Such is the common idea, and yet I cannot accept it, for it does not explain all the recorded phenomena. You are familiar with a searchlight, are you not?"

"In a general way, yes."

"A searchlight is merely a source of light, and of course, of heat, which is placed at the focus of a parabolic reflector so that all of the rays emanating from the source travel in parallel lines. A searchlight, of course, gives off heat. If we place a lens of the same size as the searchlight aperture in the path of the beam and concentrate all the light, and heat, at one spot, the focal point of the lens, the temperature at that point is the same as the temperature of the source of the light, less what has been lost by radiation. You understand that, do you not?"

"Certainly."

"Suppose that we place at the center of the aperture of the searchlight a small opaque disc which is permeable neither to heat nor light, in such a manner as to interrupt the central portion of the beam. As a result, the beam will go out in the form of a hollow rod, or pipe, of heat and light with a dark, cold core. This core will have the temperature of the surrounding air plus the small amount which has radiated into it from the surrounding pipe. If we now pass this beam of light through a lens in order to concentrate the beam, both the pipe of heat and the cold core will focus. If we place a temperature measuring device near the focus of the dark core, we will find that the temperature is lower than the surrounding air. This means that we have focused or concentrated cold."

"That sounds impossible. But I can offer no other criticism."

*   *   *   *   *

"Nevertheless, it is experimentally true. It is one of the facts which lead me to consider cold as negative heat. However, this is true of cold, as it is of the other negative forces; they exist and manifest themselves only in the presence of the positive forces. No one has yet concentrated cold except in the presence of heat, as I have outlined. How this cold belt which the T. A. C. plane encountered came to be there is another question. The thing which we have to determine is whether it was caused by natural or artificial forces."

"Both of the packets which the plane carried are gone, Doctor," observed Carnes.

"Yes, and that seems to add weight to the possibility that the cause was artificial, but it is far from conclusive. The packets might not have been on the men when the plane fell, or someone may have passed later and taken them for safekeeping."

The doctor's remarks were interrupted by the guides.

"Someone has been here since the wreck, Doctor," said Bill. "Walter and I found tracks where two men came up here and prowled around for some time and then left by the way they came. They went off toward the northwest, and we followed their trail for about forty rods and then lost it. We weren't able to pick it up again."

"Thanks, Bill," replied the doctor. "Well, Carnes, that seems to add more weight to the theory that the spot of cold was made and didn't just happen. If a prospecting party had just happened along they would either have left the wreck alone or would have made some attempt to inter the bodies. That cold belt must have been produced artificially by men who planned to rob this plane after bringing it down and who were near at hand to get their plunder. Is there any chance of following that trail?"

"I doubt it, Doc. Walter and I scouted around quite a little, but we couldn't pick it up again."

"Is there any power line passing within twenty miles of here?"

"None that Walter and I know of, Doc."

"Funny! Such a device as must have been used would need power and lots of it for operation. Well, I'll try my luck. Carnes, help me unpack and set up the rest of my apparatus."

*   *   *   *   *

With the aid of the operative, Dr. Bird unpacked two of the burros and extracted from cases where they were carefully packed and padded some elaborate electrical and optical apparatus. The first was a short telescope of large diameter which he mounted on a base in such a manner that it could be elevated or depressed and rotated in any direction. At the focal point of the telescope was fastened a small knot of wire from which one lead ran to the main piece of apparatus, which he sat on a flat rock. The other lead from the wire knot ran into a sealed container surrounded by a water bath under which a spirit lamp burned. From the container another lead led to the main apparatus. This main piece consisted of a series of wire coils mounted on a frame and attached to the two leads. The doctor took from a padded case a tiny magnet suspended on a piece of wire of exceedingly small diameter which he fastened in place inside the coils. Cemented to the magnet was a tiny mirror.

"What is that apparatus?" asked Carnes as the doctor finished his set-up and surveyed it with satisfaction.

"Merely a thermocouple attached to a D'Arsonval galvanometer," replied the doctor. "This large, squat telescope catches and concentrates on the thermocouple and the galvanometer registers the temperature."

"You're out of my depth. What is a thermocouple?"

"A juncture of two wires made of dissimilar metals, in this case of platinum and of platinum-iridium alloy. There is another similar junction in this case, which is kept at a constant temperature by the water bath. When the temperatures of the two junctions are the same, the system is in equilibrium. When they are at different temperatures, an electrical potential is set up, which causes a current to flow from one to the other through the galvanometer. The galvanometer consists of a magnet set up inside coils through which the current I spoke of flows. This current causes the magnet to rotate and by watching the mirror, the rotation can be detected and measured.

"This device is one of the most sensitive ever made, and is used to measure the radiation from distant stars. Currents as small as .000000000000000000000000001 ampere have been detected and measured. This particular instrument is not that sensitive to begin with, and has its sensitivity further reduced by having a high resistance in one of the leads."

"What are you going to use it for?"

"I am going to try to locate somewhere in these hills a patch of local cold. It may not work, but I have hopes. If you will manipulate the telescope so as to search the hills around here, I will watch the galvanometer."

*   *   *   *   *

For several minutes Carnes swung the telescope around. Twice Dr. Bird stopped him and decreased the sensitiveness of his instrument by introducing more resistance in the lines in order to keep the magnet from twisting clear around, due to the fluctuations in the heats received on account of the varying conditions of reflection. As Carnes swung the telescope again the magnet swung around sharply, nearly to a right angle to its former position.

"Stop!" cried the doctor. "Read your azimuth."

Carnes read the compass bearing on the protractor attached to the frame which supported the telescope. Dr. Bird took a pair of binoculars and looked long and earnestly in the indicated direction. With a sigh he laid down the glasses.

"I can't see a thing, Carnesy," he said. "We'll have to move over to the next crest and make a new set-up. Plant a rod on the hill so that we can get an azimuth bearing and get the airline distance with a range finder."

On the hilltop which Dr. Bird had pointed out the apparatus was again set up. For several minutes Carnes swept the hills before an exclamation from the doctor told him to pause. He read the new azimuth, and the doctor laid off the two readings on a sheet of paper with a protractor and made a few calculations.

"I don't know," he said reflectively when he had finished his computations. "This darned instrument is still so sensitive that you may have merely focused on a deep shadow or a cold spring or something of that sort, but the magnet kicked clear around and it may mean that we have located what we are looking for. It should be about two miles away and almost due west of here."

"There is no spring that I know of, Doc, and I think I know of every water hole in this country," remarked Bill.

"There could hardly be a spring at this elevation, anyway," replied the doctor. "Maybe it is what we are seeking. We'll start out in that direction, anyway. Bill, you had better take the lead, for you know the country. Spread out a little so that we won't be too bunched if anything happens."

*   *   *   *   *

For three-quarters of an hour the little group of men made their way through the wilderness in the direction indicated by the doctor. Presently Bill, who was in the lead, held up his hand with a warning gesture. The other three closed up as rapidly as cautious progress would allow.

"What is it, Bill?" asked the doctor in an undertone.

"Slip up ahead and look over that crest."

The doctor obeyed instructions. As he glanced over he gave vent to a low whistle of surprise and motioned for Carnes to join him. The operative crawled up and glanced over the crest. In a hollow before them was a crude one-storied house, and erected on an open space before it was a massive piece of apparatus. It consisted of a number of huge metallic cylinders, from which lines ran to a silvery concave mirror mounted on an elaborate frame which would allow it to be rotated so as to point in any direction.

"What is it?" whispered Carnes.

"Some kind of a projector," muttered the doctor. "I never saw one quite like it, but it is meant to project something. I can't make out the curve of that mirror. It isn't a parabola and it isn't an ellipse. It must be a high degree subcatenary or else built on a transcendental function."

He raised himself to get a clearer view, and as he did so a puff of smoke came from the house, to be followed in a moment by a sharp crack as a bullet flattened itself a few inches from his head. The doctor tumbled back over the crest out of sight of the house. Bill and Walter hurried forward, their rifles held ready for action.

"Get out on the flanks, men," directed the doctor. "The man we want is in a house in that hollow. He's armed, and he means business."

*   *   *   *   *

Bill and Walter crawled under the shelter of the rocks to a short distance away and then, rifles ready, advanced to the attack. A report came from the hollow and a bullet whined over Bill's head. Almost instantly a crack came from Walter's rifle and splinters flew from the building in the hollow a few inches from a loophole, through which projected the barrel of a rifle.

The rifle barrel swung rapidly in a circle and barked in Walter's direction; but as it did so, Bill's gun spoke and again splinters flew from the building.

"Good work!" ejaculated Dr. Bird as he watched the slow advance of the two guides. "If we just had rifles we could join in the party, but it's a little far for effective pistol work. Let's go ahead, and we may get close enough to do a little shooting."

Pistols in hand, Carnes and the doctor crawled over the crest and joined the advance. Again and again the rifle spoke from the hollow and was answered by the vicious barks of the rifles in the hands of the guides, Carnes and the doctor resting their pistols on rocks and sending an occasional bullet toward the loophole. The conditions of light and the moving target were not conducive to good marksmanship on the part of the besieged man, and none of the attackers were hit. Presently Walter succeeded in sending a bullet through the loophole. The rifle barrel suddenly disappeared. With a shout the four men rose from their cover and advanced toward the building at a run.

As they did so an ominous whirring sound came from the apparatus in front of the house and a sudden chill filled the air.

"Back!" shouted Dr. Bird. "Back below the hill if you value your lives!"

He turned and raced at full speed toward the sheltering crest of the hill, the others following him closely. The whirring sound continued, and the concave reflector turned with a grating sound on its gears. As the path of its rays struck the ground the rocks became white with frost and one rock split with a sharp report, one fragment rolling down the slope, carrying others in its trail.

*   *   *   *   *

With panic-stricken faces the four men raced toward the sheltering crest, but remorselessly the reflector swung around in their direction. The intense cold numbed the racing men, cutting off their breath and impeding their efforts for speed.

"Stop!" cried the doctor suddenly. "Fire at that reflector! It's our only chance!"

He set the example by turning and emptying his pistol futilely at the turning mirror. Bill, Walter and Carnes followed his example. Nearer and nearer to them came the deadly ray. Bill was the nearest to its path, and he suddenly stiffened and fell forward, his useless gun still grasped in his hands. As his body struck the ground it rolled down hill for a few feet, the deadly ray following it. His head struck a rock, and Carnes gave a cry of horror as it broke into fragments.

Walter threw his rifle to his shoulder and fired again and again at the rotating disc. The cold had became intense and he could not control the actions of his muscles and his rifle wavered about. He threw himself flat on the ground, and, with an almost superhuman effort, steadied himself for a moment and fired. His aim was true, and with a terrific crash the reflector split into a thousand fragments. Dr. Bird staggered to his feet.

"It's out of order for a moment!" he cried. "To the house while we can!"

As swiftly as his numbed feet would allow him, he stumbled toward the house. The muzzle of the rifle again projected from the loophole and with its crack the doctor staggered for a moment and then fell. Walter's rifle spoke again and the rifle disappeared through the loophole with a spasmodic jerk. Carnes stumbled over the doctor.

"Are you hit badly?" he gasped through chattering teeth.

"I'm not hit at all," muttered the doctor. "I stumbled and fell just as he fired. Look out! He's going to shoot again!"

The rifle barrel came slowly into view through the loophole. Walter fired, but his bullet went wild. Carnes threw himself behind a rock for protection.

*   *   *   *   *

The rifle swung in Walter's direction and paused. As it did so, from the house came a strangled cry and a sound as of a blow. The rifle barrel disappeared, and the sounds of a struggle came from the building.

"Come on!" cried Carnes as he rose to his feet, and made his stumbling way forward, the others following at the best speed which their numbed limbs would allow.

As they reached the door they were aware of a struggle which was going on inside. With an oath the doctor threw his massive frame against the door. It creaked, but the solid oak of which it was composed was proof against the attack, and he drew back for another onslaught. From the house came a pistol shot, followed by a despairing cry and a guttural shout. Reinforced by Carnes, the doctor threw his weight against the door again. With a rending crash it gave, and they fell sprawling into the cabin. The doctor was the first one on his feet.

"Who are you?" asked a voice from one corner. The doctor whirled like a flash and covered the speaker with his pistol.

"Put them up!" he said tersely.

"I am unarmed," the voice replied. "Who are you?"

"We're from the United States Secret Service," replied Carnes who had gained his feet. "The game is up for you, and you'd better realize it."

"Secret Service! Thank God!" cried the voice. "Get Koskoff—he has the plans. He has gone out through the tunnel!"

"Where is it?" demanded Carnes.

"The entrance is that iron plate on the floor."

Carnes and the doctor jumped at the plate and tried to lift it, without result. There was no handle or projection on which they could take hold.

"Not that way," cried the voice. "That cover is fastened on the inside. Go outside the building; he'll come out about two hundred yards north. Shoot him as he appears or he'll get away."

The three men nearly tumbled over each other to get through the doorway into the bitter cold outside. As they emerged from the cabin the gaze of the guide swept the surrounding hills.

"There he goes!" he cried.

"Get him!" said Carnes sharply.

Walter ran forward a few feet and dropped prone on the ground, cuddling the stock of his rifle to his cheek. Two hundred yards ahead a figure was scurrying over the rocks away from the cabin. Walter drew in his breath and his hand suddenly grew steady as his keen gray eyes peered through the sights. Carnes and the doctor held their breath in sympathy.

* * * * *

Suddenly the rifle spoke, and the fleeing man threw up his arms and fell forward on his face.

"Got him," said Walter laconically.

"Go bring the body in, Carnes," exclaimed the doctor. "I'll take care of the chap inside."

"Did you get him?" asked the voice eagerly, as the doctor stepped inside.

"He's dead all right," replied the doctor grimly. "Who the devil are you, and what are you doing here?"

"There is a light switch on the left of the door as you come in," was the reply.

Dr. Bird found the switch and snapped on a light. He turned toward the corner from whence the voice had come and recoiled in horror. Propped in the corner was the body of a middle-aged man, daubed and splashed with blood which ran from a wound in the side of his head.

"Good Lord!" he ejaculated. "Let me help you."

"There's not much use," replied the man rather faintly. "I am about done in. This face wound doesn't amount to much, but I am shot through the body and am bleeding internally. If you try to move me, it may easily kill me. Leave me alone until your partners come."

The doctor drew a flask of brandy from his pocket and advanced toward the corner.

"Take a few drops of this," he advised.

With an effort the man lifted the flask to his lips and gulped down a little of the fiery spirit. A sound of tramping feet came from the outside and then a thud as though a body had been dropped. Carnes and Walter entered the cabin.

"He's dead as a mackerel," said Carnes in answer to the doctor's look. "Walter got him through the neck and broke his spinal cord. He never knew what hit him."

"The plans?" came in a gasping voice from the man in the corner.

"We got them, too," replied Carnes. "He had both packets inside his coat. They have been opened, but I guess they are all here. Who the devil are you?"

"Since Koskoff is dead, and I am dying, there is no reason why I shouldn't tell you," was the answer. "Leave that brandy handy to keep up my strength. I have only a short time and I can't repeat.

*   *   *   *   *

"As to who I am or what I was, it doesn't really matter. Koskoff knew me as John Smith, and it will pass as well as any other name. Let my past stay buried. I am, or was, a scientist of some ability; but fortune frowned on me, and I was driven out of the world. Money would rehabilitate me—money will do anything nowadays—so I set out to get it. In the course of my experimental work, I had discovered that cold was negative heat and reacted to the laws which governed heat."

"I knew that," cried Dr. Bird; "but I never could prove it."

"Who are you?" demanded John Smith.

"Dr. Bird, of the Bureau of Standards."

"Oh, Bird. I've heard of you. You can understand me when I say that as heat, positive heat is a concomitant of ordinary light. I have found that cold, negative heat, is a concomitant of cold light. Is my apparatus in good shape outside?"

"The reflector is smashed."

"I'm sorry. You would have enjoyed studying it. I presume that you saw that it was a catenary curve?"

"I rather thought so."

"It was, and it was also adjustable. I could vary the focal point from a few feet to several miles. With that apparatus I could throw a beam of negative heat with a focal point which I could adjust at will. Close to the apparatus, I could obtain a temperature almost down to absolute zero, but at the longer ranges it wasn't so cold, due to leakage into the atmosphere. Even at two miles I could produce a local temperature of three hundred degrees below zero."

"What was the source of your cold?"

"Liquid helium. Those cylinders contain, or rather did contain, for I expect that Koskoff has emptied them, helium in a liquid state."

"Where is your compressor?"

*   *   *   *   *

"I didn't have to use one. I developed a cold light under whose rays helium would liquefy and remain in a state of equilibrium until exposed to light rays. Those cylinders had merely enough pressure to force the liquid out to where the sun could hit it, and then it turned to a gas, dropping the temperature at the first focal point of the reflector to absolute zero. When I had this much done, Koskoff and I packed the whole apparatus here and were ready for work.

"We were on the path of the transcontinental air mail, and I bided my time until an especially valuable shipment was to be made. My plans, which worked perfectly, were to freeze the plane in midair and then rob the wreck. I heard of the jewel shipment the T. A. C. was to carry and I planned to get it. When the plane came over, Koskoff and I brought it down. The unsuspected presence of another plane upset us a little, and I started to bring it down. But we had been all over this country and knew there was no place that a plane could land. I let it go on in safety."

"Thank you," replied Carnes with a grimace.

"We robbed the wreck and we found two packets, one the jewels I was after, and the other a sealed packet, which proved to contain certain War Department plans. That was when I learned who Koskoff was. I had hired him in San Francisco as a good mechanic who had no principles. He was to get one-fourth of the loot. When we found these plans, he told me who he was. He was really a Russian secret agent and he wanted to deliver the plans to Russia. I may be a thief and a murderer, but I am not yet ready to betray my country, and I told him so. He offered me almost any price for the plans; but I wouldn't listen. We had a serious quarrel, and he overpowered me and bound me.

*   *   *   *   *

"We had a radio set here and he called San Francisco and sent some code message. I think he was waiting here for someone to come. Had we followed our original plans, we would have been miles from here before you arrived.

"He had me bound and helpless, as he thought, but I worked my bonds a little loose. I didn't let him know it, for I knew that the plane I had let get away would guide a party here and I thought I might be able to help out. When you came and attacked the house, I worked at my bonds until they were loose enough to throw off. I saw Koskoff start my cold apparatus to working and then he quit, because he ran out of helium. When he started shooting again, I worked out of my bonds and tackled him.

"He was a better man than I gave him credit for, or else he suspected me, for about the time I grabbed him he whirled and struck me over the head with his gun barrel and tore my face open. The blow stunned me, and when I came to, I was thrown into this corner. I meant to have another try at it, but I guess you rushed him too fast. He turned and ran for the tunnel, but as he did so, he shot me through the body. I guess I didn't look dead enough to suit him. You gentlemen broke open the door and came in. That's all."

"Not by a long shot, it isn't," exclaimed Dr. Bird. "Where is that cold light apparatus of yours?"

"In the tunnel."

"How do you get into it?"

"If you will open that cupboard on the wall, you'll find an open knife switch on the wall. Close it."

*   *   *   *   *

Dr. Bird found the switch and closed it. As he did so the cabin rocked on its foundations and both Carnes and Walter were thrown to the ground. The thud of a detonation deep in the earth came to their ears.

"What was that?" cried the doctor.

"That," replied Smith with a wan smile, "was the detonation of two hundred pounds of T.N.T. When you dig down into the underground cave where we used the cold light apparatus, you will find it in fragments. It was my only child, and I'll take it with me."

As he finished his head slumped forward on his chest. With an exclamation of dismay Dr. Bird sprang forward and tried to lift the prostrate form.

In an agony of desire the Doctor tightened his grip on the dying man's shoulder. But Smith collapsed into a heap. Dr. Bird bent forward and tore open his shirt and listened at his chest. Presently he straightened up.

"He is gone," he said sadly, "and I guess the results of his genius have died with him. He doesn't strike me as a man who left overmuch to chance. Carnes, is your case completed?"

"Very satisfactorily, Doctor. I have both of the lost packets."

"All right, then, come back to the wreck and help me pack my burros. I can make my way back to Fallon without a guide."

"Where are you going, Doctor?"

"That, Carnes, old dear, is none of your blankety blanked business. Permit me to remind you that I am on my vacation. I haven't decided yet just where I am going, but I can tell you one thing. It's going to be some place where you can't call me on the telephone."

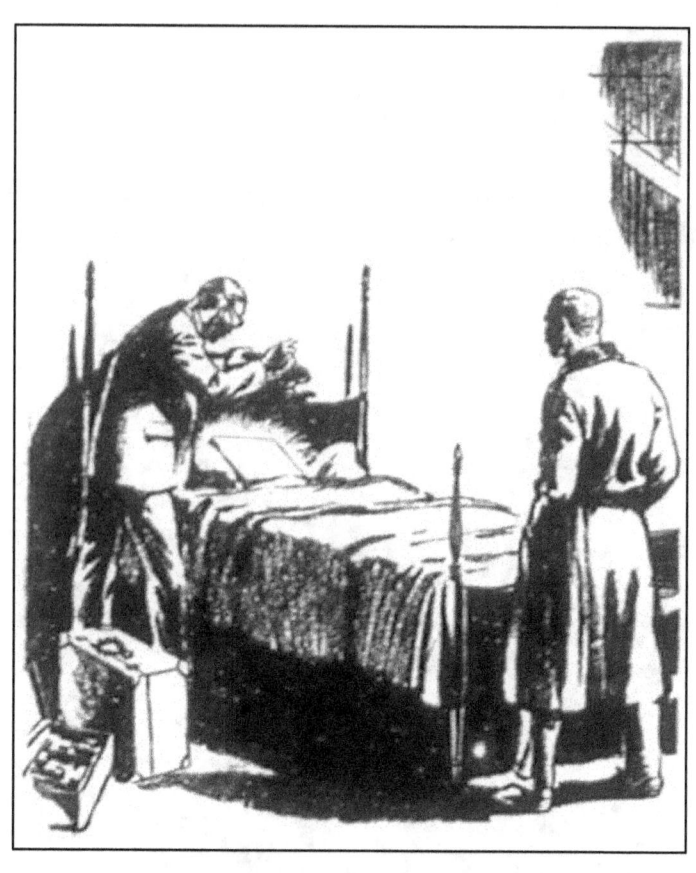

The Ray of Madness

Originally Published In *Astounding Stories Of Super-Science*,
April 1930

Dr. Bird discovers a dastardly plot, amazing in its mechanical ingenuity, behind the apparently trivial eye trouble of the President.

THE RAY OF MADNESS

A knock sounded at the door of Dr. Bird's private laboratory in the Bureau of Standards. The famous scientist paid no attention to the interruption but bent his head lower over the spectroscope with which he was working. The knock was repeated with a quality of quiet insistence upon recognition. The Doctor smothered an exclamation of impatience and strode over to the door and threw it open to the knocker.

"Oh, hello, Carnes," he exclaimed as he recognized his visitor. "Come in and sit down and keep your mouth shut for a few minutes. I am busy just now but I'll be at liberty in a little while."

"There's no hurry, Doctor," replied Operative Carnes of the United States Secret Service as he entered the room and sat on the edge of the Doctor's desk. "I haven't got a case up my sleeve this time; I just came in for a little chat."

"All right, glad to see you. Read that latest volume of the *Zeitschrift* for a while. That article of Von Beyer's has got me guessing, all right."

Carnes picked up the indicated volume and settled himself to read. The Doctor bent over his apparatus. Time and again he made minute adjustments and gave vent to muttered exclamations of annoyance at the results he obtained. Half an hour later he rose from his chair with a sigh and turned to his visitor.

"What do you think of Von Beyer's alleged discovery?" he asked the operative.

*   *   *   *   *

"It's too deep for me, Doctor," replied the operative. "All that I can make out of it is that he claims to have discovered a new element named 'lunium,' but hasn't been able to isolate it yet. Is there anything remarkable about that? It seems to me that I have read of other new elements being discovered from time to time."

"There is nothing remarkable about the discovery of a new element by the spectroscopic method," replied Dr. Bird. "We know from Mendeleff's table that there are a number of elements which we have not discovered as yet, and several of the ones we know were first detected by the spectroscope. The thing which puzzles me is that so brilliant a man as Von Beyer claims to have discovered it in the spectra of the moon. His name, lunium, is taken from Luna, the moon."

"Why not the moon? Haven't several elements been first discovered in the spectra of stars?"

"Certainly. The classic example is Lockyer's discovery of an orange line in the spectra of the sun in 1868. No known terrestrial element gave such a line and he named the new element which he deduced helium, from Helos, the sun. The element helium was first isolated by Ramsey some twenty-seven years later. Other elements have been found in the spectra of stars, but the point I am making is that the sun and the stars are incandescent bodies and could be logically expected to show the characteristic lines of their constituent elements in their spectra. But the moon is a cold body without an atmosphere and is visible only by reflected light. The element, lunium, may exist in the moon, but the manifestations which Von Beyer has observed must be, not from the moon, but from the source of the reflected light which he spectro-analyzed."

*   *   *   *   *

"You are over my depth, Doctor."

"I'm over my own. I have tried to follow Von Beyer's reasoning and I have tried to check his findings. Twice this evening I thought that I caught a momentary glimpse on the screen of my fluoroscope of the ultra-violet line which he reports as characteristic of lunium, but I am not certain. I haven't been able to photograph it yet. He notes in his article that the line seems to be quite impermanent and fades so rapidly that an accurate measurement of its wave-length is almost impossible. However, let's drop the subject. How do you like your new assignment?"

"Oh, it's all right. I would rather be back on my old work."

"I haven't seen you since you were assigned to the Presidential detail. I suppose that you fellows are pretty busy getting ready for Premier McDougal's visit?"

"I doubt if he will come," replied Carnes soberly. "Things are not exactly propitious for a visit of that sort just now."

*   *   *   *   *

Dr. Bird sat back in his chair in surprise.

"I thought that the whole thing is arranged. The press seems to think so, at any rate."

"Everything is arranged, but arrangements may be cancelled. I wouldn't be surprised to hear that they were."

"Carnes," replied Dr. Bird gravely, "you have either said too much or too little. There is something more to this than appears on the surface. If it is none of my business, don't hesitate to tell me so and I'll forget what you have said, but if I can help you any, speak up."

Carnes puffed meditatively at his pipe for a few minutes before replying.

"It's really none of your business. Doctor," he said at length, "and yet I know that a corpse is a chatterbox compared to you when you are told anything in confidence, and I really need to unload my mind. It has been kept from the press so far; but I don't know how long it can be kept muzzled. In strict confidence, the President of the United State acts as though he were crazy."

"Quite a section of the press has claimed that for a long time," replied Dr. Bird, with a twinkle in his eye.

"I don't mean crazy in that way, Doctor, I mean *really* crazy. Bugs! Nuts! Bats in his belfry!"

*   *   *   *   *

Dr. Bird whistled softly.

"Are you sure, Carnes?" he asked.

"As sure as may be. Both of his physicians think so. They were non-committal for a while, especially as the first attack waned and he seemed to recover, but when his second attack came on more violently than the first and the President began to act queerly, they had to take the Presidential detail into their confidence. He has been quietly examined by some of the greatest psychiatrists in the country, but none of them have ventured on a positive verdict as to the nature of the malady. They admit, of course, that it exists, but they won't classify it. The fact that it is intermittent seems to have them stopped. He was bad a month ago but he recovered and became, to all appearances, normal for a time. About a week ago he began to show queer symptoms again and now he is getting worse daily. If he goes on getting worse for another week, it will have to be announced so that the Vice-President can take over the duties of the head of the government."

*   *   *   *   *

"What are the symptoms?"

"The first we noticed was a failing of his memory. Coupled with this was a restlessness and a habit of nocturnal prowling. He tosses continually on his bed and mutters and at times leaps up and rages back and forth in his bedchamber, howling and raging. Then he will calm down and compose himself and go to sleep, only to wake in half an hour and go through the same performance. It is pretty ghastly for the men on night guard."

"How does he act in the daytime?"

"Heavy and lethargic. His memory becomes a complete blank at times and he talks wildly. Those are the times we must guard against."

"Overwork?" queried the Doctor.

"Not according to his physicians. His physical health is splendid and his appetite unusually keen. He takes his exercise regularly and suffers no ill health except for a little eye trouble."

Dr. Bird leaped to his feet.

"Tell me more about this eye trouble, Carnes," he demanded.

"Why, I don't know much about it, Doctor. Admiral Clay told me that it was nothing but a mild opthalmia which should yield readily to treatment. That was when he told me to see that the shades of the President's study were partially drawn to keep the direct sunlight out."

*   *   *   *   *

"Opthalmia be sugared! What do his eyes look like?"

"They are rather red and swollen and a little bloodshot. He has a tendency to shut them while he is talking and he avoids light as much as possible. I hadn't noticed anything peculiar about it."

"Carnes, did you ever see a case of snow blindness?"

The operative looked up in surprise.

"Yes, I have. I had it myself once in Maine. Now that you mention it, his case does look like snow blindness, but such a thing is absurd in Washington in August."

Dr. Bird rummaged in his desk and drew out a book, which he consulted for a moment.

"Now, Carnes," he said, "I want some dates from you and I want them accurately. Don't guess, for a great deal may depend on the accuracy of your answers. When was this mental disability on the part of the President first noticed?"

Carnes drew a pocket diary from his coat and consulted it.

"The seventeenth of July," he replied. "That is, we are sure, in view of later developments, that that was the date it first came on. We didn't realize that anything was wrong until the twentieth. On the night of the nineteenth the President slept very poorly, getting up and creating a disturbance twice, and on the twentieth he acted so queerly that it was necessary to cancel three conferences."

*   *   *   *   *

Dr. Bird checked off the dates on the book before him and nodded.

"Go on," he said, "and describe the progress of the malady by days."

"It got progressively worse until the night of the twenty-third. The twenty-fourth he was no worse, and on the twenty-fifth a slight improvement was noticed. He got steadily better until, by the third or fourth of August, he was apparently normal. About the twelfth he began to show signs of restlessness which have increased daily during the past week. Last night, the nineteenth, he slept only a few minutes and Brady, who was on guard, says that his howls were terrible. His memory has been almost a total blank today and all of his appointments were cancelled, ostensibly because of his eye trouble. If he gets any worse, it probably will be necessary to inform the country as to his true condition."

When Carnes had finished, Dr. Bird sat for a time in concentrated thought.

"You did exactly right in coming to me, Carnes," he said presently. "I don't think that this is a job for a doctor at all—I believe that it needs a physicist and a chemist and possibly a detective to cure him. We'll get busy."

"What do you mean, Doctor?" demanded Carnes. "Do you think that some exterior force is causing the President's disability?"

*   *   *   *   *

"I think nothing, Carnes," replied the Doctor grimly, "but I intend to know something before I am through. Don't ask for explanations: this is not the time for talk, it is the time for action. Can you get me into the White House to-night?"

"I doubt it, Doctor, but I'll try. What excuse shall I give? I am not supposed to have told you anything about the President's illness."

"Get Bolton, your chief, on the phone and tell him that you have talked to me when you shouldn't have. He'll blow up, but after he is through exploding, tell him that I smell a rat and that I want him down here at once with *carte blanche* authority to do as I see fit in the White House. If he makes any fuss about it, remind him of the fact that he has considered me crazy several times in the past when events showed that I was right. If he won't play after that, let me talk to him."

"All right, Doctor," replied Carnes as he picked up the scientist's telephone and gave the number of the home of the Chief of the Secret Service. "I'll try to bully him out of it. He has a good deal of confidence in your ability."

* * * * *

Half an hour later the door of Dr. Bird's laboratory opened suddenly to admit Bolton.

"Hello, Doctor," exclaimed the Chief, "what the dickens have you got on your mind now? I ought to skin Carnes alive for talking out of turn, but if you really have an idea, I'll forgive him. What do you suspect?"

"I suspect several things, Bolton, but I haven't time to tell you what they are. I want to get quietly into the White House as promptly as possible."

"That's easy," replied Bolton, "but first I want to know what the object of the visit is."

"The object is to see what I can find out. My ideas are entirely too nebulous to attempt to lay them out before you just now. You've never worked directly with me on a case before, but Carnes can tell you that I have my own methods of working and that I won't spill my ideas until I have something more definite to go on than I have at present."

"The Doctor is right, Chief," said Carnes. "He has an idea all right, but wild horses won't drag it out of him until he's ready to talk. You'll have to take him on faith, as I always do."

Bolton hesitated a moment and then shrugged his shoulders.

"Have it your own way, Doctor," he said. "Your reputation, both as a scientist and as an unraveller of tangled skeins, is too good for me to boggle about your methods. Tell me what you want and I'll try to get it."

*   *   *   *   *

"I want to get into the White House without undue prominence being given to my movements, and listen outside the President's door for a short time. Later I will want to examine his sleeping quarters carefully and to make a few tests. I may be entirely wrong in my assumptions, but I believe that there is something there that requires my attention."

"Come along," said Bolton. "I'll get you in and let you listen, but the rest we'll have to trust to luck on. You may have to wait until morning."

"We'll cross that bridge when we get to it," replied the Doctor. "I'll get a little stuff together that we may need."

In a few moments he had packed some apparatus in a bag and, taking up it and an instrument case, he followed Bolton and Carnes down the stairs and out onto the grounds of the Bureau of Standards.

"It's a beautiful moon, isn't it?" he observed.

Carnes assented absently to the Doctor's remark, but Bolton paid no attention to the luminous disc overhead, which was flooding the landscape with its mellow light.

"My car is waiting," he announced.

"All right, old man, but stop for a moment and admire this moon," protested the Doctor. "Have you ever seen a finer one?"

"Come on and let the moon alone," snorted Bolton.

"My dear man, I absolutely refuse to move a step until you pause in your headlong devotion to duty and pay the homage due to Lady Luna. Don't you realize, you benighted Christian, that you are gazing upon what has been held to be a deity, or at least the visible manifestation of deity, for ages immemorial? Haven't you ever had time to study the history of the moon-worshipping cults? They are as old as mankind, you know. The worship of Isis was really only an exalted type of moon worship. The crescent moon, you may remember, was one of her most sacred emblems."

*　*　*　*　*

Bolton paused and looked at the Doctor suspiciously.

"What are you doing–pulling my leg?" he demanded.

"Not at all, my dear fellow. Carnes, doesn't the sight of the glowing orb of night influence you to pious meditation upon the frailty of human life and the insignificance of human ambition?"

"Not to any very great degree," replied Carnes dryly.

"Carnesy, old dear, I fear that you are a crass materialist. I am beginning to despair of ever inculcating in you any respect for the finer and subtler things of life. I must try Bolton. Bolton, have you ever seen a finer moon? Remember that I won't move a step until you have carefully considered the matter and fully answered my question."

Bolton looked first at the Doctor, then at Carnes, and finally he looked reluctantly at the moon.

"It's a fine one," he admitted, "but all full moons look large on clear nights at this time of the year."

"Then you *have* studied the moon?" cried Dr. Bird with delight. "I was sure–"

*　*　*　*　*

He broke off his speech suddenly and listened. From a distance came the mournful howl of a dog. It was answered in a moment by another howl from a different direction. Dog after dog took up the chorus until the air was filled with the melancholy wailing of the animals.

"See, Bolton," remarked the Doctor, "even the dogs feel the chastening influence of the Lady of Night and repent of the sins of their youth and the follies of their manhood, or should one say doghood? Come along. I feel that the call of duty must tear us away from the contemplation of the beauties of nature."

He led the way to Bolton's car and got in without further words. A half-hour later, Bolton led the way into the White House. A word to the secret service operative on guard at the door admitted him and his party, and he led the way to the newly constructed solarium where the President slept. An operative stood outside the door.

"What word, Brady?" asked Bolton in a whisper.

"He seems worse, sir. I doubt if he has slept at all. Admiral Clay has been in several times, but he didn't do much good. There, listen! The President is getting up again."

*   *   *   *   *

From behind the closed door which confronted them came sounds of a person rising from a bed and pacing the floor, slowly at first, and then more and more rapidly, until it was almost a run. A series of groans came to the watchers and then a long drawn out howl. Bolton shuddered.

"Poor devil!" he muttered.

Dr. Bird shot a quick glance around.

"Where is Admiral Clay?" he asked.

"He is sleeping upstairs. Shall I call him?"

"No. Take me to his room."

The President's naval physician opened the door in response to Bolton's knock.

"Is he worse?" he demanded anxiously.

"I don't think so, Admiral," replied Bolton. "I want to introduce you to Dr. Bird of the Bureau of Standards. He wants to talk with you about the case."

"I am honored, Doctor," said the physician as he grasped the scientist's outstretched hand. "Come in. Pardon my appearance, but I was startled out of a doze

when you knocked. Have a chair and tell me how I can
serve you."

Dr. Bird drew a notebook from his pocket.

"I have received certain dates in connection with the
President's malady from Operative Carnes," he said, "and
I wish you to verify them."

"Pardon me a moment, Doctor," interrupted the
Admiral, "but may I ask what is your connection with the
matter? I was not aware that you were a physician or
surgeon."

*   *   *   *   *

"Dr. Bird is here by the authority of the secret
service," replied Bolton. "He has no connection with the
medical treatment of the President, but permit me to
remind you that the secret service is responsible for the
safety of the President and so have a right to demand
such details about him as are necessary for his proper
protection."

"I have no intention in obstructing you in the proper
performance of your duties, Mr. Bolton," began the
Admiral stiffly.

"Pardon me, Admiral," broke in Dr. Bird, "it seems to
me that we are getting started wrong. I suspect that
certain exterior forces are more or less concerned in this
case and I have communicated my suspicions to Mr.
Bolton. He in turn brought me here in order to request
from you your cooperation in the matter. We have no idea
of demanding anything and are really seeking help which
we believe that you can give us."

"Pardon me, Admiral," said Bolton. "I had no
intention of angering you."

"I am at your service, gentlemen," replied Admiral
Clay. "What information did you wish, Doctor?"

"At first merely a verification of the history of the case
as I have it."

*   *   *   *   *

Dr. Bird read the notes he had taken down from Carnes and the Admiral nodded agreement.

"Those dates are correct," he said.

"Now, Admiral, there are two further points on which I wish enlightenment. The first is the opthalmia which is troubling the patient."

"It is nothing to be alarmed about as far as symptoms go, Doctor," replied the Admiral. "It is a rather mild case of irritation, somewhat analogous to granuloma, but rather stubborn. He had an attack several weeks ago and while it did not yield to treatment as readily as I could have wished, it did clear up nicely in a couple of weeks and I was quite surprised at this recurrent attack. His sight is in no danger."

"Have you tried to connect this opthalmia with his mental aberrations?"

"Why no, Doctor, there is no connection."

"Are you sure?"

"I am certain. The slight pain which his eyes give him could never have such an effect upon the mind of so able and energetic a man as he is."

"Well, we'll let that pass for the moment. The other question is this: has he any form of skin trouble?"

*   *   *   *   *

The Admiral looked up in surprise.

"Yes, he has," he admitted. "I had mentioned it to no one, for it really amounts to nothing, but he has a slight attack of some obscure form of dermatitis which I am treating. It is affecting only his face and hands."

"Please describe it."

"It has taken the form of a brown pigmentation on the hands. On the face it causes a slight itching and subsequent peeling of the affected areas."

"In other words, it is acting like sunburn?"

"Why, yes, somewhat. It is not that, however, for he has been exposed to the sun very little lately, on account of his eyes."

"I notice that he is sleeping in the new solarium which was added last winter to the executive mansion. Can you tell me with what type of glass it is equipped?"

"Yes. It is not equipped with glass at all, but with fused quartz."

"When did he start to sleep there?"

"As soon as it was completed."

"And all the time the windows have been of fused quartz?"

"No. They were glazed at first, but the glass was removed and the fused quartz substituted at my suggestion about two months ago, just before this trouble started."

"Thank you, Admiral. You have given me several things to think about. My ideas are a little too nebulous to share as yet but I think that I can give you one piece of very sound advice. The President is spending a very restless night. If you would remove him from the solarium and get him to lie down in a room which is glazed with ordinary glass, and pull down the shades so that he will be in the dark, I think that he will pass a better night."

*   *   *   *   *

Admiral Clay looked keenly into the piercing black eyes of the Doctor.

"I know something of you by reputation, Bird," he said slowly, "and I will follow your advice. Will you tell me why you make this particular suggestion?"

"So that I can work in that solarium to-night without interruption," replied Dr. Bird. "I have some tests which I wish to carry out while it is still dark. If my results are negative, forget what I have told you. If they yield any information, I will be glad to share it with you at the proper time. Now get the President out of that solarium and tell me when the coast is clear."

The Admiral donned a dressing gown and stepped out of the room. He returned in fifteen minutes.

"The solarium is at your disposal, Doctor," he announced. "Shall I accompany you?"

"If you wish," assented Dr. Bird as he picked up his apparatus and strode out of the room.

In the solarium he glanced quickly around, noting the position of each of the articles of furniture.

"I presume that the President always sleeps with his head in this direction?" he remarked, pointing to the pillow on the disturbed bed.

The Admiral nodded assent. Dr. Bird opened the bag which he had packed in his laboratory, took out a sheet of cardboard covered with a metallic looking substance, and placed it on the pillow. He stepped back and donned a pair of smoked glasses, watching it intently. Without a word he took off the glasses and handed them to the Admiral. The Admiral donned them and looked at the pillow. As he did so an exclamation broke from his lips.

"That plate seems to glow," he said in an astonished voice.

*　　*　　*　　*　　*

Dr. Bird stepped forward and laid his hand on the pillow. He was wearing a wrist watch with a radiolite dial. The substance suddenly increased its luminescence and began to glow fiercely, long luminous streamers seeming to come from the dial. The Doctor took away his hand and substituted a bottle of liquid for the plate on the pillow. Immediately the bottle began to glow with a phosphorescent light.

"What on earth is it?" gasped Carnes.

"Excitation of a radioactive fluid," replied the Doctor. "The question is, what is exciting it. Somebody get a stepladder."

While Bolton was gone after the ladder, the Doctor took from his bag what looked like an ordinary pane of glass.

"Take this, Carnes," he directed, "and start holding it over each of those panes of quartz which you can reach. Stop when I tell you to."

*   *   *   *   *

The operative held the glass over each of the panes in succession, but the Doctor, who kept his eyes covered with the smoked glasses and fastened on the plate which he had replaced on the pillow, said nothing. When Bolton arrived with the ladder, the process went on. One end and most of the front of the solarium had been covered before an exclamation from the Doctor halted the work.

"That's the one," he exclaimed. "Hold the glass there for a moment."

Hurriedly he removed the plate from the pillow and replaced the phial of liquid. There was only a very feeble glow.

"Good enough," he cried. "Take away the glass, but mark that pane, and be ready to replace it when I give the word."

From the instrument case he had brought he took out a spectroscope. He turned back the mattress and mounted it on the bedstead.

"Cover that pane," he directed.

Carnes did so, and the Doctor swung the receiving tube of the instrument until it pointed at the covered pane. He glanced into the eyepiece, and then held a tiny flashlight for an instant opposite the third tube.

"Uncover that pane," he said.

Carnes took down the glass plate and the Doctor gazed into the instrument. He made some adjustments.

"Are you familiar with spectroscopy, Admiral?" he asked.

"Somewhat."

"Take a squint in here and tell me what you see."

* * * * *

The Admiral applied his eye to the instrument and looked long and earnestly.

"There are some lines there, Doctor," he said, "but your instrument is badly out of adjustment. They are in what should be the ultra-violet sector, according to your scale."

"I forgot to tell you that this is a fluoroscopic spectroscope designed for the detection of ultra-violet lines," replied Dr. Bird. "Those lines you see are ultra-violet, made visible to the eye by activation of a radioactive compound whose rays in turn impinge on a zinc blende sheet. Do you recognize the lines?"

"No, I don't."

"Small wonder; I doubt whether there are a dozen people who would. I have never seen them before, although I recognize them from descriptions I have read. Bolton, come here. Sight along this instrument and through that plate of glass which Carnes is holding and tell me what office that window belongs to."

Bolton sighted as directed up at the side of the State, War and Navy Building.

"I can't tell exactly at this time of night, Doctor," he said, "but I'll go into the building and find out."

"Do so. Have you a flashlight?"

"Yes."

"Flash it momentarily out of each of the suspected windows in turn until you get an answering flash from here. When you do, flash it out of each pane of glass in the window until you get another flash from here. Then come back and tell me what office it is. Mark the pane so that we can locate it again in the morning."

* * * * *

"It is the office of the Assistant to the Adjutant General of the Army," reported Bolton ten minutes later.

"What is there in the room?"

"Nothing but the usual desks and chairs."

"I suspected as much. The window is merely a reflector. That is all that we can do for to-night, gentlemen. Admiral, keep your patient quiet and in a room with *glass* windows, preferably with the shades drawn, until further notice. Bolton, meet me here with Carnes at sunrise. Have a picked detail of ten men standing by where we can get hold of them in a hurry. In the mean time, get the Chief of Air Service out of bed and have him order a plane at Langley Field to be ready to take off at 6 A. M. He is not to take off, however, until I give him orders to do so. Do you understand?"

"Everything will be ready for you, Doctor, but I confess that I don't know what it is all about."

"It's the biggest case you ever tackled, old man, and I hope that we can pull it off successfully. I'd like to go over it with you now, but I'll be busy at the Bureau for the rest of the night. Drop me off there, will you?"

At sunrise the next morning, Bolton met Dr. Bird at the entrance to the White House grounds.

"Where is your detail?" he asked.

"In the State, War and Navy Building."

"Good. I want to go to the solarium, put a light on the place where the President's pillow was last night, and mark that pane of quartz we were looking through. Then we'll join the detail."

*   *   *   *   *

Dr. Bird placed the light and walked with Carnes across the White House grounds. Bolton's badge secured admission to the State, War and Navy Building for the party and they made their way to the office of the Assistant to the Adjutant General.

"Did you mark the pane of glass through which you flashed your light last night, Bolton?" asked the Doctor.

The detective touched one of the panes.

"Good," exclaimed the Doctor. "I notice that this window has hooks for a window washer's belt. Get a life belt, will you?"

When the belt was brought, the Doctor turned to Carnes.

"Carnes," he said, "hook on this life saver and climb out on the window ledge. Take this piece of apparatus with you."

He handed Carnes a piece of apparatus which looked like two telescopes fastened to a base, with a screw adjustment for altering the angles of the barrels.

* * * * *

Carnes took it and looked at it inquiringly.

"That is what I was making at the Bureau last night," explained Dr. Bird. "It is a device which will enable me to locate the source of the beam which was reflected from this pane of glass onto the President's pillow. I'll show you how to work it. You know that when light is reflected the angle of reflection always equals the angle of incidence? Well, you place these three feet against the pane of glass, thus putting the base of the instrument in a plane parallel to the pane of glass. By turning these two knobs, one of which gives lateral and the other vertical adjustment, you will manipulate the instrument until the first telescope is pointing directly toward the President's pillow. Now notice that the two telescope barrels are fastened together and are connected to the knobs, so that when the knobs are turned, the scopes are turned in equal and opposite amounts. When one is turned from its present position five degrees to the west, the other automatically turns five degrees to the east. When one is elevated, the other is correspondingly depressed. Thus, when the first tube points toward the pillow, the other will point toward the source of the reflected beam."

"Clever!" ejaculated Bolton.

"It is rather crude and may not be accurate enough to locate the source exactly, but at least it will give us a pretty good idea of where to look. Given time, a much more accurate instrument could have been made, but two telescopic rifle sights and a theodolite base were all the materials I could find to work with. Climb out, Carnesy, and do your stuff."

*　　*　　*　　*　　*

Carnes climbed out on the window and fastened the hooks of the life saver to the rings set in the window casings. He sat the base of the instrument against the pane of glass and manipulated the telescope knobs as Dr. Bird signalled from the inside. The scientist was hard to please with the adjustment, but at last the cross hairs of the first telescope were centered on the light in the solarium. He changed his position and stared through the second tube.

"The angle is too acute and the distance too great for accuracy," he said with an air of disappointment. "The beam comes from the roof of a house down along Pennsylvania Avenue, but I can't tell from here which one it is. Take a look, Bolton."

The Chief of the Secret Service stared through the telescope.

"I couldn't be sure, Doctor," he replied. "I can see something on the roof of one of the houses, but I can't tell what it is and I couldn't tell the house when I got in front of it."

"It won't do to make a false move," said the Doctor. "Did you arrange for that plane?"

"It is waiting your orders at the field, Doctor."

"Good. I'll go up to the office of the Chief of Air Service and get in touch with the pilot over the Chief's private line. There are some orders that I wish to give him and some signals to be arranged."

*   *   *   *   *

Dr. Bird returned in a few minutes.

"The plane is taking off now and will be over the city soon," he announced. "We'll take a stroll down the Avenue until we are in the vicinity of the house, and then wait for the plane. Carnes will take five of your men and go down behind the house and the rest of us will go in front. Which building do you think it is, Bolton?"

"About the fourth from the corner."

"All right, the men going down the back will take station behind the house next to the corner and the rest of us will get in front of the same building. When the plane comes over, watch it. If you receive no signal, go to the next house and wait for him to make a loop and come over you again. Continue this until the pilot throws a white parachute over. That is the signal that we are covering the right house. When you get that signal, Carnes, leave two men outside and break in with the other three. Get that apparatus on the roof and the men who are operating it. Bolton and I will attack the front door at the same time. Does everybody understand?"

Murmurs of assent came from the detail.

"All right, let's go. Carnes, lead out with your men and go half a block ahead so that the two parties will arrive in position at about the same time."

*   *   *   *   *

Carnes left the building with five of the operatives. Dr. Bird and Bolton waited for a few minutes and then started down Pennsylvania Avenue, the five men of their squad following at intervals. For three-quarters of a mile they sauntered down the street.

"This should be it, Doctor," said Bolton.

"I think so, and here comes our plane."

They watched the swift scout plane from Langley Field swing down low over the house and then swoop up into the sky again without making a signal. The party walked down the street one house and paused. Again the plane swept over them without sign. As they stopped in front of the next house a white parachute flew from the cockpit of the plane and the aircraft, its mission accomplished, veered off to the south toward its hangar.

"This is the place," cried Bolton. "Haggerty and Johnson, you two cover the street. Bemis, take the lower door. The rest come with me."

*   *   *   *   *

Followed closely by Dr. Bird and two operatives, Bolton sprinted across the street and up the steps leading to the main entrance of the house. The door was barred, and he hurled his weight against it without result.

"One side, Bolton," snapped Dr. Bird.

The diminutive Chief drew aside and Dr. Bird's two hundred pounds of bone and muscle crashed against the door. The lock gave and the Doctor barely saved himself from sprawling headlong on the hall floor. A woman's scream rang out, and the Doctor swore under his breath.

"Upstairs! To the roof!" he cried.

Followed by the rest of the party, he sprinted up the stairway which opened before him. Just as he reached the top his way was barred by an Amazonian figure in a green bathrobe.

"Who th' divil arre yer?" demanded an outraged voice.

"Police," snapped Bolton. "One side!"

"Wan side, is it?" demanded the fiery haired Amazon. "The divil a stip ye go until ye till me ye'er bizness. Phwat th' divil arre yer doin' in th' house uv a rayspictable female at this hour uv th' marnin'?"

"One side, I tell you!" cried Bolton as he strove to push past the figure that barred the way.

"Oh, ye wud, wud yer, little mann?" demanded the Irishwoman as she grasped Bolton by the collar and shook him as a terrier does a rat. Dr. Bird stifled his laughter with difficulty and seized her by the arm. With a heave on Bolton's collar she raised him from the ground and swung him against the Doctor, knocking him off his feet.

"Hilp! P'lice! Murther!" she screamed at the top of her voice.

"Damn it, woman, we're on—"

*　　*　　*　　*　　*

Dr. Bird's voice was cut short by the sound of a pistol shot from the roof, followed by two others. The Irishwoman dropped Bolton and slumped into a sitting position and screamed lustily. Bolton and Dr. Bird, with the two operatives at their heels, raced for the roof. Before they reached it another volley of shots rang out, these sounding from the rear of the building. They made their way to the upper floor and found a ladder running to a skylight in the roof. At the foot of the ladder stood one of Carnes' party.

"What is it, Williams?" demanded Bolton.

"I don't know, Chief. Carnes and the other two went up there, and then I heard shooting. My orders were to let no one come down the ladder."

As he spoke, Carnes' head appeared at the skylight.

"It's the right place, all right, Doctor," he called. "Come on up, the shooting is all over."

*　　*　　*　　*　　*

Dr. Bird mounted the ladder and stepped out on the roof. Set on one edge was a large piece of apparatus, toward which the scientist eagerly hastened. He bent over it for a few moments and then straightened up.

"Where is the operator?" he asked.

Carnes silently led the way to the edge of the roof and pointed down. Dr. Bird leaned over. At the foot of the fire escape he saw a crumpled dark heap, with a secret service operative bending over it.

"Is he dead, Olmstead?" called Carnes.

"Dead as a mackerel," came the reply. "Richards got him through the head on his first shot."

"Good business," said Dr. Bird. "We probably could never have secured a conviction and the matter is best hushed up anyway. Bolton, have two of your men help me get this apparatus up to the Bureau. I want to examine it a little. Have the body taken to the morgue and shut up the press. Find out which room the chap occupied and search it, and bring all his papers to me. From a criminal standpoint, this case is settled, but I want to look into the scientific end of it a little more."

"I'd like to know what it was all about, Doctor," protested Bolton. "I have followed your lead blindly, and now I have a housebreaking without search-warrant and a killing to explain, and still I am about as much in the dark as I was at the beginning."

"Excuse me, Bolton," said Dr. Bird contritely; "I didn't mean to slight you. Admiral Clay wants to know about it and so does Carnes, although he knows me too well to say so. As soon as I have digested the case I'll let you know and I'll go over the whole thing with you."

*   *   *   *   *

A week later Dr. Bird sat in conference with the President in the executive office of the White House. Beside him sat Admiral Clay, Carnes and Bolton.

"I have told the President as much as I know, Doctor," said the Admiral, "and he would like to hear the details from your lips. He has fully recovered from his malady and there is no danger of exciting him."

"I cannot read Russian," said Dr. Bird slowly, "and so was forced to depend on one of my assistants to translate the papers which Mr. Bolton found in Stokowsky's room. There is nothing in them to definitely connect him with the Russian Union of Soviet Republics, but there is little doubt in my mind that he was a Red agent and that Russia supplied the money which he spent. It would be disastrous to Russia's plans to have too close an accord between this country and the British Empire, and I have no doubt that the coming visit of Premier McDougal was the underlying cause of the attempt. So much for the reason.

"As to how I came to suspect what was happening, the explanation is very simple. When Carnes first told me of your malady, Mr. President, I happened to be checking Von Beyer's results in the alleged discovery of a new element, lunium. In the article describing his experiments, Von Beyer mentions that when he tried to observe the spectra, he encountered a mild form of opthalmia which was quite stubborn to treatment. He also mentions a peculiar mental unbalance and intense exhilaration which the rays seemed to cause both in himself and in his assistants. The analogy between his observations and your case struck me at once.

*   *   *   *   *

"For ages the moon has been an object of worship by various religious sects, and some of the most obscene orgies of which we have record occurred in the moonlight. The full moon seems to affect dogs to a state of partial hypnosis with consequent howling and evident pain in the eyes. Certain feeble minded persons have been known to be adversely affected by moonlight as well as some cases of complete mental aberration. In other words, while moonlight has no practical effect on the normal human in its usual concentration, it does have an adverse effect on certain types of mentality and, despite the laughter of medical science, there seems to be something in the theory of 'moon madness.' This effect Von Beyer attributed to the emanations of lunium, which element he detected in the spectra of the moon, in the form of a wide band in the ultra-violet region.

*   *   *   *   *

"I obtained from Carnes a history of your case, and when I found that your attacks grew violent with the full moon and subsided with the new moon, I was sure that I was on the right track, although I had at that time no way of knowing whether it was from natural or artificial causes that the effect was being produced. I interviewed Admiral Clay and found that you were suffering from a form of dermititis resembling sunburn, and that convinced me that an attack was being made on your sanity, for an excess of ultra-violet light will always tend to produce sunburn. I inquired about the windows of your solarium, for ultra-violet light will not pass through a lead glass. When the Admiral told me that the glass had been replaced with fused quartz, which is quite permeable to ultra-violet and that the change had been almost coincident with the start of your malady, I asked him to get you out of the solarium and let me examine it.

"By means of certain fluorescent substances which I used, I found that your pillow was being bathed in a flood of ultra-violet light, and the fluoro-spectroscope soon told me that lunium emanations were present in large quantities. These rays were not coming to you directly from their source, but one of the windows of the State, War and Navy Building was being used as a reflector. I located the approximate source of the ray by means of an improvised apparatus, and we surrounded the place. Stokowsky was killed while attempting to escape. I guess that is about all there is to it."

"Thank you, Doctor," said the President. "I would be interested in a description of the apparatus which he used to produce this effect."

*   *   *   *   *

"The apparatus was quite simple, Sir. It was merely a large collector of moonlight, which was thrown after collection onto a lunium plate. The resultant emanations were turned into a parallel beam by a parabolic reflector and focused, through a rock crystal lens with an extremely long focal length, onto your pillow."

"Then Stokowsky had isolated Von Beyer's new element?" asked the President.

"I am still in doubt whether it is a new element or merely an allotropic modification of the common element, cadmium. The plate which he used has a very peculiar property. When moonlight, or any other reflected light of the same composition falls on it, it acts on the ray much as the button of a Roentgen tube acts on a cathode ray. As the cathode ray is absorbed and an entirely new ray, the X-ray, is given off by the button, just so is the reflected moonlight absorbed and a new ray of ultra-violet given off. This is the ray which Von Beyer detected. I thought that I could catch traces of Von Beyer's lines in my spectroscope, and I think now that it is due to a trace of lunium in the cadmium plating of the barrels. Von Beyer could have easily made the same mistake. Von Beyer's work, together with Stokowsky's opens up an entirely new field of spectroscopic research. I would give a good deal to go over to Baden and go into the matter with Von Beyer and make some plans for the exploitation of the new field, but I'm afraid that my pocketbook wouldn't stand the trip."

"I think that the United States owes you that trip, Dr. Bird," said the Chief Executive with a smile. "Make your plans to go as soon as you get your data together. I think that the Treasury will be able to take care of the expense without raising the income tax next year."

STOLEN BRAINS

ORIGINALLY PUBLISHED IN *ASTOUNDING STORIES OF SUPER-SCIENCE,* OCTOBER 1930

Dr. Bird, scientific sleuth extraordinary,
goes after a sinister stealer of brains.

Stolen Brains

"I hope, Carnes," said Dr. Bird, "that we get good fishing."

"Good fishing? Will you please tell me what you are talking about?"

"I am talking about fishing, old dear. Have you seen the evening paper?"

"No. What's that got to do with it?"

Dr. Bird tossed across the table a copy of the *Washington Post* folded so as to bring uppermost an item on page three. Carnes saw his picture staring at him from the center of the page.

"What the dickens?" he exclaimed as he bent over the sheet. With growing astonishment he read that Operative Carnes of the United States Secret Service had collapsed at his desk that afternoon and had been rushed to Walter Reed Hospital where the trouble had been diagnosed as a nervous breakdown caused by overwork. There followed a guarded statement from Admiral Clay, the President's personal physician, who had been called into conference by the army authorities.

The Admiral stated that the Chief of the Washington District was in no immediate danger but that a prolonged rest was necessary. The paper gave a glowing tribute to the detective's life and work and stated that he had been given sick leave for an indefinite period and that he was leaving at once for the fishing lodge of his friend, Dr. Bird of the Bureau of Standards, at Squapan Lake, Maine. Dr. Bird, the article concluded, would accompany and care for his stricken friend. Carnes laid aside the paper with a gasp.

*　　*　　*　　*　　*

"Do you know what all this means?" Carnes demanded.

"It means, Carnsey, old dear, that the fishing at Squapan Lake should be good right now and that I feel the need of accurate information on the subject. I didn't want to go alone, so I engineered this outrage on the government and am taking you along for company. For the love of Mike, look sick from now on until we are clear of Washington. We leave to-night. I already have our tickets and reservations and all you have to do is to collect your tackle and pack your bags for a month or two in the woods and meet me at the Pennsy station at six to-night."

"And yet there are some people who say there is no Santa Claus," mused Carnes. "If I had really broken down from overwork, I would probably have had my pay docked for the time I was absent, but a man with official pull in this man's government wants to go fishing and presto! the wheels move and the way is clear. Doctor, I'll meet you as directed."

"Good enough," said Dr. Bird. "By the way, Carnes," he went on as the operative opened the door, "bring your pistol."

Carnes whirled about at the words.

"Are we going on a case?" he asked.

"That remains to be seen," replied the Doctor enigmatically. "At all events, bring your pistol. In answer to any questions, we are going fishing. In point of fact, we are—with ourselves as bait. If you have a little time to spare this afternoon you might drop around to the office of the *Post* and get them to show you all the amnesia cases they have had stories on during the past three months. They will be interesting reading. No more questions now, old dear, we'll have lots of time to talk things over while we are in the Maine woods."

*   *   *   *   *

Late the next evening they left the Bangor and Aroostook train at Mesardis and found a Ford truck waiting for them. Over a rough trail they were driven for fifteen miles, winding up at a log cabin which the Doctor announced was his. The truck deposited their belongings and jounced away and Dr. Bird led the way to the cabin, which proved to be unlocked. He pushed open the door and entered, followed by Carnes. The operative glanced at the occupants of the cabin and started back in surprise.

Seated at a table were two figures. The smaller of the two had his back to the entrance but the larger one was facing them. He rose as they entered and Carnes rubbed his eyes and reeled weakly against the wall. Before him stood a replica of Dr. Bird. There was the same six feet two of bone and muscle, the same beetling brows and the same craggy chin and high forehead surmounted by a shock of unruly black hair. In face and figure the stranger was a replica of the famous scientist until he glanced at their hands. Dr. Bird's hands were long and slim with tapering fingers, the hands of a thinker and an artist despite the acid stains which disfigured them but could not hide their beauty. The hands of his double were stained as were Dr. Bird's, but they were short and thick and bespoke more the man of action than the man of thought.

The second figure arose and faced them and again Carnes received a shock. While the likeness was not so, striking, there was no doubt that the second man would have readily passed for Carnes himself in a dim light or at a little distance. Dr. Bird burst into laughter at the detective's puzzled face.

"Carnes," he said, "shake yourself together and then shake hands with Major Trowbridge of the Coast Artillery Corps. It has been said by some people that we favor one another."

"I'm glad to meet you, Major," said Carnes. "The resemblance is positively uncanny. But for your hands, I would have trouble telling you two apart."

*   *   *   *   *

The Major glanced down at his stubby fingers.

"It is unfortunate but it can't be helped," he said. "Dr. Bird, this is Corporal Askins of my command. He is not as good a second to Mr. Carnes as I am to you but you said it was less important."

"The likeness is plenty good enough," replied the Doctor. "He will probably not be subjected to as close a scrutiny as you will. Did you have any trouble in getting here unobserved?"

"None at all, Doctor. Lieutenant Maynard found a good landing field within a half mile of here, as you said he would, and he has his Douglass camouflaged and is standing by. When do you expect trouble?"

"I have no idea. It may come to-night or it may come later. Personally I hope that it comes later so that we can get in a few days of fishing before anything happens."

"What do you expect to happen, Doctor?" demanded Carnes. "Every time I have asked you anything you told me to wait until we were in the Maine woods and we are there now. I read up everything that I could find on amnesia victims during the past three months but it didn't throw much light on the matter to me."

"How many cases did you find, Carnes?"

"Sixteen. There may have been lots more but I couldn't find any others in the *Post* records. Of course, unless the victim were a local man, or of some prominence, it wouldn't appear."

"You got most of them at that. Did any points of similarity strike you as you read them?"

"None except that all were prominent men and all of them mental workers of high caliber. That didn't appear peculiar because it is the man of high mentality who is most apt to crack."

"Undoubtedly. There were some points of similarity which you missed. Where did the attacks take place?"

"Why, one was at–Thunder, Doctor! I did miss something. Every case, as nearly as I can recall, happened at some summer camp or other resort where they were on vacation."

"Correct. One other point. At what time of day did they occur?"

"In the morning, as well as I can remember. That point didn't register."

"They were all discovered in the morning, Carnes, which means that the actual loss of memory occurred during the night. Further, every case has happened within a circle with a diameter of three hundred miles. We are near the northern edge of that circle."

*   *   *   *   *

Carnes checked up on his memory rapidly.

"You're right, Doctor," he cried. "Do you think–?"

"Once in a while," replied Dr. Bird dryly, "I think enough to know the futility of guesses hazarded without complete data. We are now located within the limits of the amnesia belt and we are here to find out what did happen, if anything, and not to make wild guesses about it. You have the tent set up for us, Major?"

"Yes, Doctor, about thirty yards from the cabin and hidden so well that you could pass it a dozen times a day without suspecting its existence. The gas masks and other equipment which you sent to Fort Banks are in it."

"In that case we had better dispense with your company as soon as we have eaten a bite, and retire to it. On second thought, we will eat in it. Carnes, we will go to our downy couches at once and leave our substitutes in possession of the cabin. I trust, gentlemen, that things come out all right and that you are in no danger."

Major Trowbridge shrugged his heavy shoulders.

"It is as the gods will," he said sententiously. "It is merely a matter of duty to me, you know, and thank God, I have no family to mourn if anything does go wrong. Neither has Corporal Askins."

"Well, good luck at any rate. Will you guide Carnes to the tent and then return here and I'll join him?"

*   *   *   *   *

Huddled in the tiny concealed tent, Dr. Bird handed Carnes a haversack on a web strap.

"This is a gas mask," he said. "Put it on your neck and keep it ready for instant use. I have one on and one of us must wear a mask continually while we are here. We'll change off every hour. If the gas used is lethane, as I suspect, we should be able to detect it before its gets too concentrated, but some other gas might be used and we must take no chances. Now look here."

With the aid of a flash-light he showed Carnes a piece of apparatus which had been set up in the tent. It consisted of two telescopic barrels, one fitted with an eye-piece and the other, which was at a wide angle to the first, with an objective glass. Between the two was a covered round disc from which projected a short tube fitted with a protecting lens. This tube was parallel to the telescopic barrel containing the objective lens.

"This is a new thing which I have developed and it is getting its first practical test to-night," he said. "It is a gas detector. It works on the principle of the spectroscope with modifications. From this projector goes out a beam of invisible light and the reflections are gathered and thrown through a prism of the eye-piece. While a spectroscope requires that the substance which it examines be incandescent and throw out visible light rays in order to show the typical spectral lines, this device catches the invisible ultra-violet on a fluorescent screen and analyzes it spectroscopically. Whoever has the mask on must continually search the sky with it and look for the three bright lines which characterize lethane, one at 230, one at 240 and the third at 670 on the illuminated scale. If you see any bright lines in those regions or any other lines that are not continually present, call my attention to it at once. I'll watch for the first hour."

*   *   *   *   *

At the end of an hour Dr. Bird removed his mask with a sigh of relief and Carnes took his place at the spectroscope. For half an hour he moved the glass about and then spoke in a guarded tone.

"I don't see any of the lines you told me to look for," he said, "but in the southwest I get wide band at 310 and two lines at about 520."

Dr. Bird advanced toward the instrument but before he reached it, Carnes gave an exclamation.

"There they are, Doctor!" he cried.

Dr. Bird sniffed the air. A faint sweetish odor became apparent and he reached for his gas mask. Slowly his hands drooped and Carnes grasped him and drew the mask over his face. Dr. Bird rallied slightly and feebly drew a bottle from his pocket and sniffed it. In another instant he was shouldering Carnes aside and staring through the spectroscope. Carnes watched him for an instant and then low whirring noise attracted his attention and he looked up. Silently he caught the Doctor's arm in a viselike grip and pointed.

Hovering above the cabin was a silvery globe, faintly luminous in the moonlight. From its top rose a faint cloud of vapor which circled around the globe and descended toward the earth. The globe hovered like a giant humming bird above the cabin and Carnes barely stifled an exclamation. The door of the cabin opened and Major Trowbridge, walking stiffly and like a man in a dream, appeared. Slowly he advanced for ten yards and stood motionless. The globe moved over him and the bottom unfolded like a lily. Two long arms shot silently down and grasped the motionless figure and drew him up into the heart of the globe. The petals refolded, and silently as a dream the globe shot upward and disappeared.

"Gad! They lost no time!" commented Dr. Bird. "Come on, Carnes, run for your life, or rather, for Trowbridge's life. No, you idiot, leave your gas mask on. I'll take the spectroscope; it'll be all we need."

Followed by the panting Carnes, Dr. Bird sped through the night along an almost invisible path. For half a mile he kept up a headlong pace until Carnes could feel his heart pounding as though it would burst his ribs. The pair debouched from the trees into a glade a few acres in extent and Dr. Bird paused and whistled softly. An answering whistle came from a few yards away and a figure rose in the darkness as they approached.

"Maynard?" called Dr. Bird. "Good enough! I was afraid that you might not have kept your gas mask on."

"My orders were to keep it on, sir," replied the lieutenant in muffled tones through his mask, "but my mechanician did not obey orders. He passed out cold without any warning about fifteen minutes ago."

"Where's your ship?"

"Right over here, sir."

"We'll take off at once. Your craft is equipped with a Bird silencer?"

"Yes, sir."

"Come on, Carnes, we're going to follow that globe. Take the front cockpit alone, Maynard; Carnes and I will get in the rear pit with the spec and guide you. You can take of your gas mask at an elevation of a thousand feet. You have pack 'chutes, haven't you?"

"In the rear pit, Doctor."

"Put one on, Carnes, and climb in. I've got to get this spec set up before he gets too high."

The Douglass equipped with the Bird silencer, took the air noiselessly and rapidly gained elevation under the urging of the pilot. Dr. Bird clamped the gas-detecting spectroscope on the front of his cockpit and peered through it.

"Southwest, at about a thousand more elevation," he directed.

"Right!" replied the pilot as he turned the nose of his plane in the indicated direction and began to climb. For an hour and a half the plane flew noiselessly through the night.

"Bald Mountain," said the pilot, pointing. "The Canadian Border is only a few miles away."

"If they've crossed the Border, we're sunk," replied the doctor. "The trail leads straight ahead."

*   *   *   *   *

For a few minutes they continued their flight toward the Canadian Border and then Dr. Bird spoke.

"Swing south," he directed, "and drop a thousand feet and come back."

The pilot executed the maneuver and Dr. Bird peered over the edge of the plane and directed the spectroscope toward the ground.

"Half a mile east," he said, "and drop another thousand. Carnes, get ready to jump when I give the word."

"Oh, Lord!" groaned Carnes as he fumbled for the rip cord of his parachute, "suppose this thing doesn't open?"

"They'll slide you between two barn doors for a coffin and bury you that way," said Dr. Bird grimly. "You know your orders, Maynard?"

"Yes, sir. When you drop, I am to land at the nearest town—it will be Lowell—and get in touch with the Commandant of the Portsmouth Navy Yard if possible. If I get him, I am to tell him my location and wait for the arrival of reenforcements. If I fail to get him on the telephone, I am to deliver a sealed packet which I carry to the nearest United States Marshal. When reenforcements arrive, either from the Navy Yard or from the Marshal, I am to guide them toward the spot where I dropped you and remain, as nearly as I can judge, two miles away until I get a further signal or orders from you."

"That is right. We'll be over the edge in another minute. Are you ready, Carnes?"

"Oh, yes, I'm ready, Doctor, if I have to risk my precious life in this contraption."

"Then jump!"

*   *   *   *   *

Side by side, Carnes and the doctor dropped toward the ground. The Douglass flew silently away into the night. Carnes found that the sensation of falling was not an unpleasant one as soon as he got accustomed to it. There was little sensation of motion, and it was not until a sharp whisper from Dr. Bird called it to his attention that he realized that he was almost to the ground. He bent his legs as he had been instructed and landed without any great jar. As he rose he saw that Dr. Bird was already on his feet and was eagerly searching the ground with the spectroscope which he had brought with him in the jump.

"Fold your parachute, Carnes, and we'll stow them away under a rock where they can't be seen. We won't use them again."

Carnes did so and deposited the silk bundle beside the doctor's, and they covered them with rocks until they would be invisible from the air.

"Follow me," said the doctor as he strode carefully forward, stopping now and then to take a sight with the spectroscope. Carnes followed him as he made his way up a small hill which blocked the way. A hiss from Dr. Bird stopped him.

Dr. Bird had dropped flat on the ground, and Carnes, on all fours, crawled forward to join him. He smothered an exclamation as he looked over the crest of the hill. Before him, sitting in a hollow in the ground, was the huge globe which had spirited away Major Trowbridge.

"This is evidently their landing place," whispered Dr. Bird. "The next thing to find is their hiding place."

* * * * *

He rose and started forward but sank at once to the ground and dragged Carnes down with him. On the hill which formed the opposite side of the hollow a line of light showed for an instant as though a door had been opened. The light disappeared and then reappeared, and as they watched it widened and against an illuminated background four men appeared, carrying a fifth. The door shut behind them and they made their way slowly toward the waiting globe. They laid down their burden and one of them turned a flash-light on the globe and opened a door in its side through which they hoisted their burden. They all entered the globe, the door closed and with a slight whirring sound it rose in the air and moved rapidly toward the northeast.

"That's the place we're looking for," muttered Dr. Bird. "We'll go around this hollow and look for it. Be careful where you step; they must have ventilation somewhere if their laboratory is underground."

Followed by the secret service operative, the doctor made his way along the edge of the hollow. They did not dare to show a light and it was slow work feeling their way forward, inch by inch. When they had reached a point above where the doctor thought the light had been he paused.

"There must be a ventilation shaft somewhere around here," he whispered, his mouth not an inch from Carnes' ear, "and we've got to find it. It would never do to try the door; if any of them are still here it is sure to be guarded.

You go up the hill for five yards and I'll go down. Quarter back and forth on a two hundred yard front and work carefully. Don't fall in, whatever you do. We'll return to this point every time we pass it and report."

The operative nodded and walked a few yards up the hill and made his way slowly forward. He went a hundred yards as nearly as he could judge and then stepped five yards further up the hill and made his way back. As he passed the starting point he approached and Dr. Bird's figure rose up.

"Any luck?" he whispered.

Dr. Bird shook his head.

"Well try further," he said. "I think it is probably beyond us, so suppose you go fifteen yards up and quarter the same as before."

*   *   *   *   *

Carnes nodded and stole silently away. Fifteen yards up the hill he went and then paused. He stood on the crest of the hill and before him was a steep, almost precipitous slope. He made his way along the edge for a few yards and then paused. Faintly he could detect a murmur of voices. Inch by inch he crept forward, going over the ground under foot. He paused and listened intently and decided that the sound must come from the slope beneath him. A glance at his watch told him that he had spent ten minutes on this trip and he made his way back to the meeting place.

Dr. Bird was waiting for him, and in a low whisper Carnes reported his discovery. The doctor went back with him and together they renewed the search. The slope of the hill was almost sheer and Carnes looked dubiously over the edge.

"I wish we had brought the parachutes," he whispered to the doctor. "We could have taken the ropes off them and you could have lowered me over the edge."

Dr. Bird chuckled softly and tugged at his middle. Carnes watched him with astonishment in the dim light, but he understood when Dr. Bird thrust the end of a strong but light silk cord into his hands. He looped it under his arms and the doctor with whispered instructions, lowered him over the cliff. The doctor lowered him for a few feet and then stopped in response to a jerk on the free end. A moment later Carnes signaled to be drawn up and soon stood beside the doctor.

"That's the place all right," he whispered. "The whole cliff is covered with creepers and there is a tree growing right close to it. If we can anchor the cord here, I think that we can slide down to a safe hold on the tree."

A tree stood near and the silk cord was soon fastened. Carnes disappeared over the cliff and in a few moments Dr. Bird slid down the cord to join him. He found the detective seated in the crotch of a tree only a few feet from the face of the cliff. From the cliff came a pronounced murmur of voices. Dr. Bird drew in his breath in excitement and moved forward along the branch. He touched the stone and after a moment of searching he cautiously raised one corner of a painted canvas flap and peered into the cliff. He watched for a few seconds and then slid back and silently pulled Carnes toward him.

* * * * *

Together the two men made their way toward the cliff and Dr. Bird raised the corner of the flap and they peered into the hill. Before them was a cave fitted up as a cross between a laboratory and a hospital. Almost directly opposite them and at the left of a door in the farther wall was a ray machine of some sort. It was a puzzle to Carnes, and even Dr. Bird, although he could grasp the principle at a glance, was at a loss to divine its use. From a set of coils attached to a generator was connected a tube of the Crookes tube type with the rays from it gathered and thrown by a parabolic reflector onto the space where a man's head would rest when he was seated in a white metal chair with rubber insulated feet, which stood beneath it. An operating table occupied the other side of the room while a gas cylinder and other common hospital apparatus stood around ready for use.

Seated at a table which occupied the center of the room were three men. The sound of their voices rose from an indistinct murmur to audibility as the flap was raised and the watchers could readily understand their words. Two of them sat with their faces toward the main entrance and the third man faced them. Carnes bit his lip as he looked at the man at the head of the table. He was twisted and misshapen in body, a grotesque dwarf with a hunched back, not over four feet in height. His massive head, sunken between his hunched shoulders, showed a tremendous dome of cranium and a brow wider and even higher than Dr. Bird's. The rest of his face was lined and drawn as though by years of acute suffering. Sharp black eyes glared brightly from deep sunk caverns. The dwarf was entirely bald; even the bushy eyebrows which would be expected from his face, were missing.

*   *   *   *   *

"They ought to be getting back," said the dwarf sharply.

"If they get back at all," said one of the two figures facing him.

"What do you mean?" growled the dwarf, his eyes glittering ominously. "They'll return all right; they know they'd better."

"They'll return if they can, but I tell you again, Slavatsky, I think it was a piece of foolishness to try to take two men in one night. We got Bird all right, but it is getting late for a second one, and they had to take Bird over a hundred miles and then go nearly three hundred more for Williams. The news about Bird may have been discovered and spread and others may be looking out for us. Carnes might have recovered."

"Didn't he get a full dose of lethane?"

"So Frick says, and Bird certainly had a full dose, but I can't help but feel uneasy. Our operations were going too nicely on schedule and you had to break it up and take on an extra case in the same night as a scheduled one. I tell you, I don't like it."

"I'm sorry that I did it, Carson, but only because the results were so poor. We had planned on Williams for a month and I wanted him. And Bird was so easy that I couldn't resist it."

"And what did you get? Not as much menthium as would have come from an ordinary bookkeeper."

"I'll admit that Bird is a grossly overrated man. He must have worked in sheer luck in his work in the past, for there was nothing in his brain to show it above average. We got barely enough menthium to replace what we used in capturing him."

"We ought to have taken Carnes and left Bird alone," snorted Carson. "Even a wooden-headed detective ought to have given us a better supply than Bird yielded."

"We are bound to meet with disappointments once in a while. I had marked Bird down long ago as soon as I could get a chance at him."

"Well, you ran that show, Slavatsky, but I'll warn you that we aren't going to let you pull off another one like it. I take no more crazy chances, even on your orders."

*   *   *   *   *

The hunchback rose to his feet, his eyes glittering ominously.

"What do you mean, Carson?" he asked slowly, his hand slipping behind him as he spoke.

"Don't try any rough stuff, Slavatsky!" warned Carson sharply. "I can pull a tube as fast as you can, and I'll do it if I have to."

"Gentlemen, gentlemen!" protested the third man rising, "we are all too deep in this to quarrel. Sit down and let's talk this over. Carson is just worried."

"What is there to be worried about?" grunted the dwarf as he slid back into his chair. "Everything has gone nicely so far and no suspicion has been raised."

"Maybe it has and then again maybe it hasn't," growled Carson. "I think this Bird episode to-night looks bad. In the first place, it came too opportunely and too easily. In the second place Bird should have yielded more menthium, and in the third place, did you notice his hands? They weren't the type of hands to expect on a man of his type."

"Nonsense, they were acid stained."

"Acid stains can be put on. It may be all right, but I am worried. While we are talking about this matter, there is another thing I want cleared up."

"What is it?"

"I think, Slavatsky, that you are holding out on us. You are getting more than your share of the menthium."

Again the dwarf leaped to his feet, but the peace-maker intervened.

"Carson has a right to look at the records, Slavatsky," he said. "I am satisfied, but I'd like to look at them, too. None of us have seen them for two months."

The dwarf glared at first one and then the other.

"All right," he said shortly and limped to a cabinet on the wall. He drew a key from his pocket and opened it and pulled out a leather-bound book. "Look all you please. I was supposed to get the most. It was my idea."

"You were to get one share and a half, while Willis, Frink and I got one share each and the rest half a share," said Carson. "I know how much has been given and it won't take me but a minute to check up."

*   *   *   *   *

He bent over the book, but Willis interrupted.

"Better put it away, Carson," he said, "here come the rest and we don't want them to know we suspect anything."

He pointed toward a disc on the wall which had begun to glow. Slavatsky looked at it and grasped the book from Carson and replaced it in the cabinet. He moved over and started the generator and the tube began to glow with a violet light. A noise came from the outside and the door opened. Four men entered carrying a fifth whom they propped up in the chair under the glowing tube.

"Did everything go all right?" asked the dwarf eagerly.

"Smooth as silk," replied one of the four. "I hope we get some results this time."

The dwarf bent over the ray apparatus and made some adjustments and the head of the unconscious man was bathed with a violet glow. For three minutes the flood of light poured on his head and then the dwarf shut off the light and Carson and Willis lifted the figure and laid it on the operating table. The dwarf bent over the man and inserted the needle of a hypodermic syringe into the back of the neck at the base of the brain. The needle was an extremely long one, and Dr. Bird gasped as he saw four inches of shining steel buried in the brain of the unconscious man.

Slowly Slavatsky drew back the plunger of the syringe and Dr. Bird could see it was being filled with an amber fluid. For two minutes the slow work continued, until a speck of red appeared in the glass syringe barrel.

"Seven and a half cubic centimeters!" cried the dwarf in a tone of delight.

"Fine!" cried Carson. "That's a record, isn't it?"

"No, we got eight once. Now hold him carefully while I return some of it."

*   *   *   *   *

Slavatsky slowly pressed home the plunger and a portion of the amber fluid was returned to the patient's skull. Presently he withdrew the needle and straightened up and held it toward the light.

"Six centimeters net," he announced. "Take him back, Frink. I'll give Carson and Willis their share now and we'll take care of the rest of you when you return. Is the ship well stocked?"

"Enough for two or three more trips."

"In that case, I'll inject this whole lot. Better get going, Frink, it's pretty late."

The four men who had brought the patient in stepped forward and lifted him from the table and bore him out. Dr. Bird dropped the canvas screen and strained his ears. A faint whir told him that the globe had taken to the air. He slid back along the limb of the tree until he touched the rope and silently climbed hand over hand until he gained the crest. He bent his back to the task of raising Carnes, and the operative soon stood beside him on the ledge surmounting the cliff.

"What on earth were they doing?" asked Carnes in a whisper.

"That was Professor Williams of Yale. They were depriving him of his memory. There will be another amnesia case in the papers to-morrow. I haven't time to explain their methods now: we've got to act. You have a flash-light?"

"Yes, and my gun. Shall we break in? There are only three of them, and I think we could handle the lot."

"Yes, but the others may return at any time and we want to bag the whole lot. They've done their damage for to-night. You heard my orders to Lieutenant Maynard, didn't you?"

"Yes."

"He should be somewhere in these hills to the south with assistance of some sort. The signal to them is three long flashes followed in turn by three short ones and three more long. Go and find them and bring them here. When you get close give me the same light signal and don't try to break in unless I am with you. I am going to reconnoitre a little more and make sure that there is no back entrance through which they can escape. Good luck. Carnes: hurry all you can. There is no time to be lost."

* * * * *

The secret service operative stole away into the night and Dr. Bird climbed back down the rope and took his place at the window. Willis lay on the operating table unconscious, while Slavatsky and Carson studied the now partially emptied syringe.

"You gave him his full share all right," Carson was saying. "I guess you are playing square with us. I'll take mine now."

He lay down on the operating table and the dwarf fitted an anesthesia cone over his face and opened the valve of the gas cylinder. In a moment he closed it and rolled the unconscious man on his face and deftly inserted the long needle. Instead of injecting a portion of the contents of the syringe as Dr. Bird had expected to do, he drew back on the plunger for a minute and then took out the needle and held the syringe to the light.

"Well, Mr. Carson," he said with a malignant glance at the unconscious figure, "that recovers the dose you got a couple of weeks ago while Willis watched me. I don't think you really need any menthium; your brain is too active to suit me as it is."

He gave an evil chuckle and walked to the far side of the cave and opened a secret panel. He drew from a recess a flask and carefully emptied a portion of the contents of the syringe into it. He replaced the flask and closed the panel, and with another chuckle he limped over to a chair and threw himself down in it. For an hour he sat motionless and Dr. Bird carefully worked his way back along the branch and climbed the rope and started for the hollow.

*   *   *   *   *

A faint whirring noise attracted his attention, and he could see the faintly luminous globe in the distance, rapidly approaching. It came to a stop at the spot where it had previously landed and four men got out. Instead of going toward the cave, they towed the globe, which floated a few inches from the earth, toward the side of the hill farthest from where the doctor stood. Three of them held it, while the fourth went forward and bent over some controls on the ground. A creaking sound came through the night and the men moved forward with the globe. Presently its movement stopped and men reappeared. Again came the creaking sound and the glow faded out as though a screen had been drawn in front of it. The four men walked toward the door of the cave.

Dr. Bird dropped flat on the ground and saw them pause a few yards below him on the hill and again work some hidden controls. A glare of light showed for an instant and they disappeared and everything was again quiet. Dr. Bird debated the advisability of returning to the window but decided against it and moved down the face of the hill.

Inch by inch he went over the ground, but found nothing. In the darkness he could not locate the door and he made his way around to the back of the hill. The precipice loomed above him and he swept it with his gaze, but he could locate no opening in the darkness and he dared not use a flash-light. As he turned he faced the east and noted with a start of surprise that the sky was getting red. He glanced at his watch and found that Carnes had been gone for nearly three hours.

"Great Scott!" he exclaimed in surprise. "Time has gone faster than I realized. He ought to be back at any time now."

*   *   *   *   *

He mounted the highest point of the hill and sent three long flashes, followed in turn by three short and three more long to the south and watched eagerly for an answer. He waited five minutes and repeated the signal, but no answering flashes came from the empty hills. With a grunt which might have meant anything, he turned and made his way toward the opposite side of the hollow where the globe had disappeared. Here he met with more luck. He had marked the location with extreme care and he had not spent over twenty minutes feeling over the ground before his hand encountered a bit of metal. As he pulled on it his eyes sought the side of the hill.

The dawn had grown sufficiently bright for him to see the result of his action. A portion of the hill folded back and the faintly glowing ship became visible. With a muttered exclamation of triumph he approached it.

The globe was about nine feet in diameter and was without visible doors or windows. Around and around it the doctor went, searching for an entrance. The ship now rested solidly on the ground. He failed to find what he sought and his sensitive hands began to go over it searching for an irregularity. He had covered nearly half of it before his finger found a hidden button and pressed it. Silently a door in the side of the craft opened and he advanced to enter.

"Keep them up!" said a sharp voice behind him.

Dr. Bird froze into instant immobility and the voice spoke again.

"Turn around!"

Dr. Bird turned and looked full into the eye of a revolver held by the man the dwarf had addressed as Frink. Behind Frink stood the dwarf and three other men.

As his eye fell on Dr. Bird, Frink turned momentarily pale and staggered back, the revolver wavering as he did so. Dr. Bird made a lightning-like grab for his own weapon, but before he could draw it Frink had recovered and the revolver was again steady.

"Dr. Bird!" gasped Slavatsky. "Impossible!"

"Get his gun, Harris," said Frink.

*   *   *   *   *

One of the men stepped forward and dextrously removed the doctor's automatic and frisked him expertly to insure himself that he had no other weapon concealed.

"Bring him to the cave," directed Slavatsky, who, though obviously still shaken, had just as obviously recovered enough to be a very dangerous man. Two of the men grasped the doctor and led him along toward the entrance to the laboratory cave which stood wide open in the gathering daylight. Frink paused long enough to shut the side of the hill and conceal the ship, and then followed the doctor. In the cave the door was shut and the doctor placed against the wall under the window through which he had peered earlier in the night. Slavatsky took his seat at the table, his malignant black eyes boring into the Doctor. Carson and Willis sat on the edge of the operating table, evidently still partially under the effects of the anesthetic that had been administered to them.

"How did you get back here?" demanded Slavatsky.

"Find out!" snapped Dr. Bird.

The dwarf rose threateningly.

"Speak respectfully to me; I am the Master of the World!" he roared in an angry voice. "Answer my questions when I speak, or means will be found to make you answer. How did you get back here?"

Dr. Bird maintained a stubborn silence, his fierce eyes answering the dwarf's, look for look, and his prominent chin jutting out a little more squarely. Carson suddenly broke the silence.

"That's not the Bird we had here earlier," he cried as he staggered to his feet.

"What do you mean?" demanded Slavatsky whirling on him.

"Look at his hands!" replied Carson pointing.

* * * * *

Slavatsky looked at Dr. Bird's long mobile fingers and an evil leer came over his countenance.

"So, Dr. Bird," he said slowly, "you thought to match wits with Ivan Slavatsky, the greatest mind of all the ages. For a time you fooled me when your double was operated on here, but not for long. I presume you thought that we had no way of detecting the substitution? You have discovered differently. Where is your friend, Mr. Carnes?"

"Didn't your men leave him in the cabin when you kidnapped me?"

Slavatsky looked at Frink inquiringly.

"He stayed in the cabin if he was in it when we got there," the leader of the kidnapping gang replied. "He got a full shot of lethane and he's due to be asleep yet. I don't know how this man recovered. I left him there myself."

"Fool!" shrieked Slavatsky. "You brought me a double, a dummy whom I wasted my time in operating on. Was the other a dummy, too?"

"I didn't enter the cabin."

Slavatsky shrugged his shoulders.

"If that is all the good the menthium I have injected has done you, I might as well have saved it. It doesn't matter, however: we have the one we wanted. Dr. Bird, it was very thoughtful of you to come here and offer your marvelous brain to strengthen mine. I have no doubt that you will yield even more menthium than Professor Williams did this evening especially as I will extract your entire supply and reduce you to permanent idiocy. I will have no mercy on you as I have on the others I have operated on."

Dr. Bird blanched in spite of himself at the ominous words.

"You have the whip-hand for the moment, Slavatsky, but my time may come—and if it does, I will remember your kindness. I saw your operation on Professor Williams this evening and know your power. I also know that you stole the idea and the method from Sweigert of Vienna. I saw you inject the fluid you drew into Willis' brain. Shall I tell what else I saw?"

It was the dwarf's turn to blanch, but he recovered himself quickly.

"Into the chair with him!" he roared.

*　　*　　*　　*　　*

Three of the men grasped the doctor and forced him into the chair and Slavatsky started the generator. The violet light bathed Dr. Bird's head and he felt a stiffness and contraction of his neck muscles, and as he tried to shout out his knowledge of Slavatsky's treachery, he found that his vocal chords were paralyzed. Through a gathering haze he could see Carson approaching with an anesthesia cone and the sweet smell of lethane assailed his nostrils. He fought with all his force, but strong hands held him, and he felt himself slipping—slipping—slipping— and then falling into an immense void. His head slumped forward on his chest and Slavatsky shut off the generator.

"On the table," he said briefly.

Four men picked up the herculean frame of the unconscious doctor and hoisted him up on the table. Carson seized his head and bent it forward and the dwarf took from a case a syringe with a five-inch needle. He touched the point of it to the base of the doctor's brain.

"Slavatsky! Look!" cried Frink.

With an exclamation of impatience the dwarf turned and stared at a disc set on the wall of the cave. It was glowing brightly. With an oath he dropped the syringe and snapped a switch, plunging the cave into darkness. A tiny panel in the door opened to his touch and he stared out into the light.

"Soldiers!" he gasped. "Quick, the back way!"

As he spoke there came a sound as of a heavy body falling at the back of the cave. Slavatsky turned the switch and flooded the cave with light. At the back of the cave stood Operative Carnes, an automatic pistol in his hand.

"Open the main door!" Carnes snapped.

*   *   *   *   *

Slavatsky made a move toward the light, and Carnes' gun roared deafeningly in the confined space. The heavy bullet smashed into the wall an inch from the dwarf's hand and he started back.

"Open the main door!" ordered Carnes again.

The men stared at one another for a moment and the dwarf's eyes fell.

"Open the door, Frink," he said.

Frink moved over to a lever. He glanced at Slavatsky and a momentary gleam of intelligence passed between them. Frink raised his hand toward the lever and Carnes gun roared again and Frink's arm fell limp from a smashed shoulder.

"Slavatsky," said Carnes sternly, "come here!"

Slowly the dwarf approached.

"Turn around!" said Carnes.

He turned and felt the cold muzzle of Carnes' gun against the back of his neck.

"Now tell one of your men to open the door," said the detective. "If he promptly obeys your order, you are safe. If he doesn't, you die."

Slavatsky hesitated for a moment, but the cold muzzle of the automatic bored into the back of his neck and when he spoke it was in a quavering whine.

"Open the door, Carson," he whimpered.

There was moment of pause.

"If that door isn't open by the time I count three," said Carnes, "–as far as Slavatsky is concerned, it's just too bad. I'll have four shots left–and I'm a dead shot at this range. One! Two!"

His lips framed the word "three" and his fingers were tightening on the trigger when Carson jumped forward with an oath. He pulled a lever on the wall and the door swung open. Carnes shouted and through the opened door came a half dozen marines followed by an officer.

"Tie these men up!" snapped Carnes.

*   *   *   *   *

In a trice the six men were securely bound and Frink's bleeding shoulder was being skilfully treated by two of the marines. Carnes turned his attention to the unconscious doctor.

He rolled him over on his back and began to chafe his hands. An officer in a naval uniform came through the door and with a swift glance around, bent over Dr. Bird. He raised one of the doctor's eyelids and peered closely at his eye and then sniffed at his breath.

"It's some anesthetic I don't know," he said. "I'll try a stimulant."

He reached in his pocket for a hypodermic, but Carnes interrupted him.

"Earlier in the evening Dr. Bird said they were using lethane," he said.

"Oh, that new gas the Chemical Warfare Service has discovered," said the surgeon. "In that case I guess it'll just have to wear off. I know of nothing that will neutralize it."

Without replying, Carnes began to feverishly search the pockets of the unconscious scientist. With an exclamation of triumph he drew out a bottle and uncorked it. A strong smell as of garlic penetrated the room and he held the opened bottle under Dr. Bird's nose.

The doctor lay for a moment without movement, and then he coughed and sat up half strangled with tears running down his face.

"Take that confounded bottle away, Carnes!" he said. "Do you want to strangle me?"

He sat up and looked around.

"What happened?" he demanded. "Oh, yes, I remember now. That brute was about to operate on me. How did you get here?"

"Never mind that, Doctor. Are you all right?"

"Right as a trivet, old dear. How did you get here so opportunely?"

"I was a little slow in locating Lieutenant Maynard and the marines. When we got here I was afraid that we couldn't find the door, so I took Maynard and a detail around to the back and I went up to the top and slid down our cord and looked in the window. You were unconscious and Slavatsky was bending over you with a needle in his hand. I was about to try a shot at him when something called their attention to the men in front and I squeezed through the window and dropped in on them. They didn't seem any too glad to see me, but I overlooked that and insisted on inviting the rest of my friends in to share in the party. That's all."

"Carnes," said the Doctor, "you're probably lying like a trooper when you make out that you did nothing, but I'll pry the truth out of you sooner or later. Now I've got to get to work. Send for Lieutenant Maynard."

*   *   *   *   *

One of the marines went out to get the flyer, and Dr. Bird stepped to the cabinet from which Slavatsky had taken his record book earlier in the evening and took out the leather-bound volume. He opened it and had started to read when Lieutenant Maynard entered the cave.

"Hello, Maynard," said the Doctor, looking up. "Are the rest of the party on their way?"

"They will be here in less than two hours, Doctor."

"Good enough! Have some one sent to guide them here. In the meanwhile, I'm going to study these records. Keep the prisoners quiet. If they make a noise, gag them. I want to concentrate."

For an hour and a half silence reigned in the cave. A stir was heard outside and Admiral Clay, the President's personal physician, entered leading a stout gray-haired man. Dr. Bird whistled when he saw them and leaped to his feet as another figure followed the admiral.

"The President!" gasped Carnes as the officers came to a salute and the marines presented arms.

The President nodded to his ex-guard, acknowledged the salute of the rest and turned to Dr. Bird.

"Have you met with success, Doctor?" he asked.

"I have, Mr. President; or, rather, I hope that I have. At the same time, I would rather experiment on some other victim of their deviltry than the one you have brought me."

"My decision that the one I have brought shall be the first to be experimented on, as you term it, is unalterable."

*   *   *   *   *

Dr. Bird bowed and turned to the dwarf who had been a sullen witness of what had gone on.

"Slavatsky," he said slowly, "your game is up. I have witnessed one of your brain transfusions and I know the method. I gather from your notes that the menthium you have hidden in that cabinet is still as potent as when it was first extracted from a living brain, but in this case I am going to draw it fresh from one of your gang. Some of the details of the operation are a little hazy to me, but those you will teach me. I am going to restore this man to the condition he was in before you did your devil's work on him and you will direct my movements. Just what is the first step in removing the menthium from a brain?"

The dwarf maintained a stubborn silence.

"You refuse to answer?" asked the Doctor in feigned surprise. "I thought that you would rather instruct me and have me try the operation first on other men. Since you prefer that I operate on you first, I will be glad to do so."

He stepped to the opposite wall and in a few moments had opened the dwarf's hiding place and taken out the flask of menthium.

"Carson," he said, "after you had watched Slavatsky inject menthium into Willis, you took lethane and expected him to inject menthium into your brain. Instead of doing so he withdrew a portion from your brain and put it in this flask. I have reason to believe from his secret records which I found in the cabinet with this flask that he has done so regularly. Are you willing to instruct me while I remove the menthium from him?"

"The dirty swine!" shouted Carson. "I'll do anything to get even with him, but I have never performed the operation. Only Slavatsky and Willis have operated."

"Will you help me, Willis? asked Dr. Bird.

"I'll be glad to, Doctor. I am sick of this business anyway. At first, Slavatsky just planned to give us abnormally keen brains, but lately he has been talking of setting himself up as Emperor of the World, and I am sick of it. I think I would have broken with him and told all I know, soon, anyway."

"Throw him in that chair," said Dr. Bird.

*　　*　　*　　*　　*

Despite the howlings and strugglings of the dwarf, three of the marines strapped him in the chair beneath the tube. The dwarf howled and frothed at the mouth and directed a final appeal for mercy to the President.

"Spare me, Your Excellency," he howled. "I will put my brains at your service and make you the greatest mentality of all time. Together we can conquer and rule the world. I will show you how to build hundreds of ships like mine–"

The President turned his back on the dwarf and spoke curtly.

"Proceed with your experiments, Dr. Bird," he said.

Slavatsky directed his appeals to the doctor, who peremptorily silenced him.

"I told you a few hours ago, Slavatsky, that the time might come when I would remember your threats against me. I will show you the same mercy now as you promised me then. Carnes, put a cone over his face."

Despite the howls of the dwarf, the operative forced an anesthesia cone over his face and Dr. Bird turned to the valve of the lethane cylinder. With Willis directing his movements, he turned on the ray for three minutes and removed the unconscious dwarf to the operating table. He took the long-needled syringe from a case and sterilized it and then turned to the President.

"I am about to operate," he said, "but before I do so, I wish to explain to all just what I have learned and what I am about to do. With that data, the decision of whether I shall proceed will rest with you and Admiral Clay. Have I your permission to do so?"

*   *   *   *   *

The President nodded.

"When I first read of these amnesia cases, I took them for coincidences–until you consulted me and gave me an opportunity to examine one of the victims. I found a small puncture at the base of the brain which I could not explain, and I began to dig into old records. I knew, of course, of Sweigert of Vienna, and the extravagant claims he had put forward in 1911. He was far ahead of his time, but he mixed up some profound scientific discoveries with mysticism and occultism until he was discredited. Nevertheless, he continued his experiments with the aid of his principal assistant, a man named Slavatsky.

"Sweigert's theory was that intellectuality, brain power, intelligence, call it what you will, was the result of the presence of a fluid which he called 'menthium' in the brain. He thought that it could be transferred from one person to another, and with the aid of Slavatsky, he experimented on himself. He removed the menthium from an unfortunate victim, who was reduced to a state of imbecility, and Slavatsky injected the substance into Sweigert's brain. The experiment resulted fatally and Slavatsky was tried for murder. He was acquitted of intentional murder but was imprisoned for a time for manslaughter. He was released when the Austro-Hungarian Empire was broken up, and for a time I lost track of him.

"I found translations of both the records of the trials and of Sweigert's original reports, and the thing that attracted my attention was that the puncture I found in the victim corresponded exactly with the puncture described by Sweigert as the one he made in extracting the menthium. I asked the immigration authorities to check over their records and they found that a man named Slavatsky whose description corresponded with the ill-fated Sweigert's assistant had entered the United States under Austria's quota about a year ago. The chain of evidence seemed complete to me, and it only remained to find the man who was systematically robbing brains.

"If such a thing was really going on, I felt that my reputation would make me an attractive bait and I secured a double, as you know, and placed him in a position where his kidnapping would be an easy matter. I was sure that the victims were being taken away by air and that lethane was being used to reduce the neighborhood to a state of profound somnolence, so I hid myself near my double with a gas detector which would find even minute traces of lethane in the air.

"My fish rose to the lure and came after the bait last night. When his ship arrived, I found a strange gas in the air, and followed the ship by the trail of the substance which it left behind it. Carnes was with me, and we got here in time to witness the extraction of the menthium from my friend, Professor Williams of Yale, and to see it injected into one of Slavatsky's gang. I sent Carnes for help and messed around until I was captured myself–and help arrived just in time. That's about all there is to tell. I am now about to reverse the process and try to remove the stolen brains from the criminals and restore them to their rightful owners. I have never operated and the result may be fatal. Shall I proceed?"

The President and Admiral Clay consulted for a moment in undertones.

"Go on with your experiments, Dr. Bird," said the President, "and we will hold you blameless for a failure. You have worked so many miracles in the past that we have every confidence in you."

Dr. Bird bowed acknowledgment to the compliment and bent over the unconscious dwarf. With Willis directing every move, he inserted the needle and drew back slowly on the plunger. Twenty-three and one-half cubic centimeters of amber fluid flowed into the syringe before a speck of blood appeared.

"Enough!" cried Willis. Dr. Bird withdrew the syringe and motioned to Admiral Clay. The man the Admiral had brought in was placed in the chair and lethane administered. He was laid on the table, and, with a silent prayer, Dr. Bird inserted the needle and pressed the plunger. When five and one-quarter centimeters had flowed into the man's brains, he withdrew the needle and held the bottle which Carnes had used to revive him under the man's nose. The patient coughed a moment and sat up.

"Where am I?" he demanded. His gaze roved the cave and fell on the President. "Hello, Robert," he exclaimed. "What has happened?"

With a cry of joy the President sprang forward and wrung the hand of the man.

"Are you all right, William?" he asked anxiously. "Do you feel perfectly normal?"

"Of course I do. My neck feels a little stiff. What are you talking about? Why shouldn't I feel normal? How did I get here?"

"Take him outside, Admiral, and explain to him," said the President.

Admiral Clay led the puzzled man outside and the President turned to Dr. Bird.

"Doctor," he said, "I need not tell you that I again add my personal gratitude to the gratitude of a nation which would be yours, could the miracles you work be told off. If there is ever any way that can serve you, either personally or officially, do not hesitate to ask. The other victims will be brought here to-day. Will you be able to restore them?"

"I will, Mr. President. From Slavatsky's records I find that I will have enough if I reduce all of his men to a state of imbecility except Willis. In view of his assistance, I propose to leave him with enough menthium to give him the intelligence of an ordinary schoolboy."

"I quite approve of that," said the President as Willis humbly expressed his gratitude. "Have you had time to make an examination of that ship of Slavatsky's, yet?"

"I have not. As soon as the work of restoration is completed, I will go over it, and when I master the principles I will be glad to take them up with the Army-Navy General Board."

"Thank you, Doctor," said the President. He shook hands heartily and left the cave. Carnes turned and looked at the Doctor.

"Will you answer a question, Doctor?" he asked. "Ever since this case started, I have been wondering at your extraordinary powers. You have ordered the army, the navy, the department of justice and everyone else around as though you were an absolute monarch. I know the President was behind you, but what puzzles me is how he came to be so vitally interested in the case."

Dr. Bird smiled quizzically at the detective.

"Even the secret service doesn't know everything," he said. "Evidently you didn't recognize the man whose memory I restored. Besides being one of the most brilliant corporation executives in the country, he has another unique distinction. He happens to be the only brother of the President of the United States."

The Sea Terror

Originally Published In *Astounding Stories Of Super-Science*, December 1930

*The trail of mystery gold leads Carnes and
Dr. Bird to a tremendous monster of the deep.*

THE SEA TERROR

"I beg your pardon, sir. I'm looking for Dr. Bird."

The famous Bureau of Standards scientist appraised the speaker rapidly. Keen blue eyes stared questioningly at him from a mahogany brown face, criss-crossed with a thousand tiny wrinkles. The tattooed anchor on his hand and the ill-fitting blue serge suit smacked of the sea while the squareness of his shoulders and the direct gaze of his eye spoke eloquently of authority.

"I'm Dr. Bird, Captain. What can I do for you?"

"Thank you, Doctor, but I'm not a captain. My name is Mitchell and I am, or was, the first mate of the *Arethusa*."

"The *Arethusa!*" Operative Carnes of the United States Secret Service sprang to his feet. "You said the *Arethusa?* There *were* no survivors!"

"I believe that I am the only one."

"Where have you been hiding and why haven't you reported the fact of your rescue to the proper authorities? Tell the truth; I'm a federal officer!"

Carnes flashed the gold badge of the Secret Service and an expression of anger crossed Mitchell's face.

"If I had wished to talk to an officer I could have found plenty in New York," he said shortly. "I came to Washington in order to tell my story to Dr. Bird."

The seaman and the detective glared at one another for a moment and then Dr. Bird intervened.

"Pipe down, Carnes," he said softly. "Mr. Mitchell undoubtedly has reasons, excellent reasons, for his actions. Sit down, Mr. Mitchell, and have a cigar."

*   *   *   *   *

Mitchell accepted the cigar which the doctor proferred and took a chair. He lighted the weed and after another glance of hostility toward the detective he pointedly ignored him and addressed his remarks to Dr. Bird.

"I have no objection to telling you why I haven't spoken earlier, Doctor," he said. "When the *Arethusa* sank, I must have hit my head on something, for the next thing I knew, I was in the Marine Hospital in New York. I had been picked up unconscious by a fishing boat and brought in, and I lay there a week before I knew anything. When I knew what I was doing I heard about the loss of my ship and was told that there were no survivors, and I didn't know what to do. The story I had to tell was so weird and improbable that I hesitated to speak to anyone about it. I was not sure at first that it was not a trick of a disordered brain, but since my head has cleared I am convinced of the truth of it ... and yet I know that it *can't* be so. I have read about you and some of the things you have done, and so as soon as I was able to travel I came here to tell you about it. You will be better able to judge than I, whether what I tell you really happened or was only a vision."

Dr. Bird leaned back in his chair and put the tips of his fingers together. Long, tapering fingers they were, sensitive and well shaped, though sadly marred by acid stains. It was in his hands alone that Dr. Bird showed the genius in his make-up, the artistry which inspired him to produce those miracles of experimentation which had made his name a household word in the realm of science. Aside from those hands he more resembled a pugilist than a scientist. A heavy shock of unruly black hair surmounted a face with beetling black brows and a prognathous jaw. His enormous head, with a breadth and height of forehead which were amazing, rose from a pillar-like neck which sprang from a pair of massive shoulders and the arching chest of the trained athlete. Dr. Bird stood six feet two inches in his socks, and weighed over two hundred stripped. As he leaned back a curious glitter, which Carnes had learned to associate with keen interest, showed for an instant in his eyes.

"I will be glad to hear your story, Mr. Mitchell," he said softly. "Tell it in your own way and try not to omit any detail, no matter how trivial it may be."

*   *   *   *   *

The seaman nodded and sat silent for a moment as though marshaling his thoughts.

"The story really starts the afternoon of May 12th," he said, "although I didn't realize the importance of the first incident at the time. We were steaming along at good speed, hoping to make New York before too late for quarantine, when a hail came from the forward lookout. I was on watch and I went forward to see what was the matter. The lookout was Louis Green, an able bodied seaman and a good one, but a confirmed drunkard. I asked him what the trouble was and he turned toward me a face that was haggard with terror.

"'I've seen a sea serpent, Mr. Mitchell,' he said.

"'Nonsense!' I replied sharply. 'You've been drinking again.'

"He swore that he hadn't and I asked him to describe what he had seen. His teeth were chattering so that he could hardly speak, but he gasped out a story about seeing a monstrous head, a half mile across, he said, with a long snake body stretching out over the sea until the end of it was lost on the horizon. I turned my glass in the direction he pointed and of course there was nothing to be seen. The man's condition was such as to make him worse than useless as a lookout, so I relieved him and ordered him below. I took it for a touch of delirium tremens.

"We were bucking a head wind, although not a very stiff one, and we didn't make port until after dark, so we anchored at quarantine, just off Staten Island, in forty fathoms of water, and Captain Murphy radioed for a

Coast Guard boat to come out and lay by us for the night. As you have probably heard, we were carrying four millions in bar gold consigned to the Federal Reserve Bank of New York from the Bank of England."

*   *   *   *   *

Dr. Bird and Carnes nodded. The inexplicable loss of the *Arethusa* had occupied much space in the papers ten days earlier.

"The cutter came out, signalled, and dropped anchor about three hundred yards away. So far, everything was exactly as it should be. I walked to the stern of the boat and looked out across the Atlantic and then I realized that Green wasn't the only one who could see things. The wind had fallen and it was getting pretty dark, but not too dark to see things a pretty good distance away. As I looked I saw, or thought I saw, a huge black leathery mass come to the surface a mile or so away. There were two things on it that looked like eyes, and I had a feeling as though some malignant thing was staring at me. I rubbed my eyes and looked again, but the vision persisted, and I went forward to get a glass. When I came back the thing, whatever it was, had disappeared, but the water where it had been was boiling as though there were a great spring or something of the sort under the surface.

"I trained my glass on the disturbed area, and I will take my oath that I saw a huge body like a snake emerge from the water. It lay in long undulations on the waves, and moved with them as though it were floating. It was quite a bit nearer than the first thing had been and I could see it plainly with the glass. I would judge it to be fifteen or twenty feet thick, and it actually seemed to disappear in the distance as Green had described it. The sight of the thing sent shivers up and down my spine, and I gave a hoarse shout. The lookout hurried to my side and asked me what the trouble was. I pointed and handed him the glass. He looked through it and handed it back to me with a curious expression.

"'I can't see nothing, sir,' he said.

"I took the glass from him and tried to level it but my hands were trembling so that I was forced to rest it on the rail. The lookout was right. There was absolutely nothing to be seen and the peculiar appearance of the sea had subsided to normal. The lookout was staring at me rather curiously and I knew that he was thinking the same thing about me as I had thought about Green in the afternoon. I made some kind of an excuse and went below to pull myself together. I caught a glimpse of myself in the glass. I was as white as a sheet, and the sweat was running off my face in drops.

*   *   *   *   *

"I shook myself together after a fashion and managed to persuade myself that the whole thing was just a trick of my mind, inspired by Green's vivid description of his delirious vision of the afternoon. Eight bells struck, and when Mr. Fulton, the junior officer, relieved me, I laid down and tried to quiet myself. I didn't have much luck. Just before I took the deck again at midnight I slipped down to the forecastle to see how Green was coming along. He was lying in his bunk, wide awake, with staring eyes.

"'How are you feeling now, Green?' I asked.

"He looked up at me with an expression of a man who has looked death in the face.

"'Ain't there no chance of dockin' to-night, Mr. Mitchell?' he asked.

"'Of course not,' I said rather sharply. 'What's the matter with you? Are you afraid your sea serpent will get us?'

"'He'll get us if we stay out here to-night, sir,' he replied with an air of conviction. 'I saw the horrible mouth on him, large enough to bite this ship in half; and it had a beak like a bird, like a bloody parrot, sir. I saw its horrible body, too, with great black ulcers on the under side of it where the sharks had been after it. For all the shark takes a man now and then, he's the seaman's friend, sir, because he kills off the sea serpents who would take ship and all.'

"'Nonsense, Green!' I said sharply. 'Don't talk any more such foolishness or I'll have you ironed. You've been drinking so much that you are seeing things, and I won't have the crew disturbed by your crazy talk.'

"'You won't think it's talk when those big eyes stare into yours to-night, Mr. Mitchell, and that body twists around you and squeezes the life out of you. I don't care whether you iron me or not; I know that I'm doomed and so is everyone else; but I won't talk about it, sir. The crew might as well rest easy while they can, for there's no escape if we have to stay out here to-night.'

"'Well, be sure you keep a tight mouth then,' I said, and left rather hurriedly. I was in a cold sweat, for his air of conviction, together with what I had seen, had shaken me pretty badly. I heard the watch changing up above, and knew there would be men in the forecastle in a minute. I didn't want to face them right then.

*   *   *   *   *

"Mr. Fulton reported everything quiet when I went on deck to relieve him, and although I surveyed the water through a night glass for as far as I could see, there was nothing out of the way. The Coast Guard's lights were shining less than a quarter of a mile away, and things looked peaceful enough. The wind had gone down with the sun; the sea was almost glassy, and there was a bright moon.

"After going around the ship, I relieved all of the watch except two men for lookouts, and sent them below to get a good night's sleep. If I hadn't done that, some of them might be alive now.

"I paced the deck for an hour trying to quiet my nerves, but really getting more nervous every minute. Three bells struck and I walked forward and leaned on the rail to watch the water. I saw a peculiar swirl as though some large body were coming to the surface from below, and then I saw—it.

"Dr. Bird, I take a drink once in a while when I am on shore, but never at sea and never in excess, and I know it wasn't a vision of drink delirium. I felt perfectly normal aside from my nervousness, and I don't think it was fever. Either I saw it or I am insane, for it is as vivid to me as though I were standing on the *Arethusa's* deck and that monstrous horror was rising once more before my eyes."

The seaman's face had become drawn and white as he talked, and drops of sweat were trickling from his chin. Carnes sat forward absorbed in his narrative while Dr. Bird sat back with a glitter in his black eyes and an expression of great attention on his face.

"Go on, Mr. Mitchell," the doctor said soothingly. "Tell me just what you saw."

*   *   *   *   *

Mitchell shuddered and glanced quickly around the laboratory as though to assure himself that he was safe within four walls.

"From the surface of the sea," he went on, "rose a massive body, black, and of the appearance of wet leather. It must have been a couple of hundred yards across, although the size of objects is often magnified by moonlight and my terror may have added to its size. In the midst of it were two great discs, thirty feet across, which glowed red with the reflected moonlight. It stared for a moment and then rose higher until it towered above the ship; and then I saw, or thought I saw, a huge gaping beak like a parrot's. It was as Green had described it, large enough to bite the *Arethusa* in half, and she was a ship of three thousand tons.

"I was frozen with horror and couldn't move or cry out. As I watched, I saw the long snake-like body emerge from the water, and the estimate I had made of the size in the afternoon seemed pitifully inadequate. Presently a second and a third snake arose from the water, and then more, until the whole sea and the air above it seemed a writhing mass of huge snakes. I remember wondering why the watch of the Coast Guard cutter didn't sound an alarm, and then I realized that the thing had arisen on our port side and the cutter was on the starboard.

"The mass of snakes writhed backward and forward, and then two of them rose in the air and hung over the ship. I could see the under side and I saw what Green had called the scars where the sharks had attacked. They were great cup-shaped depressions with vile white edges, and they did resemble huge sores or ulcers. They wavered over the ship for an instant, and then both of them dropped down on the deck.

"I found my voice and I think that I gave a yell, but even as I opened my mouth, I realized the futility of it. The *Arethusa* was sucked down into the sea as though it had been a tiny chip. I saw the water rising to the rail, and I think I cried out again. The ship tilted and I felt myself falling. The next thing I knew was when I was in the hospital and was told that I had been raving for a week. I was afraid to tell my story for fear I would be put in an asylum, so I kept a tight tongue in my head until I was discharged."

*   *   *   *   *

Dr. Bird mused for a moment as the seaman's voice stopped.

"You cried out all right, Mr. Mitchell," he said. "You gave two distinct shouts, both of which were heard by the watch on the *Wren*, the Coast Guard cutter. They reported that at 1:30, the *Arethusa* sank without warning. As soon as he heard your shouts, the watch gave the alarm and the crew piled on deck. The *Arethusa* was gone completely and the *Wren* was tossing about like 'a chip in a whirlpool' as they graphically described it. The *Wren* had steam up and they fought the waves and steamed over your anchoring ground looking for survivors, but they found none. The sea gradually subsided and they did the only thing they could do— dropped a buoy, to guide the salvage people, and radioed for assistance. The *Robin* came out and joined them, and both cutters stood by until daylight, but nothing unusual was seen. The insurance people are trying to salvage the wreck now, but so far they have made little headway."

"That brings me to the rest of the story, the part that made me decide to come to you, Doctor," said the seaman. "Did you see what happened to the divers yesterday?"

Dr. Bird nodded.

"I saw a brief account of it," he said. "It seems that two of them were lost through their lines getting fouled and their air connections severed in some way. I don't believe the bodies have been recovered yet."

"They never will be recovered, Doctor. I was discharged from the hospital yesterday and the papers were just out with an account of it. I went down to the dock where the *John MacLean*, the salvage ship, ties up, and I talked to Captain Starley who commands it. I have known him casually for some years, although not intimately, and he gave me a few more details than the press got. He didn't connect me up at first with the Mitchell who was reported lost on the *Arethusa*.

"The first man to go down from the *MacLean* was Charley Melrose, an expert diver. He went down in a pressure outfit to the bottom and started to work. Everything was going along fine until the telephone suddenly rang and the man who answered it heard him say, 'Raise me, for God's sake! Hurry!' The signal for raising was given, but they hadn't got him more than thirty feet from the bottom before there came a tug on the line and he was gone! The air line, the lifting cable and

the telephone cord floated free and were reeled in.
Melrose had been plucked off the end of that line as you
or I would pluck off a grape."

*   *   *   *   *

Dr. Bird leaned forward with the curious glitter again
in his eye.

"Go on," he said tersely.

"Blake, the other diver, donned a suit and insisted on
being lowered at once. Starley tried to dissuade him but
he insisted on going down. They lowered him over the
side with a twelve-foot steel-shod pike in his hand. He
never got to the bottom. He had not been lowered more
than a hundred feet when a scream came over the
telephone, and again there was a jerk on the lines which
threatened to wreck the reel—and the line came aboard
with no diver on the end of it. At the same time, Starley
told me, the sea boiled and churned as though the whole
bottom were coming up, and his ship was tossed about as
though it were in a violent storm, although it was calm
enough for forty fathom salvage work and that is pretty
quiet, you know. Half the time his screws were out of
water and he had a hard time to keep from being
capsized. He fought his way out of the disturbed area,
and as soon as he did, it started to quiet down, and in ten
minutes it was calm again.

"Starley was pretty badly shaken and besides he had
lost both of his divers, so he came in and I saw him at the
dock. When I heard his yarn, I took him into my
confidence and told him what I had seen and that I
proposed coming to you and asking your advice. I was
afraid until I heard his story that it was merely a vision
that I had had, but it certainly was no vision that plucked
those two divers off their lines."

"Has Captain Starley told that story to anyone else
yet?"

"No, Doctor, he hasn't. He promised not to talk until after I had seen you. I'll vouch for him; he'll keep his word through anything; and he is keeping his whole crew on board until he hears from me."

*   *   *   *   *

Dr. Bird sprang to his feet.

"Mr. Mitchell," he said energetically, "you have shown excellent judgment. Wire Captain Starley that you have seen me and that he is to hold his crew on board and to talk to no one until I get there. Carnes, telephone the Chief of Naval Operations and ask him to receive me in conference at once. Have him get the Secretary of the Navy in, too, if he is available. When you have finished that, telephone Bolton that you will be away from Washington indefinitely."

"I'll telephone Admiral Buck for you, Doctor, but I don't dare telephone any such message to Bolton; he'd take my head off. He has been running the whole service ragged lately, and this is my first afternoon off duty in a fortnight."

"What's the trouble, a flood of new counterfeits?"

"No, the counterfeit division is getting along all right. In point of fact, they have lent us a dozen men. The trouble is a sudden big increase in Communist activity throughout the country, with the Young Labor party behind it. Bolton has been pretty jumpy since that Stokowski affair last August and he is afraid of another attempt of some sort on the President."

"The Young Labor party? I thought that gang was bankrupt and out of business, since the Coast Guard broke up their alien smuggling scheme."

"They were down and out for a while, but they are in funds again–and how! They must have three or four millions at least."

"Where did they get it?"

"That's what we have been trying to find out. The
leaders have presented bars of gold to a dozen banks
throughout the country and demanded specie. The banks
shipped the gold to the mint and it was good gold, nine
hundred and twenty-five fine. What we are trying to find
out is how that gold got into the United States."

"A shipment of that size should be easy to trace."

"It would seem so, but it hasn't been. We have
accounted for every pound of every shipment that has
come in through a port of entry, and we have checked
almost that close on the output of every mine in the
United States. If the gold came from Russia, it would
have had to cross Europe, and we can't get any trace of it
from abroad. It looks as though they were *making* it."

*   *   *   *   *

Dr. Bird rubbed his head thoughtfully.

"Possible, but hardly probable," he said. "How much
did you say they had?"

"Over three millions in thirty-pound bars. Each bar
shows signs of having a mint mark chiselled off, but that
don't help much for they have done too good a job. It has
us pretty well bluffed."

Again Dr. Bird rubbed his head.

"Telephone Admiral Buck, and then phone Bolton and
tell him exactly what I told you to: that you will be away
indefinitely. When he gets through exploding, tell him
that you are going with me and that possibly, just barely
possibly, we might be on the trail of that gold shipment."

"On the trail of the gold!" gasped Carnes. "Surely,
Doctor, you don't think—"

"Once in a while, old dear," replied the Doctor with a
chuckle, "which is more than anyone in the Secret Service
does. You might tell Bolton that I said that, but hang up
quickly if you do. I don't want the wires of my telephone
melted off. No, Carnesy, I have no miraculous inspiration
as to where that gold is coming from; I just have a plain

old-fashioned hunch, and that hunch is that we are going to have lots of fun and more than our share of danger before we see Washington again. After you get through bearding Bolton in his den, you might call the Chief of the Air Corps and ask him to have a bomber held at Langley Field subject to my orders. If he squawks any, I'll talk to him."

He turned to a telephone which stood on his desk and lifted the receiver.

"Get Mr. Lambertson on the wire," he said. "He is the chief technician of the Pyrex Glass Works at Corning, New Jersey."

*   *   *   *   *

The *U.S.S. Minneconsin* steamed out of New York harbor and headed down toward the lower bay. On her forward deck rested a huge globe. The bottom quarter of the sphere was made of some dark opaque substance but the upper portion was transparent as crystal. Through the walls could be seen a quantity of apparatus resting on the opaque bottom portion. Two mechanics from the Bureau of Standards were making final adjustments of one of the pieces of apparatus, which resembled a tank fitted with a piston geared to an electric motor. From the tank, tubes ran to four hollow pipes, an inch and a half in diameter, which ran through the skin and extended thirty inches from the outer skin of the twenty-foot sphere. Dr. Bird stood near talking with the executive officer of the ship and from time to time giving a brief word of direction to the mechanics.

"It's safer than you might think, Commander," he said. "In the first place, that globe is not made of ordinary glass; it is made of vitrilene, a new semi-malleable glass which was developed at the Bureau and which is being made on an experimental scale for us by the Pyrex people. It is much stronger than ordinary glass, and is not sensitive to shock. It is also perfectly transparent to ultra-violet light, being superior even to rock crystal or fused quartz in that respect. The walls, as you have noticed, are four inches thick, and I have calculated that the ball will stand a uniform external pressure of thirty-five hundred atmospheres, the pressure which would be encountered at a depth of about twenty miles. I believe that it will stand a squeeze of six thousand tons without buckling, and it is impossible to fracture it by shock. It could be dropped from the top of the Woolworth Building, and it would just bounce."

"It seems incredible that it could stand such a pressure as you have named."

"My figures are conservative ones. Lambertson calculated them even higher, but we allowed for the fact that this is the first large mass of the material to be cast, and lowered them."

*   *   *   *   *

"But suppose your lifting cable should break?" objected the naval officer. "The outfit weighs a good many tons."

"You notice that the lower quarter is made of lead. The specific gravity of the entire globe when sealed up tight with two men in it is only a little more than unity. In the water its weight is so little that a three-inch manilla hawser would raise it, let alone a steel cable. I have another safety device. Granted that the cable should snap, I can detach the lead from it and it would shoot to the surface like a rocket."

"How long can you remain under water in it?"

"A week, if necessary. I have an oxygen tank and a carbon dioxide removing apparatus which will keep the air in good condition. The globe is electrically lighted, and can be heated if necessary. Should my telephone line become fouled and broken, I have a radio set which will enable me to communicate with you. I can't see that it is especially dangerous; not nearly as much so as a submarine."

"What is your object in going down, if I may ask?"

"To take pictures and to explore the wreck if we can. The globe is equipped with huge floodlights and excellent cameras. The salvage people are having a little trouble and we are trying to help them out."

"You mentioned exploring. Can you leave the globe while it is under water?"

"Yes. There is a locking device for doing so. A man in a diving suit can enter the lock and fill it with water. Once the external pressure is released he can open the outer door and step out. Coming back, he seals the outer door and the man inside blows out the lock and compressed air and then the inner door can be opened. It is the same principle as a torpedo tube."

*   *   *   *   *

A jangle of bells interrupted them and the *Minneconsin* slowed down. Commander Lawrence stepped to the rail and gave a sharp order to the navigating officer on the bridge. The bells jangled again and the ship's engines stopped.

"We are almost over the buoy, Doctor," he said.

Dr. Bird nodded and spoke to the two mechanics. With a few final touches to the apparatus they emerged from the globe and Dr. Bird entered.

"Come on, Carnes," he called. "No backing out at the last minute."

Carnes stepped forward with a sickly smile and joined the Doctor in the huge sphere.

"All right, boys; close her up."

The mechanics swung the outer door into place with a crane. Both the edge of the door and the surface against which it fitted had been ground flat and were in addition faced with soft rubber. Bolts were fastened in the door which passed through holes in the main sphere, and Dr.

Bird spun nuts onto them and tightened them with a heavy wrench. He and Carnes lifted the smaller inner door into place and bolted it tight. Dr. Bird stepped to the telephone.

"Lower away," he directed.

From a boom attached to the *Minneconsin's* forward fighting top, a huge steel cable swung down, and the latch at the end of the cable was closed over a vitrilene ring which was fastened to the top of the sphere. The cable tightened and the globe with the two men in it was lifted over the side of the battleship and lowered gently into the water. Carnes involuntarily ducked and threw up his hand as the waters closed over them. Dr. Bird laughed.

"Look up, Carnes," he said.

Carnes gasped as he looked up and saw the surface of the water above him. Dr. Bird laughed again and turned to the telephone.

"Lower away," he said. "Everything is tight."

                    *   *   *   *   *

The globe descended into the depths of the sea. Darker and darker it grew until only a faint twilight glow filled the sphere. A dark bulk loomed before them. Dr. Bird snapped on one of his huge floodlights and pointed.

"The *Arethusa*," he said.

The ill-fated vessel lay on her side with a huge jagged hole torn in her fabric amidships.

"That's where her boilers burst," explained the Doctor. "Luckily we have a hard bottom to deal with. Let's see if we can locate any of Mitchell's sea serpents."

He turned on other flood lights and swept the bottom of the sea with them. The huge beams bored out into the water for a quarter of a mile, but nothing unusual was to be seen. Dr. Bird turned his attention again to the wreck.

"Things look normal from this side," he said after a prolonged scrutiny. "I'll have the *Minneconsin* steam around it while we look it over."

In response to his telephone orders the ship above them swung around the wreck in a circle, and Carnes and the Doctor viewed each side in turn. But nothing of a suspicious nature made its appearance. The sphere stopped opposite the hole in the side and Dr. Bird turned to Carnes.

"I'm going to put on a diving suit and explore that wreck," he said. "If there ever was any danger, it isn't apparent now; and I can't find out anything until I get inside."

"Don't do it, Doctor!" cried Carnes. "Remember what happened to the other divers!"

*   *   *   *   *

"We don't know what happened to them, Carnes. No matter what it was, there is no danger apparent right now, and I've got to get into that ship before I can get any real information. We could have lowered an under-sea camera and learned as much as we have so far."

"Let me go instead of you, Doctor."

"I'm sorry to refuse you, old dear, but frankly, I wouldn't trust your judgment as to what you had seen if you went alone; and we can't both go."

"Why not?"

"If we both went, who would work the air to let us back in? No, this is a one-man job and I'm the one to do it. While I am gone, keep a sharp lookout, and if you see anything unusual call me at once."

"How can I call you?"

"On this small radio phone. A pair of receivers tuned to the right wave-length are in my diving helmet, and I will be able to hear you although I can't reply. I won't be gone long: I have only a small air tank, large enough to keep me going for thirty minutes. Now help me into my suit and keep a sharp watch. A timely warning may save my life if anything happens."

With Carnes' assistance, Dr. Bird donned a deep-sea diving outfit and screwed down the helmet. He crawled through the inner door into the lock and lifted the inner door into place. Carnes fastened the door with nuts and the Doctor opened a pair of valves in the outer door and filled the lock with water. He removed the outer door; and, taking in one hand a steel-shod twelve-foot pike with a hook on the end, and in the other a waterproof flashlight, he sallied forth. As he left the shell he paused for a moment, and then returned and picked up the heavy wrench with which he had removed the nuts holding the outer door into place. He fastened the tool to the belt of his suit. Then, with a wave of his hand toward the detective, he approached the hulk.

The hole in the side was too high for him to reach, but he hooked the end of his pike in one of the joints of the *Arethusa's* plates and climbed slowly and painfully up the side of the vessel. As he disappeared into the hull, Carnes realized with a sudden start that he had been watching his friend and neglecting the duty imposed on him of keeping a sharp watch. He turned quickly to the floodlights and searched the sea bottom.

$$* \quad * \quad * \quad * \quad *$$

Nothing appeared, and the minutes moved as slowly as hours should. Carnes felt that he had been submerged alone for weeks, and his nerves grew so tense that he felt that he would scream in another instant. A sudden thought sobered him like a dash of cold water. If he screamed, Dr. Bird would take it for an alarm signal and possibly be afraid to emerge from the vessel. His watch showed him that the Doctor had been gone for twenty-five minutes and he moved slowly to the radio transmitter.

"Dr. Bird," he said slowly and distinctly, "you have been gone nearly thirty minutes. Nothing alarming has appeared but I will feel better when I see you coming back."

He glued his eyes on the opening in the ship's side and waited. Five minutes passed, and then ten, with no signs of the Doctor. Carnes moved again to the receiver.

"It has been over half an hour. Doctor," he cried in a pleading voice. "If you are all right, for God's sake show yourself. I am frantic with worry."

Another five minutes passed, and the sweat dripped in a steady stream from the detective's chin. Suddenly he gave a sob of relief and sank back against the side of the globe. A bulky figure showed at the edge of the hole, and Dr. Bird climbed slowly and heavily out of the hold and dropped to the sea bottom. He lay prone for a moment before he rose and made his way with evident effort toward the sphere. He entered the compartment and with a heroic effort lifted the outer door into place, and feebly and with fumbling fingers placed nuts on the bolts. His hands wandered uncertainly toward the valves and closed the upper one. He waved his hand toward Carnes and sank in a heap on the floor of the lock.

*   *   *   *   *

With trembling hands Carnes connected the air and opened the valve. Air flowed into the lock and the water was gradually forced out. When the lock was empty, he waited for Dr. Bird to close the outer valve but the Doctor did not move. Carnes tore at the bolts which held the inner door and threw his weight against it. It held against his assault, and he thought frantically. An inspiration came to him, and he disconnected the air valve. With a whistling rush, the air from the lock rushed into the sphere and he forced open the inner door. A stream of sea water drove against his feet through the open valve, and he reached for the valve to close it. The force of the water held it open for a moment, but he threw every ounce of his strength into the effort. The valve slowly closed.

It was beyond his strength to haul the heavy Doctor with his pressure diving suit through the restricted confines of the inner door, so Carnes wormed his way into the lock and with trembling fingers unscrewed the helmet of the Doctor's diving suit. The helmet clanged to the floor and Carnes scooped up his hands full of water and dashed it into the Doctor's face. There was no response and he was at his wit's end. He sprang for the radio to order the sphere hauled up when his glance fell on the oxygen tank. It took him only a moment to connect a rubber hose to the tank, and in a few seconds a blast of the life-giving gas was blowing into the scientist's face. Dr. Bird gave a convulsive gasp or two and opened his eyes.

"Shut off the juice, Carnes," he said faintly. "Too much of that's bad."

Carnes shut off the oxygen and Dr. Bird struggled to a sitting position and inhaled deep breaths.

"That was a narrow squeak, old dear," he said faintly. "Give me a hand and I'll climb in."

*   *   *   *   *

With the detective's aid he climbed into the sphere and Carnes fastened the inner door. Slowly the Doctor rid himself of the diving suit and lay prone on the floor, his breath still coming in gasps.

"Thanks for your warning about the time, Carnes," he said. "I knew that my air supply was running short but I was caught down there and couldn't readily free myself. I thought for a while that my time had come, but it wasn't so written. By the looks of things, I freed myself just in time."

"Did you find out anything?" asked the detective eagerly.

"I did," replied Dr. Bird grimly. "For one thing, the gold is no longer in the hold of the *Arethusa*."

"It's gone?"

"Clean as a whistle, every bar of it. A hole has been cut in the vault around the combination, and the bars slid back and the door opened. The gold has been stolen."

"Might it not have been stolen before the vessel sank?"

"The idea occurred to me of course, and I examined things pretty carefully. I know that the theft occurred after the vessel sank."

"How could you tell?"

"For one thing, the hole was cut with an under-water cutting torch. For the second, look here."

* * * * *

The Doctor rolled up his trousers and showed the detective his leg. Carnes cried out as he saw huge purple welts on it.

"What caused that?" he cried.

"As I entered the vault, I stepped full into a steel bear trap which was set there for the purpose of catching and holding anyone who entered. Someone has visited the *Arethusa*, since she sank, and looted her, and also arranged so that any diver who got as far as the vault would never return to the surface to tell of it. Luckily for myself, I carried a heavy wrench and was able to free myself. Most divers don't carry such a thing."

"But who could have done it?"

"That's what we have got to find out, and we aren't going to do it down here. Give the word to have us hauled up; and, Carnes, don't mention anything about the looting of the vessel. Allow it to be understood that I couldn't get into the hold. We'll head back for New York at once. I want to have a few small changes made in this sphere before we use it again. While I am doing that, I want you to get hold of the Coast Guard or the Immigration Service or whoever it is that has the complete records in that case of alien smuggling, by the Young Labor party. When you get the information, report to me and we'll go over it. You might also drop a hint to Captain Starley that will stop all further attempts at salvage operations for a few days. Tell him that I'll arrange to have a Coast Guard cutter guard the locality of the wreck."

"Won't that be rather risky for the cutter?"

"I think not. The gold is gone and there is no reason to apprehend any further danger in that locality, at least for the present."

*   *   *   *   *

At nine o'clock next morning Carnes and Dr. Bird sat in the office of Lieutenant Commander Minden of the United States Coast Guard, listening intently to the history of the alien smuggling case. Commander Minden was saying:

"Their boats would load up and clear ostensibly for Rio de Janeiro or some other South American port, but once they were in the Atlantic, they would alter their course and head from the Massachusetts coast. Of course, we had no right to interfere with them on the high seas, and they never came closer than fifty miles of our coast line. When they got that close, they would cruise slowly back and forth for a few days and then steam away south to the port they had cleared for. When they got there, of course there were no passengers on board.

"We patrolled the coast carefully while they were around but we never got any indication of any landing of aliens and yet we knew they were being landed in some way. We drew lines so close that a cork couldn't get by without being seen and we even had the air patrolled, but with no results. Eventually the air patrol was the thing that gave them away.

"They had been operating so successfully that they evidently got careless and started a load off late in the night so they didn't reach the coast by dawn. A Navy plane was flying along the coast-line about twelve miles off when they spotted a submarine running parallel with the coast, headed north. It didn't look like an American craft and they went on and radioed Washington and found that we had no under-sea craft in that neighborhood. They returned to their patrol and followed the sub for a matter of thirty or forty miles up the coast, and then it turned in right toward the shore. The shore line there is rocky, and, at the point where the sub was heading, it falls sheer about two hundred fathoms. The sub ran right at the cliff and disappeared from view."

*   *   *   *   *

Lieutenant Commander Minden paused impressively. Carnes and Dr. Bird set forward in their chairs, for it was evident that the crux of the story was at hand.

"When the plane reported what they had seen, we knew how those aliens were being landed. The point where the sub went in gave us a good idea of the location of their base and we threw a cordon of men around and searched. A Navy sub was sent to the scene and they reported that there was a tunnel opening into the rock, about a hundred fathoms under water, running for they had no idea how far under the land. They stayed to guard the hole while we combed the land. It took us a week to locate the place, but we traced some truck loads of food and finally found it. This tunnel ran under the land for a mile and then ended in a large cave underground. The Young Labor party had established a regular receiving depot there, and took the aliens from the sub and kept them for a day or two until they had a chance to load them into trucks and run them into Boston or some other town in the night.

"Once we had the place spotted, we sent a gang in and captured the whole works without any trouble. The underground cavern had no natural opening to the surface, but one had been made by blasting. We captured the whole lot and then sealed the end of the hole with rock and concrete. That was the end of the affair."

"Thank you, Commander; you have given us a very graphic description of it. I suppose you could find the entrance which was sealed up?"

*   *   *   *   *

"Easily. I led the raiding party. I forgot to mention one blunder we made. Evidently some word of our plans leaked out, for the sub which was guarding the outer end of the tunnel was called away by a radio message supposed to be from the Navy Department. It had gone only a short distance, however, when the commander smelled a rat and made his way back. He was too late. He was just in time to see the sub emerge from the hole and head into the open sea. He gave chase, but the other sub was faster than the Navy boat and it got clear away. The leader of the gang must have been on it, for we didn't get him."

"Who was the leader?"

"From some records we captured, his name was Ivan Saranoff. I never saw him."

"Saranoff?" said Dr. Bird thoughtfully. "The name seems familiar. Where have I—Thunder! I know now. He was at one time a member of the faculty of St. Petersburg. He was one of the leading biologists of his time. Carnes, we've found our man."

"If you are thinking of Saranoff, I am afraid you are mistaken, Doctor," said Commander Minden. "Neither he nor his submarine have ever been heard of since and it has been generally conceded that they were lost at sea. We had some pretty rough weather just after that affair."

"Rough weather doesn't mean much to a sub, Commander. I expect that he's our man. At any rate, the place we want to go is the end of that tunnel."

"I'm at your service, Doctor."

"Carnes, get the location of that tunnel entrance from Commander Minden and order the *Minneconsin* to proceed north along the coast to that vicinity and stand by for radio orders. I am going to telephone Mitchell Field and get a plane. We have no time to lose."

*   *   *   *   *

The plane from Mitchell Field roared down to a landing, and Carnes, Dr. Bird and Commander Minden dismounted from the rear cockpit and looked around. They had landed in a smooth field at the base of a rise almost rugged enough to be called a mountain. A group of three men were standing near them as they got out of the plane. One of the men approached.

"Dr. Bird?" asked the newcomer. "I am Tom Harron, United States Marshal. These two men are deputies. I understand that I am to report to you for orders."

"I'm glad to know you, Mr. Harron. This is Operative Carnes of the Secret Service and Commander Minden of the Coast Guard. We are going to explore an underground cavern that is located in this vicinity."

"Do you mean the one where they used to smuggle aliens? That is closed up. I was in charge of that work and we closed it tight as a drum two years ago."

"Can you find the entrance?"

"Sure. It isn't over a mile from here."

"Lead the way, then. We want to take a look at it."

The marshal led the way toward the eminence and took a path which led up a gully in its side. He paused for a moment to take his bearings and then turned sharply to his left and climbed part way up the side of the ravine.

"Here it is," he announced. An expression of astonishment crossed his face and he examined the ground closely. "By Golly, Doc," he went on as he straightened up, "this place has been opened since I left it!"

*   *   *   *   *

Dr. Bird hurried forward and joined him. The heavy stone and concrete with which the entrance to the cavern had been sealed were undisturbed, but in the side of the hill was set a steel door beside the concrete. There was no sign of a keyhole or other means of entering it.

"Was this steel door part of your work?" asked Carnes.

"No, sir, it wasn't. We sealed it solid. That door has been put there since."

Dr. Bird closely examined the structure. He tapped it and went around the edges and then straightened up and took a small pocket compass from his pocket and opened the case. The needle swung crazily for a moment and then pointed straight toward the door.

"A magnetic lock," he exclaimed. "If we could find the power line it would be easy to force, but finding that line might take us a week. At any rate, we have found out what we were after. This is their base from which they are operating. Mr. Harron, I want you to station a guard armed with rifles at this door day and night until I personally relieve you. Remember, until I relieve you, in person. Verbal or written orders don't go. Capture or kill anyone who tries to enter or leave the cavern through this entrance. Just now we'll find that cavern more vulnerable from the sea end, and that is where I mean to attack. We'll force that door and explore from this end later. Commander Minden, you may stay here with Mr. Harron, if you like, or you may come with Carnes and me. We are going on board the *Minneconsin*."

*   *   *   *   *

The Mitchell Field plane roared to a take-off and bore south along the coast. Half an hour of flying brought them in view of the battleship steaming at full speed up the coast. Dr. Bird radioed instructions to the ship, and an hour later a launch picked them up from the beach and took them out. As soon as they were on board they resumed their progress, and in two hours the peak that Dr. Bird had marked as a landmark was opposite.

"Steam in as close to the shore as you can safely," he said, "and then lower us. Once we are down, you will be guided by our telephoned instructions. Come on, Carnes, let's go."

The detective followed him into the sphere as the *Minneconsin* edged up toward the shore. The huge ball was lifted from the deck and lowered gently into two hundred fathoms of water. It was pitch dark at that depth, and Dr. Bird switched on one floodlight and studied the cliff which rose a hundred yards from them.

"We have missed the place, Carnes," he said. "We'll have them pull us up a few hundred feet and then steam along the coast."

He turned to the telephone and the sphere rose while the battleship steamed slowly ahead, the vitrilene ball following in her wake. For a quarter of a mile they continued on their way, and then Dr. Bird halted the ship.

"What depth are we?" he asked. "Eighty fathoms? All right, lower us, please."

*　　*　　*　　*　　*

The ball sank until it rested on the sea bottom, and Dr. Bird turned on two additional floodlights and studied the surroundings. The bed of the ocean was literally covered with lobster and crab shell, with the bones of fish scattered here and there among them. A few bones of land animals were mixed with the debris and Carnes gave a gasp as Dr. Bird pointed out to him a diving helmet.

"We are on the right track," said the scientist grimly. He stepped to the telephone and ordered the sphere raised to one hundred fathoms. The ship moved forward along the coast until Dr. Bird again stepped to the telephone and halted it. Before them yawned the entrance to the underground tunnel. It was about two hundred feet high and three hundred across, and their most powerful beams would not penetrate to the end of it. A pile of debris could be seen on the floor of the tunnel and Carnes fancied that he could see another diving helmet among the litter. Dr. Bird pointed toward the side of the cavern.

"See those floodlights fastened to the cliff so that their beams will sweep across the mouth of the tunnel when they are lighted?" he said. "Apparently the cave is used as a prison and the light beams are the bars. The creature is not at home just now or the bars would be up. My God! Look at that, Carnes!"

Carnes stared and echoed the Doctor's cry of surprise. Clinging to a shelf of rock which extended out from the wall of the cavern and half hidden among the seaweed was a huge marine creature. It looked like a huge black slug with rudimentary eyes and mouth. The thing was fifty feet in length and fully fifteen feet in diameter. It hung there, moving sluggishly as though breathing, and rudimentary tentacles projecting from one end moved in the water.

"What is it, Doctor?" asked Carnes in a voice of awe.

"It is a typical trochosphere of the giant octopus, the devil fish of Indian Ocean legend, multiplied a thousand times," he replied. "When the octopus lays its eggs, they hatch out into the larval form. The free swimming larva is known as a trochosphere, and I am positive that that is what we see; but look at the size of the thing! Man alive, if that ever developed, I can't conceive of its dimensions!"

*   *   *   *   *

"I have seen pictures of a huge octopus pulling down a ship," said Carnes, "but I always fancied they were imaginary."

"They are. This monstrosity before us is no product of nature. A dozen of them would depopulate the seas in a year. It is a hideous parody of nature conceived in the brain of a madman and produced by some glandular disturbance. Saranoff spent years in glandular experimentation, and no doubt he has managed to stimulate the thyroid of a normal octopus and produce a giant. I fancy that the immediate parent of the thing before us was of normal size, and so, probably, are its brothers and sisters. The phenomenon of giantism of this nature occurs in alternate generations and then only in rare instances. Its grandparent may not be far away, however. I wish it was safe to use a submarine to explore that cavern."

"Why isn't it?"

"Any creature powerful enough to pull the *Arethusa* under water would crush a frail submarine without effort. Anyway, a Navy sub isn't built for under-water exploration like this ball is. The window space is quite limited and they aren't equipped with powerful floodlights. I would like to be able to reach that thing and destroy it, but it can wait until later. The best thing we can do is to put out our lights and wait."

His hand sought the light switch, and the globe became dark. Only a tiny glimmer of light came down to them from the surface, a hundred fathoms above. In the darkness they stared into the depths of the sea.

* * * * *

For an hour they waited and then Dr. Bird grasped Carnes by the shoulder and pointed. Far in the distance could be seen a tiny point of light. It wavered and winked and at times disappeared, but it was gradually approaching them. Dr. Bird stepped to the telephone and the *Minneconsin* moved a hundred yards further from the shore. The light disappeared again as though hidden by some opaque body. Their eyes had become accustomed to the dim light and they could dimly see a long snake-like body approach the globe and then suddenly withdraw.

The light appeared again only a few hundred yards away. The water swirled and the sphere swayed drunkenly as some gigantic body moved past it with express train speed and entered the mouth of the cavern. The light turned toward them and they could see the dim outlines of a small submarine on which it was mounted. Another rush of water came as the object which had entered the cave started to leave it, and the light swung around. It bore on a huge black body, and was reflected with a red glow from huge eyes, and the creature backed again into the cave. Back and forth across the mouth of the cavern the light played, and the watchers caught a glimpse of a huge parrot beak which could have engulfed a freight car. From the cavern projected twisting tentacles of gargantuan dimensions, and red eyes, thirty feet in diameter, glared balefully at them. For several minutes the light of the submarine played across the mouth of the cave, and then the floodlights on the cliff sprang into full glow and bathed the ball and the mouth of the tunnel in a flood of light.

Before their horrified gaze was an octopus of a size to make them disbelieve their eyes. The submarine had moved up to within a few feet of them, and the light from it played full on the ball. The submarine maneuvered in the vicinity, keeping the ball full in the beam of its light, and then drew back. As it did so, the floodlights on the cliff died out and the beam of the submarine's light was directed away from them. Dr. Bird jumped to the telephone.

"Head straight out to sea and full speed ahead!" he shouted. "Don't try to pull us in; tow us!"

*   *   *   *   *

The ball swayed as the *Minneconsin's* mighty engines responded to his orders and the cliff wall disappeared.

"As long as they know we're here, we might as well announce our presence in good style," said the doctor grimly as he closed a switch and threw all of the sphere's huge lights into action. He had turned on the lights just in time, for even as he did so a mighty tentacle shot out of the darkness and wrapped itself around the ball. For a moment it clung there and then was withdrawn.

"The thing can't stand light," remarked the doctor as he threw off the switch. "That sub was herding it like a cow by the use of a light beam. As long as we are lighted up we are safe from attack."

"Then for God's sake turn on the lights!" cried Carnes.

"I want it to attack us," replied the doctor calmly. "We have no offensive weapons and only by meeting an attack can we harm the thing."

As he spoke there came a soft whisper of sound from the vitrilene walls and they were thrown from their feet by a sudden jerk. Dr. Bird stumbled to the switch and closed it, and the ball was flooded with light. Two arms were now on them but they were slowly withdrawn as the lights glared forth. The huge outlines of the beast could be seen as it followed them toward the surface. Its great eyes glared at them hungrily. The submarine was visible only as a speck of light in the distance.

*   *   *   *   *

The *Minneconsin's* speed was picking up under the urge of her huge steam turbines, and the ball was nearing the surface. The sea was light enough now that they could see for quite a distance. The telephone bell jangled and Dr. Bird picked the receiver from its hook.

"Hello," he said. "What's that? You can? By all means, fire. Yes, indeed, we're well out of danger; we must be thirty or forty feet down. Watch the fun now," he went on to Carnes as he replaced the receiver. "The beast is showing above the surface and they're going to shell it."

They watched the surface and suddenly there came a flash of light followed by a dull boom of sound. The huge

octopus suddenly sank below them, thrashing its arms
about wildly.

"A hit!" shouted Dr. Bird into the telephone. "Get it
again if it shows up. I want it to get good and mad."

He turned off the lights in the ball and the octopus
attacked again. The shell had taught it caution and it
kept well down, but three huge arms came up from the
depths of the sea and wrapped themselves about the ball.
The forward motion stopped for a moment, and then came
a jerk that threw them down. The ball started to sink.

"Our cable has parted!" cried the doctor. "Turn on the
lights!"

*   *   *   *   *

Carnes closed the switch. The ball was so covered
with the huge tentacles that they could see nothing, but
the light had its usual effect and they were released. The
ball sank toward the bottom and they could see the huge
cephalopod lying below watching them. Blood was flowing
from   a   wound   near   one   of   its   eyes   where   the
Minneconsin's shell had found its mark.

Toward the huge monster they sank until they lay on
the bottom of the ocean and a few yards from it. In an
instant the sea became opaque and they could see
nothing.

"He has shot his ink!" cried the doctor. "Here comes
the real attack. Strap yourself to the wall where you can
reach one of the motor switches."

Through the darkness huge arms came out and
wrapped themselves around the ball. The heavy vitrilene
groaned under the enormous pressure which was applied,
but it held. The ink was clearing slightly and they could
see that the sphere was covered by the arms. The mass
moved and the huge maw opened before them. The pipes
projecting from the sides of the ball were buried in the
creature's flesh.

"Good Lord, he's going to swallow us!" gasped the doctor. "Quick, Carnes, the motor switch."

He closed one of them as he spoke, and the powerful little electric motors began to hum, forcing forward the piston attached to the tank connected to the hollow rods. Steadily the little motors hummed, and the tank emptied through the rods into the body of the giant cephalopod.

"I hope the stuff works fast," groaned the doctor as they approached closer to the giant maw. "I never tried giving an octopus a hypodermic injection of prussic acid before, but it ought to do the business. There's enough acid there to kill half New York City."

*   *   *   *   *

Carnes blanched as the ball approached the mouth. One by one the arms unwound until only one was holding them and the jaws opened wider. They were almost in them when the motion stopped. They could feel a shudder run through the arm which held them. For a moment the arm alternately expanded and contracted, almost releasing them only to clutch them again. Another arm came from the depths and whipped about the ball, and again the vitrilene groaned at the pressure which was applied. The arms were suddenly withdrawn and the ball started to sink.

"Drop the lead, Carnes!" cried the doctor. With the aid of the detective he operated the electric catches which held the huge mass of lead to the bottom, and the sphere shot up through the water like a rocket. It leaped clear of the water and fell back with a splash. A half mile away the *Minneconsin* was swinging in a wide circle to head back toward them. They turned their gaze toward the shore.

As they looked a giant arm shot a hundred yards up into the air, twisting and writhing frantically. It disappeared, and another, and then half a dozen flashed into the air. The arms dipped below the surface. A huge black body reared its bulk free from the water for a moment, and the sea boiled as though in a violent storm. The body sank and again the arms were thrown up, twisting and turning like a half dozen huge snakes. The whole creature sank below the waves and the ball tossed back and forth, often buried under tons of water and once tossed thirty feet into the air by the huge waves.

*   *   *   *   *

A momentary lull came in the waves. Carnes gave a cry of astonishment and pointed toward the shore. With an effort, Dr. Bird twisted himself in his lashing and looked in that direction. The huge body had again come to the surface, and three of the arms were towering into the air. Grasped in them was a long, black, cigar-shaped object. As they watched the object was torn into two parts and the fragments crushed by the enormous power of the octopus. Again the arms writhed in torment, and then they stiffened out. For a moment they towered in the air and then slowly sank below the surface of the sea.

"The cyanide has worked," cried the doctor, "and in its last agonies the creature has turned on its creator and destroyed him. It is a shame, for Saranoff was a brilliant although perverted genius, and besides, I would have liked to have learned his method. However, I may find something when we open the land end and raid the cave; and really, he was too brilliant a man to hang for murder. Once we open the cave and I get any data that is there, my connection with the case will end. Trailing down the gold and recovering it is a routine matter for Bolton, and one in which he won't need my help."

"What about that creature we saw in the cave, Doctor? Won't it hatch into another terror of the sea like the thing that destroyed the ship?"

"The trochosphere? No, I'm not worried there. It won't try to leave the cave for some days yet, and by that time we'll have the land end opened and the floodlights turned on. They will keep it there and it will starve to death. We could send down a sub to feed it a torpedo, but there's no need. Nature will dispose of it. Meanwhile, I hope the *Minneconsin* rigs up a jury tackle pretty soon and takes us on board. I'm getting seasick."

THE BLACK LAMP
ORIGINALLY PUBLISHED IN *ASTOUNDING STORIES OF SUPER-SCIENCE,*
FEBRUARY 1931

*Dr. Bird and his friend Carnes unravel
another criminal web of scientific mystery.*

THE BLACK LAMP

"The clue, Carnes," said Dr. Bird slowly, "lies in those windows."

Operative Carnes of the United States Secret Service shook his head before he glanced at the windows of the famous scientist's private laboratory on the top floor of the Bureau of Standards.

"I usually defer to your knowledge, Doctor," he said, "but this time I think you are off on the wrong foot. If the thieves came in through the windows, what was their object in cutting that hole through the roof? The marks are very plain and they indicate that the hole was cut in some manner from the inside."

Dr. Bird smiled enigmatically.

"That is too evident for discussion," he replied. "I grant you that the thieves entered from the roof through that hole. After they had secured their booty they left by the same route. I presume that you have noticed the marks on the roof where an aircraft of some sort, probably a helicopter, landed and took off. A question of much greater moment is that of what they did before they landed and cut the hole."

"I don't follow your reasoning, Doctor."

"Carnes, that hole was cut through the roof with a heavy saw. In cutting it, the workers dislodged quite a little plaster which fell to the floor and must have made a great deal of noise. Why wasn't that noise heard?"

"It was heard. The watchman heard it, but knew that Lieutenant Breslau was working here and he thought that he made the noise."

"Surely, but why didn't Breslau hear it?"

"How do we know that he didn't? He was taken to Walter Reed Hospital this morning with his mind an absolute blank and with his tongue paralyzed. He must have seen the thieves and they treated him in some way to ensure his silence. When he is able to talk, if he ever is, he'll probably give us a good description of them."

*   *   *   *   *

Dr. Bird shook his head.

"Too thin, Carney, old dear," he said. "Breslau is a very intelligent young man. He was perfectly normal when I left him shortly after midnight last night. He was working alone in here on a device of the utmost military importance. On the desk is a push button which sets ringing a dozen gongs in the building. Surely a man of that type would have had sense enough when he heard and saw intruders cutting a hole through the roof to sound an alarm which would have brought every watchman on the grounds to his assistance. He must have been knocked out before the hole was started, probably before the helicopter's landing."

"How? Gas of some sort?"

"The windows were all closed and locked and I have already ascertained that the gas and water lines have not been tampered with. Gas won't penetrate through a solid roof in sufficient concentration to knock out a man like that. It was something more subtle than gas."

"What was it?"

"I don't know yet. The clue to what it was lies, as I told you, in those windows."

Carnes moved over and surveyed the windows closely.

"I see nothing unusual about them except that they need washing rather badly."

"They were washed last Friday, but they do look rather dirty, don't they? Suppose you take a rag and some scouring soap and clean up a pane."

The detective took the proffered articles and started his task. He wet a pane of glass, rubbed up a thick lather of scouring soap and applied it and rubbed vigorously. With clear water he washed the glass and then gave an exclamation of astonishment and examined it more closely.

"That isn't dirt, Doctor," he cried. "The glass seems to be fogged."

Dr. Bird chuckled.

"So it seems," he admitted. "Now look at the rest of the glass around the laboratory."

Carnes looked around and then walked to a table littered with apparatus and examined a dozen pieces carefully.

"It's all fogged in exactly the same way, Doctor," he said. "The only piece of clear glass in the room is that piece of plate glass on your desk."

*   *   *   *   *

Dr. Bird picked up a hammer and struck the plate on his desk a sharp blow. Carnes ducked instinctively, but the hammer rebounded harmlessly from the plate.

"That isn't glass, Carnes," said the doctor. "That plate is made of vitrilene, a new product which I have developed. It looks like glass, but it has entirely different properties. It is of enormous strength and is quite insensitive to shock. It has one most peculiar property. While ultra-violet and longer rays will penetrate it quite readily, it is a perfect screen for X-rays and other rays of shorter wave length. It appears to be the only piece of transparent substance in my laboratory which has not been fogged, as you call it."

"Do short waves fog glass, Doctor?"

"Not so far as I know at present, but you must remember that very little work has been done with the short wave-lengths. In the vast range of waves whose lengths lie between zero and that of the X-ray, only a few points have been investigated and definitely plotted. There may be in that range a wave-length which will fog glass."

"Then your theory is that some sort of a ray machine was put in operation before the helicopter landed?"

"It is too early to attempt any theorizing, Carnes. Let us confine ourselves to the known facts. Lieutenant Breslau was normal at midnight and was working in this room. Some time between then and seven this morning he underwent certain mental and physical changes which prevent him from telling us what he observed. During the same period, a hole was cut in the roof and things of great importance stolen. At the same time, all the glass in the laboratory became semi-opaque. The problem is to determine what connection there is between the three events. I will handle the scientific end here, but there is some outside work to be done, and that will be your share."

*   *   *   *   *

"Give your orders, Doctor," said the detective briefly.

"To understand what I am driving at, I will have to tell you what has been stolen. Naturally this is highly confidential. Some rumors have leaked out as to my experiments with 'radite,' as I have named the new radium-containing disintegrating explosive on which I have been working, but no one short of the Secretary of War and the Chief of Ordnance and certain of their selected subordinates knows that my experiments have been successful and that the United States is in a position to manufacture radite in almost unlimited quantities from the pitchblende ore deposits of Wyoming and Nevada. The effects of radite will be catastrophic on the unfortunate victim on whom it is first used. The only thing left to do was to develop a gun from which radite shells could be fired with safety and precision.

"Ordinary propellant powders are too variable for this purpose, but I found that radite B, one form of my new explosive, can be used for propelling the shells from a gun. The ordinary gun will last only two or three rounds, due to the erosive action of the radite charge on the barrel, and ordinary ordnance is heavier and more cumbersome than is necessary. When this was found to be the case, the Chief of Ordnance detailed Lieutenant Breslau, the army's greatest expert on gun design, to work with me in an attempt to develop a suitable weapon. Breslau is a wizard at that sort of work and he has made a miniature working model of a gun with a vitrilene-lined barrel which is capable of being fired with a miniature shell. The gun will stand up under the repeated firing of radite charges and is very light and compact and gives an accuracy of fire control heretofore deemed impossible. From this he planned to construct a larger weapon which would fire a shell containing an explosive charge of two and one-half ounces of radite at a rate of fire of two hundred shots per minute. The destructive effect of each shell will be greater than that of the ordinary high-explosive shell fired from a sixteen-inch mortar, and all of the shells can be landed inside a two-hundred foot circle at a range of fifteen miles. The weight of the completed gun will be less than half a ton, exclusive of the firing platform. It is Breslau's working model which has been stolen."

*   *   *   *   *

Carnes whistled softly between his teeth.

"The matter will have to be handled pretty delicately to avoid international complications," he said. "It's hard to tell just where to look. There are a great many nations who would give any amount for a model of such a weapon."

"The matter must be handled delicately and also in absolute secrecy, Carnes. We are not yet ready to announce to the world the fact that we have such a weapon in our armory. It is the plan of the President to have a half dozen of these weapons manufactured and give a demonstration of their terrible effectiveness to representatives of the powers of the world. Think what an argument the existence of such a weapon will be for the furtherance of his plans for disarmament and universal peace! Public sentiment will force disarmament on the world, for even the worst jingoist could no longer defend armaments in the face of America's offer to scrap these super-engines of destruction and to destroy the plans from which they were made. If the model has fallen into the hands of any civilized power the damage is not irreparable, for public opinion would force its surrender and return. It is among the uncivilized powers that our search must first be made."

"That makes the problem of where to start more complicated."

"On the contrary, it simplifies it immensely. At the head of the uncivilized powers stands one which has the brains, the scientific knowledge and the manufacturing facilities to make terrible use of such a weapon. In addition, the aim of that power is to overthrow all world governments and set up in their stead its own tyrannical disorder. Need I name it?"

"You refer to Russia."

"Not to Russia, the great slumbering giant who will some day take her place in the sun in fellowship with the other nations, but to Bolsheviki, that empire within an empire, that horrible power which it holding sleeping Russia in chains of steel and blood. It is there that our search must first be made."

*   *   *   *   *

"Of course, they have no official representative in America."

"No, but the Young Labor Party is as much their accredited representative as the British Ambassador is of imperial Britain. Your first task will be to trail down and locate every leader of that group and to investigate his present activities."

"I can tell you where most of them are without investigation. Denberg, Semensky and Karuska are in Atlanta; Fedorovitch and Caspar are in Leavenworth; Saranoff is dead—"

"Presumably."

"Why, Doctor, I saw with my own eyes the destruction of the submarine in which he was riding!"

"Did you see his dead body?"

"No."

"Neither did I, and I will never be sure until I do. Once before we were certain of his death, and he bobbed up with a new fiendish device. We cannot eliminate Saranoff."

"I will include him in my plans."

"Do so. Besides a hypothetical Saranoff, there are a half dozen or more of the old leaders of the gang who are alive and at liberty, so far as we know. They fled the country after the Coast Guard broke up their alien smuggling scheme, but some of them may have returned. There are also thirty or forty underlings who should be located and checked up on, and, in addition, we must not lose sight of the fact that new heads of the organization may have been smuggled into the United States. It is no simple task that I am setting you, Carnes, but I know that you and Bolton will see it through if anyone can."

"Thanks, Doctor, we'll do our best. If I am not speaking out of turn, what are you planning to do in the mean time?"

*   *   *   *   *

"I am going to start Taylor off on an ultra-short wave generator and try a few experiments along that line.

Breslau is at Walter Reed and they are doing all they can for him, but until I can get some definite information as to the underlying cause of his condition, they are more or less shooting in the dark."

"How are they treating him?"

"By electric stimulations and vibratory treatments and by keeping him in a darkened room. By the way, Carnes, if I am correct in my line of thought, it would be well to have an extra guard put over Karuska. He was the only real expert in ordnance that the Young Labor party had, and if they have Breslau's model they'll need him to supervise the construction of a gun."

"I'll attend to that at once, Doctor. Is there anything else?"

"Not that I know of. I am going out to Takoma Park this afternoon and have another look at Breslau, but it is too soon to hope for any change in his condition. Aside from the time I will be out there, you can find me either here or at my home, in case anything develops."

"I'll get on the job at once, Doctor."

"Thanks, old dear. Remember that speed must be the keynote of your work."

* * * * *

The telephone bell at the head of Dr. Bird's bed woke into noisy activity. The doctor roused himself and took down the instrument sleepily. A glance at the clock showed him that it was four in the morning and he muttered a malediction on the one who had called him.

"Hello," he said into the receiver. "Dr. Bird speaking."

"Doctor," came a crisp voice over the wire, "wake up! This is Carnes talking. Something has broken loose!"

All trace of sleep vanished from Dr. Bird's face and his eyes glowed momentarily with a peculiar glitter which Carnes would at once have recognized as indicative of the keenest interest.

"What has happened, Carnes?" he demanded.

"I telephoned Atlanta this morning and arranged to have an extra guard put over Karuska as you suggested. The matter was simplified by the fact that he and nine others were confined in the prison infirmary. The warden agreed to do as I told him, and, in addition to the regular guards, a special man was placed in the ward near Karuska's bed. At 2 A. M. the lights in the ward went out."

"Accidentally, or were they put out?"

"They haven't found out yet. At any rate they are all right now, but Karuska and all of the other inmates and all the guards of that particular ward have gone crazy."

"The dickens you say!"

"Not only that, they are also partially paralyzed. The description I got over the telephone corresponds exactly with the condition of Lieutenant Breslau as you described it to me. Here is the most interesting part of the whole affair. The special guard over Karuska was only lightly affected and has already recovered and is in a position to tell you exactly what happened. I got a garbled account of the affair from the warden, something about a goldfish bowl or something like that, the warden wouldn't take it seriously enough to give me details. I didn't press for them much for I knew that you would rather get them at first hand."

"I certainly would. I'll be ready to leave for Atlanta in less than ten minutes."

"I expected that, Doctor, and a car is already on its way to pick you up. I'll meet you at Langley Field where a plane is already being tuned up and will be ready to take off by the time we get there."

"Good work, Carnes. I'll see you at the field."

*   *   *   *   *

A car was waiting for Carnes and Dr. Bird when the Langley Field plane slid down to a landing at Atlanta. At the penitentiary, Dr. Bird went direct to the infirmary where Karuska had been confined. As he entered, he shot a keen glance around and gave an exclamation of satisfaction.

"Look at the windows, Carnes," he cried.

Carnes went over to the nearest window and moistened his finger tip and applied it experimentally to the glass. The moisture produced no effect, for the glass of the windows was permanently clouded as was that of the doctor's laboratory.

"Whatever happened in my laboratory the night before last was repeated here last night with a similar object," said the doctor. "The object there was to steal a gun model; here it was to steal a man who could construct a full-sized gun from the model. I understand that one of the guards escaped the fate which overtook the rest of the persons in the infirmary?"

"Not altogether, Doctor," replied the warden. "I think that his mind is somewhat affected, for he tells a wild yarn and insists on trying to wear a goldfish bowl on his head. I have him under observation in the psychopathic ward."

Dr. Bird shot a scornful glance at the warden.

"'There are none so blind as those who will not see'," he murmured.

"By all means, I wish to see him," he went on aloud. "Will you have him brought here at once, please?"

*   *   *   *   *

The warden nodded and spoke to one of the attendants. In a few moments a tall, fair-haired young giant stood before the doctor. Dr. Bird pushed back his unruly shock of black hair with his fingers, those long slim mobile fingers which alone betrayed the artist in his make-up, and shot a piercing glance from his black eyes into the blue ones, which returned the gaze unabashed.

"What is your name?" he asked.

"Bailley, sir."

"You were on guard here last night?"

"Yes, sir. I was detailed as a special guard over No. 9764."

"Tell me in your own words just what happened. Don't be afraid to speak out; I'm not going to disbelieve you; and above all, tell me everything, no matter how unimportant it may seem to you. I'll judge the importance of things for myself. I'm Dr. Bird of the Bureau of Standards."

The guard's face lighted up at the doctor's words.

"I've heard of you, Doctor," he said in a relieved tone, "and I'll be glad to tell you everything. At ten o'clock last night, I relieved Carragher as special guard over No. 9764. Carragher reported that the prisoner was somewhat restless and hadn't been asleep as yet. I sat down about fifteen feet from his bed and prepared to keep an eye on him until I was relieved at six o'clock this morning.

"Nothing happened until about two o'clock. No. 9764 was restless as Carragher had said, but toward midnight he quieted down and apparently went to sleep. I was sleepy myself, and I got up and took a turn around the room every five minutes to be sure that I kept awake. That's how I am so sure of the time, sir."

*   *   *   *   *

Dr. Bird nodded.

"At five minutes to two, just as I got up, I heard a noise outside like a big electric fan. It sounded like it came from directly overhead and I went to the window and looked out. I couldn't see anything, although I could hear it pretty plainly, and then I heard a noise like something had fallen on the roof. Almost at the same time there came a sort of high-pitched whine, a good deal like the noise an electric motor makes when it is running at high speed.

"I thought of giving an alarm, but I didn't want to stir things up unless I was sure that there was some necessity for it, so I started for the door to ask one of the outside guards if he had heard anything. As I turned toward No. 9764 I saw that he had been sitting up in bed while my back was turned. As soon as he saw that I noticed him, he lay back real quick and pulled the covers over his head. He moved pretty quick, but not so quick that I couldn't see that he had something that glittered like glass before his face. I started over toward his bed to see what he was doing and then it was that the lights started to get dim!"

"Go on!" said the doctor as Bailley paused. His eyes were glittering brightly now.

"Well, sir, Doctor, I don't hardly know how to describe what happened next. The lights were getting dim, but not as they ordinarily do when the current starts to go off. The filaments were shining as bright as they ever did, but the light didn't seem to be able to penetrate the air. The whole room seemed to be filled with a blackness that stopped the light. No, sir, it wasn't like fog; it was more like something more powerful than the lights was in the room and was killing them.

*   *   *   *   *

"It wasn't only the lights which were affected, it was me as well. This blackness, whatever it was, was getting into me as well as into the room, and I couldn't seem to make myself think like I wanted to. I tried to yell to give an alarm, and I found that I could hardly whisper. I went toward the bed and then I saw No. 9764 sit up again. He had a goldfish bowl pulled down over his head and it was evident that it was keeping the blackness away, for I could see him plainly and his eyes were as bright as ever.

"The nearer I got to him, the funnier I felt, and I began to be afraid that I would go out. No. 9764 got up out of bed, and I could see him grinning at me through the bowl. He reached up and adjusted that bowl, and all of a sudden I realized that whatever was knocking me out was not affecting him because he had that thing on. I jumped for him with the idea of taking the bowl off and putting it on my own head. He saw what I was up to and he fought like a cornered rat, but the blackness hadn't affected my muscles. I'm a pretty big man, sir, and No. 9764 is a little runt, and it didn't take me long to get the bowl off his head and pulled on over mine. As soon as I did that, I seemed to be able to think clearer. I was sitting on No. 9764 and was ready to tap him with a persuader if he started anything, but I didn't have to. In a few minutes he stopped struggling and lay perfectly quiet.

"The lights kept getting dimmer and dimmer until they went out altogether and the room became pitch dark. It wasn't exactly as if the lights had gone out, sir; I seemed to know that they were still there and were burning as bright as ever, but they couldn't penetrate the blackness in the room, if you understand what I mean."

*   *   *   *   *

"I think I do," said Dr. Bird slowly. "It was a good deal as if you had seen a glass filled with a pale red liquid and someone had dumped black ink into the fluid and hid the red color. You would know that the red was still there, but you wouldn't be able to see it through the black."

"That's exactly what it was like, Doctor; you have described it better than I can. At any rate, after it got real dark I heard a low whistle from the roof. No. 9764 made a struggle to get up for a moment and then lay quiet again. The whistle sounded again and then I heard some one call 'Caruso.' Everything was quiet for a while and then the same voice called again and said some stuff in a foreign language that I couldn't understand. I kept perfectly quiet to see what would happen.

"For about ten minutes the room remained perfectly dark, as I have said, and all the while I could hear that whining noise. All of a sudden it began to sound in a lower note and then I could see the lights again, very dimly and like the black ink you spoke of was fading out. The note got lower until it stopped altogether, and the lights came on brighter until they were normal again. Then I heard a scraping noise on the roof and the noise I had heard at first like a big electric fan. I looked at the clock. It was two-twenty.

"For a few minutes I wasn't able to collect my wits. When I got up off of No. 9764 at last he stared at me as though he didn't know a thing, and I heaved him back into his bed and ran to the door to summon an outside guard. I could still talk in a husky whisper, but not loud, and I wasn't surprised when no one heard me. My orders were not to let No. 9764 out of my sight, but this was an emergency, so I left the ward and found a guard. It was Madigan and he was standing on his beat staring at nothing. When I touched him he looked at me and there was the same vacant look in his eyes that I had seen in the prisoner's. I talked to him in a whisper, but he didn't seem to understand, so I left him and went to a telephone and called for help. Mr. Lawson, the warden, got here with guards in a couple of minutes and I tried to tell him what had happened, but I couldn't talk loud, and I was afraid to take the fish bowl off my head."

*   *   *   *   *

"What happened next?"

"Mr. Lawson took me to his office, and on the way we passed under an arc light. As soon as I got under it I begin to feel better, and my voice came stronger. I saw that it was doing me some good and I stopped under it for an hour before my voice got back to normal. It seemed to clear the fog from my brain, too, and I was able, about four o'clock, to tell everything that had happened. Mr. Lawson seemed to think that my brain was affected as well as the others' and he sent me to the hospital. That's all, Doctor."

"Do you feel perfectly normal now?"

"Yes, sir."

"There is no need for confining this man longer, Mr. Lawson. He is as well as he ever was. Carnes, get the Walter Reed Hospital on the telephone and tell them that I said to treat Lieutenant Breslau with light rays, rich in ultra-violet. Tell them to give him an overdose of them and not to put goggles on him. Keep him in the sun all day and under sun-ray arcs at night until further orders. Mr. Lawson, give the same treatment to the men who were disabled last night. If you haven't enough sun-ray arcs in your hospital, put them under an ordinary arc light in the yard. Bailley, have you still got that goldfish bowl?"

"It is in my office, Doctor," said the warden.

"Good enough! Send for it at once. By the way, you have two more communists here, Denberg and Semensky, haven't you?"

"I think so, although I will have to consult the records before I can be positive."

"I am sure that you have. Look the matter up and let me know."

*　　*　　*　　*　　*

The warden hurried away to carry out the doctor's orders, and an orderly appeared in a few moments with a hollow globe made of some crystalline transparent substance. Despite its presence in the infirmary the evening before, there was no trace of clouding apparent. Dr. Bird took it and examined it critically. He rapped it with his knuckles and then stepped to the door and hurled it violently down on the concrete floor of the yard. The globe rebounded without injury and he caught it.

"Vitrilene, or a good imitation of it," he remarked to Carnes. "After you get through talking to the hospital, get

Taylor on the wire. There is plenty of loose vitrilene in the Bureau, and I want him to send down about fifty square feet of it by a special plane at once."

As Carnes left the room, the warden reappeared.

"The men are all lying in the sun now, Doctor," he said. "I find that we have the two men you mentioned confined here. They are both in Tier A, Building 6."

"Is that an isolated building?"

"No, it is one wing of the old main building."

"On which floor?"

"The second floor. It is a six-story building."

"Have they been moved there recently?"

"They have been there for nearly a year."

*   *   *   *   *

"In that case there will be little chance of another attack of this sort to-night. At the same time, I would advise you to station extra guards there to-night and every night until I notify you otherwise. Caution them to watch the lights carefully and to give an alarm at once if they appear to get dim. In such a case, send men to the roof with rifles with orders to shoot to kill anyone they find there. I am going back to Washington and I am going to take Karuska, your No. 9764 with me. You had better have one of the guards in the corridor, where Denberg and Semensky are, wear this goldfish bowl, as you call it. A lot of plate glass—at least it will look like that—will come from Washington by plane. Cut it into sheets a foot square and use surgeon's plaster to make some temporary glass helmets for your men. I want all your guards to wear them until I either settle this matter or else send you some better helmets. Do you understand?"

"I understand all right, but I'm afraid that I can't do it. The wearing of such appliances would interfere with the efficiency of my men as guards."

"Brain and tongue paralysis would interfere rather more seriously, it seems to me. In any event, I have sufficient authority to enforce my request. If you are at all doubtful, call up the Attorney General and ask him."

The warden hesitated.

"If you don't mind, I think I will call Washington, Doctor," he said. "I will have to get authority to turn No. 9764 over to you in any event."

"Call all you wish, Mr. Lawson. Mr. Carnes is talking to Washington now and we'll have a clear line through for you in a few minutes. Meanwhile, get a set of shackles on Karuska and get him ready to travel by plane. He appears to be suffering from mental paralysis, but I don't know how his case will develope. He may go violently insane at any moment and I don't care to be aloft in a plane with an unbound maniac."

* * * * *

Major Martin looked up from the prone figure of Karuska.

"His condition duplicates that of Lieutenant Breslau, Dr. Bird," he said. "We received your telephoned message this afternoon and we kept Breslau in a flood of sunlight until dusk, and then put him under sun-ray lamps. I don't know how you got on to that treatment, but it is having a very beneficial effect. He can already make inarticulate sounds, and his eyes are not quite as vacant at they were. If he keeps on improving as he has, he should be able to talk intelligently in a few days. If you wish to question this man, why not give him the same treatment?"

"I haven't time, Major. I must make him talk to-night if it is humanly possible. I called you in because you are the most eminent authority on the brain in the government service. Is there any way of artificially stimulating this man's brain so that we can force the secrets of his subconscious mind from him?"

The major sat for a moment in profound thought.

"There *is* a way, Doctor," he said at length, "but it is a method which I would not dare to use. By applying high frequency electrical stimulations to the medulla oblongata, at the same time bathing the cerebellum with ultra-violet, it might be done, but the chances are that either death or insanity would result. I would not do it."

"Major Martin, this man is a reckless and dangerous international criminal. If his gang carries out the plan which I fear they have formed, the lives of thousands, yes, of millions, may pay for your hesitation. I will assume full responsibility for the test if you will make it, and I have the authority of the President of the United States behind me."

"In that case, Doctor, I have no choice. The President is the Commander-in-chief of the army, and if those are his orders the experiment will be carried out. As a matter of form, I will ask that your orders be reduced to writing."

"I will write them gladly, Major. Please proceed with the experiment without delay."

*   *   *   *   *

Major Martin bowed and spoke to a waiting orderly. The prostrate figure of Karuska was wheeled down a corridor into the electrical laboratory, and with the aid of the laboratory technician the surgeon made his preparations. The Moss lamp was arranged to throw a flood of ultra-violet over the Russian's cranium while the leads from a deep therapy X-ray tube was connected, one to the front of Karuska's throat and the other to the base of his brain. At a signal from the major, a nurse began to administer ether.

"I guarantee nothing, Dr. Bird," said the major. "The paralysis of the vocal cords may be physical, in which case the victim will still be unable to speak, regardless of the brain stimulation. If, however, the evident paralysis is due to some obscure influence on the brain, it may work."

"In any, event I will hold you blameless and thank you for your help," replied the doctor. "Please start the stimulation."

Major Martin closed a switch, and the hum of a high tension alternator filled the laboratory. The Russian quivered for a moment and then lay still. Major Martin nodded and Dr. Bird stepped to the side of the operating table.

"Ivan Karuska," he said slowly and distinctly, "do you hear me?"

The Russian's lips quivered and an unintelligible murmur came from them.

"Ivan Karuska," repeated Dr. Bird, "do you hear me?"

*   *   *   *   *

There was a momentary struggle on the part of the Russian and then a surprisingly clear voice came from his lips.

"I do."

"Who is the present head of the Young Labor party?"

Again there was a pause before the name "Saranoff" came from the lips of the insensible figure. Carnes gave a sharp exclamation but a gesture from the doctor silenced him.

"Is Saranoff alive?"

"Yes."

"Is he in the United States?"

"No, he is in London."

"Is he coming to the United States?"

"Yes."

"When?"

"I don't know. Soon. As soon as we are ready for him."

"Where is he living in London?"

"I don't know."

"How did you get word that you were to be rescued from Atlanta?"

"A message was smuggled in to me by O'Grady, a guard in our pay."

"What was that vitrilene helmet for?"

"To protect me from the effects of the black lamp."

"What is the black lamp?"

"I don't know exactly. Saranoff invented it. It gives a black light and it kills all other light except sunlight, and it paralyses the brain."

"Did you know that the model of the Breslau gun had been stolen?"

"Yes."

"What were you going to do after you were rescued from jail?"

"I was going to make a full-sized gun. We have a disappearing gun platform built in the swamps at the juncture of the Potomac and Piscataway Creek. The gun was to be mounted there and we would shell Washington and institute a reign of terror. It would be a signal for uprisings all over the country."

"Is there a black lamp at that gun platform?"

"Yes. The black lamp will kill both the flash and the report."

"Where did you get the formula for radite?"

"We got it from one of Dr. Bird's assistants. His name—"

*   *   *   *   *

As he spoke the last few sentences, Karuska's voice had steadily risen almost to a shriek. As he endeavored to give the name of the doctor's treacherous helper his voice changed to an unintelligible screech and then died away into silence. Major Martin stepped forward and bent over the prone figure. Hurriedly he tore away the electrical connections and placed a stethoscope over the Russian's heart. He listened for a moment and then straightened up, his face pale.

"I hope that the information you obtained is worth a life, Dr. Bird," he said, his voice trembling slightly, "because it has cost one."

"It may easily save thousands of lives. I thank you, Major, and I will see that no blame attaches to you for your actions. I only wish that he had lived long enough to tell me the name of my assistant who has sold me to Saranoff. However, we'll get that information in other ways. Carnes, telephone Lawson at Atlanta to slam O'Grady into a cell pending investigation while I get Camp Meade on the wire and order up a couple of tanks. We are going to attack that gun emplacement at daybreak."

The telephone bell in the laboratory jangled sharply. Major Martin answered it and turned to Carnes.

"You're wanted on the telephone, Mr. Carnes."

The detective stepped forward and took the transmitter.

"Carnes speaking," he said. "Yes. Oh, hello, Bolton. Yes, we have Karuska here, or rather his body. Yes, Dr. Bird is here right now. You've what? Great Scott, wait a minute."

"Dr. Bird," he cried eagerly turning from the telephone, "Bolton has located the Washington headquarters of the Young Labor party."

Dr. Bird sprang to the instrument.

"Bird speaking, Bolton," he cried. "You've located their headquarters? Who's running it? Stanesky, eh? You're on the right track; he used to be Saranoff's right hand man. Where is the place located? I don't seem to recollect the spot. You have it well surrounded? Where are you speaking from? All right, we'll join you as quickly as we can. Keep your patrols out and don't let anyone get away."

He hung up the receiver and turned to Carnes.

"Did you have the car wait?" he asked. "Good enough; we'll jump for the Bureau and pick up all the vitrilene

laying around loose and then join Bolton. He thinks that
he has the whole outfit bottled up."

*   *   *   *   *

Bolton was waiting as the car rolled up and Dr. Bird
leaped out.

"Where are they?" demanded the doctor eagerly.

"In an abandoned factory building about three
hundred yards from here," replied the Chief of the Secret
Service. "I traced them through New York. We have been
watching the place ever since yesterday noon, and I know
that Stanesky is in there with half a dozen others. No one
has tried to leave since we set our watch. One funny thing
has happened. About an hour ago a peculiar red glow
suffused the whole building. It has died down a good deal
since, but we can still see it through the windows. Could
you tell us what it means?"

"No. I couldn't, Bolton, but we'll find out. How many
men have you?"

"I have sixteen stationed around."

"That's more than we'll need. I have only vitrilene
shields and helmets enough to equip six men. Pick out
your three best men to go with us and we'll make a try at
entering."

Bolton strode off into the darkness and returned in a
few moments with three men at his heels. Dr. Bird spoke
briefly to the operatives, all of them men who had been
his companions on other adventures. He explained the
need for the vitrilene helmets and shields, and without
comment the six donned their armor and followed Bolton
as he strode toward the building. As they approached, a
dull red glow could be plainly seen through the windows,
and Dr. Bird paused and studied the phenomenon for a
moment.

"I don't know what that means, Bolton," he said softly,
"but I don't like the looks of it. Stanesky is up to some
devilment or other. I wouldn't be a bit surprised to find

out that he knows all about your pickets and is ready for a raid."

"We'd better rush the place, then," muttered Bolton.

*   *   *   *   *

Dr. Bird nodded agreement and with a sharp command to his men Bolton broke into a run. Not a shot was fired as they approached, and the front door gave readily to Bolton's touch. At it opened there came a grating sound from the roof followed by the whir of a propeller. Dr. Bird ran out of the building and glanced up.

"A helicopter!" he cried. "They were expecting us and have escaped!"

He drew his pistol and fired ineffectually at the great bird-like ship which was rising almost noiselessly into the air. He cursed and turned again to the building.

Bolton still stood in the room which they had first entered. His flashlight showed it to be empty, but from under a door on the opposite side a line of dull red light glowed evilly. With his pistol ready in his hand, Bolton approached the door on hands and knees. When he reached it he threw his shoulder against it and dropped flat to the floor as the door swung open. No shot greeted him, and he stared for a moment and then rose to his feet.

"Nothing in here but some glass statues," he announced.

Dr. Bird followed him into the room. As he looked at what Bolton had called glass statues he gasped and shielded his eyes.

"God in Heaven!" he ejaculated. "Those were living men!"

*   *   *   *   *

Before them were three men or what had been three men. All stood in strained attitudes with a look of horror frozen on their faces. The thing that made the spectators shudder was that their bodies had, by some diabolical method, been rendered semi-transparent. The dull red light which suffused the room emanated from the three bodies. Dr. Bird examined them closely, being careful not to touch them.

"The identity of my treacherous assistant is known," he said grimly as he pointed at the middle figure. "It was Gerond. What is this?"

He took an envelope from the hand of the middle figure and opened it. A sheet of paper fell out and he picked it up and read it.

"My dear Mr. Bolton," ran the note. "Your methods of tracing and picketing my headquarters are so crude as to be almost laughable. This base has served its purpose and we were ready to abandon it in any event, but I couldn't resist the temptation to let you almost nab us. The three men whom you will find here are agents who failed in their duty. If you are interested in learning the method of their execution, you might take to heart the words of your colleague, Dr. Bird: 'The clue lies in those windows.'"

Carnes glanced at the windows and gave a cry of surprise. The glass was opaque, as had been the glass in the doctor's laboratory and the glass in the infirmary at Atlanta. The fogging however, was much more pronounced, and the opaque glass gave faintly the same red effulgence which came from the three bodies.

"What does it mean, Doctor?" he asked.

"I don't know, Carnes," said Dr. Bird slowly. "I foresee that I am going to have to do a great deal of work on short wave-lengths soon. It is doubtless the effect of some modification of the black lamp which has done it. Look out!"

*   *   *   *   *

He leaped to one side as he spoke, drawing Bolton and Carnes with him. A panel in the side of the wall opposite the doorway had slid silently open and through the opening poured out a beam of fiery red. Full on the three bodies it fell, and then spread out to fill the room. Dr. Bird had drawn the two nearest men out of the direct beam, but one of the secret service men stood full in its path. In the excitement of entering he had dropped his vitrilene shield and the livid ray fell full on his defenceless body. As they watched an expression of horror spread over his face and he strove to move to one side, but he was held helpless. Slowly he stiffened; and, as the ray bored through him, his body became semi-transparent and the same dull red glow which emanated from the three bodies they had found began to shine forth from him. Bolton strove to break from the doctor's grasp and rush to the rescue but Dr. Bird held him with a grip of iron.

"Too late," he said grimly. "Chalk up another murder to the arch fiend who has committed the others. I don't know the nature of that ray and vitrilene may not be an adequate defence against its full force. We had better get out of here and attack the place from the rear."

Carefully edging their way around the sides of the room, the five men made their way out through the door. Dr. Bird slammed the door shut behind him and led the way out of the building and around to the rear. A door loomed before them and he cautiously tried it. It gave to his touch and he entered. As he set his foot on the threshold a terrific explosion came from the interior of the building.

"Run!" he shouted as he led the way in retreat. "If that is a radite explosion it will act for several seconds!"

From a safe distance they watched. One corner of the building had been torn off by the force of the explosion, and as they watched the rest of the building gradually collapsed and sank into a pile of ruins.

"They had planned on a visit from us all right," said Dr. Bolton grimly. "They had a surprise for us any way we jumped. If we went in the front door, that devil's ray was to finish us, and if we went in the back door the whole place was arranged to blow up as we entered. I only hope that Stanesky thinks that he has got us all and doesn't expect an attack on his next base in the morning. If he doesn't, I think we may give him a rather unpleasant surprise. Of course, that lamp is smashed into atoms and buried under the debris, but I don't know what other devil's contraptions that ruin holds. Bolton, have your men picket it and allow no one near until I get back. I've got to get to a telephone and get a couple of tanks from Meade and a plane or two from Langley Field."

*   *   *   *   *

Two tanks made their way slowly across country. The front of each tank was protected by a heavy sheet of vitrilene, while from the turrets of the tanks projected the wicked looking muzzles of thirty-seven millimeter guns. Overhead two airplanes from Langley Field soared, scouting the country. Dr. Bird and Carnes rode in the leading tank.

"It ought to be somewhere near here, unless Karuska lied," said Carnes as he swept the country with a pair of binoculars.

"He didn't lie," returned Dr. Bird. "It was his subconscious mind that spoke and it never lies. He spoke of the gun emplacement as being in a swamp and I have a strong idea that it is submersible. Of course, it is bound to be well camouflaged, both from land and from air observation."

The planes circled around again and again, quartering the air like a pair of well-trained bird dogs will quarter a hunting field. First high and then low they swooped back and forth, the tanks lumbering slowly along in the same direction. Presently the occupants of the leading tank saw one of the planes bank sharply and swing around. It dropped to an altitude of only a few hundred feet and turned and went back over the ground it had just crossed.

"I believe that fellow sees something!" exclaimed Carnes.

As he spoke, three green Very lights came from the cockpit of the plane. The tank driver gave a grunt of satisfaction and turned the nose of his vehicle in that direction. The second tank followed.

Hardly had they turned in the new direction before the ground began to get soft under their tracks and the heavy vehicles began to sink. The driver of the Doctor's tank forced it ahead, but the tank sank deeper in the mire until water flowed in around the feet of the occupants.

"I reckon we'll have to get out and walk pretty soon, Doctor," said the driver.

*   *   *   *   *

Dr. Bird grunted in acquiescence. The tank made its way forward a few yards before the engine sputtered and died. The second tank stopped when the first one did, fifty yards behind it. Donning vitrilene helmets and taking vitrilene shields in their hands, the crews of both tanks climbed out into the waist-deep water and gathered around the Doctor for orders.

"Form a skirmish line at ten-pace intervals and cross the swamp," he directed. "We may meet with no opposition, but if there is, the more scattered we are, the safer we will be. You all have hand grenades as well as your rifles?"

A murmur of assent answered him and the line formed and started across the swamp. They had gone perhaps a hundred yards when three red lights came from one of the planes circling overhead.

"Down!" cried the doctor, dropping to his knees in the muck.

Four hundred yards ahead of them a concrete platform emerged from the marsh and rose slowly into the air. It was roofed with a dome of what looked like plate glass, but which the doctor shrewdly suspected was vitrilene. When the base of the platform was two-feet above the level of the water the dome slid silently aside disclosing two men bending over a tiny gun. Dr. Bird leveled his binoculars.

"That's the Breslau gun model that was stolen as sure as I'm a foot high!" he cried. "They must have made some miniature shells and be planning to fire it."

Slowly a pall of intense blackness rose from the marsh and enveloped the platform and hid it from view. A whining noise came from overhead, and then a crash like a thunderbolt. The blast of the explosion threw the attackers face down in the swamp, and when they arose and looked back there was merely a gaping hole where the leading tank had been. The second tank suddenly seemed to rise in the air and fly into millions of tiny fragments, and a second thunderous blast sent them again to their knees.

"Radite!" bellowed Dr. Bird to Carnes. "Imagine the effect if that had been a full charge fired from a completed Breslau gun! Watch the planes, now. I think they are going to drop a few eggs on them."

*   *   *   *   *

The black mist cleared as if by magic and the platform was in plain view. The big glass dome rolled back into place as the two planes swept over at an elevation of two thousand feet. From each one a small black cigar-shaped object was released and fell in a long parabola toward the earth. The glass dome which had been closing over the gun platform rolled quickly back and a long beam of intense blackness pierced the heavens. First one and then the other of the falling bombs disappeared from view into it, and then the black column faded from view. The two bombs fell with increasing speed but the dome closed over the platform before they struck. The two hit the dome at almost the same instant and instead of the blinding crash they expected, the watchers saw the bombs rebound from the dome and fall harmlessly into the water.

"Stymied!" muttered the doctor. "I wonder what other properties that confounded lamp has."

He resumed his advance, Carnes and the soldiers keeping abreast of him. When they were within two hundred yards of the platform it rose again and the transparent dome rolled back. A beam of black shot forth over the swamp, searching them out and hiding them from view. First one and then another felt the effects of the black beam; but the vitrilene which the Doctor had provided stood them in good stead, and, aside from a slight shortening of their breath, none of the attackers felt any the worse.

"Come on, men!" cried the Doctor as his athletic figure plowed forward through the breast-deep water. "That is their worst weapon and it is harmless against us!"

Cheering, they fought their way toward the platform. It sunk for a moment and then rose again. As the dome swung back a sharp crackle of machine-gun fire sounded and the water before them was whipped into foam by the plunging bullets. One of the soldiers gave a sharp cry and slumped forward into the water.

"Fire at will!" shouted the lieutenant in command.

*   *   *   *   *

A crackle of rifle fire answered the tattoo of the machine-gun, and the sharp ping of bullets striking on the dome could be plainly heard. An occasional shot kicked up a spurt of white dust from the concrete, but the machine-gun kept up a steady rattle of fire and the soldiers kept their heads almost at the level of the water.

There came the roar of an airplane motor, and one of the planes swept over the platform, a hundred yards in the air, with two machine-guns spraying streams of bullets onto the platform. Two men abandoned their machine-gun and crouched under the partially folded-back dome as the second plane swept over, and Dr. Bird took advantage of the lull to advance his party a few yards nearer. Again the defenders of the platform rushed to their gun, but the first plane had turned and swooped down with both guns going, and again they were forced to take shelter while the Doctor and his force made another advance.

The second plane had turned and followed the first, but the defenders had had enough. The transparent dome closed over them and the platform sank into the marsh. With a shout, Dr. Bird led the way forward again.

The attackers were within a hundred yards of the platform when it again rose above the surface of the water. The guns had disappeared, but in their place stood an airship. It was a small affair with stubby wings above which were two helicopter blades revolving at high speed. No sound of a motor could be heard.

The transparent dome rolled back and like a bullet the little craft shot into the air, followed by a futile volley from the soldiers. Hardly had it appeared than the two airplanes bore down on it with machine-guns going. The helicopter paid no attention to them for a moment, and then came a puff of smoke from its side. The leading plane swerved sharply and the helicopter fired again. The leading plane maneuvered about, trying to get a machine-gun to bear, while the second plane climbed swiftly to get above the helicopter and pour a deadly stream of fire down into it. It gained position and swooped down to the attack, but another puff of smoke came from the side of the helicopter and there was a thunderous report and a blinding flash in the sky. As the smoke cleared away, no trace of the ill-fated plane could be seen. The helicopter hung motionless in the air as though daring the remaining plane to attack.

*   *   *   *   *

The plane accepted the challenge and bore down at full speed on the stranger. Again came a puff of smoke, but the plane swerved and an answering shot came from its side. It was above the helicopter, and the shell which missed its mark plunged to the ground. When it struck there came a roar and a flash and the whole earth seemed to shake. The helicopter shot upward into the air and forward, both its elevating fans and its propellers whirling blurs of light. The airplane followed at its sharpest climbing angle, but was helpless to compete with its swifter climbing rival.

"He's got away!" groaned Carnes.

"Not yet, old dear!" cried the Doctor hopping with excitement. "He isn't safe yet. I never told you, but one Breslau gun had been made and it is on that plane. It has deadly accuracy and is good for fifteen miles. That's Lieutenant Dreen at the controls and Mason at the gun."

As he spoke the plane swung around and made a half loop. For a few yards it flew upside down and then whirled swiftly. As it turned there came a sharp report and a puff of smoke from its rear cockpit. High above, the helicopter had ceased climbing and hovered motionless. As the plane fired, the helicopter shot forward like an arrow from a bow, and thereby spelled its doom. Not for nothing did Captain Mason bear the title of the best aerial gunner in the Air Corps. He had foreseen what the action of his opponent would be and had allowed for just such a move. Far up in the sky came a blinding flash and a cloud of smoke. When the smoke cleared the sky was empty, except for a little scattered debris falling slowly to the ground.

*   *   *   *   *

"And that's that!" exclaimed Dr. Bird as he finished his examination of the underground laboratory with which the gun platform connected. "The lamp has gone to glory with Breslau's gun model and two of the best brains of the Young Labor party. I am sure that Stanesky was one of those two men. I wish the whole gang had been on board."

"Don't you think that this is the end of it, Doctor?" asked Carnes.

"No, Carnes, I don't. We know that the real brains of this outfit is Saranoff, and Saranoff is still alive. He probably won't try to use his black lamp again, because I will have a defence against it in a short time, now that I have seen it in action, but he'll try something else. The whole object of life to a loyal citizen of Bolshevikia is to reduce the whole world to the barbarous level in which they hold Russia, and they will spare no pains or effort to accomplish it. The greatest obstacle to their success at present is the President of the United States. He is loved and respected by the whole world, and if he is spared he will forge the world into a great machine for the preservation of peace and universal good will. That would be fatal to Bolshevikia's plans, and they will spare no effort to remove him. By the grace of God, we have saved him from harm so far, but until we remove Saranoff permanently from the scene, I will never feel safe for him."

"What do you suppose they'll try next, Doctor?"

"That, Carnes, time alone will tell."

When Caverns Yawned

Originally Published In *Astounding Stories Of Super-Science*,
May 1931

*Only Dr. Bird's super-scientific sleuthing
stands in the way of Ivan Saranoff's latest
attempt at wholesale destruction.*

When Caverns Yawned

Bells jangled discordantly. A whistle split the air with a piercing note. A band blared away on the platform. With a growing rumble of sound, the Presidential special slowly gathered headway. The President waved a final farewell to the crowds at the platform and sat down. He chatted cheerily with his companions until the train was clear of Charleston, then rose, and with a word to the others stepped into the car. Operative Carnes of the United States Service slumped back in his chair with a sigh of relief.

"Thank Goodness, that's over," he said. "I was never so glad to get him safely away from a place in my life."

Haggerty of the secret service nodded in agreement. Colonel Holmes, the military aide, looked up inquiringly.

"Why so? Do you think Charleston an especially dangerous place for him to be?"

"Not ordinarily. Charleston is a very patriotic and loyal city, but I have been worried. There have been vague rumors going around. Nothing definite that we could pin down, but enough to make me pretty uneasy."

"I think you've worried needlessly. I have been in constant touch with the Military Intelligence Division and they have reported nothing alarming."

Haggerty chuckled at the look of disgust that spread over Carnes' face. Colonel Holmes bridled visibly.

"Now look here, Carnes," he began.

"Oh, horse-feathers!" interrupted Carnes. "The M.I.D. is all right in its place—Good Lord! What's that?"

*   *   *   *   *

The train gave a sudden sickening lurch. Colonel Holmes sprawled in an undignified heap in one corner of the observation platform. Carnes and Haggerty kept their feet by hanging on to the rails. From the interior of the car came cries of alarm. The train righted itself for a moment and then lurched worse than before. There was a scream of brakes as the engineer strove to halt the forward progress. The train swayed and lurched like a ship in a storm. Carnes sprang for the telephone connected with the engine cab and rang excitedly.

"Hello, Bemis," he cried when an answer came: "take off the brakes! Keep moving at full speed, no matter what happens. What? Use your gun on him, man! Keep moving even if the train tips over!"

The train swayed and rocked worse than ever as it began to gather momentum. Carnes looked back along the track and gasped. For three hundred yards behind them, the track was sinking out of sight. The train forged ahead, but it was evident that it also was sinking into the ground. The track behind them suddenly gave. With a roar like a hundred buildings collapsing, it sank out of sight in a cloud of dust. The rear car of the train hung partially over the yawning cavern in the earth for an instant before the laboring engine dragged it to solid ground. The swaying and lurching grew less. For a mile it persisted to a slight degree. With a face the color of a sheet, Carnes made his way into the train. The President met him at the door.

"What's the trouble, Carnes?" he demanded.

"I am not sure, Mr. President. It felt like an earthquake. A great cavern opened in the earth behind us. Our train was almost trapped in it."

"An earthquake! We must stop the train at once and take charge of the situation. An emergency of that sort demands immediate attention."

"I beg you to do nothing of the sort, sir. Your presence would add little to the rescue work and your life is too precious to risk."

"But my duty to the people—"

"Is to keep yourself alive, sir! Mr. President, this may well be an attempt on your life. There are persons who would give anything to do away with you, especially at present. You have not endeared yourself to a certain class in calling for a conference of the powers to curb Russia's anti-religious tactics."

* * * * *

The President hesitated. He knew Carnes well enough to know that he usually spoke from accurate knowledge and with good judgment.

"Mr. President," went on the operative earnestly, "I am responsible to the American people for your safety. I beg you to follow my advice."

"Very well, Carnes," replied the President, "I'll put myself in your hands for the present. What is your program?"

"Your route is well known. Other attempts may be planned since this one failed. Let me have you transferred incognito to another train and hurried through to Washington secretly. I am going to drop off and go back. That earthquake needs to be looked into."

Again the President hesitated.

"My desertion of the stricken area will not be favorably regarded. If I sneak away secretly as though in fear, it will be bad for the public morale."

"We'll let the special go through. No one need know that you have left it."

"Well—I guess you're right. What are you going to do about it?"

"My first move will be to summon Dr. Bird from Washington."

"That's a good move. You'd better have him bring Dr.
Lassen with him. Lassen is a great volcano and
earthquake specialist, you know."

"I will, sir. If you will get ready to drop of at the next
connecting point, I'll send Haggerty and Bemis with you.
The rest of the party can remain on the special."

"All right, Carnes, if you insist."

*   *   *   *   *

Carnes went forward to the operator of the train's
radio set. In half an hour the special came to a stop at a
junction point and four men got off. Ten minutes later
three of them climbed aboard another train which
stopped for them. Carnes, the fourth man, hurried to a
telephone. Fifteen minutes later he was talking to Dr.
Bird at the latter's private laboratory in the Bureau of
Standards.

"An earthquake, Carnes?" exclaimed the doctor as the
operative described the happenings. "Wait a few minutes,
will you?"

In five minutes he was back on the telephone.

"It was no earthquake, old dear, whatever it may have
been. I have examined the records of all three of the
Bureau's seismographs. None of them record even a
tremor. What are you going to do?"

"Whatever you say, Doctor. I'm out of my depth
already."

"Let me think a moment. All right, listen. Go back to
Charleston as quickly as you can and get in touch with
the commanding officer at Fort Moultrie. I'll have the
Secretary of War telephone him and give him orders. Get
troops and go to the scene of the catastrophe. Allow no
one near it. Proclaim martial law if necessary. Stop all
road and rail traffic within a radius of two miles. Arrest
anyone trying to pass your guard lines. I'll get a plane
from Langley Field and come down on the run. Is that all
clear?"

"Perfectly, Doctor. By the way, the President suggested that you bring Dr. Lassen with you."

"Since it wasn't an earthquake, he wouldn't be of much value. However, I'll bring him if I can get hold of him. Now start things moving down there. I'll get some apparatus together and join you in five hours; six at the outside. Have a car waiting for me at the Charleston airport."

*   *   *   *   *

Carnes commandeered a passing car and drove back to Charleston. He made a wide sweep to avoid the disturbed area and went direct to Fort Moultrie. Dr. Bird had been good at his word. The troops were assembled in heavy marching order when the detective arrived. A few words to the commanding officer was sufficient to set the trucks loaded with soldiers in motion. Carnes, accompanied by the colonel and his staff, went direct to the scene of the catastrophe.

He found a hole in the ground, a hundred feet wide and a quarter of a mile long, sunk to a depth of fifty feet. He shuddered as he thought of what would have happened had the Presidential train been in the center of the devastated area instead of at the edge. The edges of the hole were ragged and sloping as though the earth had caved in to fill a huge cavern underground.

State and local authorities were already on the ground, striving to hold back sightseers. They were very glad to deliver their responsibility to the representative of the federal government. Carnes added their force to that of the military. In an hour a cordon of guards were stationed about the cavern while every road was picketed two miles away. Fortunately there had been no loss of life and no rescue work was needed. The earth-shaking had been purely a local matter, centered along the line of the railroad track.

There was nothing to do but wait, Carnes thought furiously. He had worked with Dr. Bird long enough to have a fair idea of the scientist's usual lines of investigation.

"The first thing he'll want to do is to explore that hole," he mused. "Probably, that'll mean some excavating. I'd better get a wrecking train with a crane on it and a steam shovel here. A gang of men with picks and shovels might be useful, too."

He hurried to the railroad officials. The sight of his gold badge had the desired result. Telegraph keys began to click and telephones to ring. Carnes was sorely tempted to explore the hole himself, but he resisted the temptation. Dr. Bird was not always pleasant when his colleagues departed from the orders he had given.

*   *   *   *   *

The morning passed, and the first part of the afternoon. Two wrecking trains stood with steam up at the edge of the hole. Grouped by the trains were a hundred negroes with shovels and picks. Carnes sat at the edge of the hole and stared down into it. He was roused from his reverie by the sound of a motor.

From the north came an airplane. High over the hole it passed, and then swerved and descended. On the under side of the wings could be seen the insignia of the Air Corps. Carnes jumped to his feet and waved his hat. Lower came the plane until it roared across the cavern less than a hundred feet above the ground. Two figures leaned out and examined the terrain carefully. Carnes waved again. One of the figures waved a hand in reply. The plane rose in the air and straightened out toward Charleston.

"We'll have the doctor here in a few minutes now," said Carnes to the Colonel. "It might be a good plan to send a motorcycle out along the Charleston road to bring him in. We don't want the guards to delay him."

The colonel gave an order and a motorcycle shot off down the road. In half an hour it came sputtering back with a huge Cadillac roaring in its wake. The car drew up and stopped. From it descended two men. The first was a small, wizened figure with heavy glasses. What hair age had left to him was as white as snow. The second figure, which towered over the first, was one to merit attention anywhere.

*　　*　　*　　*　　*

Dr. Bird was as light on his feet and as quick and graceful as a cat, but there was nothing feline about his appearance. He stood well over six feet in his stockings and tipped the beam close to the two hundred mark. Not one ounce of fat was on his huge frame. So fine was he drawn that unless one looked closely he would never suspect the weight of bone and muscle that his unobtrusive tweed suit covered. Piercing black eyes looked out from under shaggy brows. His face was lean and browned, and it took a second glance to realize the tremendous height and breadth of his forehead. A craggy jutting chin spoke of stubbornness and the relentless following up of a line of action determined on. His head was topped with an unruly shock of black hair which he tossed back with a hand that commanded instant attention.

His hands were the most noteworthy thing about the famous Bureau scientist. Long slender hands, they were, with slim tapering fingers–the hands of an artist and a dreamer. The acid stains that marred them could not hide their slim beauty, yet Carnes knew that those hands had muscles like steel wire and that the doctor boasted a grip that could crush the hand of a professional wrestler. He had seen him tear a deck of playing cards in half and, after doubling, again in half, with as little effort as the ordinary man would use in tearing a bare dozen of the cards. As he climbed out of the car his keen black eyes swept around in a comprehensive glance. Carnes, trained observer that he was, knew that in that one glance every essential detail which it had taken him an hour to place had been accurately noted and stored away in the doctor's mind. He came forward to the detective.

"Has anything happened since you telephoned me?" was his first question.

"Nothing, Doctor. I followed your instructions and also assembled a crew of men with excavating tools."

"You're improving, Carnes. This is Dr. Lassen. This is a little out of your line. Doctor, but you may see something familiar. What does it look like to you?"

"Not like an earthquake, Bird, at all events. Offhand I would say that a huge cavern had been washed in the earth and the ground had caved in."

"It looks that way. If you are right, we should find running water if we dig deep enough. Have you been down in the hole, Carnes?"

"No, Doctor."

"Then that's the first thing to do. You have ropes, of course?"

*   *   *   *   *

Carnes called to the waiting gang of negroes and a dozen of these hurried up with ropes. Dr. Bird slung a rope around his body under his arms and was lowered into the hole. The rope slackened as he reached bottom. Carnes lay on his stomach and looked over the edge. Dr. Bird was gingerly picking his way across the ground. He turned and called up.

"Carnes, you and Lassen can come down if you care to."

In a few minutes the detective and the volcanologist joined him in the cavern. The top surface of the ground was rolled up into waves like the sea. The sides of the hole were almost sheer. The naked rock was exposed for thirty feet. Above the rock could be seen the subsoil, and then the layer of top soil and vegetation. Dr. Bird was carefully examining the rock wall.

"What do you make of these, Lassen?" he asked, pointing to a row of horizontal striations in the rock. The volcanologist studied them.

"They might be water marks but if so they are different from any that I have seen before," he said doubtfully. "It looks as though some force had cut the rock away in one sharp stroke."

"Exactly. Notice this yellow powder on the ridges. Water would have washed it away."

Dr. Bird stepped forward to the wall and idly attempted to pick up a pinch of the yellow powder he had referred to in his fingers. He gave an exclamation of surprise as he did so. The powder was evidently fast to the wall. He drew his knife from his pocket and pried at the stuff. It fell readily. He scraped again and caught a speck of the falling powder in his hand. He gave a cry of surprise, for his hand sank as though borne down by a heavy weight. With an effort he lifted his hand and examined the substance.

"Come here, Carnes," he said. "Hold your hand up to catch some of this powder as I scrape it off."

*   *   *   *   *

The detective held up his hand. Dr. Bird pried with his knife and a shower of dull yellow particles fell. Carnes' hand sank as though the bits of dust had been a lead bar. He placed his other hand under it and with an effort lifted both hands up a few inches.

"What on earth is this stuff, Doctor?" he cried. "It's as heavy as lead."

"It's a great deal heavier than lead, Carnesy, old dear. I don't know what it is. I am inclined to think you did a wise thing when you sent for me. Lassen, take a look at this stuff. Did you ever run into anything like it?"

The aged volcanologist shook his head. The yellow powder was something beyond his ken.

"I have been poking around volcanos all my life," he said, "and I have seen some queer things come out of the ground—but nothing like that."

Dr. Bird poked tentatively at the substance for a moment, his brow furrowed in lines of thought. He suddenly threw back his shoulders in a gesture of decision.

"Send a gang of excavators down here," he cried. "Never mind the power shovel at present."

*   *   *   *   *

Down the ropes swarmed the gang of negroes. Dr. Bird indicated an area at one end of the cavern and directed them to dig. The blacks flew to work with a will. The top soil and subsoil were rapidly tossed into buckets and hauled to the surface. When bare rock lay before them, the negroes ceased their efforts.

"What next, Doctuh, suh?" asked the foreman.

"Get dynamite!" cried the doctor. "If I'm right, this underground cavern is entered by a tunnel. We'll blast away this caved-in rock until we locate it."

Then occurred a strange thing.

"There is no need to go to that trouble, Dr. Bird," spoke a metallic voice, from nowhere, it seemed. The negroes looked at one another. Picks and shovels fell from nerveless hands.

"Your guess about a tunnel is correct, Doctor," went on the Voice. "There is a tunnel leading away from the spot where you are, but to find the end would be useless to you. I have prepared for that."

From the blacks came a low moan of fear.

"Ha'nts!" cried one of them. The cry was taken up and spread into a rolling chorus of fear. With one accord they dropped their tools and stampeded in a mad rush toward the dangling ropes. Carnes sprang forward to stop them.

"Let them go, Carnes!" cried the doctor. "Their work is done for the present. Let's locate that radio receiver."

"That also will be a useless search. Doctor," spoke up the Voice again. "I have perfected a transmitter which will send my voice through space and make it audible without the aid of the clumsy apparatus you depend on. I am also able to see you through the miles of intervening rock without the aid of any instruments at your end."

*   *   *   *   *

"I presume that you can hear me as well?"

"Certainly, Doctor. To save you trouble—and I dislike to see you waste the efforts of your really good brain on minor problems—I will tell you that your surmise is correct. A tunnel does lead both to and from the place where you stand. It twists and turns so that even you would be puzzled to plot a general direction. You would have to follow it inch by inch. If you tried that, naturally I would cause it to collapse before you, or on top of you, if you got too close. Be content with what you have seen and seek a better way to trace me."

"Who are you, anyway?" blurted out Carnes.

"Is it possible that you do not know? Such is fame. I thought that at least my friend Mr. Carnes would suspect that Ivan Saranoff had done this."

"But you're dead!" protested the detective. "We killed you when we destroyed your helicopter."

"You killed merely an assistant who had disobeyed my orders. Had I not decreed his death, he would be alive to-day. I could kill you as you stand there; you into nothingness; but I do not choose to do so—yet. Other attempts I have made you have frustrated, but this time I shall succeed. I will institute a reign of terror which will bring your rich, foolish country to its knees. Listen, while I give you a taste of my power. The city of Charleston is about to be destroyed."

A thunderous roaring filled the air. Crash followed crash in rapid succession. It sounded as though all the noise of the universe had been concentrated in the cavern. The earth shook and rocked like a restless sea. From above came cries of terror.

The three men in the cavern were thrown to the ground. Shaken by the fall and deafened by the tumult, they hung onto irregularities of the rock on which they lay. Gradually the tumult and the shaking subsided. The cries from above became more apparent. Silence finally reigned in the cavern and the metallic Voice spoke again.

"Go back now and look at Charleston and you will see what to expect. The rest of your cities will soon share the same fate. Beware of trying to trace my movements, for your lives are in the hollow of my hand."

*   *   *   *   *

The voice died away in silence. From the edge of the hole came a cry. A Fort Moultrie officer was peering down at them.

"Are you all right down there?" he hailed.

"Right as hops," called Dr. Bird cheerfully. "What happened up above?"

"I don't know, Doctor. There seems to be a lot of smoke and fire over in the direction of the city. I expect the quake shook them up a little this time. What shall we do now?"

"We're ready to come up. First I'm going to send up a wheelbarrow full of yellow powder. Rig a crane to lift it, for it's too heavy to try to hoist with ropes."

With the aid of Carnes and Dr. Lassen, Dr. Bird collected a few cubic inches of the yellow powder from the ridges in the rock. He made the wheelbarrow containing it fast to the wire cables of the crane and gave the signal. Slowly it was raised to the surface. When it had safely reached there he turned to his companions.

"Grab a rope and let's go," he said.

In a few moments they were on the upper level. With the efforts of half a dozen men, the body of the wheelbarrow was lifted into the car. With a few final words of instruction to the colonel, Dr. Bird and his companions entered the car and were whisked away to the city.

A spectacle of destruction and ruin awaited them. Fully one-fourth of the city had sunk thirty feet into the ground. The sinking was not even nor uniform. The sunken ground was rolled into huge waves while buildings which had collapsed lay in confused heaps on all sides. From a dozen places in the area, columns of fire rose in the air.

*   *   *   *   *

Dr. Bird wasted little time on the scene before him. His car skirted the edge of the huge hole and took the road toward the Charleston airport, which was in a section which had suffered little. In half an hour the army transport roared into the air carrying Dr. Bird's precious load of yellow powder. Four hours later they dropped to a landing at Langley Field.

"Now, Carnes," said the doctor as they debarked from the plane, "there is work ahead. It may be too late to do much to-night, but we have no time to waste. Get Bolton on the wire and tell him that we have positive evidence that Saranoff is still alive and still up to his devil's tricks. Start every man of the secret service and every Department of Justice agent that can be spared on the trail. He can't live underground all the time, and you ought to get on his tracks somehow. I'm going up to the laboratory and see what I can do with this stuff. Report to me there to-morrow morning."

Carnes hurried away. Bolton, the chief of the United States Secret Service, had long ago recovered from any professional jealousy he had ever felt of Dr. Bird. The doctor's message that Ivan Saranoff, the arch-enemy of society, the head of the Young Labor party, the unofficial chief of the secret Soviet forces in the United States, was alive and again in the field against law and order was enough to set in motion every force that he controlled. Waving aside precedent and crashing his way past secretaries, he set in motion not only the agents of the Department of Justice but also the post-office forces and the specialized but highly efficient Military and Naval Intelligence Divisions. The telephone and telegraph wires from Washington were kept busy all night carrying orders and bringing in reports. But despite all this activity, it was with a disappointed face that Operative Carnes sought the doctor in the morning.

*   *   *   *   *

Dr. Bird was in his private laboratory on the third floor of the Bureau of Standards. When Carnes entered he was seated in a chair at his desk. His black eyes shone out from a chalky face like two burned holes in a blanket. Carnes started at the appearance of utter weariness presented by the famous scientist. Dr. Bird straightened up and squared his shoulders as the detective entered.

"Any luck, Carnes?" he asked eagerly.

"None at all, Doctor. We haven't been able to get a single trace of his corporeal existence since that submarine was destroyed off the Massachusetts coast. All we have is Karuska's word that he is still alive."

"We heard his voice yesterday."

"His or another's."

"True. Have you set in motion every agency that the government has?"

"Every one. Either Bolton or I have talked to the Chief of Police in every large city in the United States and Canada. Every known member of the Young Labor party who is above the mere rank and file is under close surveillance."

"Good enough. Keep at it and you'll trace him eventually. As soon as I get a few quarts of black coffee into my system, I'll start another line of search going."

"What did you find out last night?"

"I found that our seismograph recorded the Charleston disaster. It was merely a faint jog, about what should be caused by a severe landslide. The disaster did not affect the earth's crust, but was purely local. That gives me a clue to his method."

"I described the affair to Bolton and he suggested that it might be caused by a disintegrating ray."

* * * * *

Dr. Bird snorted. "When will people learn that there is not, and in the nature of things never can be, a disintegrating ray?" he exclaimed. "Of course a ray can be made which will tear things down to their constituent elements, but matter is indestructible, and the idea of wiping matter out of existence is absurd."

"But I have heard you say that matter and energy were interchangeable."

"That is a different proposition. I believe they are. In fact, if you remember, Carmichael proved it, although the proof was lost at his death. Nothing of the sort was done at Charleston, however. Do you know how much energy is contained in matter? Well, a cubic inch of copper would drive the largest ship afloat around the world twice, and across the Atlantic to boot. The energy contained in the cubic yards of rock that were removed under Charleston would have blown the world to fragments."

"Then what did happen?"

"Matter, as you know, is composed of atoms. These atoms are as far from one another, compared to their size, as the stars and planets of the universe. Each atom in turn is composed of electrons, negative particles of electrical energy, held in position about a fixed central nucleus of positive electricity known as a proton. I speak now of the simplest element. Most of them have many protons and electrons in their make-up. The space between these particles compared with their size is such that the universe would be crowded in comparison."

"What does that lead to?"

"I have described the composition of lead, the densest known element, over thirteen times as heavy as water, bulk for bulk. Conceive what it would mean if some force could compress together these widely separated particles until they touched. The resulting substance would be an element of almost inconceivable density. Such a condition is approached in the stars, some of which are as high as four thousand times as dense as the earth. What Saranoff has done is to find some way of compressing together the atoms into that yellow powder which we found in the cavern. He has not gone to the limit, for the stuff is only a little over four thousand times as dense as water. A cubic inch of it weighs one hundred and thirty-two pounds. With its density increased to that extent, the volume is reduced accordingly. That was what accounted for those caverns into which the earth tumbled."

"I'll believe you, Doctor," replied the detective; "but I'd believe you just as quickly if you swore that the moon was made of cream cheese made from the milk taken from the milky way. One would be just as understandable to me as the other."

$$* \quad * \quad * \quad * \quad *$$

They were interrupted by the entrance of a waiter who bore a huge pot of steaming coffee. Dr. Bird's eyes lighted up as a cup was poured. Carnes knew enough not to interrupt while the doctor poured and drank eight cups of the strong black fluid. As he drank, the lines of fatigue disappeared from the scientist's face. He sat up as fresh as though he had not been working at high pressure the entire night.

"Dr. Fisher tells me that the amount of caffeine I drink would kill a horse," he said with a chuckle; "but sometimes it is needed. I feel better now. Let's get to work."

"What shall we do?"

"Despite Saranoff's words, it must be possible to trace him. He is undoubtedly releasing his energy from some form of subterranean borer, and such a thing can be located. The energy he uses must set up electrical disturbances which instruments will detect. I have had work started on a number of ultra-sensitive wave detectors which will record any wave-length from zero to five millimeters. We'll send them to various points along the seacoast. They ought to pick up the stray waves from the energy he is using to blast a path through the earth. I'm not going to bother with the waves from his motor; they may be of any wave-length, and there would be constant false alarms. I have another idea."

"What is it?"

"I am judging Saranoff from his previous actions. You remember that he used a submarine in that alien-smuggling scheme the Coast Guard broke up, and also when he loosed that sea monster on the Atlantic shipping? He seems to be rather fond of submarines."

"Well?"

*　　*　　*　　*　　*

"The amount of energy he uses must be almost inconceivable," Dr. Bird went on. "He can hardly carry an amount of fuel which will enable him to bore underground for very many miles, Charleston is on the coast. I have an idea that he uses a submarine to transport his borer from point to point. After using the borer he must return to the submarine for recharging and transportation to the point where he plans to strike next. I already have two hundred planes scouring the sea looking for such a craft."

"Where do you expect him to strike next?"

"I have no idea. New York and Washington will undoubtedly be targets eventually, but neither of them may be next. Meanwhile, would you like to do a little more flying?"

"Surely."

"A plane is waiting for us at Langley Field. I want to look over the coast in the vicinity of Charleston Harbor and some of the sounds near there. If he is using a sub, he must have a base somewhere."

*   *   *   *   *

With a competent pilot at the stick, Carnes and the Doctor spent the day in exploring. The day yielded no results, and with the coming of dusk they landed at Savannah for the night. Carnes talked with Bolton over the telephone, but the secret service chief could report no favorable progress. Tired and disgusted, they retired early, but they were not destined to enjoy a night of uninterrupted sleep. At one o'clock a telegram was brought to their room. Dr. Bird tore it open and glanced sleepily at it.

"Get up, Carnes," he cried sharply. "Read this!"

The yawning detective glanced at the telegram. It contained only two words and a signature. It was signed "Ivan," and read simply, "Watch Wilmington."

"What the dickens?" he exclaimed as he studied the yellow slip. Dr. Bird was hurriedly pulling on his clothes.

"Saranoff has slipped a cog this time," said the doctor. "He sent that as a night message, but it was delivered as a straight message through error. He has got further north than I expected. We will turn out our pilot and take off. We should make Wilmington by daybreak. I'll telephone Washington and have a couple of destroyers started up Delaware Bay at once. We ought to give him a first class surprise party. I suppose that Philadelphia was meant to be his next stop."

In an hour the army plane took off into the night. At seven o'clock they were circling over Wilmington. The city had not been disturbed. For an hour they flew back and forth before they landed. Startling news awaited them. At six that morning an earthquake had struck Wilmington, North Carolina. Half the town had sunk into the earth. Dr. Bird struck his brow with his clenched fist.

"Score one for the enemy," he said grimly. "We were too sure of ourselves, Carnes. We should have realized that he would hardly be so far north yet. Well, I've got to use the telephone while we're refueling."

*   *   *   *   *

Within an hour after landing they were again in the air One o'clock found them over the stricken city. Dr. Bird wasted no time on Wilmington but headed north along the coast. For a hundred miles he skirted the shore, two miles out. With an exclamation of disappointment he ordered the pilot to turn the plane and retrace his route southward, keeping ten miles from the shore. Fifty miles south he ordered the plane further out and again turned north. From time to time they passed a ship of the air patrol which was steadily skirting the coast, but none of them had seen a submarine. Off Cape Hatteras the pilot asked for orders.

"The gas is running low. Doctor," he said. "I think we had better put in somewhere and refuel. If we are going to keep the air much longer, you had better get a relief pilot. I have been flying for thirty hours out of the last thirty-six and I'm about done."

"Head back for Washington," said the doctor with a sigh. "I seem to have gone off on a false scent."

At Cape Charles the pilot swung east over Chesapeake Bay. Hardly had he turned than Dr. Bird gave a cry. Excitedly he pointed toward the water. Carnes grasped a pair of binoculars and looked in the direction

Dr. Bird was indicating. Sliding along under the water was a long cigar-shaped shadow.

"It's a submarine!" exclaimed Carnes. "Is it a navy ship or the one we're after?"

"It's no navy sub," said the doctor positively. "It's not the right shape. Look at that bump on the side!"

The symmetry of the craft was marred by a huge projection on one side that could not be explained by the pattern of any known type of under-water craft.

"He's towing the borer!" cried the doctor in exultation. He took up the speaking tube. "Turn back to sea!" he cried. "We passed four destroyers less than ten miles out. We want to get in touch with them."

The plane roared out to sea while Dr. Bird feverishly sounded the "Alnav" call on the radio sending set. In a few minutes an answer came. From their point of vantage they could see flags break out at the peak of the destroyer leader. The four ships turned into column formation and stormed at full speed into the bay. The plane raced ahead to guide them.

"We've got him this time, Doctor!" cried Carnes in exultation. He pointed to the bay below where the submarine was still making its way slowly forward. Dr. Bird shook his head.

"I hope so," he said, "but I have my doubts. Saranoff is no fool. He wouldn't walk into a trap like this unless he had some means of escape. Here comes the first destroyer. We'll soon know the truth."

*   *   *   *   *

With the radio set he directed the oncoming boat. The destroyer reduced to half speed and changed direction slightly. From side to side she maneuvered until she was less than half a mile behind the submarine and headed straight for it. Dr. Bird tapped a few words on his key. With a belch of smoke, the destroyer lurched forward. She cut the waters with her sharp bow, throwing up a wave higher than her decks. Dr. Bird watched anxiously.

The destroyer was almost over the submarine and Dr. Bird's fingers trembled on the key. One word from him would send a half dozen depth charges into the water. On came the destroyer until it was directly over the underseas craft. Dr. Bird pounded his key rapidly.

"Good Lord!" cried Carnes.

From the bump on the side of the submarine came a flash of red light. The destroyer staggered for a moment, and the entire central section of the ill-fated ship disappeared. The bow and stern came together with a rush and went down in a swirling maelstrom of water. The plane lurched in the air as a thundering crash rose from the sea.

The second destroyer, in no way daunted by the fate of her colleague, rushed to the attack. Dr. Bird pounded his key frantically in an attempt to turn her back. His message was too late or was misunderstood. Straight over the submarine went the second ship. Again came the red flash. The forward half of the destroyer disappeared and the stern slid down into a huge hole which had opened in the water.

"He's invulnerable!" cried the doctor. He pounded his key with feverish rapidity. The two remaining destroyers slackened speed and veered off. Slowly, as though loath to turn their backs on the enemy, they headed out for the broad Atlantic and comparative safety.

The submarine went slowly on her way. She did not turn west at the mouth of the Potomac but continued on up the bay. As long as there was light enough, the doctor's plane kept above her but the fading light soon made it impossible to see her. When she had disappeared from view, the doctor reluctantly gave the word to return to Washington.

*   *   *   *   *

"Where do you suppose he will attack next, Doctor?" asked Carnes when they sat again in the doctor's private laboratory.

"Washington, of course," said Dr. Bird absently as he looked up from a pile of telegrams he was running through.

"Why Washington?"

"Use your head. Representatives of every civilized power are in Washington now at the President's invitation to consider means of halting the anti-religious activities of the Soviets. The destruction of the city and the killing of these men would be a telling blow for Russia to strike."

"But, Doctor, you don't think—"

"Excuse me, Carnes; that will keep. Let me read these telegrams."

For half an hour silence reigned in the laboratory. Dr. Bird laid down the last message with a sigh.

"Carnes," he said, "I'm check-mated. I sent out a hundred ultra-sensitive short wave receivers yesterday. Four of them were located within fifty miles of Wilmington, North Carolina. One of these four was destroyed, but none of the others detected a sign of a wave during the attack. One of them was within a hundred feet of the edge of the hole. If he isn't using a ray of some sort, what on earth is he using?"

"It looked like a flash of red light when it came from the submarine."

"Yes, but it couldn't be light. Let me think."

The doctor sat for a few minutes with corrugated brows. Suddenly he sprang to his feet.

"I deserve to be beaten," he cried. "Why didn't I think of that possibility before?"

*   *   *   *   *

He hurried into his laboratory and brought out a small box with a glass front. From the top projected a spike topped with a ball. Through the glass, Carnes could see a thin sheet of metal hanging pendant from the spike.

"An electroscope," explained the doctor. "That sheet of metal is really two sheets of gold-leaf, at present stuck together. If I rub a piece of hard rubber with a woolen cloth, the rod will become charged with static electricity. If I then touch the ball with it, the charge is transferred to the electroscope and causes the two sheets of gold-leaf to stand apart at an angle. Watch me."

He took a hard rubber rod and rubbed it briskly on his coat sleeve. As he touched the ball of the electroscope the sheets of gold-leaf separated and stood apart at a right angle.

"As long as the air remains non-conducting, the two bits of gold-leaf will hold that position. The air, however, is not a perfect insulator and the charge will gradually leak off. If I bring a bit of radioactive substance, for instance, pitchblende, near the electroscope, the charge will leak rapidly. Do you understand?"

"Yes, but how is that going to help us?"

"Saranoff is accomplishing his result by artificially compressing the atoms. It is inevitable that he will do it imperfectly, and some electrons will be loosened and escape. These electrons, traveling up through the earth will make the air conducting. To-morrow we will have a means of locating the borer under ground."

"Once you locate it, how will you fight it?"

"That is the problem I must work out to-night."

"Could we bury a charge of explosive and blow it up?"

* * * * *

"Ordinary explosives would be useless," the doctor answered. "They would react in the same manner as other substances, and would be rendered harmless. Radite might do the work if it could be placed in the path, but it couldn't be. We may locate the position and depth of the borer, but long before we could dig and blast a hole deep enough to place a charge of radite before it, it would have passed on or changed direction. No, Carnes, old dear, the only solution that I can see is to turn his own guns on him. If I can, before morning, duplicate his device, we can train it on the spot where he is and reduce him and his machine to a pinch of yellow powder."

"Can you do it, Doctor?"

"What one man's brain can device, another man's brain can duplicate. The only question is that of time. I am confident that Saranoff will attack Washington to-morrow. If I can do the job to-night, we may save the city. If not—At any rate, Carnes, your job will be to see that the President and all of the heads of the government are out of the city by morning. The President may refuse to leave. Knowing him as I do, I rather expect he will."

"In that case, the issue is in the hands of the gods. Now get out of here. I want to work. Report back at daybreak with a car."

Dr. Bird turned back to his laboratory.

"He must be using a ray of some sort, possibly a radium emanation," he muttered to himself. "That would have no wave motion and might accomplish the result, although I would expect the exact opposite from it. The first thing to do is to examine that powder with a spectroscope and see if I can get a clue to the electronic arrangement."

*　　*　　*　　*　　*

When Carnes arrived at the Bureau of Standards at dawn be rubbed his eyes in astonishment. The buildings were lighted up and the grounds swarmed with workmen. Before the buildings were lined up a dozen trucks and twice that many touring cars. A cordon of police held back the curious. Carnes' gold badge won him an entrance and he hurried up the stairs to Dr. Bird's laboratory. The doctor's face was drawn and haggard, but his eyes glowed with a feverish light. Workmen were carrying down huge boxes.

"What's up, Doctor?" demanded the detective.

"Oh, you got here at last, did you? You're just in time. If you'd been fifteen minutes later, you would have found us gone."

"Gone where?"

"Out into Maryland in an attempt to stop Saranoff in his progress toward Washington."

"Have you found your means of combating him?"

"I hope so, although it is not what I started out to get. Did you bring a car as I told you?"

"It's waiting below."

"Good enough. I'll go in it. Williams, are those projectors all loaded?"

"Yes, Dr. Bird. The magnet will be ready to go in five minutes. The electroscopes and the other light stuff are all loaded and ready to move."

"You have done well. I'll let you bring the trucks and heavy equipment while I go ahead with the instruments. Take the road out toward Upper Marlboro. If I don't meet you before, stop there for orders."

"Very well, Doctor."

"Come on, Carnes, let's go."

* * * * *

He raced down the stairs with the detective at his heels. He went along the line of touring cars and spoke briefly to the drivers. He climbed into the car which Carnes had brought. As it started the other cars fell in behind it. At a speed of forty miles an hour, with a detachment of motorcycle police leading the van, the cavalcade rolled out through the deserted streets of Washington. Once clear of the city, the speed was increased.

"Did you persuade the President to leave?" asked the doctor.

"There wasn't a chance. The papers panned him so much for following my advice at Charleston that he has turned stubborn. He says that if all the forces of the government can't protect him against one man, he is willing to die."

"We've got to save him," said Dr. Bird grimly. "Hello, there's the Chesapeake ahead."

The doctor studied the country.

"We are about opposite the place where we left that sub last night. I fancy that Saranoff will operate from there, for it didn't move during the last half hour we watched it. We'll go back inland a mile or two and spread out. I have no idea how far his radiations will affect the electroscopes, but we'll try four hundred-yard intervals to start. That will enable us to cover a line twelve miles long."

He picked up a megaphone and spoke to the line of cars behind him.

"Take up four hundred yard intervals when we spread out," he said. "Every man keep his headphone on and listen for orders. Follow my car until it stops, then turn north and south and drop your men at intervals."

He reentered the car and led the way back for two miles. He halted his car at a crossroad. The cars following him turned and went to the north and south. Besides Carnes and the doctor, the car held two men from the Bureau. As they climbed out, Carnes saw that one of them carried a portable radio sending set, while the other bore an electroscope and a rubber rod. The radio operator set up his device, while the other man rubbed his coat sleeve briskly with the hard rubber and then touched the ball of the electroscope with it. The two bits of gold-leaf spread out.

"While we're waiting, I'll explain something of this to you, Carnes," said the doctor. "At four hundred-yard intervals are men with electroscopes like this one. My attempt to locate Saranoff by means of wave detectors was a failure. That proved that the ray he was using is not of the wave type. The other common ray is the cathode ray type which does not consist of vibrations but of a stream of electrons, negative particles of electricity, traveling in straight lines of high velocity. He must be knocking loose some of the electrons when he collapses the atoms. The rate of discharge of these electroscopes will give us a clue to the nearness of his device."

* * * * *

"Once you locate him, how do you propose to attack him?"

"The obvious method, that of using his own ray against him, fell down. However, in attempting to produce it, I stumbled on another weapon which may be equally effective. I am going to try to use an exact opposite of his ray. The cathode ray, when properly used, will bombard the atoms and knock electrons loose. I perfected last night a device on which I have been working for months. It is a super-cathode ray. I tested it on the yellow powder and find that I can successfully reverse Saranoff's process. He can contract matter together until it occupies less than one one-thousandth of its original volume. My ray will destroy this effect and restore matter to something like its original condition."

"And the effect will be?"

"Use your imagination. He blasts out a hole by condensing the rock to a pinch of yellow powder. He moves forward into the hole he has made. I come along and reverse his process. The yellow powder expands to its original volume and the hole he has made ceases to exist. What must happen to the foreign body which had been introduced into the hole that is no longer a hole?"

Carnes whistled.

"At any rate, I hope that I am never in a hole when that happens."

"And I devoutly hope that Saranoff is. I met with one difficulty. My ray will not penetrate the depth of solid rock which separates his borer from the surface."

"Then how will you reach him to crush him? You don't expect to drill down ahead of him?"

"That is my stroke of genius, Carnes. I am going to make him bore the hole down which my ray will travel to accomplish his destruction. The cathode ray and rays of that type–"

*   *   *   *   *

"Pardon me, Doctor," interrupted the radio operator. "I have just received a message from the squadron leader of the planes patrolling the bay. He states that every inch of the Chesapeake Bay and the Potomac River have been examined and no submarine is visible."

"I expected that. He will have opened a cavern under the earth, in which his craft is safe from aerial observation. Once the borer has left it, it is invulnerable no longer."

"What reply shall I make?"

"Tell him to keep up a constant patrol. Three navy subs with radite-charged torpedos are on their way up the bay, together with half a dozen destroyers. The subs will scout for such a hole as I have described and will attack his sub if they find it. The destroyers will stand by and support them."

The operator turned to his instrument. The electroscope observer claimed the doctor's attention.

"There is a steady leak here, Doctor," he said. "I get a discharge in eleven minutes."

"Probably a result of his work in opening the hiding place for his submarine last night. Keep it charged, Jones."

"What did you say about the cathode ray, Doctor?" asked Carnes.

"The cathode ray? Oh, yes. I said that rays of that type were attracted by—Hello, look there!"

From a point a mile to the north a ball of red fire streaked up into the air. A moment later similar signals rose from other watchers in the line.

"It works, Carnes!" cried the doctor as he rushed for the car. "We've got him this time!"

* * * * *

The car raced along the road. At the first man who had signalled, it slackened speed. The doctor leaned out.

"What is your discharge rate?" he called.

"Eight minutes. Doctor."

The car rolled on. Dr. Bird repeated the question at the next post and was told that the electroscope there was losing its charge in seven minutes. The next man reported four minutes and the next man, one minute. The following station reported three minutes.

"It's right along here somewhere!" cried the doctor. "Summon everyone to this point and take up twenty-yard intervals."

From the north and south the cars came racing in. The instruments were spread out along a new line twenty yards apart. As the borer was located the intervals were decreased to fifteen feet. Dr. Bird thrust a long white rod into the ground.

"His path lies under here," he said. "Into the cars and go back a mile and test again."

The borer was making slow progress, and it was half an hour before Dr. Bird drove the second stake in the ground. With a transit he took the bearing of the path and laid it out on a large scale map.

"We'll stop him between Marr and Ritchie," he announced. "Jones, I am going back and set up my apparatus. Keep track of his movements. If he changes direction, let me know at once."

*   *   *   *   *

The doctor's car tore off to the west. Near Upper Marlboro, he met the convoy of trucks and led them to the selected spot. The trucks were unloaded and the apparatus laid out. Attached to a huge transformer were a dozen strange-looking projectors. What puzzled Carnes most was a huge built-up steel bar wound about with heavy cable. Dr. Bird had this bar erected on a truck and located it with great exactness. The projectors were set up in a battery just east of the bar.

"How about power?" asked the doctor.

"We'll have it in five minutes," replied one of the men. "A power transmission line carrying twenty-two thousand passes within two hundred yards of here. We are phoning now to have the power cut off. As soon as the line is dead we'll cut it and bring the ends here."

The electrician was good at his word. In five minutes the power line had been cut and cables spliced to the ends. The cables were brought to the doctor's apparatus and the main lines were rigged to the ends of the cable wound around the bar. In parallel on taps, the projectors were connected. Huge oil-switches were placed in both lines.

"All ready, Doctor," reported the electrician.

"Good work, Avent. He'll be here soon, I fancy."

A car whirled up and a man leaped out with a surveyor's rod. He set it up on the ground while a companion watched through binoculars. He moved it a hundred yards to the north and then back twenty. When he was satisfied he turned to Dr. Bird.

"The direction of movement has not changed," he said. "The path will pass under this stake."

Under the doctor's supervision, the truck carrying the bar moved forward until it stood over the surveyor's stake. The battery of projectors moved to a new location a few feet east of the rod. Other cars came racing up.

"He's less than half a mile away, Doctor!" cried Jones.

"Get your electroscopes out and spot him a hundred yards from this truck."

"Very well, Doctor."

*   *   *   *   *

The men with the instruments spread out along the path of the borer. Briskly they rubbed their sleeves with the rubber rods and charged their instruments. Almost as fast as they charged them, the tiny bits of gold-leaf collapsed together. Presently the man on the end of the line shouted.

"Maximum discharge!" he cried.

Dr. Bird looked around. Every man stood ready at his post. The next man signalled that the borer was under him. Carnes felt himself trembling. He did not know what the doctor was about to do, but he felt that the fate of America hung in the balance. Whether it remained free or became the slave of Soviet Russia would quickly be decided.

Slowly the borer made its way forward. With a pale face, Jones signalled the news that it had reached the point the doctor had indicated. Dr. Bird raised his hand.

"Power!" he cried.

The electrician closed a switch and power surged through the cables around the bar. The earth rocked and quivered. A hundred yards east of the bar a flash of intolerable red light sprang from the ground with a roar like that of Niagara. Toward the bar it moved with gathering momentum.

"Back, everyone!" roared Dr. Bird.

*   *   *   *   *

The men sprang back. The searing ray approached the bar. It touched it, and bar and truck disappeared into thin air. A splutter of sparks came from the severed ends of the wire. The ray disappeared. Carnes rubbed his eyes.

Where the truck had rested on solid ground was now a gaping wound in the earth.

"Projector forward!" cried the doctor. "Hurry, men!"

The trucks bearing the battery of projectors moved forward until they were at the edge of the hole. Portable cranes swung the lamps out, and men swarmed over them. The projectors were pointed down the hole. Carnes joined the doctor in peering down. A hundred yards below them the terrible ray was blazing. As they watched, its end came in sight. The ray was being projected forward from the end of a black cigar-shaped machine which was slowly moving forward.

"That's your target, men!" cried the doctor. "Align on it and signal when you are ready!"

One by one the projector operators raised their hands in the signal of "ready." Still the doctor waited. Suddenly the forward movement of the black body ceased. The ray was stationary for a moment and then moved slowly upward. A terrific roaring came from the cavern.

"Projector switch!" roared the doctor, his heavy voice sounding over the tumult.

"Ready, sir!" a shrill voice answered.

"Power!"

*   *   *   *   *

From each of the projectors a dazzling green ray leaped forth as the switch was closed. There was a crash like all the thunder of the universe. Before the astonished eyes of the detective, the hole closed. Not only did it close but the earth piled up until the trucks were overturned and the green rays blazed in all directions.

"Power off!" roared the doctor.

The switch was opened and the ray died out. Before them was a huge mound where a moment before had been a hole.

"You see, Carnes," said Dr. Bird with a wan smile. "I made him bore his own hole, as I promised."

"I saw it, but I don't understand. How did you do it?"

"Magnetism. Rays of the cathode type are deflected from their course by a magnet. His ray proved unusually susceptible, and I drew it toward a huge electro-magnet which I improvised. When the magnet was destroyed, the ray dropped back ... to its original ... direction. That's the end ... of Saranoff. That is ... I hope ... it is."

Dr. Bird's voice had grown slower and less distinct as he talked. As he said the last words, he slumped gently to the ground. Carnes sprang forward with a cry of alarm and bent over him.

"What's the matter, Doctor?" he demanded anxiously, shaking the scientist. Dr. Bird rallied for a moment.

"Sleep, old dear," he murmured. "Four days—no sleep. Go 'way, I'm ... going ... to ... sleep...."

THE PORT OF MISSING PLANES

ORIGINALLY PUBLISHED IN *ASTOUNDING STORIES OF SUPER-SCIENCE*, AUGUST 1931

*In the underground caverns of the Selom,
Dr. Bird once again locks wills with the
subversive genius, Saranoff.*

THE PORT OF MISSING PLANES

So that's the "Port of Missing Planes," mused Dick
Purdy as he looked down over the side of his cockpit. "It
looks wild and desolate all right, but at that I can't fancy
a bus cracking up here and not being found pronto. Gosh,
Wilder cracked in the wildest part of Arizona and he was
found in a week."

The mail plane droned monotonously on through
perfect flying weather. Purdy continued to study the
ground. Recently transferred from a western run, he was
getting his first glimpse of that section of ill repute.
Below him stretched a desolate, almost uninhabited
stretch of country. By looking back he could see
Bellefonte a few miles behind him, but Philipsburg, the
next spot marked on his map, was not yet visible. Twelve
hundred feet below him ran a silver line of water which
his map told him was Little Moshannon Run. As he
watched he suddenly realized that the ground was not
slipping by under him as rapidly as it should. He glanced
at his air-speed meter.

"What the dickens?" he cried in surprise. For an hour
his speed had remained almost constant at one hundred
miles an hour. Without apparent cause it had dropped to
forty, less than flying speed. He realized that he was
falling. A glance at his altimeter confirmed the
impression. The needle had dropped four hundred feet
and was slowly moving toward sea-level.

*　　*　　*　　*　　*

With an exclamation of alarm, Purdy advanced his throttle until the three motors of his plane roared at full capacity. For a moment his air-speed picked up, but the gain was only momentary. As he watched, the meter dropped to zero, although the propellers still whirled at top speed. His altimeter showed that he was gradually losing elevation.

He stood up and looked over the side of his plane. The ground below him was stationary as far as forward progress was concerned, but it was slowly rising to meet him. He fumbled at the release ring of his parachute but another glance at the ground made him hesitate. It was not more than three hundred feet below him.

"I must be dreaming!" he cried. The ground was no longer stationary. For some unexplained reason he was going backward. The motors were still roaring at top speed. Purdy dropped back into his seat in the cockpit. With his ailerons set for maximum lift he coaxed every possible revolution from his laboring motors. For several minutes he strained at the controls before he cast a quick glance over the side. His backward speed had accelerated and the ground was less than fifty feet below him. It was too close for a parachute jump.

"As slow as I'm falling, I won't crack much, anyway," he consoled himself. He reached for his switch and the roar of the motors died away in silence. The plane gave a sickening lurch backwards and down for an instant. Purdy again leaned over the side. He was no longer going either forward or back but was sinking slowly down. He looked at the ground directly under him. A cry of horror came from his lips. He sat back mopping his brow. Another glance over the side brought an expression of terror to his white face and he reached for the heavy automatic pistol which hung by the side of the control seat.

*   *   *   *   *

"He cleared Bellefonte at nine in the morning, Dr. Bird" said Inspector Dolan of the Post Office Department, "and headed toward Philipsburg. He never arrived. By ten we were alarmed and by eleven we had planes out searching for him. They reported nothing. He must have come to grief within a rather restricted area, so we sent search parties out at once. That was two weeks ago yesterday. No trace of either him or his plane has been found."

"The flying conditions were good?"

"Perfect. Also, Purdy is above suspicion. He has been flying the mail on the western runs for three years. This is his first accident. He was carrying nothing of unusual value."

"Are there any local conditions unfavorable to flying?"

"None at all. It is much uninhabited country, but there is no reason why it shouldn't be safe country to fly over."

"There are some damnably unfavorable local conditions, Doctor, although I can't tell you what they are," broke in Operative Carnes of the United States Secret Service. "Dick Purdy was rather more than an acquaintance of mine. After he was lost I looked into the record of that section a little. It is known among aviators as 'The Port of Missing Planes.'"

"How did it get a name like that?"

"From the number of unexplained and unexplainable accidents that happen right there. Dugan of the air mail, was lost there last May. They found the mailbags where he had dropped them before he crashed, but they never found a trace of him or his plane."

"They didn't?"

"Not a trace. The same thing happened when Mayfield cracked in August. He made a jump and broke his neck in landing. He was found all right, but his ship wasn't. Trierson of the army, dropped there and *his* plane was never found. Neither was he. He was seen to go down in a forced landing. He was flying last in a formation. As soon as he went down the other ships turned back and circled over the ground where he should have fallen. They saw nothing. Search parties found no trace of either him or his ship. Those are the best known cases, but I have heard rumors of several private ships which have gone down in that district and have never been seen or heard of since."

*   *   *   *   *

Dr. Bird sat forward with a glitter in his piercing black eyes. Carnes gave a grunt of satisfaction. He knew the meaning of that glitter. The Doctor's interest had been fully aroused.

"Inspector Dolan," said Dr. Bird sharply, "why didn't you tell me those things?"

"Well, Doctor, we don't like to talk about mail wrecks any more than we have to. Of course, the loss of so many planes in one area is merely a coincidence. Probably the wrecked planes were stolen as souvenirs. Such things happen, you know."

"Fiddlesticks!" said Dr. Bird sharply. He raised one long slender hand with beautifully modeled tapering fingers and threw back his unruly mop of black hair. His square, almost rugged jaw, protruded and the glitter in his eyes grew in intensity. "No souvenir hunting vandals could cart away whole planes without leaving a trace. In that case, what became of the bodies? No, Inspector, this has gone beyond the range of coincidence. There is some mystery here and it needs looking into. Fortunately, my work at the Bureau of Standards is in such shape that I can safely leave it. I intend to devote my entire time to clearing this matter up. The ramifications may run deeper than either you or I suspect. Please have all of your records dealing with plane disappearances or wrecks in that locality sent to my office at once."

The Post Office inspector stiffened.

"Of course, Dr. Bird," he said formally, "we are very glad to hear any suggestion that you may care to offer. When it comes, however, to a matter of surrendering control of a Post Office matter to the Department of Commerce or to the Treasury Department, I doubt the propriety. Our records are confidential ones and are not open to everyone who is curious. I will inform the proper authorities of your desire to help, but I doubt seriously if they will avail themselves of your offer."

* * * * *

Dr. Bird's black eyes shot fire. "Idiot!" he said. "If you're a specimen of the Post Office Department, I'll have the entire case taken out of your hands. Do you mean to cooperate with me or not?"

"I fail to see what interest the Bureau of Standards can have in the affair."

"The Bureau isn't mixed up in it; Dr. Bird is. If necessary, I will go direct to the President. Oh, thunder! What's the use of talking to you? Who's your chief?"

"Chief Inspector Watkins is in charge of all investigations."

"Carnes, get him on the telephone. Tell him we are taking charge of the investigation. If he balks, have Bolton go over his head. Then get the chief of the Air Corps on the wire and arrange for an army plane to-morrow. There is something more than a mail robbery back of this or I'm badly fooled."

"Do you suspect–"

"I suspect nothing and no one, Carnes–yet! I'll get a few instruments together to take with us to-morrow. We'll fly over that section until something happens if it takes us until this time next year."

* * * * *

A three-seated scout plane rose from Langley Field at eight the next morning. Captain Garland was at the controls. In the rear cockpit sat Dr. Bird and Carnes. Inside his flying helmet, the doctor wore a pair of headphones which were connected to a box on the floor before him. Carnes carried no apparatus but his hand rested carelessly on the grip of a machine-gun.

The plane cleared Bellefonte at nine-thirty and bore east toward Philipsburg. Captain Garland kept his eyes on his instrument board and on a map. Less than six hundred feet above the ground, he was following the air-mail route as exactly as possible. Overhead a mail plane winged its way east, three thousand feet above them.

Fifteen minutes brought them to Philipsburg. Captain Garland shot his plane upward a few hundred feet.

"Turn back, Captain," said Dr. Bird into the speaking tube. "Retrace your course a quarter of a mile farther north. At Bellefonte, turn back and go over the same ground another quarter of a mile north. Keep flying back and forth, working your way north, until I tell you to stop."

The plane swung around and headed back toward Bellefonte.

"Of course, we can't tell exactly what route he followed," said the doctor to Carnes, "but he was new on this run and it is safe to assume that he didn't stray far. We'll quarter the whole area before we stop."

Carnes watched the ground below them carefully. There was nothing about it to distinguish it from any other wooded mountainous country and his interest waned. He glanced aloft. The mail plane had disappeared in the distance and the sky was clear of aircraft. He turned again to the ground. It looked closer than it had before. He turned and looked at the duplicate altimeter. The plane had lost nearly a hundred feet elevation.

*   *   *   *   *

"There's something wrong about this plane, Doctor," came Captain Garland's voice through the speaking tube. "It doesn't behave like it should."

"I guess we've found what we were looking for, Carnes," said Dr. Bird grimly. "What seems to be the matter, Captain?"

"Blessed if I know," was the answer. "It feels like a drag of some sort, like an automobile going through heavy sand. We're slowing down, though I am giving her all the gun I've got!"

"Cut your motor!" said the doctor shortly. He bent over the duplicate instrument board as the roar of the motor died away. Carnes rose and looked over the side.

"Look, Doctor!" he cried in a strained voice. Directly below them yawned a hole sixty feet in diameter and extending down into the bowels of the earth. The plane hovered over the hole for a moment and then slowly descended into it.

"What is it?" cried the detective.

"It's the secret of the Port of Missing Planes," replied Dr. Bird. "Throw off your parachute. Keep your gun and light handy but don't fire unless I do first. The same holds good for you, Captain."

The plane sunk until it was fifty feet below the level of the ground. Carnes looked up. Gradually the circle of sky became blurred and hazy as though the air were heavy with dust. The rasp of Dr. Bird's flashlight key aroused him and he hastily wound his own. The haze above them grew thicker. Suddenly the light died and then came darkness, a darkness so thick and absolute that it bore down on them like a weight. Dr. Bird's light stabbed a path through it.

*   *   *   *   *

They were in a tunnel or tube reaching into the ground. The sides were smooth and polished, as though water worn. The plane sank deeper and deeper into the earth. Suddenly Dr. Bird's light went out.

"What's the matter, Doctor?" asked Carnes, "did your light fail?"

"No," came a strained voice. "I turned it out."

"Why?"

"I don't know. Light yours."

Carnes reached into his pocket. Dr. Bird could hear his breath come in panting sobs as though he were exerting his whole strength.

"I can't do it, Doctor," he gasped. "I want to, but some power greater than my will prevents me."

"Are you affected, Captain?" asked the Doctor.

"I—can't—move," came in muffled accents from the front cockpit.

"Some power beyond my knowledge has us in its grasp," said the doctor. "All we can do is sit tight and see what happens. We are no longer falling at any rate."

From the forward cockpit came a rustling sound. There was a slight jar in the ship, and it gave as though a weight had been applied to one side.

"What are you doing, Garland?" asked the doctor sharply.

There was no reply. Again came the rustling sound. The ship gave a sudden lurch as though a weight had left the side. Carnes suddenly spoke.

"Good-by, Doctor," he said. "I'm going over the side."

"I have been fighting it but I'm going myself in a minute," replied the doctor grimly. "Something is pulling me over. It's the same power that keeps me from turning on my light."

"It's perfectly safe to go over," said Carnes suddenly. "The plane is resting on a solid base."

"I have the same feeling. Catch hold of my belt and let's go."

*   *   *   *   *

They climbed over the side of the plane and dropped to the ground. Their descent made absolutely no sound. Dr. Bird stopped and felt the floor.

"Crepe rubber, or something of the sort," he murmured. "At any rate, it's noise and vibration proof."

"Now what?" asked Carnes.

"This way," replied the doctor confidently. "I'm beginning to get the hang of understanding this. The way is perfectly level and open before us. Keep your hand on my shoulder and step right out."

"How do you know where we're going?"

"I don't, but something tells me that the road is level and open. It is the same thing that brought us over the side. I can't explain it but it is some sort of a telepathic control exerted by an intelligence. Whether the sending mind is reinforced by instruments I don't know, but I rather fancy not."

"Where is Garland?"

"He went off in another direction. I could feel the power that guided him although it was not directed at us. Something tells me that he is safe for the present."

For half a mile they made their way through the darkness before they stopped. This time Carnes could plainly understand the command which came to both of them.

"There is a table before us," said Dr. Bird. "Lay your flashlight and pistol on it."

Carnes struggled against the order but the power guiding him was stronger than his will. He strove to turn on his light. When he could not, he tried to cock his pistol. With a sigh, he laid his gun and light on the table before him. Without words, the two men walked forward a few feet and sat confidently down on a bench that something told them was there.

*   *   *   *   *

For a moment they sat quietly. A cry, choked in the middle, came from the detective's throat. Cold clammy hands touched his face. He strove again to cry out, but his voice was paralyzed. The hands went methodically over his body, evidently searching for weapons. Mustering up his will, Carnes made a grab for one of them. His captor apparently had no objection to the detective's action for Carnes seized the hand without effort. But he almost dropped it. The hand was as large as a ham. He reached for the other hand but could not locate it. A movement on the part of his captor brought it to him and he made the startling discovery that the palms were directed outward. The hand had only four fingers, which were armed with long curved claws instead of nails. Carnes ran his hand up the palm to search for a thumb but found none. He found, however, that, while the hands were naked, the wrists were covered with short thick fur.

"Doctor!" he cried, "there's–"

Again came the overpowering will and his speech died away in silence. He sat dumb and motionless while his captor moved over to Dr. Bird. A second animal came forward and felt the detective over. He was not allowed to move this time, nor was he while a third and fourth animal went carefully over him. The four drew back some distance.

"Doctor," whispered Carnes as the influence grew fainter.

"Shh!" was the answer, and as the doctor's demand for silence was reinforced by another wave of the paralyzing power, Carnes had no choice. As he sat there silent, the power which held him again seemed to grow less. He found that he could move his arms slightly. He edged forward to get his gun and light. Before he reached them, a beam of light split the darkness. Dr. Bird stood, electric torch in hand, staring before him.

At a distance of a few feet stood a group of half a dozen animals about the height of a man as they stood erect on their short hind legs. They were covered with heavy brown fur. Their lower limbs were thin and light, but their shoulders and forelegs were heavy and powerful. Their forepaws, which had the palms facing outward, were armed with the long wicked claws he had felt. No visible ears protruded from the round skulls. Their heads appeared to rest between their shoulders, so short were their necks. Their muzzles were long and obtusely pointed. Through grinning jaws could be seen powerful white teeth.

"Talpidae!" cried Dr. Bird. "Carnes, they are a race of giant intellectual moles!"

*   *   *   *   *

Despite the fact that they had no visible eyes, the creatures were strongly affected by the light. They dropped on all fours and turned their backs to the scientist and the detective. Two of them scurried away down a long tunnel which opened from the room in which they stood. Dr. Bird turned his light up and swept the room. It was roughly circular, a hundred feet in diameter, with a roof ten feet high. Dozens of tunnels led off in every direction.

"Your light, Carnes, quick!" cried the doctor in a strained voice. Carnes reached toward the table for his light. Before he could reach it he was frozen into immobility. From the corner of his eye he could watch the doctor. Dr. Bird was struggling to bring the light back on the moles which stood before them. Great beads of sweat stood out on his forehead. Inch by inch he moved the light closer to his goal, but Carnes could see that his thumb was stealing up toward the switch button. His breath came in sobs. Suddenly the light went out.

For some time the two men sat motionless on the bench unable to speak or move. One of the moles stepped before them and gave a mental command. The two rose to their feet. For a mile or more they followed their guide, then, at a silent command, they turned to the right for a few steps and stopped. In another moment, the numbing influence had departed.

"Are you all right, Carnes?"

"Yes, right as can be. Doctor, what were those things? Where are we? What's it all about?"

"We'll find out in time, I guess," replied the doctor with a chuckle. "Carnes, isn't this the darnedest thing we've ever been through? Captured half a mile underground by a race of giant talpidae before whose mental orders we are as helpless as children. Did you understand any of their talk?"

"Talk? I didn't hear any."

"Well, mental conversation then. They made no sound."

"No. All I understood was the orders I obeyed."

*   *   *   *   *

"I got a great deal of it," the doctor said. "We are evidently in or near a sort of central community of these fellows. They spoke; thought is a better word; they thought of doing away with us but decided to wait until they consulted someone with more authority. You see, we are not airplane pilots. Captain Garland was taken at once to the place where they have other aviators imprisoned."

"What do they want of pilots underground?"

"I couldn't quite get that. There was another thought that I am not sure that I interpreted correctly. If I did, there is some man of the upper world down here in a position of considerable authority among them. He has some use for pilots, but what use, I don't know. We are to be held until he is consulted."

"Who could it be?"

"I can only think of one man. Carnes, and I hope I'm wrong. I don't have to name him."

"You mean–?"

"Ivan Saranoff. We haven't heard of him or had any activity from him for the last eight months. We know that he had a subterranean borer with which he has penetrated deep into the earth. Isn't it possible that he has, at some time in his explorations, come into contact with these fellows and made friends with them?"

"It's possible, Doctor, but I hoped we had killed him when we destroyed his borer."

"So did I, but he seems to bear a charmed life. Several times we have thought him dead, only to have him show up with some new form of devil's work. It is too much to hope that we have succeeded in doing away with him. Did you notice one thing? Those fellows were helpless while I held the light on them. The one which was holding us captive got so interested in the discussion about our fate that he momentarily forgot us. That was when I got my light. Until I turned the light away from them, we were free men."

*   *   *   *   *

"That's right," answered the secret service man.

"Remember that. The next time we get a light on a bunch of them, hold them in the beam until we can make terms."

"If we ever get hold of a light again."

"I have a light they didn't get, probably because I didn't think of it while they were around. It is one of those fountain pen battery affairs and they probably took it for a pen. I won't turn it on now, partly to save it and partly not to let them know we have it. Let's see what our prison is like."

They felt their way around the room. It proved to be eight paces by ten in size. Like the tunnels it was floored with crepe rubber or some similar substance which gave out no sound of footsteps, yet was firm underfoot. The room was furnished with two beds, a table and two chairs. There was no sign of a door.

"That's that," exclaimed the doctor when they had finished their exploration. "I'm hungry. I wonder when we eat. Hello, here comes one of the fellows now."

Carnes made no reply. As the doctor's speech ended, a wave of mental power enveloped the room. One of the moles entered, moved over to the table for an instant and then left the room. An earthly odor of vegetables pervaded the room.

"My question is answered," said the doctor. "We eat now."

He moved to the table. On it had been placed dishes containing three different types of roots. Two of them proved to be palatable, but the third was woody and bitter. The prisoners made a hearty meal from the two they relished. For an hour they sat waiting.

"Here they come again!" exclaimed the doctor. "We are going before the person I spoke of. Can't you get their thoughts?"

"No, I can't, Doctor. I can understand when I get a command, but aside from those times everything is a blank to me."

"My mental wave receiver, if that's what it is, must be attuned to a different frequency than yours, for I can hear them talking to one another. I guess I should say that I can feel them thinking to one another. At any rate, they want us to follow. Come along, the road will be open and level."

*   *   *   *   *

The doctor stepped out confidently with Carnes at his heels. For half a mile they went forward. Presently they halted.

"We are in a big chamber here, Carnes," whispered the doctor, "and there is someone before us. We'll have some light in a minute."

His prophecy was soon fulfilled. A vague glimmer of light began to fill the cavern in which they stood. As it grew stronger they could see a raised dais before them on which were seated three figures. Two of them were the giant moles. Each of the moles wore a helmet which covered his head completely, with no sign of lenses or other means of vision. It was the central figure, however, which held the attention of the prisoners.

Seated on a chair and regarding, them with an expression of sardonic amusement was a man. Above a high forehead rose a thin scrub of white hair. Keen brown eyes peered at them from under almost hairless brows. The nose was high bridged and aquiline and went well with his prominent cheekbones. His mouth was a mere gash below his nose, framed by thin bloodless lips. The lips were curled in a sneer, revealing yellow teeth. The whole expression of the face was one of revolting cruelty.

"So," said the figure slowly, "fate has been kind to me. My friends, Dr. Bird and Operative Carnes have chosen to pay me a long visit. I am greatly flattered."

The thin metallic voice with its noticeable accent struck a familiar chord.

"Saranoff!" gasped Carnes.

"Yes, Mr. Carnes, Saranoff. Professor Ivan Saranoff, of the faculty of St. Petersburg once. Now merely Saranoff, the scourge of the bourgeois."

*   *   *   *   *

"I hoped we had killed you," murmured Carnes.

"It was no fault of Dr. Bird's that he failed," replied the Russian with an excess of malevolence in his voice. "His method was a correct one. Merely the fortuitous fact that we had just pierced one of the tunnels of the Selom, and I was away from my borer exploring it, saved me. You did me a good turn, Doctor, without meaning to. You destroyed an instrument on which I had relied. In doing so, you unwittingly delivered into my hands a power greater than any I had dreamed of—the Selom."

"What can a mental cripple like you do with blind allies like them?" asked Dr. Bird with a contemptuous laugh. The Russian half rose from his seat in rage. For a moment his hand toyed with a switch before him. The sardonic sneer came back into his face and he dropped back into his seat.

"You nearly provoked me to destroy you, Doctor," he said, "but cold calculation saved you. Since you will never return to the upper world, save when and as I decree, I have no objection to telling you. The Selom are not blind. Their eyes are under the skin as is the case with many of the talpidae, but for all that they can see very well. Their eyes function on a shorter wave than ours, a wave so short that it readily penetrates through miles of earth and rock. This cavern is now flooded with it. Visible light, the light by which we see, is limited to their eyes, hence the helmets which you see. They can see through those helmets as well as you or I can see through air."

"What do you intend to do with us?"

"Ah, Doctor, there you hit me in a tender spot. I have a sore temptation to close this switch on which my hand rests. Were I to do so, both you and Mr. Carnes would vanish forevermore. I have, however, conceived a very real affection for you two. Your brains, Doctor, working in my behalf instead of against me would render me well-nigh omnipotent. Mr. Carnes has a certain low cunning which I can also use to advantage. Both of you will join me."

*　　*　　*　　*　　*

"You might as well close your switch and save your breath, Saranoff, for we will do nothing of the sort," replied the doctor sharply.

"Ah, but you will. So will Mr. Carnes. I had no hopes that you would join me willingly. In fact, I am pleased that you do not. I could never trust you. All the same, you will join my forces as have the others whom I have brought into the hands of the Selom. I have ways of accomplishing my desires. It pleases my fancy, Doctor, to use your brains in aiding me in my scientific developments. You will enjoy working with the scientists of the Selom. Among them you will find brains which excel any to be found on the surface of the earth, since we two are below. Already I have learned much from them. You, Mr. Carnes shall be taught to pilot an airplane. When my cohorts go forth from the realms of the Selom to establish the rule of Russia, you will be piloting one of the planes. Your first task will be to learn to fly."

"I refuse to do anything of the sort!" said Carnes.

"I will not be ready to have your flying lessons started until to-morrow," replied the Russian, "and you will have until then to reconsider your rash decision. It will be much easier for you if you obey my orders. If you still refuse to-morrow, you will pay a visit to the laboratory of the Selom. When you return your lessons will be started. You will now be taken to your cell. I have use for Dr. Bird this afternoon."

"I won't leave Dr. Bird and that's flat!" exclaimed Carnes. Dr. Bird interrupted him.

"Go ahead, Carnesy, old dear," he said lightly. "You might just as well toddle along under your own power as to be dragged along. You have a day for reflection, in any event. I daresay I'll see you again before they do anything to you."

Carnes glanced keenly at the doctor's face. What he saw evidently reassured him for he turned without a word and walked away. The light grew gradually dimmer until darkness again reigned in the cavern.

"Come, Doctor," said Saranoff's voice. "We have work to do."

*   *   *   *   *

Carnes sat alone in his cell for hours. The darkness and loneliness wore on him until he felt that his nerves would crack. Not a sound came to him. He threw himself on one of the beds and plugged his ears with his finger tips in an attempt to keep the silence out. Then a cheerful voice sounded in the cell and a friendly hand fell on his shoulder.

"Well, Carnesy, old dear," said Dr. Bird, "have you been lonesome?"

"Dr. Bird!" gasped Carnes in tones of relief. "Are you all right?"

"Right as can be. I learned a lot this afternoon. For one thing, you're going to start flying lessons to-morrow and you're going to do your best to become an expert pilot in a short time. It is the only thing to do."

"And fly a plane for Saranoff?"

"I hope not. The only way to avoid that very thing is to keep your mentality unimpaired so that I can call on you for help when I need it. If the Selom operate on you, you will be useless to me."

"Operate? What do you mean?"

"I'll tell you. The Selom are a very old and highly civilized people. For ages they have possessed scientific knowledge for which the upper-world scientists are now blindly groping. Among other things, they have a perfect knowledge of the workings of the brain. If they operate they will remove from your brain every speck of memory you have of past events, leaving only those things that will be useful to Saranoff. You will be his complete slave. In that condition you will be taught to fly a plane. When the time comes, you will fly one with no remembrance of anything which happened prior to the operation and with no will but his. It will be easier to teach you flying in your natural state if you are willing. You will be willing."

"If you wish it, Doctor."

                    *   *   *   *   *

"I do wish it, most decidedly," Dr. Bird went on. "Obey every order they give you. You will find that the Selom are an enlightened and civilized race. They are very kindly and would willingly harm no one."

"Then why have they taken up with Saranoff?"

"He is the first man with whom they have come into contact. He has told them a horrible tale of conditions on the surface, and they have swallowed it, hook, line and sinker. They believe that he is going to establish a new order of happiness and plenty for all with the aid of his gang of cutthroats from Russia. If they had the slightest inkling of the true state of affairs, they would turn on him in an instant."

"Why don't you tell them?"

"Remember that I am a stranger here and he has poisoned their minds against me. Although the mind of an ordinary men is an open book to them, they cannot read Saranoff's secret thoughts against his will. They can't read mine either, for that matter. I am working in the laboratory and I will pick up a great deal. When the time comes, we will strike for our liberty and for the safety of the world."

"Did you learn Saranoff's plans?"

"Yes. He is gathering planes and pilots in the underground caverns of the Selom. When he gets enough, he will bring men from Russia to man the planes. What could the United States, or the world for that matter, do against a fleet of hundreds, possibly thousands, of the best planes equipped with deadly weapons unknown to their science? That menace confronts us and we must remove it. To give you some idea of the power of the Selom, this afternoon Saranoff and I with one assistant opened a cavern in the solid rock three miles long and a mile wide and over six hundred feet in height."

"Three men! How on earth did you do it?"

"Two men and one mole. We did it with a ray, the secret of which only the Selom and Saranoff know."

*   *   *   *   *

"You have told me a disintegrating ray is an impossibility," objected Carnes.

"It is. This was not a disintegrating ray. Carnes, either I am crazy or the Selom have solved the secret of time, the fourth dimension. I haven't been able to grasp the whole thing yet. What I think we did was to remove that rock a distance, perhaps only a millionth of a second, forward or back into time. At any rate it ceased to exist, yet they can bring it back unchanged at will. That was the way they captured our plane. They sent out a magnetic ray of such power that it stopped our plane in midair and brought it to the ground. They removed the rock from beneath us and lowered us into the hole. By reversing the process they restored things to their original condition. All of these tunnels and rooms were made in that way."

"I still don't understand how they did it."

"I don't either, but I hope to in time. Now let's go to bed. It's late. To-morrow you will start your lessons with Captain Garland as an instructor. He won't know you for he was operated on this afternoon. Do your best to become a pilot. When I get ready, I want you with me in full possession of all your faculties."

The next morning the two prisoners separated and went to their duties. In the cavern which Dr. Bird had described, Captain Garland was waiting beside the plane he had flown. He did not know Carnes, but he still knew how to fly. Declining to enter into any conversation, he started expounding the theory of flying to the detective. Carnes remembered Dr. Bird's words and applied himself wholeheartedly. For four hours they worked together. At the end of that time the light faded in the cavern and Carnes was led by an unseen guide back to his cell. He threw himself on a bed and awaited Dr. Bird's return.

"I have learned a few more things about the Selom," said the doctor when he entered the cell several hours later. "We are in their largest community. They have cities or warrens scattered all over the world. Each city has its own ruler, but the whole race are ruled by an overlord or king who habitually lives here. He is away visiting a community under northern Africa just now, but he will be back in a few days. The Selom are sincere in their desire to help the upper world. They feel great pity for mankind in view of the conditions Saranoff has described to them. When the king returns. I plan to make a direct appeal to him. In the meantime, go on with your flying lessons. How did you make out to-day?"

*   *   *   *   *

The second day was a repetition of the first, as were the third and fourth. A week passed before Dr. Bird entered the cell in evident excitement.

"Has Hanac brought our evening food yet?" he asked anxiously.

"No, Doctor."

"Good. Take this light. As soon as he enters throw the light full on him and hold him until I work on him. We've got to make our escape."

"Why?"

"The king is due back to-morrow. Saranoff is frightened at the good impression I have made on the Selom. He is supreme in the monarch's absence, so he plans to operate on both of us before he returns. He is afraid to allow me to see the king with an unimpaired intellect and memory. Shh! Here comes Hanac." The door to their cell opened noiselessly. When the mole who brought their food was well inside, Carnes turned on the tiny flashlight. The mole dropped on all fours and tried to turn its back. Dr. Bird sprang forward. For an instant his slim muscular fingers worked on the mole's neck and shoulders. Silently the animal sank in a heap.

"Come on, Carnes," cried the doctor. "Turn off the light."

"Did you kill him, Doctor?" asked Carnes as he raced down a pitch dark corridor at the scientist's heels.

"No, I merely paralyzed him temporarily. He'll be all right in a day or so. Turn here."

*   *   *   *   *

For ten minutes they ran down corridor after corridor. Carnes soon lost all track of direction, but Dr. Bird never hesitated. Presently he slowed down to a walk.

"It's a good thing I have a good memory," he said. "I planned that course out from a map, and I had to memorize every turn and distance of it. We are now behind your flying hall and away from any of the regular dwellings of the Selom. Straight west about four miles is one of the time-ray machines with a guard over it. Aside from them, there isn't a mole between here and Detroit."

"What are we going to do, Doctor?"

"Keep out of their way and avoid recapture if we can. If we merely wanted to escape we would try to get possession of that time-ray machine and open a road to the surface. However, I am not content with that. I want to stay underground until Astok, their king, returns. When he comes, we will surrender to him."

"Suppose they operate without giving us a chance to present our side of the affair."

"If they do, Saranoff wins; but they won't. The more I have seen of the Selom, the more impressed I am by their sense of justice. They'll give us a hearing, all right, and a fair one."

For two hours the doctor led the way. At the end of that time he stopped.

"We've gone as far as we need to," he said. "They'll undoubtedly send out searching parties, but if we can avoid thinking they won't be able to find us. The tunnels are a perfect labyrinth. If you care to sleep, go to it. We'll be safer sleeping than awake, for we won't be sending out thoughts so fast."

*   *   *   *   *

Dr. Bird threw himself down on the rubber floor of the tunnel and was soon asleep. Carnes tried to follow his example, but sleep would not come to him. Frantically he tried to think of nothing. By an effort he would sit for a few minutes with his mind a conscious blank, but thoughts would throng in in spite of him. Time and again he brought himself up with a jerk and forced his mind to become a blank. The hours passed slowly. Carnes grew cramped from long immobility and rose. A sudden thought intruded itself into his mind. "I might as well throw that light away," he murmured to himself. "It will be no good now. The Selom won't hurt us if they do catch us."

He reached in his pocket for the light. He was about to hurl it from him when a moment of sanity came to him. He stared about. The impulse to hurl the light away came stronger. He strove in vain to turn it on.

"Doctor!" he cried suddenly. "Wake up! They're after us!"

With a bound, Dr. Bird was on his feet.

"The light!" he cried. "Where is it?"

"In—my—hand," murmured Carnes with stiffening lips.

Dr. Bird seized the light. A beam stabbed the darkness. Less than fifty feet from them stood two moles. As the light flashed on Carnes regained control of himself.

"Take the light, Carnes," snapped the doctor. "I've got to put these fellows to sleep."

Slowly he advanced toward the motionless Selom. He had almost reached them when the light flickered out. He turned and raced at full speed toward the detective. Carnes was standing rigid and motionless. Dr. Bird took the light from his hand. Despite the almost overpowering drag on his mind, he managed to turn it on. He swung the beam around in a circle. Besides the two Selom he had seen before, the light revealed a pair standing behind him. As the light struck them, the numbing influence vanished for an instant from the doctor's mind. He moved a step forward and then halted. The moles behind him were hurling waves of mental power at him. Again the light cleared him for an instant, but he got a brief glance of other moles hurrying from every direction.

"The jig's up, I guess," he muttered. He strove to free himself by the use of his light, but the tiny battery had done its duty, and gradually the light grew dimmer. The influence grew too strong for him. With a sigh he shut off the feeble ray and hurled the light from him. The moles closed in.

"All right," said the doctor audibly. "We'll go peaceably."

*   *   *   *   *

As he spoke the paralyzing power was withdrawn. With Carnes at his side he retraced the route he had taken from the cell. Before they reached it they turned off. Dr. Bird realized that they were treading the familiar path to the laboratory.

Outside the laboratory the Selom halted. A wave of mental power enveloped the prisoners and they remained silent and motionless while their escort withdrew. From the laboratory came three of the Selom scientists. As the laboratory door opened they could see that it was bathed in a flood of light, and that the moles wore helmets covering their heads. They moved inside. Clad in a white gown stood Saranoff.

"So, my friends, you would run away and leave me, would you?" gloated the Russian. "And just when I had planned a very beneficial operation for you! I will remove permanently from your brains all the delusions which now encumber them, and for your own puny wills I will substitute my own."

The power which had held the prisoners silent disappeared.

"You have caught us, Saranoff," said Dr. Bird. "I know the power you wield and that you are making no idle boast. I appeal, however, to these others, my friends. The operation you are planning to perform is not a routine one. It is one that should have the sanction of the king before it is done. I appeal from you to him."

"He is far away," laughed Saranoff. "When he returns, your plea will be presented to him, but it will be too late to do you any good. You are right, Doctor—I do not plan a mere routine operation. Not only will I remove your memory, but I'm going to use the time-ray on you and banish forever into the unknown a portion of your brains. Without knowing which adjustment I make of the infinite number possible, no one, not even the king, can ever recall it."

*　　*　　*　　*　　*

Dr. Bird turned to the Selom scientists and hurled his thoughts at them.

"This man intends to commit a horrible crime," he thought, "and one which he has no authority to perform. To you I appeal for justice. Bid him wait until Astok returns, and let him be the judge as to whether it shall be done. Jumor, you know me well. You know that my brain is the equal of one of the Selom. Even you cannot read my thoughts against my will. Are you willing to see that brain destroyed? Astok will be here soon and nothing will be lost by a short delay."

"He thinks truly," was the answering thought of Jumor. "It would be better to wait."

"We will not wait," crashed Saranoff's thought into their consciousness. "He killed Hanac when he escaped, and his punishment shall be as I have decreed. Did not the king give me full power while he was away?"

"It is true that he ordered us to obey this man in all things dealing with upper-world men," thought Jumor. "If it is true that he killed Hanac his punishment is doubtless just."

"I did not kill Hanac," returned the doctor. "He is paralyzed and will be all right in a few hours, if he isn't already. I demand that you wait until Astok returns. When an appeal is made to him, no other may judge. So says the Selom law."

"That is true," replied Jumor. "We will wait until the king returns."

"We will *not* wait," came Saranoff's thought. "The king delegated to me his powers during his absence, as far as all the world, save the Selom, were concerned. Were it one of the Selom appealing to the king, I would be powerless before the appeal. These are not bound by Selom law and are not entitled to its benefits. We will operate at once."

"Then you will operate alone," retorted Jumor. "I will not assist you."

"I need none of your help," thought Saranoff. "Asmo and Camol, will you help me? If you refuse I will report to Astok that you have disobeyed and defied his chosen delegate."

"We had better assist him, Jumor," thought Asmo. "Astok did delegate his authority. I am not of the nobility and I dare not refuse to help."

"Suit yourself, Asmo," replied Jumor. "I refuse to assist, and will appeal to Astok against him."

*   *   *   *   *

The third mole hesitated.

"You are higher in rank than we are, Jumor," he thought at length, "and like Asmo, I dare not resist him. I heard the king give this upper-earth man his authority while he was away. I will assist."

"And I will leave the room," retorted Jumor.

He moved to a door and threw it open. At the threshold he paused and sent back a final thought.

"I will appeal to Astok, our ruler. I will send now a message to him to hurry home that he may judge between us."

The door closed behind him. Saranoff chuckled audibly.

"Good-by, Carnes," said Dr. Bird sadly. "This devil can do all he says he can, and more. I'm sorry I brought you and Garland into this mess."

"Oh, well, it can't be helped, Doctor," replied the detective with an attempt at cheerfulness. "What is he going to do to us?"

"He'll have to use instruments for what he plans," said the doctor. "Ordinarily a routine mental operation is performed without the use of extraneous power. The mind of the operator is electrically connected to the mind of the victim. By means of thought waves the operator banishes from the mind of the subject such portions of his memory and mentality as he chooses. He may then substitute other things in place of what he has removed. Any of the Selom could operate on you, but I doubt whether Jumor himself could do it successfully on me without aid from power. Here come the instruments."

*   *   *   *   *

Asmo and Camol took from a cabinet on the side of the wall what looked like a cloth helmet. Attached to it were a dozen wires which they connected to a box on a table. The box was made of crystal and inside it could be seen a number of vacuum tubes and coils of various designs. Other leads ran to a similar helmet which Asmo placed on Saranoff's head. A heavy cable ran to a switch on the wall.

As Camol closed the switch the tubes in the box began to glow with weird lights. Violet, green and orange streamers of light came from them to dance in wild patterns on the laboratory walls. For five minutes Saranoff made adjustments to dials on the front of the crystal box. The colored lights died away and a gentle golden glow came from the apparatus. He threw off the helmet.

Camol left the laboratory and returned with a large coil on the top of which was mounted a parabolic reflector. A device like a clock on the front of the coil was constantly marking the passage of time. The dial had two indicators which were together. Saranoff chuckled.

"You may not have seen this device work, Doctor," he said. "In order to let you know what you are facing, I will demonstrate."

He turned the reflector so that it bore on the wall. He adjusted the moving dial so that the two indicators were no longer together. As he closed a switch, the wall before the reflector vanished. Saranoff turned off the power.

"That portion of the wall has gone back in time exactly three seconds," he announced. "As far as the present is concerned, it has ceased to exist. It is following us through time three seconds behind us, but in all eternity it will never catch up unless I aid it. Since the exact time is known, it can be restored. If I were to alter this adjustment ever so little, it could never be recalled. Watch me."

*   *   *   *   *

He again closed the switch, this time in a reverse direction. The wall instantly filled up as it had been before. He moved the time dial so that the two indicators coincided.

"After I have sent a portion of your physical brain into the past or the future as the fancy strikes me, I will change the adjustment of that dial. Since there are an infinite number of adjustments to which I might have set it, the chances that any one could ever duplicate my setting and restore it are the complement of infinity, or zero," he said. "I am now ready to remove your memory. If the impossible should happen and your physical brain be restored it would be useless. Asmo, adjust the helmet. I will operate on my friend, the Doctor, first."

Carnes strove to rush to Dr. Bird's assistance, but he was helpless before the force of Camol's will. Asmo adjusted the helmet to Dr. Bird's head and buckled it firmly in place. With an evil grin, Saranoff donned the other helmet.

"Good-by, Dr. Bird," he said mockingly. "You will continue to see me, but you won't know me, except as your master."

*   *   *   *   *

His hand reached for the switch. It had almost closed on it when Saranoff stopped convulsively. He sat motionless while the laboratory door opened and Jumor entered the room. He was followed by another mole. The newcomer was fully six inches taller than the others. His head was hidden by a helmet, but around his arms he wore strings of sparkling jewels.

"Ivan Saranoff, what means this?" his powerful thoughts dominated the room.

"I was merely engaged in rectifying some of the mental errors of this man of the upper earth," explained the Russian eagerly. "It is merely a routine operation such as you gave me authority to perform."

"An operation which uses power is not routine," replied the king. "I am told that this upper-earth man has a brain equal to those of my most advanced scientist. I am also told that you planned to do more than rectify his mental errors."

"You have been falsely informed. I was merely about to adjust his memory."

"Then what means this?" The king pointed to the time-ray machine.

"That was brought here in order that it could be used when you returned," thought the Russian eagerly. "This upper-earth man killed Hanac when he brought him food."

The door opened and Hanac entered.

"Oh, Astok," objected Hanac's thoughts, "when these upper-earth men had me at their mercy, with a light, they spared me. They paralyzed me for a time so that they might escape but they did it in such a manner that no harm came to me."

"So Jumor told me," replied the king. "Release them."

*   *   *   *   *

In an instant Carnes was on his feet removing the helmet from Dr. Bird's head. The doctor struggled to his feet.

"Dr. Bird," thought the king, "can you communicate with me easily?"

"Yes, Your Majesty, but may I ask that you alter the vibration period of my comrade, Mr. Carnes? He cannot understand you with his present low period."

The king stepped to the box with which Saranoff had been working. In response to his commands the helmet which had been on Dr. Bird's head was placed on the detective. The king made a few adjustments to the dials and signalled for the helmet to be removed.

"Can you understand me, Mr. Carnes?" he asked mentally.

The question leaped with startling clearness into the detective's head. Carefully he framed his answer.

"I can understand you," said the king. "I will now sit in judgment on the appeal made to me. Dr. Bird tell me your story."

With eloquent thoughts, Dr. Bird poured forth the history of the upper world. He told of the great war and the collapse of the Russian monarchy. He traced history to the fall of the moderate party and the rise of the Bolsheviki. He described the horrible conditions existing in Russia. At the end he reviewed the long battle he and

Carnes had fought against Saranoff. When he had finished, the king questioned Carnes.

The detective repeated the story in different words and the king turned to Saranoff. From the Russian's mind came a tissue of distorted facts and downright lies. He denied or twisted around everything that the detective and the scientist had said. When he had done with his tale, Astok sat in secret thought for a few minutes.

"The tales you tell me are so far apart that I can give credence to none of them," he announced at length. "There is but one solution. Although they are never used, for the Selom have forgotten the meaning of a falsehood, we have instruments which will drag the truth from the brain of a liar. They are powerful and their use may easily be fatal. If a man gives forth the contents of his brain willingly, the process is not painful. If he tries to conceal anything, it is torture. Will you willingly submit your brains to the searching of this instrument?"

"Gladly," came Dr. Bird's thought and Carnes reechoed it.

"And you, Ivan Saranoff?" demanded the king.

"I will not submit," thought the Russian sullenly.

"You will be examined whether you submit willingly or not," replied Astok. "I am going to learn the truth though I kill you all to get it."

*　　*　　*　　*　　*

At the king's order, Jumor hastened from the laboratory. He returned in a few minutes with an apparatus similar to the one which Saranoff had planned to use on Dr. Bird, but larger, and with more dials on the crystal box. At a command from the king, Dr. Bird donned the helmet.

The king manipulated switches and dials. Around Dr. Bird's head glowed a halo of crimson light. Twice an expression of momentary pain passed over his countenance. After half an hour, Astok cut on the power and nodded to Carnes.

"Don't try to hold anything back, Carnesy," said Dr. Bird sharply. "You couldn't if you tried, and the process is very painful, I can assure you."

With the helmet on his head the detective sat for ten minutes while the Selom king went through his brain. A dozen times he shrieked in agony but his moments of suffering were short. The king removed the helmet.

"Your minds agree well," he thought. "Now I will examine the mind of my friend."

The helmet was strapped on Saranoff. Instantly an expression of the utmost anguish crossed his face. Shriek after shriek of agony came from his writhing lips. Relentlessly the king applied more power. The cries of the Russian grew heartrending. Suddenly he grew rigid and slumped forward in his chair. Astok impassively manipulated his instrument. After half an hour, he opened the switch and removed the helmet. Under the ministrations of Jumor the Russian revived. The king sat in secret thought for an hour.

"I have examined the brains of all of you," he announced at length, "and I find hopeless contradictions. Each of you believes thoroughly in his own social order. Both tell me of hopeless misery on the part of a large portion of his people. Both tell of horrible wars and suffering beyond my comprehension. The thoughts of all of you teem with modes of bringing death to your fellow beings. Your entire science his been perverted to the ends of destruction. Nothing of the sort can be realized by the Selom where truth, justice and mercy prevail. Each of you holds that his form of government is better than the other, and will cause less suffering and misery than the others'. None of you hold out hope of happiness for your fellow beings. I do not know which system is less obnoxious. My decision is made. The Selom will not interfere in the affairs of the upper-earth. You may fight out your battles without aid and without interference.

"I will operate on both Ivan Saranoff and Dr. Bird. I will remove from their minds all knowledge of our science and instruments and leave them in the same condition that they were when they entered my realms. Each of you will then be returned to upper-earth, Ivan Saranoff to Russia, Dr. Bird and Mr. Carnes to the United States. The pilots, whom I hold prisoners, will have their mentalities restored and be returned to their homes. The planes we have captured, I will send off into time so that they can never be used for the misery of upper-earth men again. Jumor, you will carry out these orders."

* * * * *

"I wish I could remember how that time machine was built and operated," said Dr. Bird reflectively, as he sat in his private laboratory in the Bureau of Standards some time later, "but Jumor did his work well. I can't even remember what the thing looked like."

"Well, Doctor, our trip below wasn't a loss. We removed a very real menace to the established order of things and we have got rid of Saranoff temporarily. It will take him some time to return here from Russia."

"Three weeks or less," said Dr. Bird pessimistically. "However, we have gained one other thing. Did you notice this?"

He pulled what looked like a watch from his pocket. Carnes regarded it with a puzzled expression.

"No, Doctor, what is it?"

"It is a very small camera which takes pictures one-half inch by seven-eighths. I had several opportunities to use it. I wasn't sure that it would work on such short waves, but it did. When Saranoff tries to return to this country, he will find that every immigration inspector and every member of the border patrol has an excellent likeness of him. That may hinder

The Solar Magnet
Originally Published In *Astounding Stories Of Super-Science,*
October 1931

*Another episode in Dr. Bird's long
scientific duel with his country's
arch-enemy, Saranoff.*

The Solar Magnet

The milling crowd in front of the Capitol suddenly grew quiet. A tall portly figure came out onto the porch of the building and stepped before a microphone erected on the steps. A battery of press cameras clicked. A newsreel photographer ground away on his machine. Wild cheers rent the air. The President held up his hand for silence. As the cheering died away he spoke into the microphone.

"My countrymen," he said, "the Congress of the United States has met in extraordinary session and is ready to cope with the condition with which we are confronted. While they deliberate as to the steps to be taken, it is essential that you meet this danger, if it be a danger, with the bravery and the calm front which has always characterized the people of the United States in times of trial and danger. You may rest assured–"

A slightly built, inconspicuous man who had followed the President out onto the porch was surveying the crowd intently. He turned and spoke in an undertone to a second man who mysteriously appeared from nowhere as the first man spoke. He listened for a moment, nodded, and edged closer to the President. The first man slipped unobtrusively down the Capitol steps and mingled with the crowd.

"–that no steps will be neglected which may prove of value," went on the President. "The greatest scientists of the country have gathered in this city in conference and they undoubtedly will soon find a simple and natural explanation for what is happening. In the meantime–"

*   *   *   *   *

The President paused. From the crowd in front of him came a sudden disturbance. A man sprang free of the crowd and broke through the restraining cordon of police. In his hand gleamed an ugly blue steel automatic pistol. Quickly he leveled it and fired. A puff of dust came from the Capitol. The bullet had landed a few inches from one of the lower windows, fifty feet from where the President stood. He raised his weapon for a second shot but it was never fired. The man who had come down the Capitol steps sprang forward like a cat and grasped the weapon. For a moment the two men struggled, but only for a moment. From the crowd, stunned for a moment by the sheer audacity of the attack, came a roar of rage. The police closed in about the struggling men but the crowd rolled over them like a wave. The captor shouted his identity and tried to display the gold badge of the secret service but the mob was in no state of mind to listen. The police were trampled underfoot and the would-be assassin torn from the hands of the secret service operative. Every man in reach tried to strike a blow. The secret service man was buffeted and thrown aside. Realizing that the affair had been taken out of his hands, he made his way to the rear of the Capitol where his badge gained him ready passage through the cordon of police. He entered the building and reappeared in a few moments by the side of the President.

*   *   *   *   *

Two hours later he leaned forward in his chair in Dr. Bird's private laboratory in the Bureau of Standards and spoke earnestly.

"Dr. Bird," he said, "that bullet was never meant for the President. That man was after bigger game."

The famous scientist nodded thoughtfully.

"Even a very rotten pistol shot should have come closer to him," he replied. "He must have missed by a good forty feet."

"He missed by a matter of inches. Doctor, that bullet struck the Capitol only two inches from a window. In that window was standing a man. The bullet was intended for the occupant of that window. I was directly behind him when he raised his weapon for a second shot and I am sure of his aim. He deliberately ignored the President and aimed again at that window. That was when I tackled him."

"Who was standing there, Carnes?"

"*You* were, Doctor."

Dr. Bird whistled.

"Then you think that bullet was intended for me?"

"I am sure of it, Doctor. That fact proves one thing to me. You are right in your idea that this whole affair is man-made and not an accident of nature. The guiding intelligence back of it fears you more than he fears anyone else and he took this means to get rid of you unobtrusively. Attention was focused on the President. Your death would have been laid to accident. It was a clever thought."

"It does look that way, Carnes," said the doctor slowly. "If you are right, this incident confirms my opinion. There is only one man in the world clever enough to have disturbed the orderly course of the seasons, and such a plan for my assassination would appeal to his love of the dramatic."

"You mean—"

"Ivan Saranoff, of course."

"We are pretty sure that he hasn't got back to the United States, Doctor."

"You may be right but I am sure of nothing where that man is concerned. However, that fact has no bearing. He may be operating from anywhere. His organization is still in the United States."

*   *   *   *   *

A knock sounded at the door. In response to the doctor's command a messenger entered and presented a letter. Dr. Bird read it and dropped it in a waste basket.

"Tell them that I am otherwise engaged just now," he said curtly. The messenger withdrew. "It was just a summons to another meeting of the council of scientists," he said to Carnes. "They'll have to get along without me. All they'll do anyway will be to read a lot of dispatches and wrangle about data and the relative accuracy of their observations. Herriott will lecture for hours on celestial mechanics and propound some fool theory about a hidden body, which doesn't exist, and its possible influence, which would be nil, on the inclination of the earth's axis. After wasting four hours without a single constructive idea being put forward, they will gravely conclude that the sun rose fifty-three seconds earlier at the fortieth north parallel than it did yesterday and correspondingly later at the fortieth south parallel. I know that without wasting time."

"Was it fifty-three seconds to-day, Doctor?"

"Yes. This is the twentieth of July. The sun should have risen at 4:52, sixteen minutes later than it rose on June twentieth and fifty-three seconds later than it rose yesterday. Instead it rose at 4:20, sixteen minutes *earlier* than it did on June twentieth and fifty-three seconds earlier than yesterday."

"I don't understand what is causing it, Doctor. I have tried to follow your published explanations, but they are a little too deep for me."

*   *   *   *   *

"As to the real underlying cause, I am in grave doubts, Carnes, although I can make a pretty shrewd guess. As to the reason for the unnatural lengthening of the day, the explanation is simplicity itself. As you doubtless know, the earth revolves daily on its axis. At the same time, it is moving in a great ellipse about the sun, an ellipse which it takes it a year to cover. If the axis of rotation of the earth were at right angles to the plane of its orbit; in other words, if the earth's equator lay in the plane of the earth's movement about the sun, each day would be of the same length and there would be no seasons. Instead of this being the case, the axis of rotation of the earth is tipped so that the angle between the equator and the elliptic is 23-1/2 deg."

"I seem to remember something of the sort from my school days."

"This angle of tilt may be assumed to be constant, for I won't bother with the precessions, nutations and other minor movements considered in accurate computations. As the earth moves around the sun, this tilt gives rise to what we call the sun's declination. You can readily see that at one time in the year, the north pole will be at its nearest point to the sun, speaking in terms of tilt and not in miles, while at another point on the elliptic, it will be farthest from the sun and the south pole nearest. There are two midway points when the two poles are practically equidistant."

"Then the days and nights should be of equal length."

"They are. These are the periods of the equinoxes. The point at which the sun is nearest to the south pole we call the winter solstice, and the opposite point, the summer solstice. The summer solstice is on June twenty-first. At that time the declination of the sun is 23-1/2 deg. north of the equatorial line. It starts to decrease until, six months later, it reaches a minus declination of 23-1/2 deg. and is that far south of the line. The longest day in the northern hemisphere is naturally June twenty-first."

"And the shortest day when the sun has the greatest minus declination."

*   *   *   *   *

"Precisely, at the winter solstice. Now to explain what is happening. The year went normally until June twenty-first. That day was of the correct length, about fourteen hours and fifty minutes long. The twenty-second should have been shorter. Instead, it was longer than the twenty-first. Each day, instead of getting shorter as it should at this time of year, is getting longer. We have already gained some thirty-two minutes of sunlight at this latitude. The explanation is that the angle between the equator and the elliptic is no longer 23-1/2 deg. as it has been from time immemorial, but it is greater. If the continuing tilt keeps up long enough, the obliquity will be 90 deg. When that happens, there will be perpetual midday at the north pole and perpetual night at the south pole. The whole northern hemisphere will be bathed in a continuous flood of sunlight while the southern hemisphere will be a region of cold and dark. The condition of the earth will resemble that of Mercury where the same face of the planet is continually facing the sun."

"I understand that all right, but I am still in the dark as to what is causing this increase of tilt."

"No more than I am, old dear. Herriott keeps babbling about a hidden body which is drawing the earth from its normal axial rotation, but the fool ignores the fact that a body of a size sufficient to disturb the earth would throw every motion of the solar system into a state of chaos. Nothing of the sort has happened. Ergo, no external force is causing it. I am positive that the force which is doing the work is located on the earth itself. Furthermore, unless my calculations are badly off, this force is located on or very near the surface of the earth at approximately the sixty-fifth degree of north latitude."

"How can you tell that, Doctor?"

"It would take me too long to explain, Carnes. I will, however, qualify my statement a little. Either a variable force is being used or else a constant force located where I have said. The sixty-fifth parallel is a long line. The exact location and the nature of that force, we have to find. If it be man-made, and I'll bet my bottom dollar that it is, we will also have to destroy it. If we fail, we'll see this world plunged into such a riot of war and bloodshed as has never before been known. It will be literally a fight of mankind for a place in the sun. Due to its favorable location in the new position of the earth, it is more than probable that Russia would emerge as the dominant power."

"Undertaking to destroy a thing that you don't know the location of and of whose existence you aren't even sure is a pretty big contract."

*　　*　　*　　*　　*

"We've tackled bigger ones, old dear. We have the President behind us. I haven't made much headway selling my idea to that gang of old fossils who call themselves the council of scientists, but I did to his nibs. Just before that attempt at assassination, I had a chin-chin with him. The fastest battle cruiser in the Navy, the *Denver*, is to be placed at my service. It will carry a big amphibian plane, so be equipped to assemble and launch it. Bolton will relieve you from the Presidential guard to-day. We sail in the morning."

"Where for, Doctor?"

"I feel sure that the force is caused and controlled by men and I know of but one man who has the genius and the will to do such a thing. That man is Saranoff. Because he must be concealed and work free from interruption, I fancy he is working in his own country. Does that answer your question?"

"It does. We sail for Russia."

"Carnesy, old dear, at times you have flashes of such scintillating brilliance that I have hopes for the future of the secret service. In time they may even show human intelligence. Toddle along now and pay your fond farewells to the bright lights of Washington. Meet me at the Pennsy station at six. We'll sail from New York in the morning."

*   *   *   *   *

With the famous scientist and his assistant as passengers, the *Denver* steamed at her best speed across the Atlantic. As soon as New York harbor was cleared, Dr. Bird charted the course. Captain Evans raised his eyebrows when he saw the course laid out, but his orders had been positive. Had Dr. Bird ordered him to steam at full speed against the shore, he would have obeyed without question.

The *Denver* avoided the usual lanes of traffic and bore to the north of the summer lane. Not a vessel was sighted in the eight days which elapsed before the Faroe Islands came in sight on the starboard bow. The *Denver* bore still more to the north and skirted around North Cape five days later. At Cape Kanin she headed south into the White Sea. Surprisingly little ice was encountered. When Captain Evans mentioned this, Dr. Bird pointed out to him that it was August and that the days were still lengthening. Once in the White Sea, the *Denver* was made ready for instant action. A huge amphibian plane was hoisted in sections from the hold and mechanics started to assemble it. Dr. Bird spent most of his time working on some instruments he had assembled in the radio room.

"This is an ultra-short wave detector," he explained to Carnes. "It will receive vibrations to the lowest limit of waves that we have ever been able to measure. The X-ray is high on the scale and even the cosmic ray is far above its lower limit of detection. We are hunting for an electro-magnet, the largest and strangest electro-magnet that has ever been constructed. Perhaps it would be more accurate to say that we are seeking for a generator of magnetic force. It does not generate the ordinary magnetism which attracts iron and steel, nor the special type of magnetism which we call gravity, but something between the two. It attracts the sun enough to disturb the tilt of the earth's axis, but not enough to pull the earth out of its orbit. Such a device should give out a wave that can be detected, if we get a receiver delicate enough and operating on the right wave length."

*   *   *   *   *

He spent hours improving and refining the apparatus, but in the end he confessed himself beaten.

"It's no use, Carnes," he said the day after Cape Kanin faded from view to the north. "Either the apparatus we are seeking gives out no wave that we can detect or my apparatus is faulty. Luckily we have other things to guide us."

"What are they, Doctor?"

"The facts that Saranoff must have easy transportation and a source of power. The first precludes him from locating his station far from the sea-coast and the second indicates that it will be near a river or other source of power. The only Russian points on the sixty-fifth parallel that are open to water transport are the Gulf of Anadyr, north of Kamchatka, and the vicinity of Archangel. I passed up Kamchatka because it would mean too long a haul through unfriendly waters from Leningrad and because there is not much water power. Archangel is easy of access at this time of the year and it has the Dwina river for power. That will be our first line of search."

"We will explore by plane, of course?"

"Certainly. We wouldn't get far on foot, especially as neither of us speaks Russian. We'll head south for another day and then– What's that?"

*   *   *   *   *

He paused and listened. From the distance came a dull drone of sound which brought him to his feet with a start. He raced out onto deck with Carnes at his heels. Far overhead in the blue, a tiny speck of black hovered.

"We're on the right trail, Carnes," he said grimly. The plane passed over them. In huge circles it sank toward the ground. Dr. Bird turned to Captain Evans. Orders flew from the bridge and a detail of marines rapidly stripped the covers from the two forward anti-aircraft rifles.

"I dislike to fire on that craft before it makes a hostile demonstration, Dr. Bird," demurred Captain Evans. "We are at peace with Russia. My action in firing might precipitate a war, or in any event, serious diplomatic misunderstandings."

"Allow me to correct you, Captain Evans, we are at war with Russia. The whole world is at war with the man who has pulled the earth out of her course. In any event, your orders are positive and the responsibility is mine. Wait until that plane gets within easy range and then shoot it down. Do not fail to get it; it must not get back to shore with word of our approach."

Captain Evans bowed gravely. Shells came up from the magazines and were piled by the guns. From the fire control stations came a monotonous calling of firing data. The guns slowly changed direction as the plane descended. Nearer and nearer it came, intent on positive identification of the war vessel below it. It passed over the *Denver* less than five thousand feet up. As it passed it swung off to one side and began to climb sharply. Dr. Bird glanced at the fighting top of the cruiser and swore softly. From the top the stars and stripes had been broken to the breeze.

"Fire at once!" he cried, "and then court-martial the fool who broke out that flag!"

*   *   *   *   *

The two three-inch rifles barked their message of death into the sky. For agonizing seconds nothing happened. The guns roared again. Below and behind the fleeing plane, two puffs of white smoke appeared in the sky. The staccato calls of the observers came from the control station and the guns roared again and again. Now above and now below the Russian plane appeared the white puffs that told of bursting shells, but the plane droned on, unharmed.

"It's away safely," groaned the doctor. "Now the fat *is* in the fire. Saranoff will know in an hour that we are coming. If we had a pursuit plane ready to take off, we might catch him, but we haven't. Oh, well, there's no use in crying over spilt milk. How soon will that amphibian be ready to take off?"

"In twenty minutes. Doctor," replied the Engineering Officer. "As soon as we finish filling the tanks and test the motor, she'll be ready to ramble."

"Hurry all you can. Hang a half dozen hundred-pound bombs and a few twenty-fives on the racks. Lower her over the side as soon as she's ready. Where's Lieutenant McCready?"

"Below, getting into his flying togs, Doctor."

"Good enough. Come on, Carnes, we'll go below and put on our fur-lined panties, too. We'll probably need them."

*   *   *   *   *

In half an hour the amphibian rose from the water. Lieutenant McCready was at the controls, with Carnes and the doctor at the bomb racks. The plane rose in huge spirals until the altimeter read four thousand feet. The pilot straightened it out toward the south. The plane was alone in the sky. For two hours it flew south and then veered to the east, following the line of the Gulf of Archangel. The town came in sight at last.

"Better drop down a couple of thousand, Lieutenant," said Dr. Bird into the speaking tube. "We can't see much from this altitude."

The plane swung around in a wide circle, gradually losing altitude. Carnes and the doctor hung over the side watching the ground below them. As they watched a puff of smoke came from a low building a mile from the edge of the town. Dr. Bird grabbed the speaking tube.

"Bank, McCready!" he barked, "They're firing at us."

The plane lurched sharply to one side. From a point a few yards below them and almost directly along their former line of flight, a burst of flame appeared in the air. The plane lurched and reeled as the blast of the explosion reached it. From other points on the ground came other puffs.

"Get out of here," shouted Dr. Bird. "There must be a dozen guns firing at us. One of them will have the range directly."

From all around them came flashes and the roar of explosions. The plane lurched and yawed in a sickening fashion. Lieutenant McCready fought heroically with the controls, trying to prevent the sideslips which were costing him altitude. Gradually the plane came under control and started to climb. The shells burst nearer as the plane took a straighter course and strove to fly out of the danger zone. Dr. Bird looked at the air-speed meter.

"A hundred and eighty," he shouted to Carnes. "We'll be safely out of range in a minute."

*   *   *   *   *

The bursts were mostly behind them now. Suddenly a blast of air struck them with terrific force. Half a dozen holes appeared in the fabric of the wings. A bit of high explosive shell plowed a way through the after compartment and wrecked the duplicate instrument board. In another moment they were out of range.

Lieutenant McCready turned the nose of his plane toward the north.

"We came out of that well," cried Carnes. Dr. Bird dropped the speaking tube which he had held pressed to his ear and smiled grimly at the detective.

"I wish we had," he replied. "Our main gas tank is punctured."

An expression of alarm crossed the detective's face.

"Is it injured badly?" he asked.

"I don't know yet. McCready says that the gauge is dropping pretty rapidly. I'm going to go out and see what I can do."

"Can't I go, Doctor? I'm a good deal lighter than you are."

"You're not as strong or as agile, Carnes, and you haven't the mechanical ability to make the repair. Hand me that line."

He fastened one end of a coil of manila rope which Carnes handed him to his waist, while the detective fastened the other end to one of the safety belt hooks. With a word of farewell, he climbed out of the cockpit and onto a wing. In the pocket of his flying suit he carried a tool kit and repair material. Carnes shuddered as the doctor's figure disappeared under the plane. He snubbed the rope about a seat bracket and held it taut. For ten minutes the strain continued. It slackened at last, and the figure of the doctor reappeared on the wing. Slowly he climbed into the cockpit.

"I've made a temporary repair, Lieutenant," he called into the speaking tube, "and the leakage has stopped. How much gas have we left?"

"Enough for about an hour of flying, including the emergency tank."

"Thunder! No chance to get back to the *Denver*. Better head inland and follow the course of the Dwina. If we can locate the place we are looking for we may be able to drop a few eggs on it before we are washed out. In any event, it will be better to come down on land than on water."

*   *   *   *   *

McCready headed the plane south and followed the winding ribbon below him which marked the channel of the Dwina. He kept his altitude well over eight thousand feet. For a few minutes the plane roared along. Without warning the motor sputtered once or twice and died.

"Gas finished?" asked Dr. Bird into the speaking tube.

"No, there is plenty of gas for another forty-five minutes. It acted like a short in the wiring. Maybe another fragment got us that we didn't know about. I can glide to a safe landing, Doctor. Which direction shall I go?"

"It doesn't matter," replied Dr. Bird as he looked over the side. "Wait a minute, it does matter. See that long low building down there with the projection like a tower on top? I'll bet a month's pay that that is the very place we're looking for. Glide over it and let's have a look at it. If I am convinced of it, I'll drop a few eggs on it."

"Right!"

McCready glided on a long slope toward the suspected building. Dr. Bird kept his eye glued to the bomb sight.

"It's suspicious enough for me to act," he cried. "Drop one!"

Carnes pulled a lever and a hundred-pound high explosive bomb detached itself from the plane and fell toward the ground.

"Another!" cried the doctor.

A second messenger of death followed the first.

"Bank around and back over while we give them the rest."

"Right!"

The plane swung around in a wide circle.

"Volley!" cried the doctor. Carnes pulled the master lever and the rest of the bombs fell earthward.

"Now glide to the east, McCready, until you are forced down."

*   *   *   *   *

McCready banked the plane and started on a long glide toward the east. Carnes and the doctor watched the falling bombs. The doctor's aim had been perfect. The first bomb released struck the building squarely while the other landed only a few feet away. Instead of the puffs of smoke which they had expected, the bombs had no effect. The volley which Carnes had discharged fell full on the building as harmlessly as had the two pilot shots.

"Were these bombs armed, Lieutenant?" demanded the doctor.

"Yes, sir. I inspected them myself before we took off and they were fused and armed. They had always fused and should have gone off, no matter in what position they landed."

"Well, they didn't. That building is our goal all right. Saranoff would naturally expect an air raid and he has perfected some device which renders a bomb impotent before it lands. How far from the building will you land?"

"A couple of miles, Doctor."

"Get as far as you can. If you can make that line of thicket ahead, we'll take to our heels and hope to hide in it."

"I don't think we'll have much luck, Doctor," said Carnes.

"Why not?"

"Look behind."

Dr. Bird looked back toward the building they had tried to bomb. Across the country, a truck loaded with armed men followed the course of the plane. The plane was gaining slightly on the truck but it was evident that the plane's occupants would have little chance of escaping on foot. Dr. Bird gave a grim laugh.

"We're cornered all right," he said. "If we did elude the men in that truck, we would have a plane after us in no time. You might as well turn back, McCready, and land fairly near the building. We are sure to be captured and our best chance is to have the plane near us. They'll probably patch it up and if we get a chance to escape later, it may be a lifesaver. At any rate, we've lost for the present."

*   *   *   *   *

McCready turned the plane again to the west. The truck halted at their new maneuver. As the plane passed over, it turned and again followed them. The ground was approaching rapidly. With a final dip, McCready leveled off and made a landing. The machine rolled to a stop about a mile from the building. The truck was less than three hundred yards away. It came up rapidly and disgorged a dozen men armed with rifles who hurried forward. In the lead was a tall, slight figure who carried no gun. Dr. Bird stepped forward to meet them.

"Do you understand English?" he asked.

An incomprehensible jargon of Russian answered him. The men raised their rifles threateningly. Dr. Bird turned back to his companions.

"Resistance is hopeless," he said. "Surrender gracefully and we'll see what comes of it."

He faced the Russians and held one hand high above his head. The Russian leader stepped forward and confiscated the doctor's pistol. He repeated the process with Carnes and McCready, frisking them thoroughly for concealed weapons. At his command, six of the Russians stepped forward. The Americans took their place in the midst of the guard and were marched to the truck. The balance of the Russians moved over to the American's plane. The truck rolled forward and approached the low building. The projection which Dr. Bird had noticed from the air proved to be a metal tube projection from the roof, fully twenty feet in diameter and fifty feet long.

"A projection tube of some sort," said the doctor, pointing. An excited command came from the Russian in command. A rifle was leveled threateningly at the doctor. He took the hint and maintained silence while they climbed down from the truck and approached the door of the building.

It swung open as they approached. As they entered a strong garlic-like smell was evident. The hum of heavy machinery smote their ears.

* * * * *

They were led down a corridor to a flight of steps. On the floor below they went along another corridor to a heavy iron-studded door. The guide unlocked it with a huge key and swung it open. With a shrug of his shoulders, Dr. Bird led the way into the cell. The door closed behind them and they were left alone. Dr. Bird turned to his companions.

"Be careful what you say," he whispered. "I am not at all convinced that there is no one here who knows English and we are probably spied upon. There is almost sure to be a dictaphone somewhere in this room. We don't want to give them any more information than we have to."

Carnes and McCready nodded. Dr. Bird spoke aloud of inconsequential matters while they explored the cell. It was a room some twenty feet square, fitted with three bunks on one side, built into the wall like the berths on shipboard. The room was lighted by a single electric light overhead. A door opened into a lavatory equipped with running water.

"We're comfortable here, at any rate," said the doctor cheerfully. "They evidently don't mean to make us suffer. I'd like to know why they took the trouble to capture us, anyway. It would seem to be more in line with their usual policy to have shot us on sight. It must be that they want some sort of information from us."

Neither of his companions had a better reason to offer and conversation languished. For an hour they sat almost without speech. A sound at the door brought them to their feet. It opened and a Russian girl pushed in a cart laden with food. She made no reply to the remarks which Dr. Bird addressed to her but quickly and silently put their food on the table. When she had completed her task, she left the room without having spoken a word.

"Beautiful, but dumb," Dr. Bird remarked. "Let's eat."

"Do you suppose that it's safe to eat this food, Doctor?" asked Carnes in a whisper.

"I don't know, and I don't care. If we've got to go out, we might as well be poisoned as shot. If we refuse food, they can poison us through our water. We couldn't refuse that for any length of time. I'm hungry and I'm going to make a good meal. What's this stuff, *bortsch?*"

*   *   *   *   *

They soon received proof that they were under observation. Hardly had they pushed back their chairs at the completion of the meal than the door opened and the Russian girl who had brought their food removed the empty dishes. Silence settled down over the cell. For another hour they waited before the door opened again. A tall bearded Russian entered with a younger man at his heels. The bearded man dropped into a chair while his companion sat at the table and opened a notebook.

"Stand up!" barked the Russian sternly.

Carnes and McCready rose to their feet but Dr. Bird remained stretched out on a bed.

"What for?" he demanded languidly.

The Russian bristled with rage.

"When I speak to you, you shall obey," he said in curiously clipped English, "else it will be the worse for you. Would you rather be questioned while in the *strelska* than while standing?"

"Not by a long shot," replied Dr. Bird promptly as he rose to his feet. "Fire away, old fellow. I'll talk."

"What are your names?"

"I am Addison Sims of Seattle," replied Dr. Bird gravely, "and my friends are Mr. Earle Liedermann and Mr. Bernarr Macfadden. You may have read of us in the American magazines."

"Their names," said the Russian to his clerk, "are Dr. Bird, of the Bureau of Standards; Operative Carnes, of the United States Secret Service; and Lieutenant McCready, of the United States Navy. Dr. Bird, you will save yourself trouble if you will answer my future questions truthfully."

"Then ask questions to which I am not sure that you know the answer," replied the doctor dryly.

"What vessel brought you here?"

"The *Denver*."

"What is her armament?"

"Consult the Navy list. You will doubtless find a copy in your files. It may be purchased from the Superintendent of Public Documents at Washington."

*   *   *   *   *

"What is your errand here?"

"To consult with Ivan Saranoff and learn his future plans. If he means merely to bestow on the northern hemisphere additional sunshine and warmth, it is possible that the United States will not oppose him. We would benefit equally with Russia, you know. Possibly the northern countries could form some sort of an alliance against the southern hemisphere which is already threatening war."

"You chose a peculiar way of showing your peaceable intentions. You shot down our plane without warning and you dropped bombs on us at first sight."

"But they didn't explode."

"No, thanks to our ray operators. Dr. Bird, I have no time to waste. Either you will answer my questions fully and truthfully or I will resort to torture."

"You don't dare. You were merely bluffing when you mentioned the *strelska*. If you tortured us, you would have to answer to Ivan Saranoff on his return."

"How did you know that he is–" The Russian paused and bit his lip. "Shall I tell him that you refuse to talk?"

"When he returns, you may tell him that I will be glad to talk frankly with him. I came to Russia for that purpose, but I will not talk with one of his underlings. In the meanwhile, we are having lovely weather for this time of year, aren't we?"

With a muttered curse the Russian rose and left the room. Carnes turned to Dr. Bird.

"How did you know that Saranoff was away?" he demanded.

"I didn't," replied Dr. Bird with a chuckle, "it was merely a shrewd guess. We have twisted his tail so often that I figured he could not resist the temptation to come here and gloat a few gloats over us if he were here. I know his ruthless methods in dealing with his subordinates and I knew that they would never dare to resort to torture in his absence. No, old dear, we are safe until he returns. I hope he stays away a long time."

*   *   *   *   *

Four days passed monotonously. Three times a day the Russian girl appeared with ample meals. Despite their attempts to engage her in conversation, not a word would she reply or give any indication that she either heard or understood their remarks. The bearded Russian appeared daily and tried to question them, but Dr. Bird laughed at his threats and reaffirmed his intention of talking to no one but Saranoff.

"Your chance will soon come," replied the Russian with an evil leer on the fourth day. "He will be here the day after to-morrow. He will be able to make you talk."

"If he's telling the truth, the jig's about up," said Dr. Bird when the Russian had left. "I don't fancy that

Saranoff will show us much mercy when he finds out what we've attempted to do."

"How would it be to overpower our waitress and make a break?" asked McCready in a guarded whisper.

"No good at all," replied the doctor decisively. "We wouldn't have a Chinaman's chance. Our best bet is to talk turkey to Saranoff. He may spare us if I can make him believe that I am willing to work for him. What a man he is! If we could turn his genius into the right channels, he would be a blessing to the world."

*   *   *   *   *

He paused as the door swung open and the Russian girl appeared with their food. She placed the cart against the wall and suddenly turned and faced them.

"Dr. Bird," she said in excellent English, "I am Feodrovna Androvitch."

"I'm glad to know you," said Dr. Bird with a bow.

"Do you recognize my name?"

"I'm very sorry, my dear, but it simply doesn't register."

"Do you remember Stefan Androvitch?"

A sudden light came into Dr. Bird's face.

"Yes," he exclaimed, "I do. He used to work for me in the Bureau some time ago. I had to let him go under peculiar circumstances. Is he related to you?"

"He was my twin brother. The peculiar circumstances you refer to were that you caught him stealing platinum. Instead of turning him over to the police, you asked him why he stole. He told you his wife was dying for lack of things that money would buy and he stole for her. You allowed him to quit his position honorably and you gave him money for his immediate needs. For that act of mercy, I am here to reward you."

"Bread cast upon the waters," murmured Carnes. The Russian girl turned on him like a wildcat.

"Unless you wish to deprive yourself and your companions of my help, you will not quote the Bible, that sop thrown by the church to their slaves, to me," she said venomously. "I am a woman of the proletariat!"

"Respect the lady's anti-religious prejudices, Carnesy, old dear," said the doctor with a smile. "How do you propose to aid us, Miss Androvitch?"

"I will give you exactly what you gave my brother, your freedom and money for your immediate needs."

"Thanks. But, er—haven't you considered what your position here will be if you aid us to escape? Saranoff doesn't deal kindly with traitors, I fancy."

The girl spat on the floor.

"That swine!" she hissed, "I would like to kill him. I would have done so long ago had not the hope of the people rested on his genius. When the people finally triumph, I will feed his heart to my cat."

"Nice, gentle, loving disposition," murmured the doctor. "All right, my dear, we're ready for anything. What's the first move?"

*   *   *   *   *

The girl whisked the covers from the food cart and displayed three pistols and belts of ammunition.

"Put these on," she said, "and take this food with you. I will take you to a hiding place outside the walls where you may safely stay for a few days. I will bring you fresh supplies of food. As quickly as possible I will arrange for you to escape from Russia. When you have left Russia safely, my debt is paid and you are again my enemies."

"But, listen here," said Dr. Bird persuasively, "why don't you come with us? You know the object of our coming here. We aim to destroy this plant and let the earth take its normal tilt. You hate Saranoff, although I don't know why. If you'll help us to destroy him, we'll guarantee you a welcome in the United States and you can join your brother. I'll take him back into my laboratory."

"My brother is dead," she said bitterly. "After he left you, he fell into more evil times. His wife died and he swore revenge upon the society which had murdered her. An opportunity came to him to join Saranoff, and he did so. Saranoff hated him and distrusted him, although he was the soul of loyalty. As a reward for his genius and aid to Saranoff in constructing the black lamp, Saranoff abandoned him to you. It was your men who killed him when you blew into nothingness the helicopter he was piloting in your state of Maryland, near Washington."

"All the more reason why you should revenge yourself upon Saranoff," replied the doctor. "We will give you a chance to do so and aid you. We also give you an opportunity to be received in a free country with honor."

An expression of rage distorted the girl's features.

"I am a woman of the proletariat!" she cried. "I hate Ivan Saranoff for what he has done but I am loyal to him. He alone will force the bourgeoisie to their knees and establish the rule of the people. I hate your country and your government; yes, and I hate you. I aid you because I must pay my just debts. Come, the way is clear for your escape. Don't ask how I cleared it."

"Come on," said Dr. Bird with a shrug of his shoulders. "There is no arguing with convictions. She must act according to her lights, even as we must act according to ours. Grab your guns and let's go."

*   *   *   *   *

The three buckled on the weapons and belts of ammunition and followed the girl from the cell. Once outside she touched her lips for silence. A door barred their way but she opened it with a key which she withdrew from her dress. Outside the door, a guard slumbered noisily. At a motion from the girl, Carnes rolled him over on his face to quiet his snoring. He moved and stirred, but did not wake.

A few feet from the door the girl paused and faced the wall. She manipulated a hidden lever and a panel swung open in the wall. She led the way silently into the dark. As the panel closed behind her, a beam of light from an electric torch stabbed the darkness. Down a sloping tunnel they followed her for half a mile. The tunnel turned at right angles and led upward. At length they paused before another door. The girl opened it and they stepped out into the night. As they did so, a dull booming struck their ears. The girl paused.

"The ship!" she cried. "Your ship! It is attacking Fort Novadwinskaja. The factory will be awake in a moment! Run for your lives!"

Even as she spoke a pair of twinkling lights appeared far down the tunnel through which they had come. She turned as if to return down the tunnel. Dr. Bird caught her about the waist and clapped his hand over her mouth.

"Quick, Carnes, your belt," he cried. "Tie her up. She meant to go down that tunnel and give her life to delay them while we escaped. We'll save her in spite of herself."

Carnes and McCready quickly bound the struggling girl with their belts. They laid her on the ground beside the door and watched the oncoming lights.

"You two hold them back for the present," said the doctor. "I'm going to take Feodrovna away a bit and argue gently with her. If I can make her see the light, we may accomplish our mission yet. If I can't, I'll come back and help you."

*   *   *   *   *

He picked up the girl in his arms and disappeared into the darkness. Pistol in hand, the two men watched the oncoming lights. The men behind the lights could not be seen, but from the sound of their footsteps it was evident that there were quite a few of them.

"Had we better let them emerge from the door and then get them?" whispered Carnes.

"No. These heavy guns will drive a bullet through three men at short range. Level your gun down the tunnel and fire when I give the word. Remember, every one is apt to shoot high in the dark."

The lights approached slowly. When they were twenty-five yards away, Lieutenant McCready spoke. The quiet was shattered by the roar of two Luger pistols. Again and again the guns barked. A volley of fire came from the tunnel, but Carnes and the lieutenant were standing well away from the opening and they escaped unharmed. Their deadly fire poured into the shambles until they were rewarded by the sound of retreating feet.

"So ends round one," said Carnes with a laugh. "I think we win on points."

"They won't try a direct attack again," replied the lieutenant. "Look out for a flank attack or from some new weapon. I don't like the way those bombs failed to explode the other day."

Dr. Bird appeared from the darkness.

"McCready," he said in a voice vibrant with excitement, "we're in luck. We have come out less than a hundred yards from the point where our plane came down. It is still there. If the *Denver* has approached within shooting range, we will have enough gas to make it. Try to get your motor going."

"If it isn't completely washed out I'll have it going in a few minutes, Doctor," cried the pilot. "I'm going down the tunnel and get those flash-lights those birds dropped when they pulled out. Where's the girl?"

"She's back by the plane," said the doctor with a chuckle. "She is a spit-fire, all right. I took her gag off and she tried to bite me. I couldn't get a word of anything but abuse out of her. Go ahead and get the lights and I'll show you the plane."

*　　*　　*　　*　　*

In a few minutes they stood before the ship. It was apparently uninjured, but the spark was dead. Carnes went back to the tunnel mouth to guard against surprise while Dr. Bird and McCready labored over the motor. Despite the best of both of them, no spark could be coaxed from the coil. As a last resort, Dr. Bird short-circuited the cells with a screwdriver blade. No answering spark came from the terminals.

"Dead as a mackerel," he remarked. "I guess that ends that hope. Let's get the machine guns out of her. Well have another attack soon and they'll be more effective than our pistols."

It was the work of a few minutes to dismount the two Brownings from the plane. Carrying the two guns, Dr. Bird joined Carnes while McCready staggered along laden down with belts of ammunition.

"Do you remember that rocky knoll we passed just before we landed?" asked the lieutenant. "If we can get this stuff there before we are attacked, we'll have a much better chance than we will in the open."

"Good idea, Lieutenant. Carnes, connect yourself to one of these guns. I'll fasten the other on my back and carry Feodrovna. We can't leave her here to Saranoff's tender mercies."

Through the night the little cavalcade made its way. The thunder of guns from Fort Novadwinskaja kept up and the sky to the north was lighted by their flashes. McCready's bump of direction proved to be a good one for the sought-for retreat was soon located. As they deposited their burdens and looked back, the lights of two trucks could be seen approaching across the plain from the factory. Hurriedly they mounted the machine gun. Dr. Bird straightened up and listened carefully.

"The guns are sounding less frequently," he said. "Possibly the *Denver* has had enough and is pulling out."

"If I know Captain Evans as well as I think I do, the *Denver* is not retreating," replied McCready grimly.

"I hope she's hammering the fort out of existence," said the doctor. "However, our main interest just now is on the land front. Gunners to the fore. Carnes, you aren't so good at this, better let McCready and me handle them."

* * * * *

The trucks approached slowly. Presently the American plane loomed up in the glare of their headlights. A powerful searchlight mounted on the leading truck swept the country. Discovery was a matter of moments. Lieutenant McCready trained his gun carefully and pressed the trigger. A rattle of fire came from the Browning. A crash was heard from the truck and the searchlight winked out.

"Bull's-eye!" cried Carnes exultantly.

"Down, you fool!" cried the doctor as he swept the detective from his feet and threw him down behind a rock. His action was none too soon. A burst of machine gun fire came from the trucks and a hail of bullets splattered on the rocks a few yards from them. McCready crawled back to his gun.

"Wait a minute, Lieutenant," counseled the doctor. "A burst of fire from here will give them our location and probably do them little damage. Wait until they try to rush us."

They did not have long to wait. A guttural shout came from a point a few yards away and the sound of running feet came to their ears. The rush was directed toward a point a few yards to the left of where they crouched. Dr. Bird swung his gun around. As the rush passed them, he released his trigger. A volley of screams and oaths from the plain answered the crackle of the Browning. McCready's gun joined in with a staccato burst of fire. The attack could not live before that rain of death. A few running feet were heard from the darkness and a few groans. Presently the roar of a motor came from the direction of the parked trucks. It retreated into the distance and all was quiet.

"Round two goes to us on a knock-down," said Carnes jubilantly. "What will they do next, Doctor?"

"Probably nothing until daylight, now that they know we have machine guns. I wish that we could make that thicket, but it's too far to try. It'll be daylight in an hour or so."

The night was normally short in Archangel at that season of the year and the unnatural lengthening of the day which Saranoff had accomplished made it shorter still. In an hour red streamers in the east announced the approach of daylight. Hardly had they appeared than a dull drone of truck motors came from the direction of the factory.

"Round three is about to commence," announced Carnes. "I wish that I could do something."

"You can as soon as our ammunition runs out, which won't be long," replied McCready. "It will be a matter of pistols at close quarters."

*   *   *   *   *

The trucks approached to within a half mile and stopped. The distance was too great to warrant wasting any of their scanty store of ammunition at such long range. In the dim light they would see the Russians working at the trucks. Presently a flash came from the plain. A whining sound filled the air. With a crash a three-inch shell broke behind them.

"No fun," remarked the doctor. "We'll have to get better cover than this."

A second shell whined through the air and burst over their heads. A third burst a few yards in front of them.

"They have us bracketed now," said McCready. "We'd better slide back a piece before they start rapid fire."

Dragging their prisoner with them, the three men made their way to the reverse side of the knoll. A short search revealed an overhanging ledge under which they crouched in comparative safety from anything but a direct hit above them.

"We're all right here except for the fact that they may rush us under cover of the fire," said the doctor. "One man will have to keep watch all the time and it will be a dangerous detail. I'll take the first hitch."

"You will not!" exclaimed Carnes emphatically. "I have done nothing so far and I am the least important member of the party. I'll do the watching."

"Let's draw straws," suggested McCready. "I'm willing to do that, but if it's a matter of volunteering, I refuse to yield to the civilian branches of the government. The Navy has traditions to uphold, you know."

"McCready's right," replied the doctor. "Get straws, Lieutenant, and we'll draw."

McCready picked up three bits of grass and held them out.

"The shortest goes on watch," he said. Carnes and the doctor drew, McCready exhibited the remaining bit of grass. It was the shortest of the three. He waited until the next shell burst above them and then stepped out from the shelter.

"I'll relieve you in fifteen minutes," said Carnes as he left.

"Right."

*   *   *   *   *

When the lieutenant had left, Dr. Bird removed the gag from Feodrovna's mouth and tried to argue with her, but the Russian girl only glared her hatred and refused to talk other than to abuse him. With a sigh, the doctor gave over his efforts and talked to Carnes. The time passed slowly with a constant rain of shells on the knoll.

"It's time for my relief," said Carnes at length. As he spoke the hail of shells on the knoll ceased.

"What the dickens?" cried the doctor.

He and Carnes jumped from their shelter and ran over the knoll. On the plain a few hundred yards from them, a straggling line of Russians were advancing with fixed bayonets. McCready was nowhere in sight.

"Where the devil is McCready?" cried the doctor. "He must have been killed. Hello, one of the guns is gone, too. There's only a belt and a half of ammunition left. I'll try to break that attack up."

He advanced to the gun and trained it carefully. When he pressed the trigger a dull click came from the gun.

"Misfire!" he cried. He drew back the bolt and inserted a fresh cartridge. Again the gun clicked harmlessly. Dr. Bird ejected the shell and examined it. A deep indentation appeared on the primer. Hurriedly he tried a half dozen more cartridges but they refused to explode. He turned a keen gaze toward the trucks. On the ground was set a tube-like projector pointing toward them. Dr. Bird swore softly and jerked his pistol from its holster. The hammer clicked futilely on a cartridge.

"Stymied!" he exclaimed. "They have that portable ray mechanism, with them, which disabled our bombs. It's hand to hand, Carnesy, old dear. I wonder where McCready is."

*　　*　　*　　*　　*

The Russians approached slowly, keeping their lines straight. They were within two hundred yards of the knoll. Suddenly from a point a hundred yards to the left of the end of the land came a rattle of fire. The attacking line dropped in a pile of grotesque heaps.

"It's McCready!" shouted Carnes. A little ravine ran from the knoll toward the trucks. Sitting in the ravine was the lieutenant, playing a Browning machine gun on the line of attackers. When there were no more of them on their feet, he turned his gun on the trucks. Panic seized the Russians and they made a rush for their truck.

Their leader leaped among them, yelling furiously. They paused and turned to the projector tube. Slowly they swung it around. The lieutenant's gun ceased firing.

As the Russians rushed the now silent gun, Dr. Bird stepped to the gun on the knoll. He trained it and pressed the trigger. A rattle of fire came from it and two of the rushing figures fell. The attack paused for an instant. McCready had risen to his feet and was running up the ravine with his gun under his arm.

"Good head!" cried Dr. Bird, "Clever work! Watch the fun now."

He ceased firing his gun. The Russians wavered and then rushed the point from which McCready had fired. The lieutenant allowed them to get to within a short distance and then crumpled the attack with another burst of fire from the flank. With cries of alarm, the Russians turned and fled toward their trucks. McCready ran along the ravine until he was within fifty yards of the standing machines. As the Russians approached, one of them stepped to the truck crank. McCready's pistol spoke and he dropped. A second shared his fate. With cries of despair, the Russians climbed into the remaining truck whose motor was running. Rapidly it drove away across the plain. McCready rose from the ravine and ran toward the standing truck. He started the motor and headed for the knoll.

"He's got a truck," cried Carnes. "We can get away in it."

"Where to?" demanded Dr. Bird. "Archangel is between us and the *Denver*."

The truck came up.

"Come on, Doctor," cried McCready. "Hurry up. We'll take the battery out of this truck and get our plane going."

"Oh, clever!" cried Dr. Bird admiringly. "Load that gun while I get Feodrovna, Carnesy. We'll get away safely yet."

*   *   *   *   *

The truck rolled up to the plane and stopped. While Carnes transferred the prisoner and the guns to the plane, the lieutenant and Dr. Bird ripped up the floor boards of the truck and exposed the battery. It was a matter of moments to detach it and carry it to the plane. It would not fit in place but they anchored it in place with wire.

"You'd better hurry," cried Carnes. "Here come a couple more trucks over the plain."

"That'll do, Doctor," said McCready. "Get on the prop and we'll see if the old puddle jumper will take off."

Dr. Bird ran to the propeller.

"Ready!" he cried.

"Contact!" snapped McCready.

The plane motor roared into life. The ship moved slowly forward as Dr. Bird climbed on board. Toward the oncoming trucks they rushed across the plain. A crash seemed imminent. In the nick of time McCready pulled back on his joystick and the plane rose gracefully into the air, clearing the leading truck by inches. The truck halted and hastily mounted a machine gun.

"Too late!" laughed the lieutenant. "Now it's our turn for some fun."

He tapped the key of his radio transmitter. In a few seconds he received an answer.

"They have reduced Fort Novadwinskaja," he reported to the rear cockpit, "but they don't know what to fire at next. Their largest guns will reach the factory easily. Shall I start some fireworks?"

"You may fire when ready, Gridly," chuckled Dr. Bird.

Again the lieutenant depressed his key. From their altitude of four thousand feet, they could see the *Denver*. From its forward turret came a puff of smoke. There were a few moments of pause and then a cloud of black rose from the plain below them, half a mile from the factory. McCready reported the position of the burst to the ship. A second shell burst beyond the factory and the third just in front of it.

"It's a clear bracket," said McCready. "Now watch the gun. I'll give them a salvo."

*　　*　　*　　*　　*

From the side of the *Denver* came a cloud of black smoke as all of her turret guns fired in unison. The aim was perfect. For a few moments all was quiet and then the factory disappeared in a smother of bursting high explosive shells.

Hardly had the shells landed than a terrific sheet of lightning ripped across the sky. The thunderclap which seemed to come simultaneously, rocked the plane like a feather. Sheet after sheet of lightning illuminated the sky while the roar of thunder was continuous. Rain fell in solid sheets. Even as they watched, it began to turn into snow. The air grew bitterly cold.

"The solar magnet is wrecked," shouted the doctor, "and these storms are the efforts of nature to return to normal."

"If they get any worse, we're doomed."

"But in a good cause."

Through the storm the plane raced. Suddenly the motor died with sickening suddenness.

"Our haywire battery connections are gone," shouted McCready. "Say your prayers."

The wind tossed the plane about like a feather. Rapidly it lost altitude. A building loomed up before them. As a crash seemed imminent, a gust of wind caught the plane and tossed it up into the air again. For several minutes the ground could not be seen through the rain. Suddenly the plane hit an airpocket and dropped like a stone. With a splash it fell into the sea. A rift came for a moment in the curtain of rain.

"Look!" cried Carnes.

A hundred yards away, the *Denver* rode at anchor.

"I'm only sorry about one thing," said Carnes ten minutes later as they changed to dry clothes aboard the battle cruiser, "and that is that Saranoff wasn't in the factory when that salvo fell on it."

"I'm glad he was away," replied Dr. Bird. "With him absent, we succeeded in destroying it. If he had been there, our task would have been more difficult and perhaps impossible. I am an enemy of Saranoff's, but I don't underrate his colossal genius." his entrance into the country for a little while."

Poisoned Air

Originally Published In *Astounding Stories Of Super-Science*, March 1932

*Again Dr. Bird closes with the evil Saranoff—
this time near the Aberdeen Proving Ground,
in a deadly, mysterious blanket of fog.*

POISONED AIR

A telephone bell jangled insistently. The orderly on duty dropped his feet from the desk to the floor and lifted the receiver with a muttered curse.

"Post hospital, Aberdeen Proving Ground," he said sleepily, rubbing his eyes.

A burst of raucous coughing answered him. Several times it ceased for an instant and a voice tried to speak, but each time a fresh spasm of deep-chested wracking coughing interrupted.

"Who is this?" demanded the now aroused orderly. "What's the matter?"

Between intervals of coughing difficultly enunciated words reached him.

"This is—*uch! uch!*—Lieutenant Burroughs at the—*uch!*—Michaelville range. We have been—*uch!*—caught in a cloud of poison—*uch! uch!*—gas. Send an ambulance and a—*uch!*—surgeon at once. Better bring—*uch!*—gas masks."

"At the Michaelville range, sir? How many men are down there?"

"*Uch! uch! uch!*—five—all help—*uch! uch!*—helpless. Hurry!"

"Yes, sir. I'll start two ambulances down at once, sir."

"Don't forget the—*uch! uch!*—gas—*uch!*—masks."

"No, sir; I'll send them, sir."

* * * * *

Five minutes later two ambulances rolled out of the garage and took the four-mile winding ribbon of concrete which separated the Michaelville water impact range from the main front of the Aberdeen Proving Ground. On each ambulance was a hastily awakened and partially clothed medical officer. For three miles they tore along the curving road at high speed. Without warning the leading machine slowed down. The driver of the second ambulance shoved home his brake just in time to keep from ramming the leading vehicle.

"What's the matter?" he shouted.

As he spoke he gave a muttered curse and switched on his amber fog-light. From the marshes on either side of the road a deep blanket of fog rolled up and enveloped the vehicle, almost shutting off the road from sight. The forward ambulance began to grope its way slowly forward. The senior medical officer sniffed the fog critically and shouted to his driver.

"Stop!" he cried. "There's something funny about this fog. Every one put on gas masks."

He coughed slightly as he adjusted his mask. His orders were shouted to the ambulance in the rear but before the masks could be adjusted, every member of the crew was vying with the rest in the frequency and violence of the coughs which he could emit. The masks did not seem to shut out the poisonous fog which crept in between the masks and the men's faces and seemed to take bodily possession of their lungs.

"I don't believe we'll ever make the last mile to Michaelville through this, Major," cried the driver between intervals of coughing. "Hadn't we better turn back while we can?"

"Drive on!" cried the medical officer. "We'll keep going as long as we can. Imagine what those poor devils on the range are going through without masks of any sort."

*   *   *   *   *

On through the rapidly thickening fog, the two ambulances groped their way. The road seemed interminable, but at length the flood lights of the Michaelville end of the range came dimly into view. As the vehicles stopped the two surgeons jumped to the ground and groped their way forward, stretcher bearers following them closely. Presently Major Martin stumbled over a body which lay at full length on the concrete runway between the two main buildings. He stooped and examined the man with the aid of a pocket flashlight.

"He's alive," he announced in muffled tones through his mask. "Take him to the ambulance and fit a mask on him."

Three more unconscious men were carried to the ambulances before the prone form of Lieutenant Burroughs was found by the searchers. The lieutenant lay on his back not far from the telephone and directly under the glare of a huge arc-light. His eyes were open and he was conscious, but when he tried to speak, only a murmur came from his lips. There was a rattle in his chest and faint coughs tried in vain to force their way out between his stiffened lips.

"Easy, Lieutenant," said Major Martin as he bent over him; "don't try to talk just now. You're all right and we'll have a mask on you in a jiffy. That damned gas isn't as thick right here as it is down the road a way."

Two medical corps men lifted the lieutenant onto a stretcher and started to fit a mask over his face. He feebly raised a hand to stop them. His lips formed words which he could not enunciate, but Major Martin understood them.

"Your men?" he said between intervals of coughing. "We've got them all in the ambulance, I think. There were four besides yourself, weren't there?"

The lieutenant nodded.

"Right. We have them all. Now we'll take you back to the hospital and have you fixed up in a jiffy."

*   *   *   *   *

The entire rescue crew were coughing violently as the ambulances left Michaelville. For a mile they drove through fog that was thicker than had been seen in Maryland for years. They reached the point where they had encountered the congealed moisture on the way out, but now there was no diminution of its density. The main post was less than two miles away when they burst out into a clear night and increased their speed.

As the two machines drew up in front of the post hospital, the driver of the leading ambulance swayed in his seat. Blindly he pulled on his emergency brake and then slumped forward in his seat, his breath coming in wheezing gasps. Major Martin hastily tore the mask from his face and glanced at it.

"Take him in with the rest!" he cried. "His mask must have leaked."

As they entered the hospital, a sickening weakness overcame Major Martin. From all sides a black pall seemed to roll in on him and bits of ice seemed to form in his brain. He reeled and caught at the shoulder of a corps man who was passing. The orderly caught at him and looked for a moment at his livid face.

"Sergeant Connors!" he cried.

A technical sergeant hastened up. Major Martin forced words with difficulty through stiffening lips.

"Call Captain Murdock," he wheezed, "and have him get Captain Williams. I'm down and probably Dr. Briscoe will be down in a few minutes. Telephone the commanding officer and tell him to quarantine the whole proving ground. Have the telephone orderly wake everyone on the post and order them to close all windows in all buildings and not to venture outside until they get fresh orders. This seems to be the same stuff they had in Belgium last December."

As the last words came from his lips he slowly stiffened and slumped toward the ground. The sergeant and the orderly picked him up and carried him to a bed in the emergency ward. The orderly hurried away to close all of the hospital windows while Sergeant Connors took down the receiver of the telephone and began to carry out the Major's orders.

*   *   *   *   *

Dr. Bird glanced at the news-paper clipping which Operative Carnes of the United States Secret Service laid on his desk. Into his eyes came a curious glitter, sure evidence that the famous scientist's interest was aroused.

"Last December when we discussed this matter, Doctor," said the detective, "you gave it as your opinion that Ivan Saranoff was at the bottom of it and that the same plague which devastated the Meuse Valley in Belgium would eventually make an appearance in the United States. You were right."

Dr. Bird bounded to his feet.

"Is Saranoff back on this side of the Atlantic?" he demanded.

"Officially, he is not. Every customs inspector and immigration officer has his photograph and no report of his arrest has come in, but we know Saranoff well enough to discount negative evidence where he is concerned. Whether he is here or not, the plague is."

"When did it appear?"

"Last night at the Aberdeen Proving Ground in Maryland. It has killed eight or ten and twice as many more are sick. The place is quarantined and a rigid censorship has been placed over the telephones, but it is only a matter of time before some press man will get the story. I have a car waiting below and a pass signed by the Secretary of War. Grab what apparatus you need and we'll start."

Dr. Bird pressed a button on his desk. A tall, willowy girl entered, notebook in hand. Carnes glanced with keen appreciation at her slim beauty.

"Miss Andrews," said the doctor, "in five minutes Mr. Carnes and I will leave here for Aberdeen Proving Ground in the Government car which is waiting below. You will see that Mr. Davis is in that car and that traveling laboratory 'Q' is ready to follow us."

"Yes, Doctor."

"You remember that mysterious plague in Belgium last December, do you not?"

"Yes, Doctor."

"I was unable to get over to Belgium, but an army surgeon and two Public Health Service men went over. You will get copies of all reports they made, including especially any reports of autopsies on bodies of victims. I want all data on file in the Public Health Service or the War Department. You will then obtain a car and follow us to Aberdeen. Arrangements will be made for your admittance to the proving ground. The Belgian plague has made its appearance in the United States."

*   *   *   *   *

Swiftly the expression of the girl's face changed. Her dark eyes glowed with an internal fire and the immobility of her face vanished as if by magic to be replaced by an expression of fierce hatred. Her lips drew back, exposing her strong white teeth and she literally spat out her words.

"That swine, Saranoff!" she hissed.

Carnes sprang to his feet.

"Why, it's Feodrovna Androvitch!" he cried in astonishment.

In an instant the rage faded from her face and the calm, immobility which had marked it reappeared. Through the silence Dr. Bird's voice cut like a whip.

"Miss Andrews," he said sternly, "I thought that I had impressed on you the fact that even a momentary lapse from the character which you have assumed may easily be fatal to both of us. Unless you can learn to control your emotions, your usefulness to me is at an end."

Although Carnes watched closely he could not detect the slightest change of expression in the girl's face as the doctor spoke.

"I am very sorry, Doctor," she said evenly. "We were alone and I allowed the mask to slip for an instant. It will not happen again."

"It *must* not," said the doctor curtly. "Carry out your instructions."

"Yes, Doctor."

She turned on her heel and left the office. Carnes looked quickly at Dr. Bird.

"Surely that is Feodrovna Androvitch, Doctor?" he asked.

"It was. It is now Thelma Andrews, my secretary. She changed her name with her appearance and politics. I have been training her since last August. This is her first official appearance, so to speak."

"In view of her past associations, is it safe to trust her?"

"If I didn't think so, I wouldn't use her. She has ample reason to hate Ivan Saranoff and she knows how much mercy she has to hope for from him if he ever gets her in his clutches. We can't play a lone hand against Saranoff forever and I know of no better place to recruit an organization than the enemy's camp. Thelma saved our lives in Russia, you may remember."

"But even when she was rescuing us from the clutches of Saranoff's gang, she was an ardent communist, if I remember correctly."

"Theoretically I believe she still favors the world revolution, but she hates Saranoff even more than she does the bourgeoisie and I believe she had come to be willing to accept capitalistic institutions for the present, at least as far as this country is concerned. At any rate, I trust her. If you have any doubts, you can have her watched for a while."

*   *   *   *   *

Carnes thought for a moment and then picked up the telephone.

"I have plenty of confidence in your judgment, Doctor," he said apologetically, "but if you don't mind, I'll have Haggerty trail her for a few days. It won't do any harm."

"Very well; and if any of the Young Labor gang should penetrate her disguise, he'd be a mighty efficient bodyguard. Do as you see fit."

Carnes called the number of the secret service and conferred for a few moments with Bolton, the chief of the bureau. He turned to Dr. Bird with a smile of satisfaction.

"Haggerty will be on the job in a few minutes, Doctor."

"Good enough. The five minutes I allowed are up. Let's see how well she has performed her first task."

As they emerged from the Bureau of Standards, Carnes glanced rapidly around. In the front seat of the secret service car which he had left sat a young man whom the detective recognized as one of Dr. Bird's assistants. Behind the car stood a small delivery truck with two of the Bureau mechanics on the seat.

Dr. Bird nodded to the mechanics and followed Carnes into the big sedan. With a motorcycle policeman clearing a way for them, they roared across Washington and north along the Baltimore pike. Two hours and a half of driving brought them to Aberdeen and they turned down the concrete road leading to the proving ground. Two miles from the town a huge chain was stretched across the road with armed guards patrolling behind it. The car stopped and an officer stepped forward and examined the pass which Carnes presented.

"You are to go direct to headquarters, gentlemen," he said. "Colonel Wesley is waiting for you."

The commanding officer rose to his feet as Carnes and Dr. Bird entered his office.

"I am at your service, Dr. Bird," he said formally. "The Chief of Ordnance has given instructions which, as I understand them, put you virtually in command of this post." There was resentment in the colonel's tone.

* * * * *

Dr. Bird smiled affably and extended his hand. The old colonel struggled with his chagrin for a moment, but few men could resist Dr. Bird when he deliberately tried to charm them. Colonel Wesley grasped the proffered hand.

"What I want most, Colonel, is your cooperation," said the doctor suavely. "I am not competent to assume command here even if I wished to. I would like to ask a few favors but if they should prove to be contrary to your established policies, I will gladly withdraw my request."

Colonel Wesley's face cleared as if by magic.

"You have only to ask for anything we have, Doctor," he said earnestly, "and it is yours. Frankly, we are at our wit's end."

"Thank you. I have a truck with some apparatus and three men outside. Will you have them guided to your laboratory and given what aid they need in setting their stuff up?"

"Gladly."

"My secretary, Miss Andrews, will arrive from Washington later in the day with some information. I would like to have her passed through the guards and brought directly to me wherever I am. You have the place well guarded, have you not?"

"As well as I can with my small force. All roads are patrolled by motorcycles; four launches are on the waterfront, and there are seven planes aloft."

"That is splendid. Now can you tell me just what happened last night?"

"Captain Murdock, the acting surgeon, can do that better than I can, Doctor. He is at the hospital but I'll have him up here in a few minutes."

"With your permission, we'll go to the hospital and talk to him there. I want to examine the patients in any event."

"Certainly, Doctor. I will remain at my office until I am sure that I can give you no further assistance."

*　　*　　*　　*　　*

With a word of thanks, Dr. Bird left, and, accompanied by Carnes, made his way to the hospital. Captain Murdock was frankly relieved to greet the famous Bureau of Standards scientist and readily gave him the information he desired.

"The first intimation we had of trouble was when Lieutenant Burroughs telephoned from the water impact range where they were doing night firing last night at about four A.M. Two ambulances went down and brought him and his four men back, all of them stricken with what I take to be an extremely rapidly developing form of lobar pneumonia. All of the men who went down were stricken with the same disease, two of them as soon as they got back. So far we have had eight deaths among these men and all of the rest, except Lieutenant Burroughs, are apt to go at any moment.

"The trouble seemed to come from a cloud of some dense heavy gas which rolled in from the marsh. On the advice of Major Martin, every door and window in the post was kept closed until morning. The gas never reached the upper part of the post but it reached the stables. Eleven horses and mules are dead and all of the rest are stricken. The stable detachment either failed to close their barracks tightly or else the gas went in through cracks for seven out of the nine are here in the hospital, although none of them are very seriously ill. As soon as the sun came up, the gas seemed to disappear."

"Let me see the men who are sick."

Captain Murdock led the way into the ward. Dr. Bird went from man to man, examining charts and asking questions of the nurses and medical corps men on duty. When he had gone the rounds of the ward he entered the morgue and carefully examined the bodies of the men who lay there.

"Have you performed any autopsies?" he asked.

"Not yet."

"Have you the authority?"

"On the approval of the commanding officer."

"Please secure that approval at once. Have all lights taken out of the operating room and the windows shaded. I want to work under red light. We must examine the lungs of these men at once. With all due respect to your medical knowledge, Captain, I am not convinced that these men died of pneumonia."

"Neither am I, Doctor, but that is the best guess I could make. I'll have things fixed up for you right away."

*   *   *   *   *

Dr. Bird stepped to the telephone and called the laboratory. When, in half an hour, Captain Murdock announced that he was ready to proceed, Davis had arrived with an ultra-microscope and other apparatus which the doctor had telephoned for.

"Did you arrange about the horses, Davis?" asked Dr. Bird.

"Yes, sir. They will be up here as soon as the trucks can bring them."

"Good enough. We'll start operating."

An hour later, Dr. Bird straightened up and faced the puzzled medical officer.

"Captain," he said, "your diagnosis is faulty. With one possible exception, the lungs of these men are free from pneumonicocci. On the other hand there is a peculiar aspect of the tissues as though a very powerful antiseptic solution had been applied to them."

"Hardly an antiseptic, Doctor; wouldn't you say, rather, a cauterizing agent."

Dr. Bird bent again over the ultra-microscope.

"Are you familiar with the work done by Bancroft and Richter at Cornell University last November and December?" he asked.

"No, I can't say that I am."

"They were working under a Heckscher Foundation grant studying just how antiseptic solutions destroy bacteria. It has always been held that some chemical change went on, but this theory they disproved. It is a process of absorption. If enough of the chemical adheres to the living bacterium, the living protoplasm thickens and irreversibly coagulates. It resembles a boiling without heat. I have seen some of their slides and the appearance is exactly what I see in this tissue."

Captain Murdock bent over the microscope with a new respect for Dr. Bird in his face.

"I agree with you, Doctor," he said. "This tissue certainly looks as though it had been boiled. It is certainly coagulated, as I can plainly see now that you point it out to me. You believe, then, that it is a simple case of gassing?"

"If so, it was done by no known gas. I have studied at Edgewood Arsenal, and I am familiar with all of the work done by the Chemical Warfare Service in gases. No known gas will produce exactly this appearance. It is something new. Carnes, have those horses been brought up yet?"

"I'll see, Doctor."

"If they are, bring one here."

*   *   *   *   *

In a few moments the body of a dead horse was dragged into the operating room and Dr. Bird attacked it with a rib saw. He soon laid the lungs open and dragged them from the body. He cut down the middle of one of the organs and shaved off a thin slice which he placed under the lens of a powerful binocular microscope.

"Hello, what the dickens is this?" he exclaimed.

With a scalpel and a delicate pair of tweezers he carefully separated from the lung tissue a tiny speck of crystalline substance which glittered under the red light in the operating room. He carefully transferred it to a glass slide and put it under a microscope with a higher magnification.

"Rhombohedral regular," he mused as he examined it. "Colorless, friable, and cleaving in irregular planes. What in thunder can it be? Have you ever seen anything like this in a lung, Murdock?"

The medical officer bent over the microscope for a long time before he shook his head with a puzzled air.

"I never have," he admitted.

"Then that's probably what we're looking for. Start slicing every lung in this place and look for those crystals. Save them and put them in this watch glass. If we can get enough of them, we may be able to learn something. Carnes, get the rest of those horses in here and open them up."

Two hours of careful work netted them a tiny pile of the peculiar crystals. Some had come from the lungs of the dead animals and some few from the lungs of the dead soldiers. Dr. Bird placed the crystals in a glass bottle which he covered with layer after layer of black paper.

"Get me more of those crystals if you can find them, Captain Murdock," he said, "and in any case, leave the bodies here for further study. Davis and I will go to the laboratory and try to find out what they are. Carnes, hasn't Miss Andrews showed up yet?"

"No, Doctor."

"Locate her on the telephone if you can and tell her not to bother about anything except the autopsy reports and to get them here as quickly as possible. Let me know when you have that done."

* * * * *

In a dark room of the photographic laboratory, Dr. Bird removed the black wrappings from the bottle. He dropped a few of the crystals in a test tube and added distilled water. The water assumed a pink tinge as the blood with which the crystals were covered dissolved, but the crystals themselves did not change. They rose and floated on the surface of the water.

"Insoluble in water, Davis," commented the doctor. "Better wash the lot and then we'll get after the ultimate analysis. Whether we'll be able to make a proximate is doubtful in view of the small amount of sample we have. It's dollars to doughnuts that it's some carbon compound."

He heated a few of the washed crystals in a watch glass. Suddenly there was a sharp crack and the material disappeared. Dr. Bird thrust his nose toward the glass and sniffed carefully.

"The dickens!" he muttered. "Davis, have I got a cold or do you smell garlic?"

"Faintly, Doctor."

"I have a hunch. Fill a gasometer with purified argon and we'll introduce a few of these crystals and explode them. If I'm right–"

Half an hour later he straightened up and examined the tube of the gas analysis apparatus with which he was working. The level of the gas showed it to be of the original volume but the liquid under the argon was stained a light brown.

"It's impossible, Davis," cried the doctor, "but nevertheless, it's true. Expose some of those crystals to strong sunlight and see what happens."

The crystals rapidly disappeared as the light from a sun-ray arc fell on them.

"It's true, Davis," cried the doctor, positive awe in his voice. "Keep this strictly under your hat for the present. Now that you know what we're up against, fix up a couple of masks and air-collecting apparatus. That stuff will show up again in the swamp to-night and I am going down there to collect some samples. I'll telephone the hospital now."

*   *   *   *   *

As Dr. Bird emerged from the dark room, Carnes hurried up with a worried expression.

"The devil's to pay, Doctor," was his greeting.

"All right, stall him off for a minute while I telephone the hospital. I think I can save some of those poor fellows up there."

Carnes paced the floor in anxiety while Dr. Bird got Captain Murdock on the telephone.

"Bird talking, Murdock," he said crisply. "How much deep therapy X-ray apparatus have you got up there?... Too bad.... Well, at least you can give every patient a four-minute dose of maximum intensity and repeat in an hour or so. Keep them under sun-ray arcs as much as you can. Be ready for a fresh attack of the same epidemic to-night. As fast as the patients come in, give them a five-minute dose of X-rays and then sun-rays. Do you understand?... All right, then."

"Just a moment more, Carnes," he went on as he called the office of the commanding officer. "Colonel Wesley, this is Dr. Bird. I think that I have some light on your problem. You must anticipate another more virulent attack than you had last night, probably as soon as the sun goes down. Will you arrange to have everyone removed from the swamp area before that time? Never mind trying to guard the place; you'll just lose more lives if you do. Warn everyone to keep inside the buildings with all doors and windows closed tight. Get all the women and children and everyone else who isn't needed here off the post before dark. Send them to Aberdeen or Baltimore or anywhere.... No, sir, the sick had better not be moved. I think they will be safer in the hospital than they would be elsewhere.... Yes, sir, that's all. Thank you."

*   *   *   *   *

Dr. Bird turned to the waiting Carnes.

"Did you locate Miss Andrews?" he asked.

"No, I didn't and that is what I want to talk to you about. I just started to telephone when a hurry call came through from Washington for me and I took it. It was Haggerty on the wire. He followed your precious secretary from the Bureau of Standards over to the Public Health Office and waited for her to come out. She stayed in the building for about an hour and brought a bundle of papers with her when she returned. She walked toward the State, War and Navy Building and Haggerty followed.

"On Pennsylvania Avenue, she was stopped by two men whom Haggerty describes as dark, swarthy, bearded Europeans of some sort. He tried to overhear their conversation but it was in a language which he did not recognize. He got only one word. The girl called one of them 'Denberg.'"

"Denberg!" cried the doctor, "Why, he's one of the Young Labor crowd, but he's in Atlanta."

"He was, Doctor, but I telephoned Atlanta, and found that he had been released last month. After several minutes of talk the two men and your secretary went off together in perfect amity with Haggerty following. The trio got into a waiting car and Haggerty trailed them in a taxi. They drove around town rather aimlessly for some time and then left the car and walked. Haggerty was afraid he would lose them in the crowd so he closed in on them. He doesn't know what happened except that he felt a sudden stab in his arm and everything went black. He recovered in the police station twenty minutes later but the birds had flown."

"The devil!" cried Dr. Bird, consternation in his voice. "Of course, it's easy to see what happened. They spotted him and a confederate slipped a hypo into his arm. What worries me is the fact that they've got Thelma."

*   *   *   *   *

"I hope they kill her," snapped Carnes vindictively. "She was never kidnapped in broad daylight. Haggerty says she went with them quite willingly and talked and laughed with them. She has deserted, if she wasn't simply acting as a spy from the first. I didn't trust her at all."

"I hate to admit that my judgment is that rotten, Carnes, but the evidence certainly points that way. At that, I think I'll reserve final judgment until later. Now, in view of what you have learned, I have a job for you."

"It's about time, Doctor. I have been rather useless with all the high-powered science that has been flying around here."

"Well, you'll be in your element now. We know that Denberg is loose and their capture of Thelma is no coincidence. I was pretty sure that Saranoff and his gang were at the bottom of this; now I am certain. They must have introduced something onto the marshes last night which caused the trouble. They could not have come overland very well, for the place is too well patrolled. Had they come by air, they would have attracted attention, even had they used a Bird silencer on their motor, for they couldn't muffle their propeller, especially on a takeoff, and there are plenty of men here who would have recognized it. You might check up on that, but I am confident that they came by water. Launches and boats are continually passing up and down the Chesapeake and its tributaries and one more could easily have escaped

notice. The Bush River is at the far end of the
Michaelville range and it is navigable for craft of light
draft at high tide. Find out whether any strange craft
were seen in the vicinity of the proving ground last night.
If you draw a blank, go to Perryville and Havre de Grace
and see what you can find out there. I have a hunch that
their base is more likely to be up the Susquehanna than
down toward the coast. Above all, Carnes, don't approach
the proving ground by water to-night and don't get near
the mouth of the Bush River."

"All right, Doctor. What are you going to do?"

"I'm going down on the swamp and collect samples.
Oh, don't look so worried. I know just what I am up
against and I will have adequate protection. I'll be in no
danger and you would just be in the way. Toddle along,
old dear, and report to me by telephone as soon as you
have learned anything."

"As you say, Doctor. You'll hear from me the minute I
do."

*   *   *   *   *

When Carnes had left, Dr. Bird climbed into the
waiting car and was driven back to the hospital. Captain
Murdock greeted him with a smiling face.

"I don't know how you got on to that treatment, Dr.
Bird," he said, "but it is doing the men good. The worst
cases haven't been affected much, one way or the other,
but the progress of the malady in the mild cases from the
stables has been completely checked. I think they have a
chance now."

"They'll be all right if the destruction and coagulation
of tissue hadn't progressed too far before you checked it,
Captain. Treat them now for simple lung cauterization
and they ought to get well."

"I have some more of those crystals dissected out,
Doctor."

"Keep them in the dark until Mr. Davis comes after them. I want to take a few of them back to Washington for study."

"You expect another attack to-night, Doctor?"

"Yes, sometime after sundown."

"What, in heaven's name, is it?"

"Heaven has nothing to do with it, Captain; the stuff comes from the devil's regions and it is the product of a Russian chemist, who I sometimes believe is verily the devil himself. How it's done and what it is, I haven't found out yet, but I am going to investigate a little to-night. The effect is what you have seen. Are you familiar with the various forms of oxygen?"

"The forms of oxygen? Why, there is only one, oxygen gas. Wait a minute though, there is another form, ozone. Are there any more?"

"None that have been previously listed and studied, but at least one other form exists. Those crystals are pure oxygen."

"Impossible! Oxygen is a gas at all ordinary temperatures."

* * * * *

"Yes, a gas, but one whose density varies. Oxygen, to which we chemists assign the formula O{2}, *meaning that its molecule consists of two atoms of oxygen, has a weight of 32 grams per gram molecule. Ozone, to which we assign the formula* O{3}, meaning that its molecule contains three atoms of oxygen, weighs fifty per cent more or 48 grams per gram molecule. This new form has a density less than water, but tremendously greater than any known gas. I have not yet been able to determine its structure, so I will have to assign to it the formula, O{x}, meaning an indefinite number of atoms per molecule. The only name which suggests itself is oxyzone, a combination of oxygen and ozone.

"The stuff is a polymerization, or condensation, to speak roughly, of the oxygen of the air. The oxygen takes this form which the lungs cannot assimilate except with great difficulty and with great damage to the tissues. The oxyzone will break down rapidly under the influence of sunlight or of any ray whose wave-length is shorter than indigo. As a result, it disappears as soon as the sun is up and it will reappear after dark. That is why I suggested X-rays as a treatment. They have a very short wave-length and will penetrate tissues and affect the particles in the lungs themselves. Once the material is removed from the lungs, the cauterization of the tissue ceases and it is merely a matter of slow recovery."

"It is a marvelous discovery, Doctor. I can foresee great uses for it in medical science if a way can be found to produce it."

"Just now we are much more interested in stopping its production than in producing it. Carry on with the line of treatment I have prescribed and be ready for a busy time to-night."

*   *   *   *   *

From the hospital, Dr. Bird made his way to the headquarters building where he conferred with Colonel Wesley on the measures being taken to clear the proving ground of all persons not strictly necessary for its guarding. The commanding officer, when he learned Dr. Bird's plans, wished to send guards with him, but the doctor promptly vetoed the scheme.

"My assistant, Mr. Davis, won't be able to fix up more than two masks before dark, Colonel," he said, "and you would just be condemning men to death to send them with me into that fog without proper protection. I can see that you are anxious to know what is causing it, but I'm not ready to tell just yet. I had given your medical officer enough information to enable him to treat the hospital cases scientifically, and to-morrow or the next day I hope to be able to tell you all about it. Now, if you'll pardon me, I'm going to the laboratory to see how Mr. Davis is getting along. It will be dark in three-quarters of an hour and I hope that everyone will stay under cover as much as possible."

Davis looked up as Dr. Bird entered the laboratory.

"I'll have the masks completed in an hour, Doctor," he said, "but I don't know how much value they will be. If the oxygen polymerizes before it enters the body, these masks ought to stop it, but if it polymerizes under the influence of heat and moisture in the lungs, they will be useless."

"I'll have to take a chance on that, Davis. From the description of the fog, I strongly suspect that the process takes place outside the body. Have you had your supper?"

"No, Doctor."

"Neither have I. I'll go over to the officers' mess and get a bite to eat. As soon as you have those masks done, get your supper and then telephone me at the club. If Carnes isn't back, I may have to ask you to drive me down toward Michaelville."

"I'll be very glad to, Doctor."

*   *   *   *   *

Carnes had not returned when Davis called Dr. Bird at the officers' club two hours later. Night had fallen and everyone on the proving ground sat behind tightly closed windows with lights blazing on them, wondering whether the finger of death would reach in from the swamp to touch them. The fog had not yet made an appearance on the main post and Dr. Bird had no fear of it when he entered his car and drove down to pick up his assistant.

Davis came out to meet him with a curious hood made of vitiolene and rubber, pulled down well over his head. In his hand he carried a second one. Dr. Bird adjusted the second mask and the two men loaded the rear of the car with apparatus designed for collecting samples of air. The outside of each sample cylinder was heavily coated with black rubberine paint. At a word from the Doctor, Davis took the wheel and drove off along the winding ribbon of concrete which led to the upper end of the Michaelville range.

For a mile they drove through a clear, calm night with no traces of fog apparent. Dr. Bird's eyes continually searched the swamps on both sides of the road.

"Stop!" he said suddenly, his voice coming muffled through the enveloping mask. The car stopped and the Doctor pointed to the west. Over the swamp a few stray fingers of fog were curling up from the water.

* * * * *

Leaving Davis in charge of the car, Dr. Bird donned rubber hip boots and with a gas cylinder in his hand, splashed through the water toward the fog. He reached the place with no difficulty and spent ten minutes trying to collect a sample. Finally, with a muttered exclamation, he removed his mask and inhaled deeply a dozen times. Carrying the mask in his hand, he made his way back to the car.

"False alarm," he said as he pulled on his mask. "It was so thin that I couldn't get a sample so I tested it by breathing. There isn't a trace of cough in that fog. Drive on."

A half mile farther along the road, a curtain of fog swept in on them, momentarily hiding the road from view. They were through the belt of fog in a few feet and the car came to a stop. Dr. Bird sprang out, gas cylinder in hand. He returned to the car shortly.

"We may have what we are looking for, Davis," he said, "but I am not at all certain. It looked very much like ordinary fog. Let's go down to the range."

The car drew up between the two main buildings of the Michaelville front. The air was clear as far as they could see, but from under the north building, a tiny wisp of fog was coming. As it came under the glare of the three huge arc-lights which flooded the ground with light, it grew more tenuous and gradually dissipated into nothingness. With an exclamation of satisfaction, Dr. Bird bent down and thrust the end of a cylinder under the building. He removed it in a moment as the fog began to stream from the upper end. Carefully he closed the pet-cocks of the tube and replaced it in the car. He filled a half dozen tubes before he was satisfied.

"I'd like to go down to the water," he said through his mask. "What kind of a jigger do they run on that track?"

"It's a Ford scooter, I was told. It's probably in that shed."

*   *   *   *   *

Half an hour later the two men were running the scooter down the four miles of narrow gage track which separated Michaelville from the Bush River. A few scattered patches of fog could be seen on either side of the track, but none were of sufficient thickness to warrant much success in sample taking. At the water front Dr. Bird looked across the half mile wide river and grunted.

"The tide won't be in for another three hours," he said. "Right now there isn't over sixteen inches of water in there."

Carnes was waiting in the well lighted laboratory when they drove up.

"All right, Davis," said the doctor, "get busy on those samples. If you can't make out the first two, don't crack the others but leave them for me. Give Carnes your mask; he'll drive the rest of the night.

"What luck, Carnesy?" he asked, as the detective, wearing Davis' mask, drove toward the officers' club.

"No stray plane landed or even flew over here last night so far as I could learn. Most of the boats on the bay were either known or lent themselves to ready identification. There were four that I couldn't exactly place, but I think we can safely discard all but one. Some fishermen were pulling nets on the bay about half a mile outside the mouth of the Bush River last night. About eleven, a boat running without lights passed them. They said that they could not hear an engine running, but just a dull hum and the gurgle of a propeller. They hailed it, but got no answer. It faded away into the darkness and they think it was headed toward the mouth of the Bush River. They had their nets up and reset in another hour but the boat didn't reappear."

"Hmm. High tide was at ten minutes after midnight. There was plenty of water in the river at that hour. It sounds promising."

"I thought of telephoning Washington and getting a Coast Guard cutter put on patrol in the bay but I didn't like to do it without your sanction."

"It might have been a good idea, but on the whole it's probably better that you didn't. Carnes, we'll go down to the water front and see whether anything shows up to-night. High tide will be about eleven-thirty. It's about half-past nine now. We'd better get going."

*   *   *   *   *

On the second drive to Michaelville, the fog patches were quite noticeably denser than they had been earlier in the evening. Three times the car had to pass through bands of fog which covered the road. As they passed the second one Carnes suddenly began to cough.

"What's the matter, old man?" cried Dr. Bird, a note of anxiety in his voice. For a few moments Carnes could not answer for coughing. He seized the mask to tear it from his head but Dr. Bird restrained him. In a few minutes his voice became intelligible.

"It seemed like that fog bit right into my lungs, Doctor," he gasped. "I felt as if I were choking. It's better now."

"Are you sure your mask isn't leaking, Carnes? It'll be all up with you if it does. Test it."

The detective closed the intake valve of the mask and expelling all of the air from his lungs, took a deep breath. The air whistled noisily in through the outlet valve.

"The devil!" cried the doctor. "Take that mask off and let me look at it."

A few moments were enough to make the needed repairs and they drove on. Carnes still coughed from time to time. At Michaelville, they started the scooter and ran down the track to the river. They secreted the scooter under the parapet on the water pent-house and walked to the river's edge.

"There's no telling just where they may land, Carnes," said the doctor reflectively, "but this looks like the most likely place. I'll tell you what we'll do. The river narrows a good deal about half a mile east of here. You go up to the narrows and keep watch while I stay here. If any craft passes you, follow it upstream until you find me. If they land, handle the situation as well as you can alone. If you hear any shooting, come as fast as you can leg it. I'll do the same."

*   *   *   *   *

The detective stole away into the darkness and Dr. Bird settled himself for a long vigil. For an hour nothing broke the stillness of the night. Suddenly the doctor was on his feet, peering downstream. A faint purring murmur came over the water, so faint that no one with less sensitive ears than the doctor's could have detected it. Assured after a few minutes of listening that some kind of a craft was coming up the river, the doctor sank back into his hiding place, an automatic pistol firmly grasped in his long tapering fingers.

The purr came nearer, but it was not appreciably louder. The gurgle of water past the prow of the boat could be heard and Dr. Bird could see a long ribbon of white on the water where the craft was passing. He stepped from his cover and leaned forward, straining his eyes to see the boat. It passed beyond him and continued up the river. He stepped quickly along the river bank, trying to keep it in sight. Suddenly he paused. The boat had turned and was coming back. Hurriedly he returned to his hiding place.

The boat came down the river until it was opposite the point where he crouched, and then it turned and came in toward the shore. Dr. Bird gripped his pistol and waited. When the craft was less than twenty feet from shore it stopped and a guttural voice spoke. Dr. Bird started. He had expected the language to be Russian, but it came as a shock to him, nevertheless. He strained his ears and cursed his inability to make out the words. Dr. Bird had been assiduously studying Russian under the tutelage of his new secretary for some months, but he had not yet progressed to the stage where he could readily understand it. The gift of languages was one which the erudite doctor did not possess.

*   *   *   *   *

The boat lay motionless for several minutes. Nervously the doctor glanced at his wrist watch. He barely stifled a cry of amazement. From the face of the luminous dial, long streamers of faintly phosphorescent light were streaming. He whirled to meet an attack from the rear but he was too late. Even as he turned the muzzle of a pistol pressed into his back and a voice spoke behind him.

"Drop that pistol, Doctor, or I'll be under the unpleasant necessity of making a hole in you."

Reluctantly, Dr. Bird dropped his pistol and the voice went on.

"Really, I hardly expected to catch you by surprise, Doctor. I thought you were clever enough to realize that our boat would be equipped with an ultra-violet searchlight. However, even the best minds must rest sometimes, and yours is due for a nice long rest. In fact, I might almost prophesy that it will be a permanent rest."

Dr. Bird shivered despite himself at the cold mercilessness of the railing voice behind him. The accents were ones which he did not recognize. His captor chuckled for a few moments and then called out in Russian. The boat came into the shore and eight figures climbed out. Two of them bore a small chest which they set down on the wharf. One of the figures picked up the doctor's automatic and his captor stepped in front. A flashlight gleamed for an instant and Dr. Bird started in surprise. The men wore no masks but only a plate of glass which protected their cheeks and eyes. Fastened to the neck of each one, below the chin, was a long tube which gleamed like glass. They wore heavy knapsacks strapped to their backs from which wires ran to each end of the bars.

"Those protectors make your enveloping head-mask look rather clumsy, don't they, Doctor?" said his captor mockingly. "It's too bad you didn't think of them first. It must be such a blow to your pride to think that anyone had invented something better than yours. Really, that mask of yours worries me. Remove it!"

* * * * *

At his words two of the men stepped forward and tore the doctor's mask roughly from his head. The mocking voice went on.

"In view of the fact that you have only a few hours of life left, Dr. Bird, it will give me pleasure to let you know how thoroughly you have been defeated. You may not know me by sight, although my name may not be unfamiliar. I am Peter Denberg."

He turned the flashlight for an instant on his own face, and Dr. Bird gazed at him keenly.

"I'll know you the next time I see you," he muttered, half to himself.

"The next time you see me will be in the hereafter, if there be such a thing," laughed the Russian. "The sweetest blow of all is now about to fall. We expected you to be here and came prepared to capture you. Had we not known that the arch enemy of the people would be here to-night, we would have struck at a point miles away. Do you know who betrayed you? It was one we placed in your laboratory for the very purpose which she served."

He turned on the light again and it picked out of the darkness another face, a long oval face with startlingly red lips and dark oval eyes which glowed as with an internal flame. As the face became visible, the red lips drew back, exposing strong white teeth and the words were literally spat out.

"Swine!" she hissed. "Bourgeois! Did you think you could bribe me with your gifts to tolerate your vileness? I have brought about your downfall and death, Dr. Bird. I, Feodrovna Androvitch! Now will I avenge my brother's death at your hands!"

She sprang forward and spat full in the doctor's face. Dr. Bird fell back for an instant under the ferocity of her attack and long nails ripped the skin from his face. Denberg stepped forward and caught her wrists.

"Gently, sister," he warned. Feodrovna struggled for an instant but gave way to the powerful muscles of the communist leader. "There is no need for anything of that sort," he went on. "In a few moments we will open the chest which we have and then you will enjoy the amazing spectacle of the man who has temporarily checked the plans of our leader a dozen times, gasping for breath like a fish out of water. Start your protectors."

*   *   *   *   *

Each of the Russians closed a switch on the knapsack which he wore. From the bars below their chins came a dull violet glow which made their faces stand out eerily in the darkness. The flashlight was centered on the box which Dr. Bird could see was made of lead, soldered into a solid mass. At a word from Denberg, one of the Russians stepped forward with a long knife in his hand and started to cut open the box.

With a sudden effort, Dr. Bird shook himself loose from the two men who were holding him and sprang forward. Denberg turned to meet him and the doctor's fist shot out like a piston rod. Full on the Russian's chin it landed and he went down like a poled ox. Two of the Russians closed with him but the two were no match for Dr. Bird's enormous strength, fighting as he was for his life. He hurled one away and swung with all of his strength at the other. His blow struck glancingly, and while the Russian spun away under the blow, he did not fall. A man caught at him from the rear and Dr. Bird whirled, but as he did so, two men seized his arms from behind. Mightily the doctor strove but others flung themselves on him. He straightened up with a superhuman effort and then from an unexpected source came help.

One of the men holding him gave a choking gasp and reeled sideways. Dr. Bird felt his neck deluged with liquid and the smell of hot blood rose sickeningly on the air. He shook himself loose again and smote with all of his strength at his nearest opponent. His blow landed fair but at the same instant an iron bar fell across his arm and it dropped limp and helpless. Again a knife flashed in the darkness and a howl of pain came from the Russian who felt it bite home.

"We are attacked!" cried one of them. They whirled about, their flashlights cutting paths through the thickening fog. With her back to the crippled doctor's Feodrovna Androvitch held aloft a bloody knife.

Something seemed to catch Dr. Bird by the throat and shut off his breath. From a gash which had been cut in the lead box, a heavy gray fog was rising and enveloping everything in its deadening blanket. The fog penetrated into the doctor's lungs and an intolerable pain, as though hot irons were searing the tissues, tore him. He tried to cough, but the sound could not force its way through his stiffening lips. Darkness closed in on him and he swayed. He was dimly conscious that the Russians were swarming about Feodrovna, knives and clubs in their hands. Then through the night came an ear-splitting crack and a flash of orange flame. One of the Russians toppled and fell forward, knocking the weakened doctor down as he did so. Again came a flash and a report, and to the doctor's fading senses came a sound of shouts and pounding feet. Over his head another flash split the fog and then darkness swarmed in and with a sigh of pain, Dr. Bird let his head fall forward on his chest.

*   *   *   *   *

He recovered consciousness slowly and looked about him. He was in a white bed in a strange, yet somehow familiar, place with a ray of light of almost intolerable brilliance boring its way into his brain. He tried to raise his hand and found himself curiously weak. With a great effort he raised his hand until he could see it and let it fall with a cry which came from his lips only as a feeble murmur. His hand was thin almost to the point of emaciation. Blue veins stood out on the back and his long, slim, mobile fingers, the fingers of an artist and dreamer, were mere claws, with the skin drawn tight over the bones.

A man in a white uniform bent over him. "Drink this, Doctor," came in soothing tones.

He was too weak to protest and he managed to sip the drink through a glass tube. Slowly he felt himself sinking through vast unexplored reaches of darkness.

How long he lay there he did not know but when he again opened his eyes the light was no longer over him. He strove to speak and a husky whisper came from his lips. A tall woman in white hastened forward and bent over him.

"Where am I?" he asked with difficulty.

"You're in the hospital at Aberdeen Proving Ground, Doctor," said the nurse. "Everything is all right and you're doing splendidly. Just don't excite yourself and you'll get well in no time. Captain Murdock will be here in a few minutes."

"How long have I been here?" he asked.

"Oh, quite a while, Doctor. Now don't ask any more questions. You must rest and get well and strong, you know."

Strength seemed to be surging slowly back into the doctor's wasted frame. His voice came clearer and stronger.

"How long have I been here?" he demanded.

*　　*　　*　　*　　*

The nurse hesitated, but her face suddenly cleared as Captain Murdock entered the ward.

"Oh, Captain," she cried, "come here and take care of your patient. He won't keep quiet."

"Out of his head again?" asked Captain Murdock as he hastened forward.

"No more than you are," came in a husky whisper from Dr. Bird's lips.

Captain Murdock looked quickly down and smiled in relief. "You'll live, Dr. Bird," he said. "Just take it easy for a few days and then you can talk all you want to."

"I'll talk now," came in stronger tones from the doctor's lips. "How long have I been here?"

Captain Murdock hesitated, but a glance at the doctor's flushed face warned him that it was better to give in than to fight him.

"You were brought in here two weeks ago yesterday," he said. "It was touch and go for a while, and, but for the treatment you devised, you would have been a goner. We fed you X-rays until I was afraid we would burn you up, but they did the business. It will cheer you up to learn that every man who got your treatment is either well or on the high road to recovery."

"The plague?" asked the doctor faintly.

"Oh, that's all over, thanks to you. It reached the post that night but under the influence of the daylight blue bulbs you had installed, it lost most of its virulence. We had a lot of sore throats in the morning but there wasn't a man dangerously sick. It all faded when the sun hit it."

An orderly entered and spoke in an undertone to Captain Murdock. The surgeon hesitated for a moment, his eyes on Dr. Bird, and then nodded.

"Bring him in," he said quietly.

*   *   *   *   *

A small, unobtrusively dressed man entered the room and stepped to the bedside. Dr. Bird's face lighted up in one of its rare smiles and he strove to raise his hand in greeting.

"Carnesy, old dear, I'm glad to see you got out all right," he whispered. "I was afraid your mask wouldn't hold up after the trouble you had with it. Tell me what happened that night."

Carnes glanced at Captain Murdock, who nodded.

"I went down to the narrows and watched, Doctor, and when the Russian boat passed, I started to make my way back to you. The tide had come in and I had to make quite a detour to get to you. I got there a little later than I liked but still in time to do some good. You were down and Miss Andrews was standing over you with a bloody knife in her hand, fighting like a wildcat. I started shooting and ran in yelling as loud as I could. I managed to plug three of them and I guess they thought I was a dozen men. I tried to make enough noise for that many. The rest took to their heels and Miss Andrews and I rigged one of their protectors over your face and dragged you to the scooter.

The rest was plain sailing. We brought you in and Captain Murdock did the rest. That's all there was to it. If I hadn't been so slow, I could have driven them off before they opened that box and saved you all of this."

"Thelma?" asked the doctor faintly.

"Oh, she's none the worse, Doctor. I want to apologize to you for the poor opinion I had of your judgment. That girl wasn't recognized; she recognized Denberg on the streets of Washington and deliberately put her head into the lion's mouth by declaring herself. She got their whole plan and went along to try to checkmate them. If she hadn't started knifing when she did, the devils meant to hold your head directly over that box and it would have been just too bad."

"What was in the box?"

*　　*　　*　　*　　*

"She found that out. It was some kind of a microbe that Saranoff developed in a Belgian laboratory which does something to the oxygen of the air. You'll have to get Dr. Burgess to explain that to you later; he has some of the bugs shut up for you to play with when you get back on the job. When we found that you were knocked out, Davis got him to come down from Washington to take charge. He has been running ray machines over the swamps for two weeks and says that every trace of the bugs are gone except those he has in the laboratory."

"Saranoff has more."

"No, he hasn't, thanks to Miss Andrews. Every day they started a fresh colony, leaving one lot back to start the next brood with. She tipped us off where they were kept and Bolton and Haggerty raided and got the lot and turned them over to Dr. Burgess."

"That's enough for to-day, Mr. Carnes," interrupted Captain Murdock. "You can see Dr. Bird to-morrow, but he has had enough excitement for to-day."

As Carnes took his leave, the nurse spoke to Captain Murdock. He looked carefully at Dr. Bird and nodded.

"For one minute. No longer!" he said.

The nurse stepped to the door. Into the room came a slim young woman of remarkable beauty, her eyes glowing as with an internal light. Her parting lips of startling redness showed strong white teeth. Her eyes grew misty as she leaned over the doctor's bed. Dr. Bird blinked for a moment and his face grew stern.

"Miss Andrews," he said in a husky whisper, "Mr. Carnes has told me what you did. In my service, success does not excuse disobedience. I thank you for your services which may have saved my life and which may have put me in worse danger. In any event, please remember two things. Unless you can learn to entirely suppress your emotions and learn that I will tolerate nothing but implicit obedience, your usefulness to me will be at an end and I will no longer need you."

The happiness faded from the girl's face as if by magic and an expression of absolute immobility took its place. Her eyes looked as though a curtain had been drawn over them.

"Yes, Doctor," she said in a toneless voice as she turned and left the room.

THE GREAT DROUGHT

ORIGINALLY PUBLISHED IN *ASTOUNDING STORIES OF SUPER-SCIENCE*, MAY 1932

Another episode in Dr. Bird's extraordinary duel with the scientific wizard Saranoff.

THE GREAT DROUGHT

"Is the maneuver progressing as you wish. Dr. Bird?" asked the Chief of the Air Corps.

The famous scientist lowered his binoculars and smiled.

"Exactly, General," he replied. "They are keeping a splendid line."

"It is the greatest concentration of air force that this country has ever seen," said General Merton proudly.

With a nod, Dr. Bird raised his glasses to his eyes and resumed his steady gaze. Five thousand feet below and two miles ahead of the huge transport plane which flew the flag of the Chief of the Air Corps, a long line of airplanes stretched away to the north and to the south. Six hundred and seventy-two planes, the entire First Air Division of the United States Army, were deployed in line at hundred-yard intervals, covering a front of nearly forty miles. Fifteen hundred feet above the ground, the line roared steadily westward over Maryland at ninety miles an hour. At ten-second intervals, a puff of black dust came from a discharge tube mounted on the rear of each plane. The dust was whirled about for a moment by the exhaust, and then spread out in a thin layer, marking the path of the fleet.

"I hope the observers on the planes are keeping careful notes of the behavior of those dust clouds," said Dr. Bird after an interval of silence. "We are crossing the Chesapeake now, and things may start to happen at any moment."

"They're all on their toes, Doctor," replied General Merton. "I understood in a general way from the President that we are gathering some important meteorological data for you, but I am ignorant of just what this data is. Is it a secret?"

Dr. Bird hesitated.

"Yes," he said slowly, "it is. However, I can see no reason why this secret should not be entrusted to you. We are seeking a means of ending the great drought which has ravaged the United States for the past two years."

*   *   *   *   *

Before General Merton had time to make a reply, his executive officer hastened forward from the radio set which was in constant communication with the units of the fleet.

"Two of the planes on the north end of the line are reporting engine trouble, sir," he said.

Dr. Bird dropped his glasses and sat bolt upright.

"What kind of engine trouble?" he demanded sharply.

"Their motors are slowing down for no explainable reason. I can't understand it."

"Are their motors made with sheet steel cylinders or with duralumin engine blocks?"

"Sheet steel."

"The devil! I hadn't foreseen this, although it was bound to happen if my theory was right. Tell them to climb! Climb all they know! Don't let them shut off their motors for any reason, unless they are about to crash. Turn this ship to the north and have the pilot climb–fast!"

A nod from General Merton confirmed the doctor's orders. The line of planes kept on to the west, but the flagplane turned to the north and climbed at a sharp angle, her three motors roaring at full speed. With the aid of binoculars, the two ships in trouble could be picked out, falling gradually behind the line. They were flying so slowly that it seemed inevitable that they would lose flying speed and crash to the ground.

"More speed!" cried the doctor. "We've elevation enough!"

The altimeter stood at eight thousand feet when the pilot leveled out the flagplane and tore at full speed toward the laboring ships. The main fleet was twenty miles to the west.

*   *   *   *   *

They were almost above the point where the two planes had first began to slow down. As they winged along, the three motors of the flagplane took on a different note. It was a laboring note, pitched on a lower scale. Gradually the air-speed meter of the ship began to show a lower reading.

"Locate us on the map, Carnes!" snapped Dr. Bird.

Operative Carnes of the United States Secret Service bent over a large-scale map of Maryland, spread open on a table. With the aid of the navigating officer, he spotted on the map the point over which the plane was flying.

"There goes Burleigh's ship!" cried the executive officer.

There was a gasp from the occupants of the flagplane's cabin. Far below them, one of the crippled planes had slowed down until it had lost flying speed. Whirling like a leaf, it plunged toward the ground. Two small specks detached themselves from the falling mass. They hovered over the falling plane for an instant. Suddenly a patch of white appeared in the air, and then another. The two specks fell more slowly.

"Good work!" exclaimed General Merton. "They took to their 'chutes just in time."

"We'll be taking them in a few minutes if our motors don't pick up!" replied the executive officer.

Far below them, the doomed plane crashed to the ground. As it struck there was a blinding flash followed by vivid flames as the gasoline from the bursted tank ignited. The two members of the crew were drifting to the east as they fell. It was evident that they were in no danger.

"Where is Lightwood's plane?" asked General Merton anxiously.

"It's still aloft and making its way slowly north. He intends to try for an emergency landing at the Aberdeen Proving Ground field," replied the executive officer.

"That's where we had better head for," said Dr. Bird. "I hope that the charge on Captain Lightwood's plane discharges through the tail skid when he lands. If it doesn't, he'll be in serious danger. Follow him and we'll watch."

*   *   *   *   *

Five thousand feet below them, the crippled plane limped slowly along toward Aberdeen. It was gradually losing elevation. Two specks suddenly appeared in the air, followed by white patches as the parachutes opened. Captain Lightwood and his gunner had given up the unequal fight and taken to the air. As the ship struck the ground, again there was a blinding flash, followed by an inferno of roaring flames.

"We're not in much better shape than they were, General," said the executive officer as he came back from the control room where the pilots were heroically striving to keep their motors turning over fast enough to keep up flying speed. "We'd better get into our 'chutes."

"The Proving Ground is just ahead," said the doctor. "Can't we make it by sacrificing our elevation?"

"We're trying to do that, Doctor, but we're down to four thousand now and falling fast. Get ready to jump."

Dr. Bird buckled on the harness of the pack parachute which the executive officer offered him. The rest of the crew had hurriedly donned their packs and stood ready.

For another five minutes the plane struggled on. Suddenly a large flat expanse of open ground which had been in sight for some time, seemed to approach with uncanny rapidity.

"There's the landing field!" cried the General. "We'll make it yet!"

Lower and lower the plane sank with the landing field still too far away for comfort. The pilot leveled off as much as he dared and drove on. The motors were laboring and barely turning over at idling speed. They passed the nearer edge of the field with the flagplane barely thirty feet off the ground. In another moment the wheels touched and the plane rolled to a halt.

"Don't get out!" cried Dr. Bird.

He looked around the cabin and picked up a coil of bare antenna wire which hung near the radio set. He wrapped one end of the wire around the frame of the plane. To the other end, he attached his pack 'chute.

"Open the door!" he cried.

*   *   *   *   *

As the door swung open, he threw the 'chute out toward the ground. As it touched, there was a blinding flash, followed by a report which shook the plane. A strong odor of garlic permeated the air.

"All right!" cried the doctor cheerfully. "All out for Aberdeen. The danger is past."

He set the example by jumping lightly from the plane. General Merton followed more slowly, his face white and his hands shaking.

"What was it, Doctor," he asked. "I have been flying since 1912, yet I have never seen or heard of anything like that."

"Just a heavy charge of static electricity," replied the doctor. "That was what magnetized your cylinder walls and your piston rings and slowed your motors down. It was the same thing that wrecked those two ships. Unless it leaks off, the men of some of your other ships are due to get a nasty shock when they land to-night. I discharged the charge we had collected through a ground wire. Here comes a car, we'll go up to Colonel Wesley's office. Carnes, you have these maps?"

"Surely, Doctor."

"All right, let's go."

"But what about this ship, Doctor?" objected the General. "Can't something be done about it?"

"Certainly. I hadn't forgotten it. Have your crew stand by. I'll telephone Washington and have some men with apparatus sent right down from the Bureau of Standards. They'll have it ready for flying in the morning. We'll also have search parties sent out in cars to locate the crews of those abandoned ships and bring them in. Now let's go."

*   *   *   *   *

Colonel Wesley, the commanding officer of the Aberdeen Proving Ground, welcomed Carnes and Dr. Bird warmly.

"I'll tell you, General Merton," he said to the Chief of the Air Corps, "if you ever get up against something that is beyond all explanation, you want to get these two men working on it. They are the ones who settled that poisoning case here, you know."

"Yes, I read of that," replied the general. "I am inclined to think that they are up against something even queerer right now."

Colonel Wesley's eyes sparkled.

"Give your orders, Dr. Bird!" he cried. "Since our last experience with you, you can't give an order on this post that won't be obeyed!"

"Thank you, Colonel," said Dr. Bird warmly. "One reason why I came here was that I knew that I could count on your hearty cooperation. The first thing I want is two cars. I want them sent out to bring in the crews of two ships which were abandoned some eight miles south of here. Carnes will locate them on the map for your drivers."

"They'll be ready to start in five minutes, Doctor. What next?"

"Turn out every man and every piece of transportation you have to-morrow morning. I want the men armed. They will have to search a stretch of swamp south of here, inch by inch, until they find what I'm looking for."

"They'll be ready, Doctor. Would it be indiscreet for me to ask what it's all about?"

"Not at all, Colonel. I was about to explain to General Merton when trouble started. I am searching for the cause of the great drought which has been afflicting this country for the past two years. If I can find the cause, I hope to end it."

"Oh! I had a sneaking hope that we were in for another skirmish with that Russian chap, Saranoff, whose men started that poison here."

"I rather think we are, Colonel Wesley."

General Merton laughed.

"I'll swallow a good deal, Dr. Bird," he said, "but when you talk of an individual being responsible for the great drought, it's a little too much. A man can't control the weather, you know!"

*   *   *   *   *

"Yet a man, or an incarnate devil—I don't know which he is—did control the weather once, as well as the sun. But for the humble efforts of two Americans, aided by a Russian girl whose brother Saranoff had murdered, he might be still controlling it."

General Merton was silent now.

"Carnes, let me have that map," went on the doctor. When the detective had unrolled a map of the United States on Colonel Wesley's table, Dr. Bird continued, pointing to the map as he spoke.

"On this map," he said, "is plotted the deficiency in rainfall for the past year, from every reporting station in the United States. These red lines divide the country into areas of equal deficiency. The area most affected, as you can see, is longer east and west, than it is north and south. It is worst in the east, in fact in this very neighborhood. Even a casual glance at the map will show you that the center of the drought area, from an intensity standpoint, lies in Maryland, a few miles south of here."

"In fact, just about where those two planes went down," added Carnes.

"Precisely, old dear. That was why we went over that section with the fleet. Now, gentlemen, note a few other things about this drought. The areas of drought follow roughly the great waterways, the Ohio and the Potomac valleys being especially affected. In other words, the drought follows the normal air currents from this point. If something were to be added to the air which would tend to prevent rain, it would in time drift, just as the drought areas have drifted."

*   *   *   *   *

General Merton and Colonel Wesley bent over the map.

"I believe you're right, Doctor," admitted the general.

"Thank you. The President was convinced that I was before he placed the First Air Division under my orders. Frankly, that search was the real object of assembling the fleet. The maneuvers are a mere blind."

General Merton colored slightly.

"Now, I'll try to give you some idea of what I think is the method being used," went on the doctor, ignoring General Merton's rising color. "In the past, rain has been produced in several cases where conditions were right— that is, when the air held plenty of moisture which refused to fall—by the discharge from a plane of a cloud of positively charged dust particles. Ergo, a heavy negative charge in the air, which will absorb rather than discharge a positive charge, should tend to prevent rain from falling. I believe that a stream of negative particles is being liberated into the air near here, and allowed to drift where it will. That was my theory when I had the First Air Division equipped with those dust ejector tubes.

"I knew that if such a condition existed, the positively charged dust would be pulled down toward the source of the negative particle stream, which must, in many ways, resemble a cathode ray. That was why I wanted the behavior of the dust clouds watched and reported. What I did not foresee was that the iron and steel parts of the plane, accumulating a heavy negative charge, would be magnetized enough to slow down the motors and eventually wreck the ships."

"We have had eight ships wrecked unexplainably within twenty miles of here, all of them to the south, during the past year," said Colonel Wesley.

"It had slipped my notice. At any rate, the behavior of the ships this afternoon showed me that my theory is correct, and that some such device exists and is in active operation. Our next task is to locate it and destroy it."

"You shall have every man on the Proving Ground!" cried Colonel Wesley.

"Thank you. General Merton, will you detach three ships from the First Air Division by radio and have them report here? I want two pursuit ships and one bomber, with a rack of hundred-pound demolition bombs. All three must have duralumin cylinder blocks."

"I'll do it at once, Doctor," the general agreed.

"Thank you. Carnes, telephone Washington for me. Tell Dr. Burgess that I want Tracy, Fellows and Von Amburgh, with three more men down here by the next train. Also tell him to have Davis rig up a demagnetizer large enough to demagnetize the motors of a transport plane and bring it down here to fix up General Merton's ship. When you have finished that, get hold of Bolton and ask for a dozen secret service men. I want selected men with Haggerty in charge."

"All right, Doctor. Shall I tell Miss Andrews to come down as well?"

*   *   *   *   *

Dr. Bird frowned.

"Certainly not. Why would she come down here?"

"I thought she might be useful, Doctor."

"Carnes, as you know, I dislike using women because they can't control their emotions or their expressions. She would just be in the way."

"It seems to me that she saved both our lives in Russia, Doctor, and but for her, you wouldn't have come out so well in your last adventure on the Aberdeen marshes."

"She did the first through uncontrolled emotions, and the second through a flagrant disobedience of my orders. No, don't tell her to come. Tell her not to come if she asks."

Carnes turned away, but hesitated.

"Doctor, I wish you'd let me have her come down here. I didn't trust her at first when you did, but she has proved her loyalty and worth. Besides, I don't like the idea of leaving her unguarded in Washington with you and me down here, and with Haggerty coming down."

Dr. Bird looked thoughtful.

"There's something in that, Carnes," he reflected. "All right, tell her to come along, but remember, she is not in on this case. She is being brought here merely for safety, not to mix up in our work."

"Thanks, Doctor."

The detective returned in ten minutes with a worried expression.

"She wasn't in your office, Doctor," he reported.

"Who? Oh, Thelma. Where was she?"

"No one seems to know. She left yesterday afternoon and hasn't returned."

"Oh, well, since I am out of the city, I expect she decided to take a vacation. Women are always undependable. Did you get hold of the rest?"

"They'll be down at midnight, all but Davis. He'll come down in the morning."

"Good enough! Now, Colonel, if you'll have the officers who are going out to-morrow assembled, we'll divide the territory and make our plans for the search."

* * * * *

A week later, the situation was unchanged. Secret service operatives and soldiers from the Proving Ground had covered, foot by foot, square miles of territory south of the Proving Ground, but without result. Not a single unexplainable thing had been found. Sensitive instruments sent down from the Bureau of Standards, instruments so sensitive that they would detect an electric light burning a mile away, had yielded no results. As a final measure, General Merton had ordered a dozen planes with steel-cylindered motors to the Proving Ground and they had repeatedly crisscrossed the suspected territory, but had acquired no static charge large enough to affect them. It was evident that Saranoff's device, if it existed, had been moved, or else was not in operation.

Also, to Carnes' openly expressed and Dr. Bird's secret worry, Thelma Andrews had not returned to the Bureau of Standards. The Russian girl, formerly known as Feodrovna Androvitch, a tool and follower of Ivan Saranoff, had acted with Carnes and the doctor in their long drawn-out fight with the arch-communist often enough to be a marked woman.

Urged by Carnes, Bolton, the head of the Secret Service, put a dozen of his best men on her trail, but they

found nothing. She had disappeared as thoroughly as if
the earth had opened and swallowed her up. At last, as
the combing of the Aberdeen marshes yielded no results,
Dr. Bird acceded to Carnes' request, and the detective left
for Washington to take personal charge of the search. Dr.
Bird sat alone in his quarters at the Officers' Club,
futilely wracking his brains for a clue to his further
procedure.

The telephone rang loudly. With a grunt, he took
down the receiver.

A feminine voice spoke with a strong foreign accent.

"I vant der Herr Doktor Vogel, plees!"

"You want who? Oh, yes. Vogel–bird! This is Dr. Bird
speaking."

The voice instantly lost both its foreign accent and its
guttural quality.

"I thought so when you spoke, Doctor, but I wanted to
make sure. This is Thelma Andrews."

"Where the devil have you been? Half the Secret
Service is looking for you, including Carnes, who deserted
me and is in Washington."

*   *   *   *   *

"He is? I'm sorry. Listen, Doctor, it's a long story and I
can't go into details now. I got a clue on the day you left.
As I couldn't get in touch with you, I followed it myself.
I've located Saranoff's main base in the Bush River
marshes."

"You have! Where is it?"

"It's underground and you've passed over it a dozen
times during the past week. It's unoccupied now and the
machines are idle until your search is over. I know the
way to it. If you'll join me now, we can get in and
hopelessly wreck the device in a short time. To-morrow
you can bring your men down here and take charge of it."

Dr. Bird's eyes glistened.

"I'll come at once, Thelma!" he cried. "Where are you?"

"I'm down on Romney Creek. Come down to the Water Impact Range below Michaelville, and I'll meet you at the wharf. You'd better come alone, because we'll have to sneak."

"Good for you!" cried the doctor. "I'll be down in an hour."

"All right, Doctor. I'll be waiting for you."

At Michaelville, Dr. Bird left his car and stepped on the scooter which ran on the narrow gauge track connecting the range house with the wharf on Romney Creek. He started it with no difficulty and it coughed away into the night. For three and a half miles, nothing broke the monotony of the trip. Dr. Bird, his hand on the throttle, kept his eyes on the twin ribbons of steel which slid along under the headlight. The road made a sharp turn and emerged from the thick wood through which it had been traveling. Hardly had the lights shot along the track in the new direction than Dr. Bird closed the throttle and applied the brakes rapidly. A heavy barricade of logs was piled across the track.

*   *   *   *   *

The doctor pressed home on the brake lever until the steel shoes screamed in protest, but no brakes could bring the heavy scooter to a stop as swiftly as was needful to avoid a crash. It was still traveling at a good rate of speed when it rammed into the barricade and overturned.

Dr. Bird was thrown clear of the wrecked scooter. He landed on soft mud beside the track. As he strove to rise, the beam of a flashlight struck him in the eyes and a guttural, sneering voice spoke through the darkness.

"Don't move, Dr. Bird. It will be useless and will only lead to your early death, a thing I should regret."

"Saranoff!" cried Dr. Bird.

"I am flattered, Doctor, that you know my voice. Yes, it is I, Ivan Saranoff, the man whom you have so often foiled. You drove me from America and tried to bar the road against my return, but I only laughed at your efforts. I returned here only for one purpose, to capture you and to compass your death."

Dr. Bird rose to his feet and laughed lightly.

"You've got me, Saranoff," he said, "but the game isn't played out yet. I represent an organization which won't end with my death, you know."

A series of expletives in guttural Russian answered him. In response to a command from their leader, two men came forward and searched the doctor quickly and expertly, removing the automatic pistol which he carried under his left armpit.

"As for your organization, as you call it—*pouf!*" said the Russian scornfully. "Carnes, a brainless fool who does only as you tell him, a few half-wits in the Bureau of Standards, some of them already in my pay, and one renegade girl. She shall learn what it means to betray the Soviets and their leader."

"You'll have to catch her first," replied Dr. Bird, a sardonic grin on his face.

"I have but to snap my fingers and she will come whining back, licking my hand and imploring mercy," boasted the Russian. "Bring him along!"

*　*　*　*　*

TWO men approached and Seized the doctor by his arms. Dr. Bird shook them off contemptuously.

"Keep your filthy paws off me!" he cried. "I know when I'm bested, and I'll come quietly, but I won't be dragged."

The men looked at their leader for orders. From behind his light, the Russian studied his opponent. He gave vent to a stream of guttural Russian. The men fell back.

"For your information, Doctor," he said in a sneering tone. "I have told my men to follow you closely, gun in hand. At the slightest sign of hesitation, or at the first attempt to escape, they will fire. They are excellent shots."

"Lead on, Saranoff," was Dr. Bird's cheery comment.

With a shrug of his shoulders, the leader of the Young Labor party turned and made his way along the track toward the wharf. Dr. Bird looked anxiously ahead as they approached, fearing that Feodrovna Androvitch would be discerned in her hiding place. Saranoff correctly interpreted his gaze.

"Does der Herr Doktor Vogel eggspect somevun?" he asked in the voice which had first come over Dr. Bird's telephone. The doctor started and the Russian went on in the voice of the doctor's secretary. "I'm so glad you came, Dr. Bird. I am going to take you directly to the main base of our dearly beloved friend, Ivan Saranoff."

An expression that was a mixture of chagrin and relief spread over Dr. Bird's face.

"Sold, by thunder!" he cried.

The Russian laughed sardonically and tramped on in silence. Tied to the Romney Creek wharf was a boat with powerful electric motors, driven by storage batteries. At a nudge from his captors, Dr. Bird took his place in the craft. It glided silently away down the creek toward the Chesapeake's mouth.

*   *   *   *   *

In the bay, the boat veered to the south and ran along the shore until the mouth of Bush River opened before them. It turned west up the river, coming to a halt at one of the occasional bits of high ground which bordered the river.

"We get off here, Doctor," said Saranoff. "My base, which you have wasted so much time seeking, lies within a hundred yards of this point. Before I take you there, you may be interested in watching us conceal our boat."

Before the doctor's surprised gaze, the edges of a huge box rose above the surface of the water, around the electric boat. The boat was raised and water could be heard running out of the box which held it. When the box was drained, a man leaped in and made some adjustments. A cover, hinged on one side, swung over and closed the box tightly with the boat inside. Men closed clamps which held it in position. As they sprang to shore, the box sunk silently out of sight below the surface of the water.

"It is now beneath a foot of mud, Doctor," laughed the Russian, "and there is nothing to lead a searching party to suspect its existence. Now I will take you to my base."

He led the way for a hundred yards over the ground. Before them loomed an old abandoned fisherman's shack. They entered to find merely a barren room. The Russian stepped to the far side and manipulated a hidden lever. Half of the floor slid to one side, disclosing a flight of steps leading down into Stygian darkness.

Flashlight in hand, Saranoff descended, Dr. Bird following closely on his heels. They went down twenty-one steps before the stairs came to an end. Above them, the floor could be heard closing. There was a sharp click and the cavern was flooded with light.

*   *   *   *   *

Dr. Bird looked around him with keen interest. Before him stood a static generator of gigantic proportions and of a totally unfamiliar design. Attached to it was an elliptic reflector of silvery metal, from which rose a short, stubby projector tube.

"I suppose, Dr. Saranoff–" began Dr. Bird.

"*Ivan* Saranoff, if you please, Doctor," interrupted the Russian. "I have renounced the trumpery distinctions of your bourgeois civilization as far as I am concerned."

"I suppose, Ivan Saranoff," said Dr. Bird obligingly, "that this is the apparatus with which you send out a stream of negative particles."

"It is, Doctor. I had no idea that the nature of it would ever be discovered; at least not until I had changed the United States to a second Sahara desert. I reckoned without you. In point of fact, at the time that I built this device and started it in operation, I had not clashed with you. Now, I know that my plan is a failure. You have left data on which other men can work, have you not?"

"Surely."

"I would not have believed you had you said otherwise," replied the Russian with a sigh. "Yet this device has done much good. Now it shall be destroyed. It has not been a failure, for its destruction will accomplish both yours and that of your friend, Carnes."

"You haven't caught Carnes yet."

"That is easy. The same bait which caught you has caught him even more easily. I have a real sense of humor, Doctor, and before I went out of my way to bring you here, my plans were carefully laid. Mr. Carnes is now on his way here from Washington, lured by my voice. He is rushing, he thinks, to your rescue."

"What—"

Dr. Bird was suddenly silent.

*   *   *   *   *

"I am glad you comprehend my plan so readily, Doctor. Yes, indeed, Mr. Carnes knows that I have captured you. He knows the exact location of this cavern and, more important, he knows the location of the power line which feeds my device when it is in operation. He also knows that there is stored in this cavern, fifty pounds of radite, your ultra-explosive. He knows that you are chained close to the explosive and that it is rigged with a detonator, connected with the power line. In only one thing is he in error.

"He thinks, that if he can sever the power line before he attempts to penetrate the cavern, that the charge will be rendered harmless, and that you will be safe. In point of fact, the charge is set with an interrupter detonator which will explode as soon at the power line is severed. It pleases my sense of humor that it will be the hand of your faithful friend, Carnes, that will send you in fragments to eternity."

Beads of sweat shone on Dr. Bird's head as the Russian finished his speech, but his expression of amused interest did not change. Neither did his voice, when he spoke, betray any nervousness.

"And I presume that Carnes is also to be blown into bits by the explosion?" he asked.

"No, indeed, Doctor, that would frustrate one of the most humorous angles of the whole affair. He will cut the line at the base of a large rock, some two hundred yards from here, far enough away that he will not be seriously injured by the force of the explosion. Thus he will witness the explosion and realize what he has done. In order to be sure that he knows, as soon as he cuts the wire, my men will capture him. I, personally, will tell him of it. I wish to see his face when he realizes what he has unwittingly done."

"Then, I presume, you'll kill him?"

"I doubt it. I rather think I'll let him live. He should be useful to me."

"Carnes will never work for you!"

"With Feodrovna in my power, I rather think that Mr. Carnes will be an efficient and loyal servant. If not, he shall have the pleasure of watching me wreak my vengeance on her before he, himself, takes his last long trip."

* * * * *

"Saranoff," said Dr. Bird in a level voice, his piercing eyes boring straight into the Russian's, "I will remember this. Later, when you grovel at my feet and beg for mercy, it will be my friend, Operative Carnes, who will read your doom to you and choose the manner of it. I can promise you that your death will not be an easy one."

The Russian laughed, albeit the laugh had more of uneasiness than humor in it.

"When you have me in your power, Doctor, you may do as you like," he said, "but I do not fear dead men. In another two hours, you will be among the dead."

He turned to the three Russians who stood behind him.

"Seize him!" he cried.

The Russians leaped forward, but Dr. Bird was not caught napping. The first one went down like a felled tree before the doctor's fist. The other two came in cautiously. Dr. Bird sprang forward, feinting. As he leaped back, his foot struck a rod which Ivan Saranoff had thrust behind him. He staggered and fell. Before he could recover his balance, the two burly Russians were on him.

Even then, they had no easy task. Dr. Bird weighed over two hundred and there was not an ounce of fat or surplus flesh on him. First one, and then the other, of the Russians was thrown off him, but they returned to the attack, unsubdued by the crashing blows which the doctor landed on their faces and heads.

Gradually their ardor began to evaporate. With a sudden effort, Dr. Bird strove to regain his feet. A crash as of all the thunders of the universe sounded in his ears, and flashes of vivid light played before his eyes. He felt himself falling down ... down....

*　　*　　*　　*　　*

He recovered consciousness to find his feet shackled and fastened to rings set in the concrete of the cavern wall. His head throbbed horribly. He raised his hands and found a huge bump on his head, from which thickened blood trickled sluggishly down his cheek. The cavern was flooded with light. On the wall before him, a clock told off the seconds with a metallic tick. He bent down and examined his shackles.

"I'm afraid you can't unfasten them, Doctor," said a sardonic voice.

He looked up to see Saranoff.

"I'm sorry I had to hit you so hard," went on the Russian. "Your half hour of unconsciousness has lessened by that much the time which is yours to indulge in an agony of apprehension. Look."

Dr. Bird's gaze followed the Russian's finger. On the floor, twenty feet from where he was shackled, stood a yellow can with the mark of the Bureau of Standards on its side. He recognized it at once as a radite container, a can of the terrible ultra-explosive which he himself had perfected. He shuddered at the thought of the havoc which its detonation would cause.

"Yes, Doctor, that is a can of radite," said the Russian. "Allow me also to call your attention to the interrupter fuse which is attached to it. When Mr. Carnes cuts the wire outside, you know well enough what will happen. Now, let me invite your attention to the clock on the wall before you. Mr. Carnes arrived at the Bush River station of the P. B. and W. at 2:15 A.M. He had a little trouble getting a boat, but he is now on his way here. It is 2:25. I think he will arrive between 3:30 and 4:00. Perhaps five minutes later, he will find the wire.

"You have a little over an hour in which to contemplate your total extinction, an extinction which will remove from my path the one great obstacle to my domination of the world. I hope you will enjoy your remaining moments. In order to help you to enjoy them, and to realize the futility of human endeavor, I have placed the key of your shackles on the floor here in plain sight, but, alas, out of your reach. I would like to stay and watch your struggle, to see the self-control on which you pride yourself vanish, and to watch you whimper and pray for the mercy you would not find; but I am deprived of that pleasure. I must take personal charge of my men to be sure that there is no slip. Good-by, Doctor, we will never meet again, I fear."

*   *   *   *   *

"We will meet again, Saranoff," said Dr. Bird in even tones of cold ferocity which made even Saranoff shiver. "We will meet again, and when you whimper and beg for mercy, remember this moment!"

The Russian started forward with an oath, his hand raised to strike. He recovered himself and essayed a sickly smile.

"I will remember, Doctor," he said in a voice which, despite himself, had a tremor of fear in it. "I will remember—*when* we meet again."

He ran lightly up the stairs and Dr. Bird heard the floor close above him. With a grunt, he bent down and examined his shackles closely. They were tight fitting and made of hardened steel. A cursory examination showed the doctor that he could neither force them nor slip them. He turned his attention to the key which Saranoff had pointed out. It lay on the floor, about ten feet, as nearly as he could judge, from where he stood.

He knelt and then stretched himself out at full length on the floor. By straining to the uttermost, his groping fingers were still six inches from the key. Saranoff had calculated the distance well.

Convinced that he could not reach the key by any effort of stretching, Dr. Bird wasted none of his precious time in vain regrets or in useless efforts to accomplish the impossible. He rose to his feet and calmly took stock of the room, searching for other means of freeing himself. The shackles themselves offered no hope. He searched his pockets. The search yielded a pocket knife, a bunch of keys, a flashlight, a handkerchief, a handful of loose change, and a wallet. He examined the miscellany thoughtfully.

*   *   *   *   *

A light broke over his face. He tied one end of the handkerchief to the knife and again took a prone position on the floor. Cautiously he tossed the knife out before him. It fell to one side of the key. He drew it back and tried again. The knife fell beyond the key. Slowly he drew it back toward him by the handkerchief. When it reached his hand, he saw to his joy, that the key was a good inch nearer. With a lighter heart, he tried again.

His toss was good. The knife fell over the key, and again he drew it to him. To his disgust, the key had not moved. Again and again he tried it, but the knife slid over the key without moving it. He looked more carefully and saw that the key was caught on an obstruction in the flooring.

With careful aim, he threw his knife so as to drive the key further away. He threw the knife again and tried to draw the key to him from its new position. It came readily until it reached the inequality in the floor which had stopped it the first time. All of his efforts to draw it nearer were fruitless. He give vent to a muttered oath as he looked at the clock. Thirty minutes of his time had gone.

A second time he knocked the key away and strove to draw it to him with no success. The clock bore witness to the fact that another ten minutes had been wasted. He rose to his feet and carefully surveyed his surroundings.

A cry of joy burst from his lips. On the floor was a tiny metallic thread which he knew for a wire. He bent down and picked it up. It was fine and very flexible. He doubled it three times and strove to bend a hook in it. The wire was too short to offer much hope, but he threw himself prone and began to fish for the key.

The wire reached it readily enough, but it did not have rigidity enough to pull the key over the little bump which held it. A glance at the clock threw him into an agony of despair. A full hour had passed since Saranoff had left him. Carnes might even now be walking into the trap which had been laid for him.

He rose to his feet and thought rapidly, twisting the wire idly around the knife as he did so. He glanced at the work of his hands, and an oath broke from his lip.

"Fool!" he exclaimed. "I deserve to die! The means for liberation were in my hands all the time."

*   *   *   *   *

With feverish activity, he ripped open the flashlight. He held the two ends of the wire against the terminals of the light battery and touched the knife to his steel key ring. To his joy, the ring adhered to the knife. Under the influence of the battery, the wire-wrapped knife had become a small electromagnet.

In a moment the doctor was prone on the floor. He tossed the knife out to the key. His aim was good and it fell directly beyond. With trembling hands he drew the knife toward him. It reached the key. Scarcely daring to breathe, he pulled it closer. The key had risen over the ridge which had held it, and was adhering to the knife. In another moment, he stood erect, freed from the shackles which had bound him.

He made for the door at a run, but a sudden thought stopped him. The clock showed him that an hour and twenty minutes had passed.

"Carnes must be nearly here!" he cried. "If I go blundering out, I'm liable to run right into the trap they have laid for him, and then we're both gone. If I yell to warn him, the fool will come ahead at full tilt. What the dickens can I do?"

His gaze fell on the can of radite. The wires leading to the interrupter fuse gleamed a dull gold with a malign significance.

"If Carnes and I are both washed out, there will be only Thelma left. She can't fight Saranoff alone. Carnes

knows the man and his methods. There is only one way
that I can see to warn him out of the trap."

He shuddered a moment. With a steady step he
walked across the cave to the can of deadly explosive. A
pair of pliers lay on a nearby bench. He picked them up.
He dashed his hand across his face for a moment, but
looked up with steady eyes. With hands that did not
tremble, he bent down over the can. With a quick snip, he
severed the wires leading to the can of radite.

*   *   *   *   *

Operative Carnes jumped ashore as the boat reached
the bank of Bush River. Before him stretched a dismal
swamp, interspersed with occasional bits of higher
ground. He looked back over the river for a moment,
taking his bearings with great care. A luminous lensatic
compass gave him the orientation of the points he had
chosen for markers.

"Are you sure we are at the right place?" he asked in
an undertone.

"Sure as shootin', Mister," replied the boatman. "It's
the only place of its kind in five miles. The rock you're
hunting for is about a hundred rods due east."

"It looks right," said Carnes. "Come on, men."

Operatives Haggerty and Dillon scrambled out of the
boat and stood by his side.

"Follow me," said Carnes in a whisper.

Both detectives nodded silently. They drew their
pistols and fell in behind their leader. Keeping his
direction with the aid of his compass, Carnes led the way
forward, counting his steps. At five hundred he paused.

"It should be right here," he whispered.

Haggerty pointed in silence. In the starlight, a large
rock loomed up a few yards away. With an exclamation of
satisfaction, Carnes led the way to it.

"Dig on the south side," he whispered, "and hurry!
The damned thing is due to go off in less than twenty

minutes. Unless we can find and cut the wire before then, the doctor is a gone gosling."

The two detectives drew intrenching shovels from their pockets and dug feverishly. For five minutes they labored. Dillon gave an exclamation.

"Here it is, Chief!" he said.

Carnes bent down and ventured a short flash from a carefully guarded light. The detective's shovel had unearthed a powerful cable running through the earth.

"Get something to cut on!" cried Carnes.

Haggerty lifted a rock which they had unearthed and thrown to one side. Carnes raised the cable and laid it on the rock.

"Now for your ax, Dillon!" he exclaimed.

He turned on his flashlight. Dillon raised a hand-ax and took careful aim. Sparks flew as the ax fell on the rock, severing the cable cleanly. Carnes rose to his feet.

"The doctor's safe!" he cried.

*　　*　　*　　*　　*

He started at a run toward the north. He had gone only a few feet when a beam of light flashed across the marsh, picking him out of the darkness. He paused in amazement.

A flash of orange light stabbed the darkness and a heavy pistol bullet sang past his head. The detective raised his weapon to reply, but three more flashes from the darkness were followed by the vicious cracks of large caliber automatics.

"Down, Chief!" cried Haggerty.

Carnes dropped to the ground, the beam of light following his movements. Four more flashes came from the darkness. Mud was thrown up into his face. Dillon's gun joined Haggerty's in barking defiance into the night.

A groan came from Haggerty.

"Hit, Tom?" asked Carnes anxiously.

"A little, but don't let that bother you. Get that damned light!"

He fired again, groaning at he did so. There was a crash from over the marsh and the light went out.

"Good work, Tom!" cried Carnes.

He raised his pistol and fired again and again into the darkness, from which still came the flashes of orange light. A cry of pain rewarded him.

"Come on, men, rush them!" he cried.

He jumped to his feet and dashed forward. A fresh beam of light stabbed a path through the darkness. A volley of fire came from behind it. Haggerty stumbled and fell.

"They've got me, Chief!" he cried faintly.

Disregarding the storm of bullets, Carnes charged ahead, Dillon at his heels. A sudden shout came from his left. A fresh beam of light made a path through the darkness and Carnes could see his opponents lying prone on the marsh. A cry of dismay came from them. Carnes fired again as he rushed forward. The men leaped to their feet and fled away into the darkness.

"Your light, Dillon!" he cried.

Dillon's light shone out and picked up one of the fleeing figures. The beam from the left was centered on another.

"Halt!" came a stern voice from behind the light. "You are surrounded! If I give the word to fire, you are dead men!"

"Dr. Bird!" cried Carnes in amazement.

*   *   *   *   *

The fleeing man in the beam of Dillon's light paused.

"Drop your gun!" cried Carnes sharply.

There was a moment of hesitation before the man's gun fell and his hands went up.

"Get him, Carnes!" came Dr. Bird's voice. "I've got another one held out here. I hope one of them is the man we want."

As Dillon slipped handcuffs on his prisoner, Dr. Bird came forward, driving another Russian before him. In his hand was a piece of iron pipe.

"Cuff him, Carnes!" he said.

The detective slipped handcuffs on the man while Dr. Bird bent down and examined the face of each of the prisoners with his light. He straightened up with an exclamation of anger.

"These are nothing but tools," he said bitterly. "We had the arch-conspirator himself in our hands and let him escape."

"The arch-conspirator!" gasped Carnes. "You don't mean Saranoff?"

"Yes, Ivan Saranoff. He was here on this marsh tonight. There were four of his men and we got two, letting the most important one get away."

"You've got four, Dr. Bird," said a guttural voice from the dark.

Dr. Bird whirled around and shot out the beam of his light. A third Russian was revealed in its gleam.

"Hands up!" cried the doctor.

"I'm willing to be captured, Doctor," said the Russian. "Your search for Saranoff is useless. He has been gone for an hour. He is not one to risk his own skin when others will risk theirs for him. He fled after he left the cave."

"Do you know where he has gone?"

"I wish I did, Doctor. If I knew, we'd soon have him, I hope."

The Russian's voice had changed entirely. Gone were the heavy guttural tones. In their place was a rich, rather throaty contralto. Carnes gave a cry of astonishment and turned his light on the prisoner.

"Thelma!" he gasped.

*   *   *   *   *

The Russian smiled.

"Surely, Mr. Carnes," she said. "Congratulations on your acumen. Dr. Bird saw me for half an hour this evening, but he didn't recognize me. He even knocked me out with his fist back in the cavern."

"The devil I did!" gasped the doctor. "What were you doing there?"

"Helping Saranoff capture you, Doctor," she replied. "The day you left, I saw one of his men on the street. I dared not summon help lest he should escape, so I followed him. I captured him and learned from him the location of the gang headquarters.

"I disguised myself and took his place for a week, fooling them all, even Saranoff himself. I was one of those chosen to carry out your capture and your murder. This afternoon, unknown to Saranoff, I tampered with that radite can and removed the fuse. That was why there was no explosion when Mr. Carnes cut the wire. I had no chance to warn him. I managed to shoot one of Saranoff's men when they broke and ran."

Her voice trembled in the darkness.

"I hated to kill him—" she said with a half sob.

A faint hail came from the night.

"Haggerty!" cried Carnes.

"All right, Chief," came Dillon's voice. "He's got a bullet in his shoulder and one through his leg, but no bones broken. He'll be all right."

Carnes turned again to the girl.

"What about that Russian whose place you took?" he asked. "Maybe we can pump something out of him."

Thelma swayed for a moment.

"Don't, Mr. Carnes," she cried, her voice rising almost to a shriek. "Don't make me think of it! I—I had to—to stab him!"

She swayed again. Carnes started toward her, his arms outstretched. Dr. Bird's voice stopped him.

"Miss Andrews," said the doctor sternly, "you know that I demand control of the emotions from all my subordinates. You are crying like a hysterical schoolgirl. Unless you can learn to control your feelings instead of giving way to them on every occasion, I will have to dispense with your further services."

The girl swayed toward him for a moment, a look of pain in her eyes. She shuddered and then recovered herself. She straightened up and faced Dr. Bird boldly.

"Yes, Doctor," came in level expressionless tones from her lips.

And Now a Message . . .
By Greg Fowlkes

A short Story from the upcoming Book - *Back Road to the Stars*

And Now A Message...

For the third time that night Jack Olsen was about to nod off over the copy of *Statistical Information Theory* that he was attempting to read. Giving it up as a bad effort, he shut the book and looked out the window of the control room at the giant bowl of the Arecibo radio telescope. Theoretically he was running the huge instrument, but in reality all the controlling was being done by the computers in the room around him. For six months he had been working eight hour shifts every night, and his job had consisted of the five minutes a shift that it took to enter the coordinates to be examined on the control console. Other than that, he was on hand only for the off chance that the monitoring programs would recognize some pattern in the radio noise, in which case an alarm would sound. So far, in the six months, it hadn't happened.

He walked over to the coffee machine in the hopes that a cup would revive him enough so that he could continue his studies. He never made it, for as if to prove the lie of his earlier thoughts, the alarm sounded. For a moment Jack was frozen, the alarm beating raucously in his ears, then he pulled himself together and flicked off the switch on the bell. With the room returned to the relative quiet of the whoosh of the cooling fans on the equipment, Jack sat down at the console and keyed in an enquiry. Within seconds the computer had replied that it was receiving a strong periodic signal on the 42 centimeter band. Further questioning showed that it was not a program malfunction but a genuine signal.

Jack picked up the phone and dialed his boss's number. It was three in the morning, but his instructions had been clear. If anything was received that could possibly be an intelligent signal, he was supposed to contact his superior immediately.

Despite the long drive through the mountains in the cool Puerto Rican night, Professor Kraft showed up with his eyes still sleepy. Shuffling over to the coffee pot by the window he poured himself a large mug before he said anything. "You'd better have something good to get me up at this hour."

"I think so," Jack said, aware that his boss's irritation was only feigned. "I've been checking with the computer since I called you. It shows a strong periodic signal with a sharp pulse every fifty milliseconds. It runs on like that for about two and a half minutes before the signal fades below the background."

"Any chance that it might be a pulsar?" Kraft asked, referring to the radio signals of rapidly rotating neutron stars. "That's within the range of periods for them. When the first one was discovered, they thought that they had received intelligent signals."

"I thought of that, so I checked the record of the broad band receiver." Jack brought out a long strip of graph paper and pointed to the evenly spaced patterns of peaks on it. "Where the narrow band shows only a single repetitive pulse, the wide band gives us this fine structure. It's far too regular to be a pulsar and much too detailed. It's more like some sort of timing signal or spacer. And in between the pulses there is another signal. It's not as repetitive as the main pulse. That's why the program doesn't bring it out. But there definitely is some sort of transmission in between. It's weaker, but I think that we can write a processing program to pick it out from the noise."

Kraft looked at the trace in his hand thoughtfully. "I hate to make snap judgements. You can be suckered in too easily that way. But it does look like some kind of artificial signal. We'll get the team working on it in the morning. Have you received any additional signals?"

"No. I've kept the dish tracking the source, but all we get on 42 cm. is background noise. It's like there was a moment of freak atmospheric conditions that opened a window, and then it shut again. Just like you get with shortwave sometimes because of the ionosphere."

"Well, we should be grateful for what we've got. I don't think I can sleep anymore tonight, so I'll keep you company. I'd like to be here if we get any more messages from our friends out there," he said, pointing with his cup towards the star filled sky that loomed over the radio telescope's antenna.

"Frustrating, isn't it?" Prof. Kraft remarked to the team of graduate students and post doctoral fellows that were working under him on the interstellar communications project. And frustrating it had been. For six months they had continuously monitored the sky searching for signs of life finally to be rewarded by a two minute snippet of extraterrestrial conversation.

Now, another six months later, they had still made no sense of the signal, nor had they received any further transmissions from that part of the sky, though they had concentrated their efforts in that direction.

"Rumors have leaked out about our discovery, and I've been getting requests for the data. I'd sure hate to have someone else steal our thunder by deciphering the signal, but if we don't make some progress soon, we're going to have to release it." He looked around the table at the young faces of his assistants. At the moment they didn't look nearly as bright and intelligent as he knew they were.

"Why don't I summarize what we've found so far in hopes that it will give us some new ideas?"

"First, we've got this repetitive pattern of pulses every twentieth of a second as regular as clockwork. So regular, in fact, that we can't decide whether they serve as breaks in the message or were just put there to attract our attention. Remember, it was these pulses that were first recognized by the computer."

"But the pulses aren't the real message. That lays in the spaces in between. We've been able to deduce that the messages are digitized and the computer has been able to enhance them so that we have a fairly error free record of them. There is some repetitive structure to them, and they do vary in some sort of progression, but beyond that, we haven't been able to get the least notion of what they mean. Anyone have something to add?"

Bill Warden, one of the post docs, spoke up. "Well, we've tried mathematical analysis on the signals and have gotten zero results. It has already been assumed that any sort of interstellar communications would be based on sort of easily recognizable mathematical progression. Like one, two three. Something like that to show that they were rational. From there you can always build up more complicated concepts."

"With this message we don't have that, which leads us to one of two assumptions. One, we have only a fragment of a broadcast, and from a very advanced lesson at that. If that's the case, I don't see much hope of our being able to decipher the message until we can receive more signals to give us a broader base to work from."

"The other alternative is that they, whoever they are, just don't think like us. Their minds work in some fashion so that this mess we have makes sense to them. If so, I don't see any hope at all. Their minds may just be too foreign for us to hold a dialog with them."

"Thank you for that optimistic note," Prof. Kraft said wryly. "For the first time mankind has received a message from another species and we can't tell whether it is a cure for cancer, a means of achieving universal peace, or a recipe for sauerbratten. Any comments?"

"If it's sauerbratten, where do we go for a tablespoon of powdered bandersnatch egg?" quipped one of the grad students. They all laughed at the joke more than it deserved. Six months of unrewarded work had left them all a little giddy. After the giggles and comments had died down, Jack Olsen coughed, trying to get their attention.

"You've got something useful to say, Jack?" Kraft asked. "You might as well tell us. I don't think anyone else has anything useful to add," he said, pointedly looking at the wisecracker.

"I've been thinking about the signal, and I remember something that I said to you the night it came in. I don't know if you recall, but I called the pulses timing signals. Now there is one type of common transmission that has the same kind of pulses, and that's television. They use the pulses to synchronize the frames. It's possible that the message in between each pulse is a picture, and the whole transmission is meant to be viewed in sequence."

"How long have you been sitting on this while the rest of us were beating our brains out?" Kraft asked.

"It just came to me," Jack said, his face flushed. "I should have thought of it earlier, but like Bill said, we've all been conditioned to look for something like one plus one equals two."

"I think that we should all have seen it," Kraft said. "It makes as much sense as anything else that's been suggested. Do you think that you can get us a picture?"

"If it's there, I should be able to pick it out using the computer," Jack answered.

"Good. Then, since it was your idea, you're in charge. Dragoon anything or anybody that you need to help you."

Five days later they were all gathered around the conference room table again, but this time there was a TV set and a video recorder on a cart at its end. From the nervous stubbing of cigarette butts and fingers drumming on the table, it was obvious that all the members of the team were in a state of anticipation.

"It took some time to figure out exactly how the signal was put together," Jack began. "After all, we didn't know how many lines there were in each frame or how many bits made up each unit of picture. In the end, I had to have the computer run through all the likely possibilities for one of the frames. It took a lot of computer time, but I've finally got some recognizable pictures."

"It turns out that the original broadcast was in color. That threw us for a while, but we finally psyched it out. The aliens must have eyes structurally different from ours; there are only two colors, not three in the signal. Which colors they are is anybody's guess. They might be ultraviolet and infrared for all we can tell. Arbitrarily, I've assigned them red and bluish green, so keep that in mind. Also, because the video recorder uses thirty frames a second instead of the twenty in the transmission, it was necessary to compress the program a bit. This means that everything you'll be seeing has been speeded up about fifty percent.

"I guess you're all more interested in seeing the tape than in listening to me." A snort from Prof. Kraft indicated agreement. Jack flicked off the lights and started the tape. For a minute the screen showed only snow, then a face became recognizable. It was a sickly chartreuse, and there was no nose between the two large, oval eyes, but it was recognizable as a face. The figures movements were quick and jerky like an old silent movie, the result of the difference in frame speed, and the picture left a lot to be desired in clarity, the product of interstellar noise, but it was a picture, the first of an alien race.

As the tape played, a weird, sings song voice came from the speaker sounding something like a Chinese chipmunk. "I forgot to mention that there was also an audio track along with the signal. Again, it's only a reconstruction and may not bear much resemblance to the original, but then, we'll never know," Jack commented. They had determined that the source of the transmission was at least several dozen light years away. It would take twice that number of years to send a message and receive a reply, by which time they would all be dead.

They continued to watch the tape. The camera had drawn back to show the alien from the waist up revealing rounded shoulders and a pair of six fingered hands. Apparently he was standing behind a low lectern or a table of some sort. The fuzzy picture and camera angle made it hard to tell which. As he, or her, or it, spoke, the alien pointed at a chart or poster suspended on the backdrop. A pattern of red and blue that hurt the eye with violent contrasts seemed to be some sort of text. The voice continued as the picture disappeared in a sea of snow and then it broke into static. The transmission had ended.

"You've done a fine job, Jack," Prof. Kraft said after they had played the tape through a half dozen times. "It's actually far better than I thought it would be, and I think we can accept any of the shortcomings that you mentioned."

"So, we've got a face and body of what certainly is a rational creature. He seemed to be giving us a lesson or lecture of some sort, though I for one don't have the faintest idea of what he was talking about. We have an idea of what they look like which I am sure will give the biologists a lot to speculate on, so I guess that we should be thankful for small favors, but I still don't see how we're going to learn any more about them without receiving further signals."

"I wouldn't hold out much hope of that," Jack interjected. "I think that it's clear now that the signal we picked up was not meant for interstellar communication. Any such signal would have been designed with much greater noise immunity. We were able to receive it only because of an accident of atmospheric conditions. It was actually just a local TV broadcast. As we haven't received anything since, those conditions must be rare."

"So," Kraft said, "we have a message of great potential import, that at the very least could provide us with insights on a totally alien culture, and no way to decipher it."

"I've got an idea," Bill said. "We've all been looking at the problem from the point of view of hardware and computer programs. That's natural because of our backgrounds, but now that we have what amounts to an artifact, maybe we should call in a specialist. We need someone who is trained in resurrecting a culture from its fragments. I suggest that we show the tape to some archeologists and get their opinions."

Convincing an archeologist to look at the tape was harder than it had sounded. Most of them were more interested in ancient rather than alien civilizations. Jack suspected that they felt out of their depth with the computers and electronics. With some pressure and pleading, a group finally agreed to view the tape, but after the showing, only one evinced any interest in following up on it.

A visiting lecturer from Norway, she was reputed to have a good background in languages, though Jack lacked the knowledge to judge her qualifications. However, as she was young, blond, and attractive, he was quite willing to spend the time required to familiarize her with the tape and the equipment they had used to come up with it. Together, they spent hours viewing the tape, studying it frame by frame attempting to pick out the slightest piece of information.

The project team had been assembled in the conference room, and this time it was the archeologist's turn to address them. For three weeks Cristina Peterson had been studying the tape almost constantly, and now she was ready to give her opinion. With the exception of Jack, who had been working closely with her, they were all, even Prof. Kraft, eagerly awaiting the report. There had been a great deal of speculation about what her findings would be.

"First," she began, "before I get your hopes up, I want to say that I have not been able to get a word for word translation of the voice on the tape. The sample of speech is just too brief for that to be possible. If the scene had contained more action, I might have been more successful, but we were not that fortunate. I have, however, been able to form a hypothesis based on the spoken word as well as visual clues such as facial expression, setting, and so on."

"An important point to remember is that the aliens, despite certain differences in appearance, are not too dissimilar from ourselves. They are bipedal, intelligent, and possess opposable thumbs. They have binocular vision and a form of color perception as well. Brain size is about the same in relationship to total body size as in humans, and I would be greatly surprised if they were much larger or smaller than ourselves. That much can be guessed on the basis of physiology from the picture and the nature of the signal. From this information, I think that we can draw the conclusion that their planet is, within limits, earthlike."

"Probably more relevant is their state of culture. They obviously have a technology and one that is recognizable in terms of our own. That we can receive their signals is proof of that. Also, they speak, they wear clothing, we can even guess at the purpose of some of the objects visible in the tape. I might add that this is more than we can do for some of the artifacts of primitive human cultures. In some ways we have more in common with the aliens than we do with the Tasadi or Bushman."

"I want you to bear in mind that these beings are not greatly different from ourselves. If we are to properly analyze the contents of the message, we must remember that they are influenced by the same drives and forces as humans." There was an uneasy shifting in their seats on the part of the team members as they took in the meaning of her statement.

"If we accept this premise, and replace the alien with a human, we can make an educated guess as to what we are seen on the tape. I'll run it again for you so that you can make the substitution." Jack tapped the switch, and for the next minute and a half they watched the now familiar scene replay itself.

"Before I give my own opinion, would anyone else like to make a guess?" Cristina asked.

Kraft looked around the room, but it appeared as though no one had the courage to be the first to put his own views forward. To break the silence he said, "It's only a guess, but to start the discussion, I'd say that the alien might be a lecturer. He's obviously standing at some sort of podium or speaker's table."

"He seems a little too impassioned for a lecturer, at least in the physical sciences," one of the grad students remarked. "I've never seen you that excited before a class." Kraft smiled at the reference to his own low keyed classroom delivery.

"Maybe it's a political science class. They get more aroused."

Bill Warden broke in, "Why a class? It looks to me more like he's a politician trying to persuade the voters. He must be up for reelection. The sign in back could be an election poster." That brought a couple of laughs and a few less than serious comments.

"We've all had a crack at it," Prof. Kraft said. "You obviously have your own interpretation, and I think that we've been kept in suspense long enough. From the look on Jack's face, it must be a good one. Let's hear it now. After all, the communication between two species is one of the most important events in human history."

She smiled at the jibe. "All your suggestions are plausible, but I've spent more time analyzing the tape than you have. I'll play it again for you and point out the features that have led me to my interpretation."

"The first thing that caught my attention was the fact that the word 'gratach' was mentioned fourteen times, an unusually high incidence in such a brief speech. Furthermore, at least four of those times the speaker pointed to the symbols on the chart behind him. I think that we can assume that 'gratach' is a name, and the symbols form the written version."

"Now here's something that I want you to see." She froze the picture on the television. "Note the artifacts on the table, a bowl filled with a substance and a box or container. There appears to be some writing on the box, but the resolution of the picture isn't good enough to allow us to make it out. However," she said as the tape began to roll again, "as the alien points to the box and says 'gratach' it is likely that the symbols again spell out the name in the chart behind the alien. Note, too, the expression on his face. Despite the lack of a nose, the face is surprisingly human, and if that expression was on a human face, it would be one of approval or pleasure."

"I think that if you put all the clues together, you can come to only one conclusion. Dr. Warden was not far off when he suggested a political campaign. The speaker is definitely trying to persuade his audience, but it is the package, not himself, that he is trying to sell."

"Oh, god," Kraft sputtered. "You can't mean it. The first communication from another planet and it's only . . ."

"Yes, I'm afraid so," Cristina said. "The first and only signal received from another world is nothing more than a breakfast food commercial."

Also From Resurrected Press

SCIENCE FICTION AUTHORS RESURRECTED

FYFE RESURRECTED - THE STORIES OF H. B. FYFE
Stories from the Golden Age of Science Fiction by the author of D-99. dealing with the interaction of humans and aliens on far off worlds in ways that were as creative as they were imaginative.

BONE RESURRECTED - THE STORIES OF J. F. BONE
More stories from the Golden Age of Science Fiction. Includes "The Issahar Artifact," "Assassin," "To Choke an Ocean" and more.

NOURSE RESURRECTED - THE STORIES OF ALAN E. NOURSE
Stories from the Golden Age of Science Fiction. Includes "Contamination Crew." "Coffin Cure," "The Link," and more.

DICK RESURRECTED - THE EARLY STORIES OF PHILIP K. DICK
Early stories from the author of the novels that inspired "Blade Runner," "Total Recall," and through a scanner darkly. Science Fiction Authors Resurrected

OTHER CLASSIC SCIENCE FICTION NOVELS BEING RESURRECTED SOON

TALENTS, INCORPORATED - BY MURRAY LEINSTER
When a Mekinese fleet conquers his home planet, Captain Bors turns to Talents, Incorporated for help using their collection of individuals with unusual abilities to defeat the enemy and save the galaxy.

THE PIRATES OF ERSATZ - BY MURRAY LEINSTER
Bran Hodden just wanted to be an electronic engineer and marry a delightful girl. But when he's framed by the powers on Walden he's forced to turn back to his family's trade, piracy. Also published as The Pirates of Zan.

EMPIRE - BY CLIFFORD SIMAK
Spencer Chambers and Interplanetary Power owned the Solar System because they controlled the source of power. It fell to Russell Page and Harry Wilson to challenge that control if they had to cross the universe to do it.

NIGHT OF THE LONG KNIVES - THE CREATURE FROM THE CLEVELAND DEPTHS - BY FRITZ LEIBER
Two classic novellas set in the not too distant future from a classic master of science fiction.

ARMAGEDDON - 2419 A.D. - THE AIR LORDS OF HAN - BY PHILLIP FRANCIS NOWLAN
The two novels that introduced the world to that intrepid hero of the 25th Century, Buck Rogers. Buck Rogers must save the world from the clutches of the insidious Han.

Other Classic Resurrected Science Fiction
Edited by Greg Fowlkes

RESURRECTED MARTIANS
Classic Stories about Mars and Martians from the Golden Age of Science Fiction

RESURRECTED ALIENS
Classic Stories of Aliens and Alien Encounters from the Golden Age of Science Fiction

RESURRECTED FLYING SAUCERS
Classic Stories of Flying Saucers and Alien Invasions from the Golden Age of Science Fiction

RESURRECTED ROBOTS
Classic Stories of Robots, Cyborgs and Androids from the Golden Age of Science Fiction

RESURRECTED SPACE SHIPS -
Classic Stories of Space Ships from the Golden Age of Science Fiction

RESURRECTED TIME TRAVEL
Classic Stories of Time Travel from the Golden Age of Science Fiction

RESURRECTED DIMENSIONS
Classic Stories of other Dimensions from the Golden Age of Science Fiction

RESURRECTED FUTURES
Classic Stories of the Far Future from the Golden Age of Science Fiction

RESURRECTED MAD SCIENTISTS
Classic Stories of Mad Scientists and their Creations from the Golden Age of Science Fiction

RESURRECTED MONSTERS
Classic Stories of Monsters and Mayhem from the Golden Age of Science Fiction

The Fictional Detective
by Greg Fowlkes

Who killed Ezekial O. Handler?

A beautiful dame, a hard-boiled private eye – and a dead body.

It started like any other case. When a famous writer dies in a mysterious car crash, private detective Frank Slade is called in to find answers, but all he finds is more questions. Who killed Ezekial Handler? Who is Janet Nielsen and why is she so interested in finding out? Who is leaving the neatly typed clues? And as Slade tries to find answers to these questions he starts to wonder if the ultimate answer will threaten his very existence.

Read about it in
The Fictional Detective

Visit www.thefictionaldetective.com

About Resurrected Press

A division of Intrepid Ink, LLC, Resurrected Press is dedicated to bringing high quality, vintage books back into publication. See our entire catalogue and find out more at www.ResurrectedPress.com.

About Intrepid Ink, LLC

Intrepid Ink, LLC provides full publishing services to authors of fiction and non-fiction books, eBooks and websites. From editing to formatting, from publishing to marketing, Intrepid Ink gets your creative works into the hands of the people who want to read them. Find out more at www.IntrepidInk.com.

www.ingramcontent.com/pod-product-compliance
Lightning Source LLC
Chambersburg PA
CBHW071202250626
47159CB00001B/170